P9-DCD-856

3 5920 00183 6756

His bare flesh singed her fingers and curled her toes.

She opened her mouth and accepted his slow, sinuous tongue. He groaned against her, his body growing harder, tighter in her hands.

"Gillian," he spoke her name on a ragged groan, "what I want to do to ye..."

"Do what you will."

"Nae." He straightened and stared down into her eyes. "Yer life is in my hands. I won't put ye in more danger."

"Colin"—she took his face in her hands—"my life is my own. You gave it back to me."

"And now that you have it, you would hand it over to me?"

"Aye." She smiled, tilting her head up to kiss him. "Now please—"

He scooped her up off the floor and carried her down the hall.

"—take me to your room."

✳ ✳ ✳

ACCLAIM FOR
PAULA QUINN'S NOVELS

Tamed by a Highlander

"A winning mix of fascinating history and lush romance... Readers will be captivated by the meticulously accurate historical detail...and Connor and Mairi's searing passion."
—*Publishers Weekly* (starred review)

"Top Pick! Quinn's talents for weaving history with a sexy and seductive romance are showcased in her latest Highlander series book. This fast-paced tale of political intrigue populated by sensual characters with deeply rooted senses of honor and loyalty is spellbinding... Top-notch Highland romance!" —*RT Book Reviews*

"[A] must read... Paula Quinn weaves romance, suspense, and history into a story that unleashes a smoldering desire within the heart of the reader. A breathtaking romance full of history and heart-melting Highlanders."
—NightOwlReviews.com

"This series is one hit after another and I enjoy it more with each book... Paula Quinn keeps her books historically accurate, which adds to the depth."
—GoodReads.com

Seduced by a Highlander

"*Seduced by a Highlander* is sparkling, sexy, and seductive! I couldn't put it down! Paula Quinn is a rising star!"
—Karen Hawkins, *New York Times* bestselling author

"Top Pick! An engrossing story brimming with atmosphere and passionate characters... a true keeper."

—*RT Book Reviews*

"Scottish romance at its very best! Deliciously romantic and sensual, Paula Quinn captures the heart of the Highlands in a tender, passionate romance that you won't be able to put down."

—Monica McCarty, *New York Times* bestselling author

"A rich tapestry of love, rivalry, and hope...the simmering passion made for very heated scenes...I can't wait to read more of the family in future books!"

—TheRomanceReadersConnection.com

"Five Stars! Reviewer's Recommended Award Winner! Paula Quinn went above and beyond my expectations...With a hero to make a heart sigh and a heroine who can match the hero wit to wit, this story is one I highly recommend adding to your bookshelf."

—CoffeeTimeRomance.com

Ravished by a Highlander

"Deftly combines historical fact and powerful romance... There's much more than just sizzling sensuality: history buffs will love the attention to periodic detail and cameos by real-life figures, and the protagonists embody compassion, responsibility, and unrelenting, almost self-sacrificial honor. Quinn's seamless prose and passionate storytelling will leave readers hungry for future installments."

—*Publishers Weekly* (starred review)

"4½ Stars! Top Pick! Quinn once again captures the aura of the Highlands. Here is an amazing love story where characters' deep emotions and sense of honor for their countrymen will enchant readers."

—*RT Book Reviews*

"Incomparable...Paula Quinn expertly interweaves fact and fiction so well that you will come to truly believe every one of her characters can be found in the pages of history."

—SingleTitles.com

Also by Paula Quinn

Lord of Desire

Lord of Temptation

Lord of Seduction

Laird of the Mist

A Highlander Never Surrenders

Ravished by a Highlander

Seduced by a Highlander

Tamed by a Highlander

ATTENTION CORPORATIONS AND ORGANIZATIONS:
Most HACHETTE BOOK GROUP books are available
at quantity discounts with bulk purchase for educational,
business, or sales promotional use. For information,
please call or write:

Special Markets Department, Hachette Book Group
237 Park Avenue, New York, NY 10017
Telephone: 1-800-222-6747 Fax: 1-800-477-5925

Conquered
by a
Highlander

PAULA QUINN

COAL CITY PUBLIC
LIBRARY DISTRICT
85 N Garfield Street
Coal City, IL 60416

FOREVER

NEW YORK   BOSTON

This book is a work of fiction. Names, characters, places, and incidents are the product of the author's imagination or are used fictitiously. Any resemblance to actual events, locales, or persons, living or dead, is coincidental.

Copyright © 2012 by Paula Quinn
Excerpt from *Ravished by a Highlander* copyright © 2010 by Paula Quinn
All rights reserved. In accordance with the U.S. Copyright Act of 1976, the scanning, uploading, and electronic sharing of any part of this book without the permission of the publisher is unlawful piracy and theft of the author's intellectual property. If you would like to use material from the book (other than for review purposes), prior written permission must be obtained by contacting the publisher at permissions@hbgusa.com. Thank you for your support of the author's rights.

Forever
Hachette Book Group
237 Park Avenue
New York, NY 10017

www.HachetteBookGroup.com

Printed in the United States of America

First Edition: June 2012
10 9 8 7 6 5 4 3 2 1

Forever is an imprint of Grand Central Publishing.
The Forever name and logo are trademarks of Hachette Book Group, Inc.

The Hachette Speakers Bureau provides a wide range of authors for speaking events. To find out more, go to www.hachettespeakers bureau.com or call (866) 376-6591.

The publisher is not responsible for websites (or their content) that are not owned by the publisher.

To my beloved . . . Until we meet again in the sweet hereafter. I love you.

Battle Born

❖

Chapter One

*H*and over that bag and I won't run you through."

Colin MacGregor smiled behind his hood and slowed his mount to a leisurely canter. He wasn't far from his destination, a league or two at best. He could smell the sea on the crisp morning air. It put him in a good mood, inclining him toward mercy to his present company. "I should warn ye," he called out to the man hurrying to keep up with him on foot. "Ye're the seventh thief who thought to rob me this day. The six before ye are already dead." His smile, slight as it was, remained intact as he turned in his saddle. "I'll grant ye a moment to reconsider yer course."

The thief chuckled and continued on foolishly. "I'll take the horse too."

"Will ye now?" Colin brought his mount to a full stop and swept his hood off his head. "I'd like to see ye give it a try. Only, be quick about it. I'd like to reach Dartmouth before they break fast. I'm hungry fer a decent meal."

The thief did not oblige but jammed two fingers into his mouth and whistled instead. From beyond the trees five more men appeared, each eyeing Colin with snarls while they pointed their weapons at him.

"One of yer companions seems to be missing," Colin pointed out, glancing about briefly before returning his steady gaze to the leader.

The thief surveyed his small troupe, then, realizing Colin was correct—but not catching what it meant— shouted for the sixth robber to quit pissing and get ready to fight.

'Twas unnecessary really, as Colin shot the man dead when he emerged from behind a tree, the thief's own pistol in one hand and the laces of his breeches in the other. Two other men carried pistols but they didn't get the chance to fire them, or even aim, in the time it took Colin to shoot one with a second pistol he kept tucked in his boot and to fling a short sword at the other, catching him in the center of his throat. The leader watched in horror as three of his comrades fell all in the space of a few breaths. When Colin leaped from his horse, the four remaining thugs shared a fearful look between them and then, realizing his pistols would have to be reloaded before he could use them again, drew their blades and attacked.

The men were poorly lacking in any kind of skill, which didn't surprise Colin in the least. He could have shown them mercy, as he had to their leader, by letting them live a bit longer, but he was a warrior, not a priest. He'd known he was being followed since entering Devon. He'd known how many men were tailing him and where they would likely make their move. 'Twas no astounding feat he possessed to be aware of such things. 'Twas what any well-trained soldier should know.

And Colin had been training for battle since before

he could remember. The desire to conquer set fire to his veins since the day he was old enough to hold a blade in his hand. He was born to fight, and as he grew older, he grew more ready and eager to go to war for a cause he believed in. The Stuart throne had become that cause. The Catholic king James Stuart, to be exact, kin by marriage to the MacGregors of Skye. A man who had gained Colin's friendship, loyalty, and finally his respect when James first took the throne three years ago. But the king had become a tyrant lately and Colin had grown more uncertain if his liege was any less guilty and unfit to rule the kingdom than his enemy William of Orange was.

That indecision was what had led him on his journey home to Camlochlin before embarking upon this latest task: to end the threat of the Dutch prince once and for all.

He'd enjoyed his trip home more than he'd expected and suspected that the memory of the visit sparked the thread of compassion he felt now, for he made a quick end of his attackers.

Then again, he was damned hungry.

He wiped his blade on the fallen leader's tunic, then sheathed it and leaped back into his saddle. The dead were no longer his concern... or the concern of any other decent man traveling this road.

Setting his course straight ahead, he returned his hood to his head and his thoughts to his purpose of stopping Prince William from taking the throne.

A general in James's Royal Army, Colin had taken the lives of many in the past three years, though few of his enemies died on the battlefield. His victories were mostly silent, purely political ones that required the sharp edge of his mind, as well as his blade. He honed each with equal diligence. He'd traded in his warrior blood and become the king's assassin, sent to mete out justice to the guilty.

There was no one guiltier than the man who'd once ordered the massacre of an abbey full of nuns. A self-righteous, falsely pious prince who not only planned the demise of every Catholic in the kingdom, but also schemed against his wife's own father. Aye, no matter what doubts Colin was beginning to harbor toward his king, he would see his task through to completion. He would have his war.

Rubbing his growling belly, he watched the sheer fortress wall of Dartmouth Castle rise over the rocky cliff tops in the distance. The round battlemented tower and high lookout turret appeared to pierce the charcoal clouds. A gloomy sense of isolation began seeping through his mantle along with the briny scent of the Dart estuary rolling in from the southwest. He didn't mind being alone. In fact, he preferred it over the feigned niceties of court.

A cool trickle snaked down his back, but he resisted the urge to shiver.

He wasn't just the king's executioner, he was a spy. And a damned good one. He was about to change his identity, including his religion, his moral code, and his entire past, in order to fit in with his enemies and learn their secrets. He wouldn't let his nerves get the better of him. He never did.

This wasn't the first time he would be living as Colin Campbell of Breadalbane, cousin to the Campbells of Glen Orchy. The information he had gathered at various tables from France to Scotland about secret correspondences between England and William in Holland had all led back to Geoffrey Dearly, Earl of Devon and lord of Dartmouth.

Approaching along the cliffs, Colin took in the structure before him. Dartmouth was more of a fort than an actual castle. Built in the fourteenth century to guard the mouth of the estuary, it lay deep within Protestant territory and 'twas a good enough place to land an army of ships if a certain Dutch prince wished to invade England.

This was it, Colin was sure of it, the last time he would have to sit in the company of his enemies and speak like them, laugh with them. If he was correct about Devon's alliance with Prince William—and Colin was certain he was correct—the earl was going to need every available sword for hire when he betrayed the king. Fortunate for him, the deadliest mercenary ever to wield a blade or fire a pistol was about to land on his doorstep.

He scanned the gun tower and surrounding gun platforms adjoining the round tower to the square. Pity, there were no fearsome-looking guardsmen patrolling the walls. He ached for a decent fight when the time finally came. Until then, he would befriend them, and then butcher them in battle.

A movement high atop the turret caught his eye, and as he focused on what it was, his thoughts of victory scattered to the four winds.

'Twas a lass, her long flaxen tresses and flowing white gown snapping against the bracing wind as she stepped up onto the edge of the crenellated wall. Was she a woman about to leap to the jagged rocks below or an angel readying to take flight? He waited, his heart beating more wildly in his chest than it had in years, to see what the answer would be. If she was a woman, he could do nothing to save her if she fell. He had seen death, had caused much with his own blade, but he had never been witness to someone taking her own life. Why would she?

What in hell was so terrible that hurling herself over the edge was a better alternative?

When she bent her knees, his heart stalled in his chest. Damned fool. He couldn't catch her.

But she didn't jump. Instead, she nestled herself into the groove of a merlon. He watched her, unnoticed while she wrapped her arms around her knees and set her chin toward the estuary. She reminded him of a painting he'd seen in King Louis's court, of a woman looking out toward the sea, waiting for her beloved to return to her. Something about this lass above him stirred him in the pit of his gut. Was she waiting for someone? Mayhap a guardsman from Devon's garrison? She looked small and utterly alone surrounded by stone, water, and the vast sky behind her. Who was she?

A better question was, what the hell did he care who she was? He didn't. 'Twas the most vital part of this duty he was born to carry out, what made him better at it than anyone else. He attached himself to no one. Mercy could get him, or worse, the king, killed. He didn't need friends, since the men he'd been sitting with over the past three years had been traitors to the throne and could never be trusted.

What he felt in his belly were hunger pangs.

Pulling his hood back over his head, he looked at the lass one last time. She dipped her head, catching his movement. When she scrambled to her feet, he clenched his jaw to keep himself from calling out. Thankfully, she stepped back down off the wall and disappeared.

Left with nothing but the passing memory of her, Colin returned his thoughts to the duty at hand and cantered his horse through the yard of St. Petroc's Church, where a dozen or so of Devon's men were loitering and looking bored until they saw him.

Dismounting, he pushed back his hood and held up his hands as the men raced toward him.

"Stranger." One stepped out from among the rest. He was tall and broad shouldered in his stained military coat. His dark, oily hair fell over gray, bloodshot eyes, which hardened on Colin's face first, and then on the swords dangling from both sides of Colin's hips beneath his wind-tossed mantle. "What brings you to Dartmouth?"

"I seek an audience with the earl."

The man's gaze settled on the flash of a dagger hidden within the folds of Colin's open vest and the pistol tucked under his belt. "You carry many weapons." He dipped his gaze to Colin's leather boots next, where more daggers and his second pistol peeked out, and licked his lips, which had apparently gone rather dry.

"The roads are perilous," Colin explained with a slight crook of his lips, still keeping his hands up. This ill-prepared soldier was afraid of him...and that made the soldier dangerous.

"So is straying into a place you don't belong," the speaker countered, reaching around his belly to the hilt of his sheathed sword. "Who are you and what do you want with the earl?"

"I'd prefer to tell that to yer highest in command."

"Well," the soldier said, puffing up his chest, "I'm Lieutenant Gilbert de Atre, and you'll tell it to me or you'll hop onto that paltry mare you rode in on and leave while you still can."

Colin knew hundreds of men just like this one. He'd seen that same challenging smirk dozens of times before. He wasn't sure what it was about him that made some men want to test him. Mayhap 'twas his weapons and the way he carried them, or the cool, composed indifference of his expression. He feared little and it intimidated less formidable men. Usually he ignored such bravado, especially when his task was to make nice and fit in. This time though, he had to fit in to an army, not at a noble's table. He would need to earn their respect before they trusted him. Colin didn't mind having to fight to prove himself. In fact, he looked forward to it. A test of his skill would provide an excellent opportunity to learn what he was up against, and also to show these men that he would be an asset to their company. He would go easy on them all, of course. No reason to reveal too soon what *they* were up against.

His expression remained impassive, save for the spark of something feral in his eyes when he glanced at his horse and then back at de Atre. "I take offense to ye insulting my horse, Lieutenant."

"Then do something about it," de Atre said and laughed, exposing a row of yellow teeth. "But first, remove all them daggers and pistols you have hidden on you. I don't trust any Scot with two hands."

Stripping himself of his extra weapons, Colin promised himself that de Atre would be among the first to feel his blade the instant he revealed his true purpose for coming here.

"Come, stray, let us see what you've got. But be warned, I've sent all your brothers back to their mothers castrated and broken."

Colin's lip curled as he readied his blade. "Not *my* brothers, ye haven't."

His metal flashed as it came up, blocking de Atre's next strike above his head. He parried another hit, and then another, scraping the edge of his blade down de Atre's. Pushing off, he stepped back, loosened his shoulders, and rolled his wrist. The blade danced with fluid grace beneath the sun, casting a flicker of doubt in de Atre's eyes.

Not yet.

He tightened his stance, as if suffering from a bout of nerves at what he was facing. De Atre advanced and swung wide. Colin avoided the slice to his belly with a step to his left. He ducked at a swipe to his neck and parried a number of rather tedious strikes to his knees. After a few moments, it became clear that he could fight the lieutenant while he was half-asleep. He suppressed the urge to yawn, thinking about what kind of beds were given to the garrison soldiers. Hay would be a welcome reprieve from the hard, cold ground he'd been sleeping on for the past se'nnight.

A spot of bright military blue and white lace crossed his vision and he followed it while he blocked another blow. The captain of the garrison caught his gaze across the crowded courtyard and held it a moment before ordering both men to cease.

"You there," he called an instant later. "Come forward."

Colin flicked his gaze to the captain, taking in polished black boots, crisp breeches, and a clean military coat adorned in lace. He was older than the lieutenant, mayhap in his fortieth year, clean-shaven and lithe of build.

"I am Captain George Gates," he said when Colin reached him.

"Captain." Colin met his level gaze.

"Your name?" the captain asked, scrutinizing him with narrowed eyes the same way his lieutenant had, but with interest rather than challenge.

"Colin Campbell of Breadalbane."

"What do you want here?"

"I wish to offer my sword to yer lord."

Gates arched his brow at him. "Why?"

"Because my cousin the future Earl of Argyll assured me that Lord Devon would soon need more men to guard his castle."

"Did he?" the captain asked with skepticism narrowing his eyes. "What else did Argyll tell you?"

Almost everything Colin needed to know. The Dutch prince had begun to assemble an expeditionary force against the king. But he wouldn't attack without penned invitations from England's most eminent noblemen inviting him to invade. According to Argyll, Dartmouth was to be the host of the invading Dutch army, and Lord Devon, the man arranging it all. Colin's task was to discover who among King James's vassals signed their names to the invitation, when the prince meant to invade, how many men he would bring with him, and then to kill them all. His glorious war.

Colin almost couldn't help smiling slightly at the thought. "He told me why."

Gates's subtle reaction was exactly what Colin expected. A hint of surprise that a mercenary would know a prince's intentions, and then a nod of acceptance because the only way he could know it was if a prominent ally such as Duncan Campbell of Argyll had told him.

"Very well," the captain said. "I'll take you to the earl. If you wish to fight for him, let him decide if you are worthy."

"My thanks," Colin offered. He retrieved his daggers, ignored the glare de Atre flung at him, and then followed his escort toward the entrance in the square tower.

At the doors, Gates stopped and turned to him. "So that we are clear on this: I did not train or choose my lieutenant. If you are here for any other purpose than the one you claim, I will personally remove your head."

He waited until Colin nodded that he understood and then led him inside. The ground floor was smaller inside than it appeared from outdoors. The narrow windows afforded little light and were used mainly as gun ports; there were seven that Colin could count from his position.

"Gillian!" The thunderous shout reverberated through the long halls, scattering servants every which way. "Gillian!" the voice bellowed again, followed this time by the pounding of boots down the stairs. "Answer when I call for you, bitch! Ranulf! Where are my musicians, my wine?"

Colin looked up at the tall, lanky nobleman stomping toward them. His dark, perfect ringlets bounced around the shoulders of his crisp justacorps. His complexion was pale, as if painted, but not. His dark gray eyes darted about the hall before coming to rest on Colin.

"Who are you?"

"My lord Devon"—Captain Gates stepped forward—"this is Colin—"

"Captain Gates." The earl shifted his haughty gaze to the captain, his interest in the mercenary standing in his hall already gone. "Where is my cousin? I've been calling for her. Your duty is to guard her. Why are you not with her and bringing her to me?"

"She was asleep when I left her, my lord."

"Well, wake her up! And her bastard with her! No reason that brat should sleep all day."

Captain Gates offered him a brisk nod, then started toward the stairs.

"There is no need to fetch me, my good captain," came a soft voice from the top of the stairs.

Colin watched the woman descend, her pale, wheaten waves falling lightly over her white, flowing gown. 'Twas the woman from the battlements.

She didn't look at him. Her eyes, like twin blue seas, churned with a frosty glitter as she set them on the earl.

"I hope my lord will forgive me for sleeping while he bellowed for me."

Colin was tempted to smile at her. Her ability to speak such a humbling falsehood and sound so convincing while doing it impressed him. The truth lay in her eyes if one but looked.

"I won't show you mercy next time, Gillian," he promised, gloating at her surrender. "Now make haste and bring me some wine from the cellar." He lifted his manicured fingers and snapped at his captain. "Go with her, Gates, and make certain she doesn't dally or it will cost you a month's wage."

Lord Devon watched them leave the hall on their errand, and then settled his gaze on a serving girl on her way to some chore. He snatched her arm as she passed him and yanked her into his arms.

"What are you still doing here?" he demanded, lifting his mouth from her neck when he saw Colin. "Who are you?"

Verra likely yer worst enemy. Colin granted his host his most practiced bow. "I am the man who will lead yer army to victory."

Chapter Two

Lady Gillian Dearly looked over her shoulder on the way toward the wine cellar at the stranger standing with her cousin Geoffrey. She knew by his dark hooded mantle that he was the man who'd watched her from the cliffs. Who was he and what had he been doing resting on the cliff side staring up at the castle? At her? Had he told Captain Gates that he'd seen her in the turrets?

She hoped not. The only thing worse than the captain discovering that she had risked her virtue alone in the halls was Geoffrey finding out the same. She wasn't permitted to roam about unescorted for fear that one of her cousin's hired mercenaries would abduct her. It was an irrational fear—for the most part, at least. Though the men held no particular allegiance to God, the king, or the Earl of Essex's daughter, they were all too afraid of Captain Gates to touch her. In that, her constant chaperone performed his duties well. She didn't want to get him into trouble or, Heaven forbid, wake up to find one of her cousin's other men tailing her, but sometimes she needed the rush of the wind through her hair and the vast horizon filling her vision. She escaped to the turrets often to imagine a different kind of life. Truly, there was no harm in it, but if either man suspected her of possessing a more cunning nature than what she portrayed, they would watch her more intently.

Both with a completely different purpose.

George Gates was her cousin's highest in command, charged from the day she'd arrived here four years ago with the duty of guarding her virtue...or whatever was left of it. But he didn't protect her from the hounds simply because he'd been hired to. He had become her friend. The only man left in the world that she trusted.

When they reached the upper cellar, she dipped a silver pitcher into a keg of aged wine and filled it. "This keg is almost empty. We will need another brought up from below."

"Where were you when he was calling?"

She looked up at him leaning his back against the door, watching her with pity softening his expression. She didn't want it. It did her no good, save to tempt her to weep—and she would never, ever do that.

"As I said, I was asleep in my bed."

Gates regarded her in silence for a moment, knowing full well that masking her expression was a feat she'd never master. Everything, damn her...everything was always right there on her face to read. "If Devon thought for an instant that you looked for a way out..."

"You know I would never think of running away," she told him, wiping the lip of the pitcher with her apron and avoiding his gaze while she passed him on her way back to the door. Oh, but how many hundreds of times had she contemplated it, dreamed about it? Not of running—for where could she go alone and with a three-year-old babe at her hip? Edmund: the reason she breathed, schemed, and risked her life sending missives to William of Orange. No, she wouldn't run. She hoped to walk out of Dartmouth with her head held high and the power of a new king at her back, a new king who, thanks to her, knew the truth about her cousin.

"Where would I take him?" she asked softly, pausing in the hall at the bottom of the stairs and looking up longingly to where her babe slept soundly in his chamber. "I cannot return to my father. Nor do I ever want to."

"Someday"—George moved up behind her and placed a tender hand on her shoulder—"when he has forgiven you..."

"Forgiven me?" She angled her chin to have a good look at her friend, and then to offer him a disparaging sigh. Was every man her judge, even the ones who didn't condemn her? Aye, she had a child out of wedlock. Was that a good enough reason to abandon her to hell? "And how long should it take me to forgive him for casting me and my son into my cousin's cruel hands? When should I forgive my mother for caring more about the haughty opinions of her peers than about the welfare of her youngest daughter and grandchild?"

Her captain looked away from the cold, hard truth of it. Gillian didn't blame him. She wished she could, as well. She'd been found guilty of falling foolishly in love and sentenced to live under lock and key inside a fortress overlooking the sea. But she and her child would be free. She would see to it, and then she would never be so foolish again.

"Let us not speak of my parents anymore." Gillian lifted her hand to his lapel and brushed a mote of lint away. "Or of me trying to escape Dartmouth. I am strong, and I shall continue to find the strength to wake each morning because of my son. Now come, I would see to Geoffrey's thirst before Edmund wakes from his nap."

He nodded, his composure disintegrating a little at the smile she offered him.

"About the man who arrived earlier." He coughed into his fist and led her down the hall.

Gillian kept her even pace as her heart quickened along with her breath. Had the stranger told him where he'd seen her then? She'd assured George the last time he caught her alone in the turrets that she could handle any man who came upon her. He'd taught her well enough how to use her dagger. But she knew he worried about her, and she didn't want him to.

"He might be remaining here," he continued, urging her to pick up her pace. "If he does, I want you to tell me if he makes any advances toward you."

"Of course," she promised quietly. It was the same promise she made to him whenever any new guardsman joined the garrison.

"Be wary of him. He arrived as if on thin air."

Or from the sea, Gillian corrected silently. "Who is he?"

"Colin Campbell, relative of the Campbells of Argyll." He grew quiet for a moment as they walked the hall. Then said, "I don't trust the Campbells, and this one carries a great number of weapons, all of which I'm certain he knows how to use with great skill, despite his claims to the contrary."

"What purpose would he have for disguising his skill?"

"I've no idea." The captain shared his thoughts with her because there was not a man in his garrison whom he had ever befriended. He was as alone here as she. "But I will tell you this," he continued absently. "I've never seen a man strike, block, and parry while not even looking at his opponent. I will be watching him closely if Devon accepts him for hire."

"I will be wary of him," Gillian promised. Another dangerous mercenary. One more to aid Geoffrey in his quest to see William of Orange take the throne. She was glad for it. The sooner Prince William arrived, the better. She didn't care about religious upheavals or who sat on the throne. Three and a half years of obeying a cruel madman had hardened her heart to everything but her son. She would do anything to keep Edmund safe, including betraying King James and tolerating her cousin when she had to. She had learned to bend, but by God, she would never break.

They searched for Geoffrey and finally found him waiting above stairs in his solar with Colin Campbell.

"Ah, finally, my dear cousin tends to me." From his seat beside the hearth, Geoffrey lifted his hand and motioned for her to come to him.

Gillian hesitated. She knew she shouldn't, but the thought of being close to him made her ill. The Earl of Devon, son of her father's brother, had demonstrated an unnatural attraction to her from the time they were children and she'd been sent to spend the summer with her relatives. It was the worst summer of her life, having to continually fight off Geoffrey's advances. She thought he'd forgotten her as the years passed, but when she confessed her delicate condition to her father, Geoffrey had been only too eager to take her under his care. In exchange for hiding away her shame, her father had offered him his troops when Prince William came to England.

Life at Dartmouth was a nightmare in different shades of gray. Bleak and oppressive, it was no place to raise a child. Geoffrey wanted her for himself and he hated her for letting Edmund's father spoil her. His words were never tender. His breath always stank of sour wine, and often the scent of sex and sweat clung to his clothes. But she didn't hate him for those things. She hated him for hating her son.

He beckoned again, and this time she moved. He didn't appear angry. She was grateful for that at least. It wasn't that she was afraid of his temper. She could take the worst he had to offer. But once his mood went sour, there was no peace to be found until he retired to his bed. She did what she could to avoid another miserable day listening to him shout and spew threats at her.

"Pour us some wine, Gillian."

She did as she was told, keeping her eyes averted from his challenging grin and lusty gaze.

"I will decline, lady. 'Tis too early in the day."

She glanced up from the cup she offered to the mercenary and went still as her level gaze met his. Enraptured like an insect to a flame...or a pair of them, she forgot everything, including the need for breath while she stared openly at his beautiful face. His eyes were the only source of light against his dark, flinty visage. Ringed by raven lashes and painted in a dozen different shades of green and gold, they shimmered with a power that, for a moment, made her feel sorry for any who came against him. Oddly, his voice was just as beguiling. It covered her like a thick blanket, warm and husky, with a slight melodious burr belonging to the Scots. When Geoffrey announced his declaration to be nonsense, he blinked slowly, breaking the spell his penetrating gaze had cast over her.

"It is never too early to drink from my fine cellar. Isn't

that correct, Gates?" While he spoke, Geoffrey moved his palm over her knuckles and she gritted her teeth, trying not to shiver as if the cold claws of death had just come for her.

Pushing off the door, Captain Gates nodded and stepped forward to take the pitcher from Gillian and pour his own drink.

Her task done, she moved to step back, but Geoffrey's hand on the small of her back stopped her. "Unless it is tainted with poison. Captain," he said, without taking his eyes off hers, "you drink it first."

Gillian wanted to laugh in his face, though the thought of poisoning him had crossed her mind a number of times. Unfortunately, there were little or no plants in the vicinity that she knew of that would do the trick. He remained silent while George downed his wine. A moment later, when the captain didn't crumple to the floor, clutching his throat, her cousin smiled up at her. "You don't have the courage to kill me, do you, Gillian?" He traced his fingertips over the curve of her hip, then up her arm, to a curl dangling beneath her breast.

"If that is all," she murmured, stepping away from him and doing everything in her power not to bolt out of the solar, out of her gown, and into the nearest cesspit to cleanse herself of his touch, "I will go tend to—"

"You will remain exactly where you are, wench. And don't speak again." The desire in his eyes turned dark with malice.

She tightened her jaw, keeping the hatred she felt for him from spilling forth. That was what he wanted: for her to lose her control and give him an excuse to take Edmund from her. The bastard was jealous of her son—and with good reason—and since he had the power to make her worst nightmare come to pass, she did as he ordered. For the time being. Besides, she didn't mind keeping quiet, since she had little to say to him, save to tell him to rot in hell.

"You will tend to me," he warned her quietly. "Your bratling sleeps, does he not? And in a soft bed, because of my mercy. Do not tax me or I'll have him put out with the horses."

Her fists trembled at her sides, but she kept them there instead of around Geoffrey's throat. She suspected he knew that if he harmed Edmund, she would kill him. Still, that didn't stop him from threatening her babe every chance he found. He didn't need her here. He had servants to do his bidding and to see to his private needs. He simply enjoyed keeping her from the one thing that gave her any joy.

"Pay no heed to my cousin." He offered the mercenary an apologetic smile for the interruption. "She may appear a noble woman, but she is nothing more than a common whore with a bastard chained to her ankles. I was kind enough to take her in when her father cast her out and she does nothing but defy me."

Gillian breathed slowly, willing herself not to flinch. This was nothing she hadn't heard a dozen times before—spoken in front of anyone who cared to listen. Geoffrey did all to strip her of her dignity, even laughing when his men whispered the same. How else would any woman want him unless she was nothing more than a broken, empty shell?

Well, he was a fool if he thought she would ever become that woman.

"My lord," Mr. Campbell said softly, "I would prefer not to speak of war in a lady's presence."

It must have been his sheer boldness that made Geoffrey laugh. The Highlander didn't smile back. In fact, if not for the twitch of his tightened jaw, Gillian would have thought him to be carved in stone.

"Regardless of what you would prefer," Geoffrey said, sobering when the mercenary didn't share his humor, "she will remain."

"As ye wish." Campbell offered him a slight nod, then caught her gaze with an intensity that threatened to consume her and everything around her.

She felt George's hand on her arm, pulling her to stand closer to him. She went without argument, lowering her gaze, sacrificing her pride for peace and quiet, for her son's sake.

"Captain," Geoffrey said, his anger mollified for now, "Mr. Campbell here thinks to take over my army."

"I did not say that, my lord," Mr. Campbell corrected him coolly.

"What then did you say?"

"I can lead ye to victory."

"Against the king?" George put to him bluntly.

"Aye, I know the numbers of his army, his navy, and, most important, his Royal Life Guards. I know who among his highest ranking officers commands his loyalty and who does not."

Gillian listened with one ear. As many of Geoffrey's hired army already had, this mercenary, too, could provide her with useful information she could send to William. She'd found favor with the Dutch prince after corresponding with him for the last year. He confessed to owing her much and promised to free her and Edmund from her cousin's care. She hoped he would keep his word. But her hope was a fragile thing. She didn't trust men and their words. A lesson she had learned well so far.

"How do you know these things, Campbell?" Geoffrey queried, examining his fingernail.

"I fought alongside many of them as a soldier in the Life Guard."

"Why did you leave?" Captain Gates asked.

"Because when he captured the Earl of Argyll after my cousin's failed rebellion, the king executed him."

Geoffrey laughed and downed his wine. "You Scots are a loyal bunch of barbarians."

Campbell crooked his mouth ever so slightly. "Not a poor combination to have at yer back."

"Indeed," Geoffrey agreed and motioned to Gillian to refill his cup. "You will begin your training tomorrow. My steward will pay you at the end of each month."

The men continued to speak about what needed to be done to restore the kingdom to its proper glory. With Geoffrey's attention on his soon-to-be, hopeful victory over the Catholics, Gillian was free to give closer inspection to the stranger.

She liked the way he wore his dark hair sheared close to his head. It gave him a cleaner look than the rest of Geoffrey's guardsmen. He wore no beard to catch bits of his food, but a shadow remained along his jaw, defining harsh, unrelenting lines and a slightly darker dimple in his chin. His expression didn't change all that much whether he spoke of battle or his family in Breadalbane.

George was correct about him. He did carry a great number of weapons. There were two daggers—that she could see—tucked into each of his black leather boots. Two pistols in his belt and another dagger tied to his hip beside one of his two swords. Good Lord, was he readying for an all-out war that he meant to fight on his own?

Gillian sighed and looked toward the door, hoping Edmund hadn't awakened yet.

A knock sounded, startling her.

"Your pardon, my lord." Margaret, Geoffrey's favorite serving wench, curtsied after he allowed entry. "The boy awakens."

The boy. Even the servants didn't give Edmund a name. Gillian nodded, thankful to be leaving. When she moved to go though, her cousin's fingers around her wrist stayed her.

"Captain," he said, holding her still. "See to the child. Take Campbell with you and show him his sleeping quarters. I would have a word with my cousin." When George hesitated, Geoffrey's expression hardened. "I'll send for de Atre to bring her to you when I'm done with her." When neither man moved, he stood. "Leave us!"

Gillian watched the men leave from beneath the veil of her lashes and thought for a moment that the stranger might turn and give her another look before walking out the door, but he didn't. She watched the door close, leaving her alone with Geoffrey, his thumb sliding across her palm.

"You know, my dear"—his stale breath along her cheekbone made her want to retch—"life would be more pleasant here for you and your little bastard if you would simply submit to my requests and desires."

When he pressed his lips to her temple, she pulled away. "And if I submit, how do you think my father would react when he learns that I carry *your* child?"

He laughed, cooling her blood. "Better than that commoner you let defile you. But soon, it will not matter what you or your father want. When Prince William is king he will give you to me."

No. No, he won't. He vowed it.

"We are cousins," she reminded him, disgusted.

"You forget that William is wed to his cousin?"

Gillian closed her eyes to hide the moisture in them blurring her vision. She would die first. She would hurl herself into the sea, and Edmund with her, before she went to her cousin's bed. *Please God*, she prayed silently. *Please, please rescue us.*

Chapter Three

Colin shut the door to the solar, then turned to have a look at it. Whatever was going on inside was not his concern. He'd achieved the first part of his task, and 'twas simple enough. He now belonged to Devon's garrison. Gates had all but admitted that they planned to overtake the king—although Colin already knew as much. He would proceed with what he'd come here to do and not waste his time on other thoughts. Besides, this wasn't the first time he'd witnessed a lass being poorly treated. He'd sat at enough tables in England's courts and in her pubs to know that the courtly customs from his mother's knightly tales had died long ago. He'd always remained untouched by what he saw. Granted, he'd rarely seen such fight in any lass's eyes, or such mastery at holding her tongue. But what did it matter? He wasn't born to save damsels in distress.

"Campbell?"

He turned away from the door and looked at the captain. Gates had been angered by the lass's humiliation, but he hadn't intervened. Colin wouldn't either.

"He will not put his hands to her."

Colin nodded and stepped away, putting aside the memory of her gazing out over the sea and the unassuming self-control she possessed not to rip out Devon's eyes.

"He knows I will cut off his hands if he does, and yours, as well."

Colin held up his palms, having no intention of ever touching her. Gates cared for her then. Did she go to the turret to await the return of the father of her child, or was he standing here before Colin now? It didn't matter. The intricacies of relationships here were of no concern to him. The less he knew about any of them, the easier it would be to deceive them and to betray their trust.

Clearing his thoughts, he looked around, familiarizing himself with his surroundings. They were in the round tower. There was a stone stairwell that he knew led to the square tower, where they were heading now, and another stairwell, illuminated by daylight, leading down to the timber-framed opening outside the river. Possible entry and escape routes were vital in his line of work. The interior was smaller than Camlochlin. Dimly lit corridors led in every direction, east and west, north and south, with plenty of shadowy alcoves where one might rest and listen to covert talks about battles to come. The absence of tapestries and sufficient fires in the hearths lent to the castle's cold ambience. The smell of ale and wine permeated the air like stale breath against a fair lady's cheek...

"You will take your meals in the Great Hall with the rest of the garrison and Lord Devon," Gates said, interrupting his uninvited thoughts.

"The earl eats with his men?" Colin asked him.

"It affords him a feeling of safety."

"Does he have many enemies in the surrounding counties, then?"

"Less than he imagines. There are very few Catholics left in Cornwall and Essex."

Aye, Colin knew that well enough after having fought in the Battle of Sedgemoor with the king's Royal Army when they quelled the Monmouth Rebellion three years ago. So, Devon was mistrustful and mayhap overly cautious. It could serve him well to sit every night with the earl.

"You'll be sleeping in one of the two barracks in the lower part of the square tower. Lady Gillian and her son's rooms are on the landing above." The captain turned to him when they entered the square tower. "You may not venture to their rooms without me. Do you understand?" He waited until Colin nodded. "I will show you to the Great Hall after I see to Edmund."

Colin assumed Edmund was Lady Gillian's son. Hell, why hadn't anyone ever mentioned a lady and her babe lived here? He wasn't so merciless to allow either to be slaughtered along with the rest of Dartmouth when he sent for his men. He would think on what to do about them later. Now he had more important discoveries to make.

"Ye are a soldier in the Royal Horse Guards," he said, looking over Gates's blue coat as they climbed the stairs. Unlike himself, a general in the red-coated Life Guards whose duty was to serve the king, the Blues were independent troops scattered throughout England, Scotland, and Ireland, serving Parliament.

"Did ye fight at the Battle of Sedgemoor when the Duke of Monmouth was captured then?" Colin studied Gates's appearance more closely. They were of the same height, though the captain's build was a bit leaner, more elegant in his crisp uniform. His hair was the same color as the sand beyond the rocky cliffs, just like hundreds of other men, Life Guards and Horse Guards alike, who had fought at Sedgemoor to protect the king. Even if they had seen each other during the battle, Colin did not recognize him, and he was fairly certain Gates did not recognize him either.

Gates shook his head as they walked together down the hall. "I did not. Though at the time, the Horse Guards did support the king."

"How did ye come to reside here then, with mercenaries under yer command?"

The captain paused for a moment to glance at him and to consider his next words.

"I was in service to Lord Algernon Dearly, Devon's father, for many years. I remain with his son for another purpose."

"To lead William to victory?" Colin pressed innocently.

"No. As a chaperone to the daughter of his uncle, the Earl of Essex."

So, the captain's loyalty did not fall to Devon but to Lady Gillian…or her father. Essex was rumored to be a supporter of William of Orange, but Colin pressed no further, seeing that Gates was clearly uncomfortable with the topic.

The captain motioned to follow him to a door at the top of another stairway, but said nothing else. When they reached it, he pushed on the latch and stepped inside.

Colin leaned around the doorframe and looked into the room to find the bulky captain lifting a small boy from his bed with gentle, tender hands. He did not caress the child to his chest, but held him slightly away, smiling, but looking ill at ease. "We'll keep him with us until his mother returns, and then you can fill your belly."

Colin nodded and stepped away from the door when

Gates exited, the child squirming in his outstretched hands.

"Do you have a wife?"

"No," Colin answered, straining his voice over the lad's wails.

"I met my Sarah in Essex. Alas, she is barren."

That accounted for his unease with the boy. Was he not the father then? The captain was wed, but Colin knew that wasn't enough to stop most men from taking another to their bed.

"Do you have many bastards?" The captain pulled his head back just in time to avoid a small fist to the lip.

"Only nephews that I recently visited."

"Good. Here." Gates shoved the boy at him. "Your first duty is to make him cease that ungodly screeching."

Colin didn't mind holding the lad. In fact, he'd enjoyed carrying his sister's and brothers' bairns around—when they let him—on his last visit to Camlochlin. "Ye don't want to be carried, do ye, Edmund?" He set the babe on his feet and took his hand. The boy stopped crying immediately.

"No." The child tugged on Colin's arm, then tugged again until Colin squatted before him. "Who are you?"

His gaze level with Edmund's, Colin was struck by the boy's beauty. With his crown of soft yellow curls and pale blue eyes, he resembled his mother . . . and a chubby angel Colin had seen once in a painting in France. "I'm Colin."

"Where's Mummy?" Edmund lifted a dimpled fist to wipe his teary eye.

"She'll be along any moment now. Will ye be a big lad and wait fer her?"

Edmund nodded and shoved his thumb into his mouth.

"I'm impressed," Gates told him when he straightened.

Colin shrugged off the compliment and picked up his steps. "They don't like to be treated like babes."

"They grow quickly," Gates agreed, giving the boy a loving look.

Colin followed his gaze and let it settle on Edmund's tiny hand in his. "Shame," he said quietly, thinking of his kin at home on Skye. He was glad he'd returned to Camlochlin before coming here. He'd never met his nephews or nieces before that day and it had pained his heart just a little that they didn't know him. They reminded him that he was more than a warrior. He was a man. Mayhap, someday, a father. But not anytime soon.

"I'm hungry," Edmund said over his thumb.

Colin looked down at him and rubbed his growling belly. "So am I. Would ye care to join me at the table?"

Edmund nodded and the three of them made their way down the stairs to the Great Hall.

There were still a few men loitering about when Colin and his party arrived. The fiery-haired serving girl whose gown Devon had been tugging on after his cousin left to fetch his wine earlier served them each a bowl of cold mutton stew, stale bread, and a hunk of hard cheese. They ate in silence for a good twenty breaths before Colin realized the oddity of the quiet at this table. Weren't wee lads supposed to make a clatter? Hell, the constant noise from his nephews at his father's table had been enough to give a man a sore head, but Edmund did not make a sound. Colin looked from the captain to the child. Edmund's back was arrow straight in his chair. One hand was neatly tucked into his lap while he carefully spooned his stew into his mouth with the other without losing a drop down his chin. His table manners were impeccable.

Colin scowled. 'Twas unnatural. "Do ye like swords, Edmund?"

"I like puppies."

Colin scowled harder. What good would puppies do the lad if he ever found himself pressed against a wall by an enemy's blade? He glanced around the Hall, surprised to discover that there were no other children in attendance. Who did the boy play with? A better question... why the hell was he giving his thoughts over to things that were not important to the task at hand? He looked down at his spoon, then shoved it into his mouth. He didn't like distractions. He didn't like the unnatural silence even more.

Relinquishing his spoon, he slid a dagger from beneath his vest and jammed the tip into the wooden table. Gates sprang to his feet and drew his sword, but Colin held up his other palm to stave off having his throat cut while Edmund stared wide-eyed at the shiny hilt. Aye, 'twas a nice piece of metal, given to him by King Louis of France.

"Ever play Naughts and Crosses, lad?" He turned an amicable look at Gates. "'Tis merely a game I wish to show him, Captain."

Edmund shook his head and watched him dig four grooves into the surface of the table—two vertical, and two horizontal.

"My nephews play this often," Colin said, sheathing his dagger and breaking off five small chunks of bread and five pieces of cheese. He handed the cheese to Edmund and grinned at the captain, who took his seat but left his blade in his lap. "Ye will be naughts and I, crosses. I will place my bread here." He set his piece in the center of the crisscrossed grooves. "Now ye must place yer cheese somewhere in these boxes. The first to place three in a row this way, this way, or that"—he traced a vertical, horizontal, and diagonal line with his finger—"wins. Understand?"

Edmund nodded.

"Good. Yer move."

Edmund thought about it for a moment, then leaned over the table and set his cheese in the top left-hand corner of the makeshift board.

"Captain, ye mentioned yer wife," Colin said, placing his bread to the right of his first piece. "Does she reside here?"

"She does not. She prefers to remain in Essex. I visit her whenever I am able." He pointed to the game as Edmund placed his cheese left of his center bread. "What happens if neither of you is able to form a row?"

"Then 'tis a draw." Colin placed his bread in the upper right corner, giving Edmund the win if the boy placed his next piece correctly. "Nae doubt, she will worry over ye when Prince William finally returns to our shores to claim the throne."

"What makes you so certain he will?"

"I hope he will," Colin said, glancing at him. "Many of us do." 'Twas not an untruth. He wasn't there to stop the invitation to William, but to discover as much as he could about the coming invasion. King James was wise enough to know that being well prepared for battle might be their only chance for victory. If Colin stopped whatever letters went out to William, by whoever signed them, the Dutch prince would make new plans that could take Colin years to discover.

Gates's only response to that was a noncommittal nod. Then, "She does not worry. If the prince returns, I don't think there will be much resistance."

Colin smiled slightly at the makeshift board when Edmund dropped his cheese in the correct space and won the game. There would be more resistance than the captain realized. "Well done." He gave the lad a wink and then looked up to find Lady Gillian hurrying toward the table with Lieutenant de Atre keeping close pace at her side.

Was it Lady Gillian? She looked completely transformed, wearing a smile now and glowing at her son. Colin studied her as she approached, taking in the delicate angles of her face, the shapely curves of her body softly defined in her coarse wool gown. She moved with long, purposeful strides, allowing nothing to come between her and her destination. Hell, she was bonny, with skin like ivory, smoothed and softened under a master carver's hand. But even the defiant tilt of her chin in Devon's solar earlier did not compare to the radiance of her unguarded, genuine smile now. The transformation made him curious about the kind of battle taking place within her. Being a soldier himself, he couldn't help but admire the strength she'd called upon while she was being mocked earlier. That strength hardened her. But now, here she was, stripped bare of her defenses and undeniably captivating. He realized he was staring at her and blinked his gaze away, only to find Gates staring back at him.

"Did you sleep well, my darling?" Her voice was soft, as tender as a harp string.

Colin wasn't certain if it was the sound of it, or her words that drew his gaze back to her. She had gained the seat closest to Edmund's, opposite Colin, and took her son's small face in her palms to kiss each cheek with loving affection. "You did not give Captain Gates a difficult time again, did you?"

"I've learned today," Gates told her, "that Edmund does not like the way I carry him."

She arched an amused eyebrow at him. "I would have thought that was obvious after three years of toting him around like a foul-smelling skunk, Captain."

"I can be dense, lady. I would have thought that was obvious after almost four years together."

Colin watched their interaction with a bit more than mild interest. Their gazes were affectionate but not intimate, an assessment that shouldn't have caused him any sense of relief, but somehow did.

"He was hungry," Gates informed her. "Mr. Campbell has been entertaining him while we supped."

She turned her gaze to Colin, her smile still intact enough to cause his words to falter—had he been any other man. "I hope he was no trouble to you."

"None at all," Colin assured her magnanimously. "I've been teaching him Naughts and Crosses."

"I bested him, Mummy!" Edmund turned his eyes, just as wide as his mother's, on Colin and held up two chubby fingers. "Two times!"

Lady Gillian seemed to melt at the sight of the boy's grin. "May I watch you best him *three* times?"

"Again!" Edmund squealed, snatching up his cheese.

They played another game, with de Atre joining to watch. Lady Gillian studied each move with her chin resting in her palm, taking great pleasure in her son's intelligence when he blocked Colin's bread. She looked only slightly unnerved when de Atre sat his arse on the table rather than in a chair and slurped up his stew. Stealing glances at her from time to time, Colin let Edmund win again before Captain Gates rose from his seat and announced it was time for Edmund's studies.

"De Atre, show Campbell to his lodgings," the captain commissioned. "I will be along later."

"Let me have a go at this," de Atre said, falling into Edmund's chair when the lad left it and gathering up the cheese.

Colin watched Gates leave with Lady Gillian and her son, his gaze following the luminescent tumble of her blond tresses all the way to her hips.

So she was bonny and strong-willed. He knew a dozen lasses just like her. He'd never let any one of them sway his thoughts from his task. She was no different. He denied himself physical pleasure more often than most, for battle was his one true love, and victory, his mistress. He desired nothing more.

But as they were about to exit the Hall, Edmund turned and waved him farewell.

Colin smiled at him before he could stop it and waved back.

"Explain the rules to me," de Atre said, studying the board and then Colin. "But first let me explain the rules of Dartmouth to you."

Colin sat back in his chair and listened, not caring for the glint in de Atre's eyes.

"Captain Gates will slice off your balls if you ever touch her."

"I wouldn't dream of it."

"Wise."

"Does he love her then?"

De Atre shook his head. "No. He is burdened with the task of keeping eyes on her. She's pleasing to the eye and Lord Devon wants to ensure that she gives birth to no more bastards while she's here." He set a piece of cheese in the bottom left corner and crooked his mouth into a nakedly male grin. "Not that I wouldn't like to get her fat with my own. She's a cold bitch, but I'm sure I could pull a few screams out of her. Repeat a word of that to Gates and I'll have your balls."

He winked at Colin, who fought the urge to smash the lewd lieutenant's head against the table and use his teeth for his next move.

Colin offered him a friendly smile instead. "It seems to me that more of yer attention is paid to her than to the army we will soon face in England. Thankfully, ye'll have William's navy at yer back if ye're caught off guard."

De Atre looked up at him from the game he'd just lost and sneered. "I won't need them. Come outside and I'll finish showing you."

Colin stood from his chair and swept his arm out before him. "After ye, Lieutenant."

Chapter Four

Sunlight puddled through the sparse trees and fell on the small bench in St. Petroc's churchyard, where Gillian sat with her son on her lap. With her lips pressed to Edmund's downy head, she read to him from Gildas's *De Excidio et Conquestu Britanniae* of Aurelius Ambrosius, who fought against the invading Saxons. Her voice blended with the clank of wooden swords coming from across the yard and the gulls screeching over the crashing surf beyond the cliffs. She lifted her head and looked to where the new mercenary practiced his swordplay with Lieutenant de Atre while the others looked on blandly. A cool breeze wafted through the centuries-old cemetery, lifting her hair from her face and refreshing her as she returned to her book and softly recited Gildas's accolades for a hero long dead. Men like Aurelius Ambrosius no longer existed, but she didn't allow that to stop her from believing that Edmund could someday be a good and honorable man, just like him. Of course, it would help if he were being raised with the correct guidance from a good father. But if it was up to her to act as both parents, then she would.

She looked toward the lists again when she heard de Atre call out another challenge to his opponent. She didn't hear what it was, but set her gaze to the cliffs beyond, where the crashing waves brought a smile to her face and inspired a new melody she would put to her lute later. After Edmund, her lute was the second thing she loved most at Dartmouth. She'd had it since she was a child, when she preferred practicing over more practical things like sewing and manners. She'd learned to play quickly, for everything stirred her; the twinkling of a certain star amid the rest, the gentle music of rustling leaves just before the violence of a storm. She composed melodies in her head that always moved her heart. Unlike her two older sisters, she had no use for the disingenuous structure of her noble life, with all its grand motions and meaningless encounters at this ball or that. She preferred to dream of the profound and thought she'd found it in Reggie Blount, the son of one of her father's tenants. He wasn't a peer, but Gillian thought him infinitely more exciting than the sons of barons and earls.

When she learned she was carrying Reggie's child, she wept for three days before she asked herself, What is more miraculous than a babe growing in her belly? Reggie didn't agree about it being a miracle. He called it a curse and then dashed her dreams to pieces. Oh, she mended, even after her father tossed her out. But none of it mattered when Edmund was placed in her arms. She had a son and in an instant, he gave her life a new meaning and filled her heart with joy.

She longed to give him a better, more vital life than this one, surrounded by tombstones and walls, with no men of dignity from which to learn.

But she didn't need them. She didn't need a husband or

a father for her son. She'd given up those girlish dreams long ago. She would be whatever Edmund needed. She would do whatever she must to keep him safe, whatever it took to keep him with her. She didn't need a hero, but she did need help…and she needed Prince William to make haste and get here.

"Mummy, I want to play with Colin."

She stroked her son's head and let her eyes drift to Colin Campbell again, now fighting two more soldiers.

"Perhaps later, my darling."

She knew much about the art of battle, for while Geoffrey didn't permit her to touch a weapon, Captain Gates did not deny her private lessons in the abandoned church. She knew how a sword should be handled for the best outcome. She surveyed the stranger. He appeared quite at ease while wielding his heavy, carved blade, though he fought mostly in defense against his three opponents. He was curious, that one, shifting from shadows to light with a slant of his lips. In Geoffrey's solar, his steady gaze had reminded her of a wolf, the hungry kind that came silently in the dark and sank its teeth into its victim's throat. When he played his game with Edmund though, she'd seen something else entirely, something less guarded. Both were equally alluring.

A swath of dark blue blocked her vision. She blinked up at Captain Gates and realized she had stopped reading.

"Gillian, put whatever you are entertaining away. No good can come of it."

"I don't know what you mean."

His broad shoulders straightened beneath his military coat, as if resolving himself to continue. "I mean Mr. Campbell. I see the way he draws your eye. There is nothing he can offer you without your cousin's consent, and you will not get it. Consider your son and the chance that you might only end up incurring your father's wrath once again."

Gillian set Edmund on the bench and rose to her feet. She did not raise her voice or speak in a caustic tone. She was too hurt and insulted to feel angry. Many cold, unfeeling things were spoken to her here, but never before by her captain. "Captain, my every thought, word, and action is in consideration of my son." She took a step closer to him and looked up into his gray-blue eyes. "And if you are going to suggest that I would cast his well-being aside for a hired henchman, please do not do so in front of him."

He looked away, down at his boots. "My apologies."

"Do you truly think so little of me?" she asked him, the dread of it saturating her voice. He was her only friend here in this dreary dungeon. He cared for her. He defended her when he could, but how long could any man listen to her cousin's vile words against her without coming to believe them? Oh, she couldn't bear the thought of George thinking poorly of her, turning his back on her, as the other men in her life had done. Was her captain capable of betraying her? Was that why she had never told him about her secret correspondence with Prince William? "Has Geoffrey's poison infected you as well, old friend?"

"No, never," he hastened to assure her, scowling fiercely at the unshed tears blurring her vision. "I worry over you and the boy. You mean much to me."

Aye, he did worry over her, and with good reason, with men like de Atre snapping at her heels—directly behind her cousin. She shouldn't doubt him. Not George.

Letting go of the matter, she reached for Edmund's hand and then looked down when he didn't take it.

"Edmund?" Her eyes searched the churchyard, but did not see him. She turned toward the rocky bluff and her heart seized with terror. "Edmund!" she screamed and took off running.

"Edmund, come here!" The captain's commanding tone spun her on her heel to see her son running toward the lists. She nearly fell unconscious with relief, but then she saw the danger in where he was headed. He was either too far away to hear the captain's call, or he simply refused to obey it. Gillian wasn't about to wait to find out which and sprinted after him. If the men didn't see him coming...and one of them swung his weapon...

Colin Campbell reached him first. Gillian didn't know how he managed it, but one instant he was fending off four attackers, and the next, they were picking up their swords from the ground and turning to watch him run. Scooping the child up in his arms, Colin carried him a safe distance away.

George reached them the same time Gillian did—his face, equally pale. "Boy, you know better than to walk among the men while they're practicing!"

Gillian offered the mercenary a brief but grateful smile while she took her son from his arms. "Edmund, my heart, what have I told you about minding me and Captain Gates?"

"I wanted to play Crosses and Bread with Colin, Mummy."

She caught the stranger's slight smile at Edmund's incorrect name of his game. He looked quite harmless when he smiled.

"Games!" George looked heavenward, then cast her a harder look than she was sure he had intended. "Now I understand why your cousin frowns upon them."

Gillian turned to him with a cool look of her own. "It has nothing to do with concern for Edmund. Geoffrey is miserable because his father gave him this small coastal fort instead of Powderham Castle. He wants everyone around him to suffer the same."

"Whatever the reason, we will discuss these games at length later." George sighed as if he knew that arguing the point with her was useless. "I'm accompanying Devon to Kingswear Castle to have word with Captain Cavenaugh."

"Is something amiss?" Mr. Campbell asked rather casually while keeping his eyes averted from hers.

Gillian looked away, unaware that she'd been staring.

"No." George took a moment to hold up his hand to Geoffrey when he spotted him exiting the castle pulling on his riding gloves. "Kingswear is our sister castle and guards the estuary on the opposite bank. We visit occasionally to make certain the garrison and guns are in working order. We should not be absent too long. It is not far." He barked out an order to Lieutenant de Atre to guard her and Edmund while he was away, then bid her and Mr. Campbell a brief farewell and left to join her cousin.

"Well, come along then," de Atre demanded, motioning her forward. "I'll escort you to your chambers."

Not if she had anything to say about it. She didn't like the lieutenant or the way he looked at her and Edmund when they were alone, like she was the food his master kept from him while he starved—and Edmund stood in his way of eating her alive. He never dared touch her for fear of what George would do to him, but when her guardian was away, the lieutenant grew bolder. "I would prefer to remain outdoors."

"You look flushed," de Atre purred at her. "One as fair as you could easily burn beneath the sun."

He reached for her but she stepped back, avoiding his touch. "Contrary to what you believe, Lieutenant, I am capable of thinking for myself, and I wish to remain outdoors."

She caught the slant of his abashed gaze in Mr. Campbell's direction and clenched her jaw. He'd obviously boasted of his command over all, including her, to the stranger. Would he try to drag her off if she continued to refuse him? If he laid a hand on her she swore to herself she would cut off his fingers. She would hate for Edmund to witness such a thing.

"You'll do as—"

"Perhaps," Mr. Campbell gracefully interrupted, drawing Gillian's gaze back to him, "the lady would enjoy a show of yer skill against me, Lieutenant."

De Atre sized him up with a scowl and then wiped his sweaty brow. "My skill against you has already been proven this day."

"Aye, but not with an audience of one so fair." The mercenary's glance to her was brief and a bit awkward for one so seemingly confident. Whatever his background, he carried himself with the kind of conviction one would see on a conqueror. If he wore enough weapons to win the battle on his own, then surely he knew how to use them. Gillian couldn't help but find it rather charming that a man like him would lose his composure because of her.

Turning back to de Atre, the crook of his mouth returned. "Mayhap ye are too weary from our earlier practice…"

"Nonsense!" de Atre charged. Turning to look at her, he seemed to consider if watching his victory might be just what she needed to offer herself up to him on a golden platter. He turned his yellow grin on her and drew his waster with an artful swoosh. "To the lists, then, Scot."

Before following him, Mr. Campbell fit his finger under Edmund's chin to hold his attention. In the sun, his eyes shone like emeralds frosted in gold. "I know many games to teach ye. But I will not play them with ye if ye don't mind what yer mother and Captain Gates tells ye. Agreed?" He waited until Edmund promised, and then slipped his gaze to hers for a moment before he turned away.

Gillian watched him go, wondering why he would help her, and how a man could look as appealing from the back as he did from the front. His form resonated with confidence...a hint of arrogance in his leisurely pace. What sort of mercenary carried himself with such self-authority? None that she knew of among her cousin's legion of men. Her gaze stretched across his shoulders, lingered over the width of his back, then settled on the snug fit of his breeches over his—

"Mummy?"

She breathed and blushed to her roots. "Aye, Edmund?" She looked down at her babe's tender face, his thumb hovering before his lips, and she forgot all else.

"I will mind what you and Captain Gates tells me."

Her heart melted with love for him and it radiated from her smile. "Then you shall learn Mr. Campbell's games."

He gave her an enthusiastic nod and popped his thumb back into his mouth as she returned to the bench and they sat down.

So, the Highlander was pleasing to look at. She certainly wouldn't lose her wits over it. She didn't need any more protection than what she already had with George, and surely it was only a matter of time before Campbell learned her place here and ceased his aid. Still, none of the other men had ever shown any interest in Edmund. Captain Gates cared for him, but he was a soldier who had never learned how to interact with a babe. He'd never offered to teach Edmund anything at all, let alone a game. There were no other children here. She was her son's only playmate and it often broke her heart. It was why, even knowing Geoffrey and George would disapprove, she would consider finding a way for Edmund to spend time with Mr. Campbell.

"Will you teach me to play your Naughts and Crosses, darling?"

He looked up at her from eyes as wide as the heavens and nodded against her breast. She would do anything for him, risk everything to make him happy, and kill anyone who tried to hurt him. "Would you like me to continue reading to you?"

He shook his head. "I want to watch."

She let her gaze follow his to the lists and to the Highlander fending off de Atre's blows as they rained down upon him. He swung a few times, hard, resounding responses, wielded with authority and rattling the lieutenant in his boots. All too soon though, he returned to the defensive position, backing up and ducking—albeit with agility as elusive as the wind. Curious. He had rendered his previous opponents harmless in the space of two breaths in order to get to Edmund. Was he letting Lieutenant de Atre beat him for her sake?

Stop this madness! She scolded herself. She wouldn't allow a man, a *stranger* to muddle her good senses. George believed the mercenary was withholding his skills. She agreed. But why would he? He spoke of fighting in the King's Life Guard. She wondered what he knew about the king that might be valuable to William. Speaking to him again could be beneficial to her and Edmund's escape from this place.

She blinked and felt the breath catch in her chest when he set his eyes upon her across the small field. Well, in truth, it was Edmund who'd caught his attention and softened his features. Gillian looked down to find her son leaning comfortably against her, still sucking his thumb and waving with his free hand.

Edmund liked him. Should she let him grow closer to the stranger, and to what end? They'd never see him again after William took the throne. Would that be worse for Edmund? Could she keep her thoughts off him while she watched him play with her son? She didn't realize she'd gone back to staring at him until she gasped at de Atre's wooden sword striking him in the temple. She grew angry when the lieutenant declared him dead. Mr. Campbell didn't seem to care much; in fact, he looked quite pleased with himself when his victorious opponent raised his weapon and cheered for himself.

Expelling a withering sigh, Gillian girded herself up for the battle when de Atre pranced toward her. It would be even harder to defy him now.

"Colin!" her son slipped from her lap and ran to him before Gillian could stop him, or before de Atre had a moment to open his mouth to boast or demand. "Are you hawrt?"

Gillian could see clearly that Mr. Campbell was in fact bleeding slightly where de Atre's wooden sword had met his flesh.

" 'Tis nothing," the mercenary promised, then rubbed his flat belly. "I'm hungry and was distracted."

"Colin, will you teach me how to fight?"

Gillian reached for her son's hand while the mercenary tensed his limbs. It was the same reaction all the men here had whenever Edmund asked them to teach him something. Run. Escape having to waste time with a babe. "Come, Edmund—" She took hold of him to soften the blow of another refusal. "Leave Mr. Campbell to his duties now. He has—"

"Fight against what?" De Atre angled his head slightly over his shoulder and spat. "Boy's too scrawny to fight off my smallest finger."

Gillian cast the lieutenant a look that said if she had the strength of a man she would haul him up and toss him over the side of the cliffs. Oh God, she hated thinking of Edmund helpless should anything ever befall her. She was teaching him to play the lute and to read, and compassion, but who would ever teach him to wield a sword?

"I'll teach ye how to defend yerself," the stranger said as if she'd voiced her fear aloud. She looked up at him and then realized that he was speaking to Edmund. She felt an unfamiliar, unwanted stirring in her belly and stomped it out before it went any further.

"You won't hurt him?" she asked, not trusting this man or any other near her son with a weapon. But someone had to teach him.

"I will not hurt him," he assured her, convincing her with a slight dip in his voice and an unwavering gaze.

This time, Gillian looked away first and turned to Lieutenant de Atre when he began to protest. "Lieutenant, why don't you and I share a word or two on that bench while Edmund and Mr. Campbell practice?" She knew the oaf would never decline her invitation, but when he grinned at her she had to remind herself over and over why she was doing this. It was beneficial to Edmund to practice with a man. Even more wonderful was hearing him laugh.

She barely heard a word the lieutenant uttered for the remainder of the afternoon. The sounds of gently clanging sticks, the Highlander's endlessly patient round of instructions, and her son's excited shouts and cheerful delight near made her heart burst with joy.

Later, when George returned to escort her and Edmund back inside, she found herself humming, thankful for such a pleasant afternoon. There were many pleasant days at Dartmouth, despite her circumstance. For she had no intention of ever letting the gloom of this place reach her child's heart, as it had hers.

Until today though, she hadn't realized how hard she had become. Until today, she'd almost forgotten the importance of remaining that way.

✥
Chapter Five

I crept up behind him and when he turned, I relieved
him of his innards."

Colin leaned back in his chair and watched while
Lord Devon finished his tale and grabbed at a serving
wench as she made her way around the table. Around
him, the others compared tales, swore, and struck one
another, already well on their way to a deep, drunken
night's sleep.

Looking around, Colin surveyed the Great Hall,
crowded now in comparison to the last time he'd been
here with Gates and wee Edmund. Three more long
tables had been recently erected to accommodate the rest
of Devon's garrison. Captain Gates was not among them.
Neither was Lady Gillian. The sun had barely set and
most in attendance were already drunk, or on their way.
If his army broke through the front doors right now, it
would not be difficult to take them down. Hell, he could
likely take half of them on his own.

He brought his cup to his lips but did not drink. The
poor condition of the men proved that Captain Gates was

grossly overconfident about the resistance that would meet Prince William upon his arrival. He would send word to the king about attacking Dartmouth before William arrived, so that *his* men would be here waiting for the prince. It would be easier to fight William's men with Devon's already dead.

"What about you, Campbell?" Devon called over the chairs that separated them while he groped at the lass in his lap. "What's your best kill?"

Colin looked down into his bowl and sniffed. His best kill? Well, it sure as hell didn't involve creeping. "'Twas three years ago," he said, dipping his bread into his stew. "I rode with my brother after a small group of men who meant to kill someone he had sworn to protect. I watched him cut through six of them and it fevered my blood and gave strength to my arm." He took a hefty bite of his bread and washed it down with ale. Hell, why couldn't William of Orange's closest ally be a noble with a decent cook? "I waited while the lead rider thundered toward me and swung my blade through his shoulder, deep into his spine. He died instantly."

Someone clapped him on the back, almost bringing the bread back up. "Well done, stray! I once..." Colin recognized Gerald Hampton from the yard—brutishly big and missing two teeth. He proceeded to tell Colin a tale unfit for the lass who had just entered the Hall and was approaching the far end of the table with Captain Gates.

Every eye in the Hall turned to appraise her, including Lord Devon's, though his gaze was void of admiration. He pulled the server closer against his chest and watched Lady Gillian through heavy-lidded eyes as she approached.

Tonight she wore an unadorned gown of dyed blue,

fashioned, it appeared to Colin's Highland eye, from lamb's wool, though he wouldn't know for certain unless he touched it. Her hair tumbled over her shoulders in loose, luminous coils, held away from her face by a wreath of delicate white flowers. She didn't look at him, or at anyone else, but waited while Gates pulled out her chair to her cousin's right. The table was tightly packed and she appeared delicate and out of place amid the rough, robust soldiers around her. Colin watched her avoid the stretch of a beefy arm to her left when her neighbor embellished a tale not fit for her ears. Edmund was not with her.

Hell. What was he to do with her and her babe when the battle commenced? Colin hadn't thought about it. He didn't want to, but he certainly couldn't sit idly by when his men slaughtered everyone who resided at Dartmouth. He couldn't worry over her and the boy while he fought, even though slight distractions didn't impede his skills. Could he get them out before his men arrived? Damn it, why was he entertaining such thoughts? He shouldn't have spent the entire afternoon with her and her son. He'd learned never to allow his heart to rule him, never to let his emotions hamper decisions that had to be made. He hadn't wanted to hold the boy when Gates delivered him into his arms this morn. He should have stayed out of de Atre's business with the lass, and he sure as hell hadn't wanted to teach the child swordplay. Those tasks fell to Gates, but apparently the captain was lax in those duties, as well. The worst part of it all was that he had enjoyed himself this afternoon.

Hampton elbowed him in his side. "She's a vision, I agree. But she's as cold and as quiet as a rotting corpse."

Her protection against grunting swine like ye. Colin dunked more bread into his bowl and nodded while he chewed. "The child does not dine with his mother?"

"The boy is a bastard and the earl does not like to be reminded that his noble cousin is a whore."

Colin concealed his blackest look behind his cup then slid his gaze back to Lady Gillian. He'd spent the afternoon in her company. She was quiet, aye, and completely uninterested in any man at Dartmouth, save her son. She was no whore. "Who is the lad's father?" he asked before he could stop himself.

"Hell if I know," Hampton told him. "But it isn't him." He pointed to de Atre across the table.

"On that, you speak true." The lieutenant winked, wiped his mouth with his forearm, and leaned in close so that only the men closest to him could hear. "Had the cock been mine, she would have had twins."

His comrades laughed. Colin joined them in their merriment because that was what he had come here to do.

He grew quiet and leaned back in his chair, closer to the shadows, taking in bits of important information Devon's men gave him without knowing it. Unwittingly, his eyes settled on Lady Gillian again, staring into her bowl. She shared speech with no one, eating alone among an army of men, ignoring Devon's black glare on her. Against the backdrop of firelight, her profile, partially veiled behind her pale tresses, mesmerized him. He fought it for the next quarter of an hour, unsure why he couldn't seem to stop his gaze from returning to her. He didn't like not being in complete control of his actions. He wasn't swayed by a fair face, or round, shapely hips he'd like to run his palms over. Still though, he found himself watching the way she raised her spoon to her lips and blew softly on her stew. A habit she had likely picked up from feeding her babe.

"You are tardy yet again, Gillian," her cousin finally

bit out, unable to keep his anger at her abated for another instant.

The laughter around the table faded as Devon's sharp tone cut the air. Some of the men looked uncomfortable, as if they knew what was coming and were not looking forward to it, while others, like Lieutenant de Atre, grinned and listened with piqued interest.

Lady Gillian did not look up from her supper but continued eating as if her cousin wasn't there. That seemed to enrage him. He pushed the serving wench off his lap and reached for his cup.

"What have I told you about keeping me waiting? I provide you with all this." He stretched out his arms as if presenting her with all the riches and gold any lass's heart could desire. "And you refuse to obey a simple command."

"Edmund had to be fed." 'Twas Captain Gates who spoke, offering Devon a quelling look of his own. "Your cousin is a dutiful mother."

"Would that she was an appreciative one. It is my food her fatherless bratling eats."

Lady Gillian finally set down her spoon and acknowledged him. Her eyes blazed with hatred, but when she spoke, her tone remained remarkably cool. "And it is my father's gold that keeps your larder full."

"Ah, wonders!" Devon jeered. "Lord Essex's proud though tarnished daughter speaks!" The men around her laughed. She leaned to the side of her chair, narrowly avoiding a spewed piece of bread. "Pity it is to offer me cheek. Why, if I was not so gracious, I might be tempted to cast her son—"

"Her late arrival to the table is my fault," Gates cut him off. "I left her in de Atre's charge and he failed to bring her inside in time to properly attend to the boy."

Hearing them, the lieutenant immediately took offense. "She refused to leave and instead let the bast—"

"Oh?" Gates cut him off sharply. "Is *she* my lieutenant, then? Do you do a woman's bidding?"

Colin remained utterly still in his seat, but in his lap, he rubbed his fingertips together, wishing there were a hilt between them. They argued about her as if she wasn't there, and still she remained silent. Why? None of the women at Camlochlin would have tolerated such treatment from the men. Why did she? Controlling her temper was one thing. Letting another control her was another. Why too, did Gates lay blame at his own man's feet rather than at a stranger's, where it belonged? 'Twas he who had kept the lady from her duties by playing with her son overlong. He realized, following Gates's gaze to her, that he was not protecting Colin, but Lady Gillian and her child.

"You will do as *I* tell you," the captain continued, turning back to his lieutenant. "Not what she or someone else tells you. Do you understand?"

Colin watched de Atre tighten his teeth around words he knew better than to utter. "I do, Captain," he muttered roughly instead—leashed, for now.

Was Gates aware of his lieutenant's debased cravings for Lady Gillian? Colin doubted the captain would have allowed de Atre to be alone with her if he knew. He should tell Gates how desperate his second had been to get the lady alone, and the terror in her eyes at the thought of it. But he wouldn't. He couldn't without destroying any chance he had of gaining the men's trust. Lady Gillian and her son were not his concern. At least, not yet.

"Lieutenant de Atre," Devon called out, dangling his cup from his dainty fingers, "now that you've been properly reprimanded by your captain, why don't you tell me what she let the bastard do?"

Gates shut his eyes. When he opened them again he fastened them on Lady Gillian while his lieutenant spoke.

"She let him play with Campbell here all afternoon."

"Oh?" Devon's sharp gaze cut to Colin. He raised an eyebrow, looking him over as if for the first time. "The afternoon, you say? Tell me, Mr. Campbell, do you think my cousin is—what's the word you Scots use? Bonny?"

Colin's eyes went to her, hating her cousin for humiliating her for his own pleasure. He would not add to it. "Aye," he told the earl, "that is the word we Scots use."

"Well," Devon raised his cup to him and smiled. "You may admire her, but fuck her and heads will roll."

"Geoffrey!" Lady Gillian slammed her napkin on the table.

"Cousin, why so sensitive?" Devon drew back in his seat, pretending to be startled by her reaction. "Every man at this table knows you're a whore. Why, the proof of it is just up those stairs."

She shot to her feet like a wellspring and looked down at him with something darker than hatred. When he ordered her to take her seat, Colin almost smiled when she refused.

"I'm going to bed," she bit out, daring him to stop her. "Captain Gates, there is no need for escort since everyone is here."

Gates rose from his seat anyway. Before she turned to leave, she slipped her gaze to Colin's. 'Twas a brief, incidental glance that went unnoticed by all save him.

Colin returned his attention to his comrades as she left the Hall. He didn't care if she acknowledged him, proving herself as aware of his presence as he was of hers. He laughed at something someone said and pushed away the desire to kill Devon before the appointed time. A bit harder to forget was the fact that she had graced him with what she had denied her cousin and every other man at the table.

If he could, he would help her and her child get out of Dartmouth before hell arrived at its doors. But he didn't give a damn what happened to her before or after that. He desired battle and blood, and soon he would be satisfied.

He would remain focused on the prize. Practicing kept his mind sharp and his body honed for what it was meant to do. "Which one of ye will practice with me in the morn?"

"Bloody hell, Campbell." Hampton turned to him. "You'll be at it again tomorrow?"

"Of course," Colin told him. "How do ye expect us to fight against an enemy army, should we be called to do so, if we have not held a weapon in our hands in months?"

The hairy giant laughed and held up his sloshing cup to the others. "I'm not concerned with meeting what's left of James's Life Guards on the field. I'll cut through their bones two at a time."

The men around the table cheered his sentiment and emptied their cups. Colin felt a pang of disappointment at how little a challenge any one of them would offer.

"A man should not underestimate his opponent," Devon said, quieting the rest. "An army that does so is usually defeated." He caught and held Colin's gaze. "Tomorrow they will all practice with you."

The table grew quiet for the first time that night. The men weren't laughing now.

"Perhaps," Hampton growled, drawing closer to him, "we will all *practice* with you at the same time."

Colin tipped his cup to his mouth and then, setting it

back down, slanted his gaze upward at the brute. "Do ye expect me to defeat yer enemies for ye then?"

De Atre howled with laughter, dragging Hampton's searing glare off Colin and onto him. "I told you the stray was an arrogant cock, did I not?"

His bulking friend nodded and gave Colin and his chair a shove. "We'll see how arrogant you are after I get done with you."

"Go easy with me." Colin smiled and moved forward to clap him on the back. "Ye will want me alive and at yer side later."

"I've fought you, lad," de Atre reminded him with more laughter. "You'll be among the first to die."

"Then perhaps 'tis best if I practice at night, as well."

The lieutenant and his men sobered quickly enough at that and cast apprehensive glances at Devon, hoping he hadn't heard.

"Captain Gates will practice with you tonight, Campbell. Perhaps you can convince him to work the men harder before I start to believe that he wants us to lose to our enemies."

Colin nodded. Interesting. Did Devon speak true? Did his captain want them to lose?

"I will accompany you both to the yard when he returns." Devon adjusted his wig and looked up to smile at the serving wench refilling his cup. Before she left he patted her backside and then returned his attention to Colin. "I would see for myself if you are worth the coin I'm paying you."

"I hope not to disappoint, my lord," Colin offered, raising his cup to him. If fortune favored him, Devon might be tempted to raise his sword against him and Colin could make him pay for calling his cousin a whore once again.

Chapter Six

Gillian stayed in Edmund's room for most of the morning. They broke fast together, read three books, and played a dozen games of Naughts and Crosses. But he was restless to be outdoors, eager to see Colin Campbell. Edmund spoke of him without pause, gleefully retelling his mother how he'd bested the friendly stranger during their stick competition the day before. It was pitiful really. Gillian wanted nothing more than to give her son what he wished, but Mr. Campbell hadn't left the courtyard all morning. She knew this because Edmund had dragged her to the window countless times to see if his new friend had finished practicing with the garrison. They watched, with Edmund safely in her arms, while the mercenary took on six men at a time. They scowled, equally annoyed that a few of the men laughed when he was brought down to one knee. He hadn't given up though, springing back to his feet to meet the next four coming against him. He seemed driven to fight, determined to continue until he collapsed. Which didn't appear to be an imminent concern. He fought defensively again, which proved he hadn't lost to de Atre for her sake. He fought as if he meant to tire the men rather than beat them.

Captain Gates was down there with the rest, which meant she would have to send one of Geoffrey's serving wenches to the yard to fetch him if she meant to leave the room. And did she truly want to witness Mr. Campbell's defeat at closer proximity? Did she want Edmund to see?

"He said we could practice today."

Gillian smiled at her son. "I fear his practice with the men may go on all day." Perhaps she could find a pair of sticks and play with him. "Perhaps you will see him after your nap."

"I'm not sleepy."

Why would he be? Sighing, Gillian drew her son's head closer and kissed it. She really had to learn more games to play with him. "Shall we finish our story about the adventurer Columbus?"

He shook his head, staring down at the courtyard below.

Gillian followed his gaze and watched while the newest addition to Geoffrey's garrison fought off three more attackers. A Campbell. What did she know about the Highland clan? Not much, save that they were a powerful clan with strong ties in Parliament. How did Mr. Campbell end up a hired mercenary? And why couldn't she forget the way his eyes felt on her last eve through supper? Curious, scalding embers in the firelight—especially after Geoffrey opened his vile mouth. Oh, she could have killed her cousin right there in front of his entire garrison when he spoke of her so crudely. What would his men have done if she had produced her hidden dagger and plunged it into his heart?

She quickly put Geoffrey out of her thoughts, replacing

him with the memory of the mercenary's voice, the way he smiled at Edmund while they clashed sticks in the yard. Was she mad? She was afraid to wonder what Geoffrey would do if she showed the slightest bit of interest in him. And she *had* no interest in him other than any new information he might have that she could give to William. What was the point of anything else? She was no longer a foolish twit looking for the magical, the astonishing, the soul-stirring. It didn't exist. She shouldn't have allowed Edmund to play with him. It wasn't practical to waste time trying to find good in a man simply because he was kind to her child.

She smiled, as relieved as her clapping son was when Colin's last two opponents threw down their wasters and gasped a halt for the day. He'd outlasted them all. The rest of the men agreed on a rest, each looking wearier than the one before him. He may have been struck in places that would have left him dead on the field, but without a true deathblow, Colin had endured them all. Not only that, but he appeared fit and ready, despite the damp shirt clinging to his chest and shoulders, to take them all on again.

As if feeling her gaze, he looked up at the window. His chiseled features softened as he raised his hand in greeting.

Gillian certainly wasn't about to wave back at him like some needy damsel in search of her champion. But his greeting wasn't aimed at her, she realized a moment later, catching Edmund's hand swinging over his head.

"May we come down now?" her son called out, but Colin was too far below to hear.

She couldn't tell if he was looking at her or Edmund before he turned to walk the other way.

Moving away from the window, Gillian set down

her son and then returned to close and lock the shutters. "Captain Gates will come for us shortly." She bent to Edmund, leveling their matching gazes. "What have we learned about patience?"

"It's a virtue!" Edmund grinned at her, proud of himself for remembering. She was proud of him too.

"Very good." She laughed and drew closer to kiss his downy soft curls. "Now why don't we practice the lute together until the good captain comes to fetch us?"

Casting the obstructed window one last, longing look, he nodded and popped his finger into his mouth. "Will you teach me a new song, Mummy?" he asked between sucks.

She turned from reaching for her beloved instrument and feigned bewilderment. "Do you think you can learn another?"

"I can learn anything, can't I?"

"Aye, my darling." She smiled, handing a smaller lute to him. "You most certainly can. Never let anyone tell you differently."

As she waited for Edmund to sit and then pluck the first note a knock came at the door. She knew who it was when the knocker didn't enter until she bid him to do so.

"Captain," she said, setting down her lute and rising to her feet. "Thank you for coming for us so quickly."

He looked like she had just kicked him in the guts. "I deserve no gratitude for leaving you up here all day. Forgive me."

She patted his arm and offered him a tender smile. "It's perfectly understandable. The men finally show interest in something other than drink."

"Aye." His mouth crooked to one side as he looked toward the window. "A bloodlust to quiet an arrogant tongue."

"What is arrogant about one admitting he needs practice?"

George cut her a measured side look before nodding a greeting to Edmund. "Where is the humility in what he is doing to my men? They gain their victories over him, but he will not yield."

Aye, her captain was clever.

"They are weary and winded from striking him," he continued, "but when they think he's spent, he challenges more to fight him. I myself practiced with him last evening and today my body feels the effects of it, but he is out there taking on an army. It's arrogant."

Turning from him, Gillian laughed at his self-abasement and reached for the pair of nets resting against the wall. "He's young."

"Aye," George agreed, turning with her. "He's just a few years older than you, and handsome as well."

She sighed and shook her head at him. She knew he was concerned about the consequences of her actions as they pertained to Edmund. If she did anything foolish, like try to escape Dartmouth with a hired mercenary, Geoffrey would find her and take Edmund away. She was not foolish. "My good captain," she reassured him as she moved to take Edmund's hand, "you're older than me and handsome as well, and I have not asked you to take me away."

"I have thought about it."

Gillian stopped, as did her heart. The smile she offered her son faded. Never before had George said such a thing to her. Why would he say it now? She turned to him and found that his customarily rigid composure was well intact.

"If I—"

Gillian held up her palm, stopping him from uttering another word. He wanted to save her from this miserable, abusive existence, and for that, she loved him. But she cared for him too much to ask him to risk his life for her.

Even though he was their captain, the men here were not loyal to him. If he took her from Geoffrey he couldn't keep her safe and hidden from the army that would surely come for her. She would save herself, and Edmund with her. George was her only friend, and for now that was all she needed.

"I would never allow you to sacrifice your life, or the life of your dear wife, for me. Do you understand that, Captain? I spoke in jest a moment ago. Never bring it up to me again."

"As you wish, my lady." He moved his gaze to Edmund, familiar enough with her to know the moist glimmer in her eyes would embarrass her.

"What have you planned for today?" he asked, straightening his shoulders and leading her and Edmund out the door.

"Fishing." She smiled and held up her stick with a net hanging limp at the end of it.

Mimicking his mother, Edmund held up his much smaller replica. "Mummy?" He looked up as he lowered his arm. "Can Colin come with us?"

The captain eyed him with a frown, then raised the same disapproving look to her.

Oh, for goodness' sake!

"Edmund has taken a liking to him, George, not I. Where is the harm in that?"

"Where would you prefer me to begin?" he asked, folding his hands behind his back. Gillian suspected by his frown growing into a full-blown scowl that he did it to stop himself from throttling her.

"Despite what you believe," she told him briskly, "games are not dangerous, and little boys need to play them." *And I need something new to entice William of Orange to keep his vow to me.* "Unless you are willing to teach him something fun now and again, I see no harm in letting him spend time with Mr. Campbell."

"We know nothing about him," George argued.

"We know he knows how to play Naughts and Crosses, and that he is willing to do so with Edmund. I'm not a fool and will not allow him or any other man to deceive me again. Let him make Edmund's days here a bit more pleasant. You've nothing to fear from me."

George's jaw tightened around a dozen arguments fighting to be presented. "Very well," he finally managed with a touch of grace. "But I will not leave your side."

He barely ever did. He was her protector, and Gillian was thankful for it.

"Does you think he knows how to catch a fish, Mummy?"

She looked up at George and he growled something unintelligible before he muttered, "We shall find out soon enough."

Soon enough came too quickly for Gillian. When they stepped out of the castle and George beckoned the mercenary forward, she did her best to look at everything around her but him.

She failed, stealing glances at him as he came toward them. His garments weren't anywhere near as crisp as Captain Gates's, but he looked infinitely more appealing in his snug breeches and damp shirt tucked haphazardly into his weapon-laden belt. She resisted the urge to clear her throat or look up and smile like some tender-aged fool, ready and willing to believe the best in a man.

She wasn't that girl. She never would be again.

"Ah, finally a worthy opponent."

His rich, resonant voice drew Gillian's gaze back to him, and she found him to be addressing Edmund. She shifted in her place when he winked at her son.

"Campbell!" George barked, startling her back to stillness. "We're going fishing."

Edmund's friend looked up the length of her stick to her net, then briefly at her. An instant was all it took to feel the charge in his gaze that set her nerve endings afire.

"You're coming."

Mr. Campbell blinked at his captain's command, but that was the only sign that he had acknowledged it. He looked neither pleased nor irritated by the prospect of wasting his afternoon away with a net in his hands rather than a sword.

"You will need a net, Colin," Edmund pointed out and reached for his hand.

"I will, won't I?" the mercenary asked, covering Edmund's small hand with his much larger one.

"You may use mine."

All three pairs of eyes looked at her, but it was the Highlander's that captured her and made her lips go dry. His gaze softened, deepening with a hint of a smokier shade of green. He offered her the barest hint of a smile, then accepted the net she offered up.

"What kind of fish do ye catch here?" he asked, returning his attention to the captain.

"I don't know. They've never caught any."

Campbell's smile widened as unexpectedly as a spring rain that even he hadn't anticipated, exposing a row of straight, clean teeth and a slight vulnerability that made him even more beautiful than before. He shook his head and picked up his steps.

It took only an instant for Gillian's head to clear and for her to realize the sight the three of them must be making, walking together like a family heading off to enjoy the day. Silly, she chastised herself, ignoring the hollow pit that made her stomach ache for what she didn't have, for what she could not give Edmund. A family. Straightening her shoulders, she tugged on her son's hand, separating him from the mercenary, and hurried to catch up with George.

Chapter Seven

Colin didn't lack patience; in fact, he possessed stores of it. After three years of slowly chipping away his enemy's secrets, waiting day after day, month after month, for the battle his bones ached for, he'd learned the virtue well.

But he wasn't cut out for sitting on a rock for over an hour, waiting for a hapless fish to swim into his net. Even Edmund appeared bored beyond his senses. Still, it said something for the lad to be able to sit for so long without protest or too much fidgeting. Colin suspected Edmund's thumb, and the tender sucking of it, helped to yield such temperance. He tried not to look at the babe overly much, since every time he did, his heart went a little softer. Looking at the lad's mother was no better. In truth, 'twas worse. He wasn't one to give in to fear. His whole life, he'd been too busy working hard to become a better fighter to be afraid of anything. The coming war between King James and Prince William would need a warrior worthy of winning it. All that training and dedication left little time for courtship. He'd met countless women

in England, Scotland, and France, and found them all
to be quite alike. What was so different about this one
that he would interest himself in her? In her child? He
was a warrior for hell's sake, not some feeble, sniveling
pansy who lost his train of thought when he looked at a
bonny woman. These two could end up costing him much
if he wasn't careful. He wanted to put Gillian Dearly
out of his mind. He didn't like her being at Dartmouth,
distracting him. He should have objected to going fishing
with them.

Colin scowled at Captain Gates, standing far enough
away so that the splash of the waves couldn't reach him.
The wee lad wasn't unpleasant to be around but Colin
wasn't a nursemaid and he'd make sure to tell Gates that
later. Right now though, a wistful sigh to his left caught
his attention. He slipped his gaze to Lady Gillian and
allowed himself a moment to examine her unnoticed. He
had never known a lass who could sit so quietly, seemingly content to study the steady surf rolling into the
estuary. He found himself beguiled by her silence, her
presence, perched close to her son with her arms wrapped
around her knees and her long hair whipping about her
shoulders. He wasn't certain if the earthy fragrance of
spring wafting across his nostrils every so often, before
drowning in the briny scent of the estuary, came from
the primroses she'd worn in her hair the night before, but
'twas driving him a bit mad.

When she turned to him, sensing his eyes on her, he
almost dropped the end of his pole into the water and bit
out a muttered oath at his suddenly poor reflexes.

"So, Mr. Campbell, you are acquainted with the king?"

A thread of panic coursed through him for one dreaded
instant before he slowed his breathing. Why would she put

such a question to him? She couldn't know anything about his purpose here. 'Twas impossible.

When he remained silent, she offered him a patient smile—much like one she might give her son if he didn't understand her question—and clarified. "You told my cousin that you fought in the Life Guards."

"Aye." He had told Devon. He cursed himself for letting her confound him so quickly. 'Twas the curious arch of her brow that was to blame. The spark of intelligence in her eyes when she looked at him. He didn't like anyone looking too closely, as if they were trying to figure him out. Figuring him out could get him killed. And lastly, damn him, 'twas the quirk of her full lips that made him wonder how they would taste against his. "I know him," he admitted. "At least, I did, once." When he spoke the words, the truth in them struck him like a physical blow.

"What was he like? Do his men love him?"

Colin didn't want to think on him or how many of his men were still loyal to him. "He's the king. All kings are the same. Arrogant and hungry for power."

She grew quiet, almost contemplative, and then continued. "Do all the Campbells feel the same way you do?"

He looked at her, this time taking in the subtle catch of her breath, the quick flicker of her eyes under his scrutiny. "What is yer interest in the king?"

She smiled and smoothed a lock of hair away from her jaw, distracting him yet again from his train of thought. "A woman cannot be curious about the king her family would rather see dead than rule another day?"

He supposed a woman could. "Yer father is a supporter of William deposing the throne then?"

"We'll be getting back soon," Gates called out, saving her from answering.

What would her reply have been? King James suspected Essex of treason, but had no proof... yet.

"The hour grows late," Gates urged.

"But I didn't catch a fish."

Colin glanced down at Edmund, noting the soft droop of the boy's shoulders. He'd caught nothing yet again, and the short time he had outside was coming to an end.

Hell. The child and his happiness were not Colin's concern. But that didn't mean he should stand by and do nothing while the only innocent thing left in the world looked about to cry.

"Does it just have to be fish that ye're hoping to catch then, lad?"

Edmund looked up at him and shook his head.

"Well, then," Colin said, springing to his feet. "Come with me." He turned to watch Edmund follow his footsteps over the rocks without the aid of his mother, though she was close behind, with Captain Gates close behind her.

When the boy reached him, Colin brought him to the shallow edge and bent to toss a loose rock aside. Nothing. It took him and Edmund, and the lad's mother, as well, at least six stones each before he found what he was looking for.

"Edmund!" he called, and both came running. He scooped up the small crab in his hand, along with some of the sand beneath it, and held it out to the child.

"Keep yer hand open, lest his claw catch yer skin." He'd learned as a child along the bank of Camas Fhionnairigh how to catch and hold crabs such as these.

Edmund took care to follow his instructions and looked so delighted by what was crawling along his palm that Colin forgot why he should not let himself care, and smiled at him, and then at his mother, bending beside him.

"Look at how it walks sideways, Edmund," she said, as delighted by the sight as her son was.

Damn, but she was bonny, Colin thought, looking at her. Her fair skin was wind burned with just enough pink to make her almost too beguiling to look at.

"May I bring it home, Colin?" Edmund asked him hopefully.

Colin shook his head, grateful for the distraction lest she turn that smile on him again and scatter his thoughts like he was some green whelp, mute and witless in her presence. "'Twill only die," he told Edmund. "And 'tis too small to eat. But I'll make ye a proper rod to help ye catch fish."

"Will you make one for you too?"

Edmund blinked at him and Colin looked down to see the crab falling off the edge of his hand.

"And one for Mummy?"

What the hell was wrong with him? He hadn't come here to find friends—even wee ones who spoke around their thumbs. He had information to discover for the king, a war to prepare for. A war to win. How could he do any of it if he spent his afternoons fishing? He raised his gaze to the man standing over him, looking mildly ill. Captain Gates hadn't left their sides all day—or yesterday for that matter, save when he had left for Kingswear. Mayhap this could work in his favor. If Colin fished with Edmund, Gates would be there. He was certain that after a few days, he could compel the captain to give him a few answers.

"Fer that, lad, ye must ask my captain."

Gates glared at him, then glanced at Lady Gillian. "Very well," he conceded tightly. "Now come along. It's time to go."

He stepped out of their path and waited until Edmund and his mother passed him. "Campbell"—he held out his hand to stop Colin—"a word."

Colin nodded and waited until the captain picked up his pace again.

"If you touch her," Gates said in a quiet tone. He smiled at Lady Gillian when she looked over her shoulder at the two of them keeping far behind her. She scowled at him in return, but kept walking. "It could mean Edmund's life. I can assure you"—he looked Colin straight in the eye—"it will most certainly cost you yours."

Colin didn't flinch. After being here for two days, he knew that Dartmouth's captain was far less interested in the deposition of England's current king than he was in guarding Lady Gillian like she was the last living virgin in a realm besieged by dragons. But what the hell was he implying? This was the second time he'd threatened Colin in regard to putting hands on her. Did his threat now include harming Edmund? Who the hell would harm Edmund? "What do ye mean it could cost the babe his life?"

Gates studied him with a wary eye, then turned back to the pair walking ahead. "You don't ask about yourself, but about him. You care about the boy."

"Nae." Colin almost laughed at the preposterous accusation. "I'm simply curious about who ye think would harm him."

"You were not paying attention last eve, Campbell. You did not see the control Lord Devon has mastered over his cousin?"

"I did," Colin said darkly.

"He uses the child as a pawn to make her yield."

Ah, here was the chain around her neck, her ankles,

her wrists, Colin thought darkly. She submitted to Devon's cruelty to protect Edmund. 'Twas valiant, indeed. Sacrifice for the good of someone or something else was a virtue he admired highly.

"He would harm Edmund if she left him before the prince arrived."

The prince was undoubtedly arriving then. But when? When? "How much time does she have?"

"Why?" Gates eyed him again while they strolled. "Do you think you can rescue her before then? You can't. If you try, I'll kill you. Do you understand?"

"Rescue her from what?" Colin asked, ignoring yet another threat.

"You are dense then."

Not completely, Colin thought. Gates wasn't suspicious of his reasons for being here, or of his fighting skills. He didn't care if his men were prepared for battle or not, because all his thoughts, his duties, centered around one soul. Lady Gillian. He didn't want Colin getting close to her, putting his hands on her, trying to take her away. Did the captain love her?

"What makes ye think I'm the rescuing kind?" Colin asked him seriously. He didn't want Gates to mistrust him based on some misplaced fear of chivalry. "Tears do not move me. Battle does. But I would ask ye plainly, why would ye stand in the way of it if ye know she needs rescuing?"

Gates paused again to look at him. "Which of the men here do you think has considered doing anything to her other than bedding her and igniting her father's wrath against her yet again?"

Colin stared at him. That's why she was here. Because she had Edmund out of wedlock. Dartmouth was her punishment. Gates, whom Colin looked at in a whole new light, was keeping the men away from her to save her from having a more severe punishment inflicted.

They walked in silence for a moment. Then Colin said, "Why do ye tell me these things?"

"Because I want you to know why your life's blood is spilling from your body if you interfere with her life."

Colin nodded, giving him the point. The captain was single-minded in his dedication to his duty. A good trait, that, and one Colin hadn't seen in another man in many years.

"Why do ye suggest that I am any different from the other men here?"

"You're frank," Gates told him. "You'll find that I am, as well. I suggest it because, though I doubt your sincerity in certain things, I don't doubt it when you speak to him."

Colin knew whom he meant, but he looked toward Edmund anyway. His eyes settled on the babe's downy crown, his chubby arm extended to his mother's. Something swelled up in Colin like a deluge, robbing him of breath. His heart went frigid and warm at the same time. He liked the lad. Damn it to hell but he liked him. But he couldn't. He couldn't let himself become so distracted from his direction.

And certainly not by a woman. That was the most dangerous. He had seen what women had done to the men of Camlochlin. It made them soft. It made them change who they were and give up what they loved. His father, a warrior who could cut down three men at once with a sweep of his claymore, had learned how to pluck a delicate sprig of heather without losing a single bloom. His eldest brother had been willing to cast aside his birth-right for the love of a lass. His once-scoundrel, good-for-naught brother Tristan had denied his entire way of living and devoted his life to one woman. His sister's husband, Connor Grant, had left the Royal Army and England to be with his wife and dedicated himself to the task of fulfilling each of her dreams.

Colin wanted no part of such weakness. He had no time for it, nor any inclination to change.

He had to leave Edmund and his mother to their own paths.

"I'm not here to change anything," he heard himself say.

"Good," the captain muttered beside him while they walked.

How the hell was he going to tell Edmund that he wasn't going to spend any more time with him? He needed to remain distant, detached, and undiscovered. Spending time with Edmund and his mother—Colin looked at the delicacy of her profile as she turned to speak to her son—was too dangerous. Apparently, for everyone. He wasn't here to care about why. He desired her, just as he had desired other women in the past. Some he had taken. Others he had not. But 'twas nothing more than that. He wouldn't risk a child's safety for it. He hadn't grown *that* cold.

"I'll tell the lad I've come down with something and cannot fish with him."

"No," Gates said, his gaze hard on Colin but going soft as it swept over Lady Gillian. "He will be unhappy and she'll blame me."

"Ye love her," Colin ventured boldly. If the captain denied it, then he did indeed think Colin a fool.

"I will admit she is dear to me." The captain paused, watching her, then shook his head and said briskly, "No. You will not disappoint the boy."

"But I—"

"I am not asking," the captain warned. "Just make certain you form no attachments with her."

Colin was about to reassure him that forming attachments was not his habit, but just as he was about to do so, Edmund broke away from his mother and ran toward him.

Watching the babe's stubby legs and flushed cheeks, Colin wondered if Devon would truly harm him. The thought near made him choke on the anger boiling up from within. How the hell did his brothers live each day with the knowledge that something terrible could befall their bairns at any moment? He looked away and cursed silently. Babes. They were even more perilous to a man's fortitude than a woman.

"Colin, will you sup with me in my room? Mummy won't mind."

Colin looked at Lady Gillian hurrying toward them, offering him an apologetic glance. He remembered her submission to her cousin yesterday after his subtle threats against Edmund. She would do anything for her son... even risk the company of a mercenary to please him.

"I cannot," Colin refused Edmund as she reached them. "I must sit at my lord's table tonight and every night."

As he feared, the lad's eyes rounded with dejection. But he didn't cry and he didn't beg. Colin wished he had, for then he might be able to tell himself that the child was overindulged and needed a firmer hand. Instead, Edmund shoved his thumb back into his mouth and turned away.

"Forgive him." Lady Gillian caught her son and took his hand once again. "He grows bored with me. I will speak to him about his unreasonable requests."

She turned, taking Edmund with her and leaving

Colin to look after them, his jaw tight and his belly feeling oddly out of sorts. Unreasonable requests? What was so damned unreasonable about the child wanting company other than his mother? And why the hell was Edmund excluded from supping with the others as if he were a mangy dog? And while he was at it, Colin wanted to know why in damnation Gates hardly spoke to the poor lad. Fearing Devon was one thing, making a child an outcast in his own home was another.

"Why would Devon hurt him?" He turned to the captain. He didn't care if he was pushing too hard for answers. He wanted them, though they had nothing to do with battle. "And what does Prince William's arrival have to do with any of it?"

Gates stopped and smiled at him, not bothering to hide the search in his gaze when his met Colin's. "You are curious indeed."

He'd gone too far. And over a lass and a boy who had no meaning in his purpose. Already they made him careless, reckless. "Nae." Colin shook his head and continued walking. "Tell me nothing more. 'Tis not my concern."

Chapter Eight

Gillian wasn't late to the supper table that night or the one after that. She had George to thank for his caution with her time. He made certain, as he had every day over her long stay here, to have her returned inside with time enough to bathe her son and play with him while he ate. She never forced the issue of Edmund not dining with them with her cousin. She told herself that Edmund was better off away from the ill-mannered, crude company of Geoffrey's garrison. She would have preferred to stay away as well, but loose talk around the supper table had earned her William of Orange's trust. Traveling mercenaries often carried with them gossip from other nobles' kitchens.

Tonight was no different. She picked at her food and inclined her ear to the men's conversations going on around her. Geoffrey's laughter drew her attention to him. She would never wed him. But what would he do if he suspected that she'd already asked the Dutch prince not to let her cousin have her? She prayed he would never find out. Even if he did, he knew she would never obey him again in anything *after* he harmed her son. She would kill him first and leave him to the dogs.

William of Orange would protect her. He had to. What was to stop Geoffrey from sending Edmund away...or worse, after he took her for his wife?

She brought a shaky cup to her lips and cut her gaze to the farther end of the table, where Colin Campbell sat drinking with the rest of the men.

She thought for a moment that she might hate him even more than Geoffrey. What did she care that he'd stopped speaking to Edmund? Why should it surprise her that he'd offered her son his time and then deprived him of it without thought? He was no different from any other man she knew and every question Edmund put to her, asking her to explain why Colin no longer liked him, made her dislike him anew.

He turned from smiling at something someone said and met her gaze across the crowded table. She glared at him and then looked away.

"Gillian, play something for us on your lute."

She blinked at Geoffrey, who was leaning back in his chair with Margaret sprawled across his lap.

"My lute is out of tune, Cousin."

"My good man, Martin!" he bellowed to one of his musicians. "Give her your lute. My poor ears have bled enough this night from your foul lack of talent. Give it to her and listen to the music of the heavens."

She didn't want to play. Her music was her most beloved treasure after Edmund and she didn't want to share it with her cousin or his men. Besides, she was in no frame of mind to play anything Geoffrey would enjoy. "Geoffrey, I must decli—"

Martin shoved the lute in her hands and trudged away, cursing her under his breath.

"Play, Gillian."

Gillian stared at her cousin, defying him with every fiber of her being. "As you wish."

She stood and walked around her gloating cousin with her chin tilted slightly in the air, lest he think her defeated. She knew he made her tend to him, sit with him, and kept her from her son with the hope of breaking her. She would die first. She waited in the center of the Hall until one of his men brought her a chair. The man happened to be Colin Campbell.

She looked at him long enough to let him see clearly the anger she felt toward him. Then she thanked him politely when he set the chair at her feet and stepped away.

She sat, arranging her skirts neatly around her and sweeping her hair off her shoulder.

"Gillian!" Geoffrey pounded his palm on the table. "Play something, damn you!"

Casting him her worst death stare, she set her fingers to the strings and then scowled. The lute was horribly out of tune. She hastened to tune it as best she could and then began to play. She closed her eyes to the clang of cups and bawdy laughter coming from the men around her and listened only to the melody filling her ears from Martin's poorly neglected instrument. As always, when she played, she soon grew lost in the rapture of giving her heart a voice. She plucked and strummed a haunting melody that brought tears to her eyes. She did not open them, lest anyone see.

Before long, the clamber of the Great Hall faded to silence. Gillian heard nothing amid the lingering notes masterfully pulled from her fingers.

"Dear heavens, Gillian." Geoffrey's voice dripped with disdain when he interrupted her. "If I wanted to hear a death march, I would have taken one of the men outside and shot him. Play something upbeat before you sour my pleasant mood."

She'd learned how to hold her tongue, but she could never master concealing her bitterness toward him. It poured from her eyes, her taut smile, and her clenched fingers, revealing her weakness. Geoffrey basked in it.

She played something a bit more up-tempo, plucking the strings as if they were Geoffrey's eyeballs. When the other musicians picked up the tune behind her, she cringed at the missed chords and flat tone.

Soon, the merriment of getting soused returned to the Hall. Gillian's gaze drifted over her cousin, nuzzling his face into Margaret's neck. Poor girl, she had no one to protect her from Geoffrey's paws. Gillian's gaze moved down the table, past Rodrigo Alvarez, a mercenary from Spain with eyes as dark as his soul, and Philippe something or other from France sitting beside him. When her eyes found Colin Campbell, they lingered over him longer than they had on the others.

She let her gaze traverse his form, long and lean and appearing more comfortable in his hard chair than any man at Dartmouth had a right to be. The soft glow of the enormous hearth fire accentuated the rugged angles of his face, the golden shards in his eyes. Saints, but he was handsome, and not in the way that George was handsome. The Scotsman's expressions were not elegant or serene, giving the impression of complete control, though Gillian didn't doubt he possessed confidence in abundance. An air of danger clung to him like the dark mantle draping his shoulders. It could have been the way his sharp eyes noted the movements of the other men, the hint of something fierce in the curl of his amiable smile, the slow, deliberate way he moved his fingers around the rim of his cup.

Of course he was dangerous; she shivered and looked away. All the men here were. Why had she ever considered him good company for Edmund? Dear Lord, was she so desperate to hear her son laugh that she would allow him to grow fond of such a man? George had been correct to warn her about him. It was just as well. There was nothing he could do to help her and Edmund, even if he wanted to. Which he clearly didn't. But he didn't have to break Edmund's heart. Even the worst among Geoffrey's men hadn't done *that*.

She turned to glare at him one last time and found him watching her. His expression of bland interest to what was going on around him didn't change. He sized her up, boldly enough to make her miss a note on her strings. He didn't look at her with desire, but with careful consideration, as if he were trying to decide if she was worth his notice.

She tilted her chin a fraction higher, wanting to tell him she didn't want, or need, his attention.

He smiled ever so slightly while his eyes moved over her like faceted jewels caught by the flickering light, robbing her of breath and her wits.

Her gaze darted toward George. Thankfully her guardian's attention was fixed on Geoffrey, as he was leaning in to share a word with him. Neither one saw the exchange between her and the mercenary. It was fortunate, for his gaze seemed a palpable thing, a touch across the distance.

No. She wouldn't let any man touch any part of her. Never again.

Against her will, her eyes returned to him, but he'd gone back to speaking with his comrades. She let out the breath she'd been holding and set her thoughts to her music. Geoffrey snatched the lute from her hands, interrupting those thoughts.

"Enough, Gillian," he said, standing over her. "Come. I will escort you to your chambers tonight. I wish to have a word with you."

She looked to George and then rose from her chair without quarrel when her captain nodded his consent. She would have preferred being smashed against the rocks outside to spending a few moments walking alone with her cousin. He wouldn't touch her. He feared her father's retaliation, and his own captain's blade, too much to be so bold—yet. But she loathed the thought of listening to whatever new threats he'd conjured up against Edmund to satisfy his cruel delight in making her bend.

"What is it now, Geoffrey?" she asked him with a long drawn-out sigh as he led her out of the hall. George would have been angry with her for her inability to mask her disdain.

"Good news, my dear," her cousin announced gaily, choosing to ignore the slight upon his illustrious presence. "Lord Shrewsbury and the Viscount Lumley have put their names to the prince's invitation. Only one more name and the parchment can be sent to the prince."

She couldn't let him see the hope in her eyes. She had to pretend dread at William's arrival, but that didn't stop her from looking up at him, sincerely astounded at how cruel and unfeeling he believed he was being. "And why do you imagine that is good news to me?"

"Why"—he gleamed at her—"it means our wedding night may be but a few months away. Surely you are pleased with these good tidings, Gillian."

He was mad. She should pity him. But she couldn't. "I

will not wed you, no matter who commands it. I would rather die."

"I could arrange a death if you wish, but not yours."

Gillian closed her eyes to gain control over the fury and fear rumbling deep in her belly. He often threatened Edmund's residence at Dartmouth, but he'd never threatened her son's life before. She suppressed the bile rushing toward the surface and opened her eyes to look at him.

"Touch him and I will cut out the rancid heart beating worthlessly in your chest."

"Could you do it, Gillian?" he sneered, doubting that she could. She had to change that misconception, and she had better do it quickly, before he thought to act on his threats.

"Aye, I could and I will. You must sleep at some point, remember."

He laughed and whirled his lacy sleeves as he turned to leave her. "Well, now I know I must have you locked away at night when I'm done with you."

Gillian watched him return to the Great Hall. At her sides, her hands shook. She wanted to run, but her feet did not obey right away. How would she escape him if the prince changed his mind after seeing all Geoffrey had done for him? How would she protect her child from him?

She turned, finally, and, swiping a tear from her eye, she ran for her rooms.

✢

Chapter Nine

A few hundred yards from the castle, Colin waited in the shadow of a shallow cave along the shoreline. Behind him, the gently crashing waves soothed his anticipation. No one had seen him slip out of Dartmouth to meet one of the king's messengers. 'Twas the middle of the night, with no men guarding the battlements. Even if they were, they would not have seen him. He'd traveled on foot, swift and limber along the rocks, keeping close to the shadows.

'Twas the appointed night, exactly one month from the day he had left Whitehall. He had arranged with the king to meet a runner from Somerset on this night and deliver to him whatever information he had gathered. The same meetings would take place each se'nnight after that, until Colin sent word to amass the Royal Army.

He tapped the folded missive against his thigh and thought briefly about what he'd written. So far, he didn't have much. The prince did indeed intend to land in Dartmouth, but Colin had not yet discovered when. There had been no boats arriving to carry away letters to the

Netherlands, so he'd written that the king should remain patient. Devon's garrison was weak and ill prepared for a decent battle. Colin believed 'twas in their best interests to take them down before William arrived, but if they were rash in their endeavors it could put them at a dangerous disadvantage later. The invitations had to be sent. They should make no moves until then. He ended his correspondence with good wishes toward the queen and a request for pardon for the Earl of Essex's daughter and grandson. They had no part in treason and should not be tried when the war was over.

He looked out over the coastline, seeking sight of his courier and scowling when he didn't find him.

The runner was tardy, providing Colin with too much time to let his thoughts wander. And hell, but they'd been wandering all night. He couldn't get Lady Gillian's music out of his head. He heard it on the water, the gentle moan of the wind through the crevices around him. 'Twas soothing, so deeply moving it diminished the importance of everything else. He wished he'd never heard it.

She was angry with him, and he knew why. But he'd done the right thing in avoiding her and her bairn. He'd already used up too many of his thoughts on them. Still, her icy glare tonight had unsettled him a bit. It shouldn't, of course. But it had. He'd discovered that he didn't like being the object of the same contempt she offered Devon and the rest of the garrison. He did, however, enjoy the subdued pride in her chin, the boldness to hold his gaze, and och, the unearthly beauty coming from her fingers.

"General?"

Colin pushed off the wall he'd been leaning against, cursing the distractions that made him miss the courier's approach.

"Here," he whispered, and then waited for the runner to dismount and enter the shadows with him. 'Twas Henry Hammond, a well-trusted servant who had been running for Colin for the last three years.

"The good king sends greetings."

Colin nodded and peered out over the rocky enclosure, making certain they were alone. "What news of England?"

"The king has ordered seven bishops to read the Declaration of Indulgence in all Anglican churches. Being opposed to the toleration of Catholics," Hammond added quietly, "they defied him and have been arrested."

Colin's jaw tightened. Hell. James was gaining more enemies each day, making this war harder to win.

"Soon, we will not have only the Dutch to fight, but all of England, as well."

Hammond remained silent for a moment, then cleared his throat. "General MacGregor, there are some who say that the king does not sincerely desire religious tolerance. But that, in truth, his purpose with the bishops was to seek to widen the division between the Anglicans and the Catholic governor."

Colin was thankful that Hammond couldn't make out his face, for the runner certainly would have believed such rumor if he could. Of course that was James's plan. He spoke of tolerance from the left side of his mouth, and from the right, declared that every non-Catholic followed a false religion. The people would not stand for it too much longer.

"Yer duty is not to question yer king," Colin told him sternly. Mutiny was the last thing the throne needed. "Let others say what they will, but keep yer own tongue still. Do ye understand?"

"Aye, General. Do you have a message for the king?"

Colin nodded and handed him the missive. Hammond would deliver the letter to another runner in Somerset and that runner would ride to Cheshire, and so on, until the message was delivered into James's hand in London.

Colin waited until Hammond left and then pulled his hood over his head and returned to the castle. He walked slowly this time, wondering if his being here was a waste of time. Once the people began to clamor for a Protestant king, there would be little James's forces could do to stop a deposition. But surprisingly, that was not what bothered Colin most.

He'd spent the first nineteen years of his life among Catholics, learning of their persecution. He'd fought alongside his Highland brothers, ignorant of the persecution of others. But he was no longer so innocent. James did not massacre defiant Presbyterians in the fields as his brother had done before him, but he denounced them and took from them their liberties. At first, Colin had believed him just in his actions, but what man had the right to deny another his rights and beliefs? Wasn't he fighting for the same thing?

Colin didn't want to see the worst in the man he admired and had sworn to protect. If he did, if his cause was no longer the right one, what was there left to fight for?

He slipped inside the castle, making certain first that the halls were silent. He looked around, granted the opportunity to do so now at his leisure. He took in every door, every curve that led down another shadowy corridor. Some he investigated, others he did not. He didn't have all night. Risky was one thing, reckless, another.

Satisfied, for the time being, that he'd found three more ways in or out of the castle, he made his way to his quarters.

He heard a sound coming from the landing above and

moved toward it. The sound came again and he pushed back his hood and inclined his ear. Someone was crying. 'Twas a child.

Edmund.

He raced up the stairs to the child's door, but the crying had stopped. He shouldn't be here. If Gates discovered him, he would likely cast him out of Dartmouth. He turned to leave but another sound brought his steps to a halt.

Music. More specifically, a lute. Was it real, or in his mind, refusing to leave his heart untouched? The sound echoed softly from high above, as if the heavens had opened to beguile his ears...and other parts of him he fought to defy. His feet, for instance, and his eyes. He looked toward the narrow stone stairway leading to the battlements, and then farther up, to the turrets. He remembered the first time he ever saw her perched and windswept high above the world, looking like a lonely princess. Now she sounded like one, as well.

He didn't move. What reason was there to go to her? He wasn't one to offer comfort and there was nothing else he could give her. Nothing he wanted to give her. She wasn't his burden.

Edmund wailed from behind his door, whirling Colin around on his feet. He plunged into the softly lit room, his fingers clasped around the hilt of his sword. His eyes found Edmund instantly, sitting knees to chin in the corner of his bed. He appeared unharmed, but badly frightened. Colin searched the shadows first, ensuring that no one hid in them, and then went to stand by the bed. "What is it lad? Why are ye crying?"

Edmund wiped his eyes with his fists and looked up at him. "I had a bad dream. I want Mummy."

Turning to look at the open doorway, Colin thought

about going to fetch her but when he moved to the task, Edmund called him back.

"Don't go. I'm afraid."

Colin frowned, turning back to the bed. What did he know about comforting children? The same he knew about comforting their mothers. Very little. Edmund sniffed and rubbed his nose and Colin scowled up at the heavens before he sat down on the bed. "I used to have them too."

"Bad dreams?"

"Aye."

"With monsters?"

"Aye, big, green ones."

Edmund relinquished his corner and moved closer to Colin, his eyes wide as they came into the light. "Did they ever get you?"

"Never." Colin glanced down at Edmund, then looked away before he was tempted to smile. Damn his feeble heart. "I had found a magic dagger in one of the mountains—"

"Magic?" Edmund asked, popping his thumb out of his mouth to gasp.

"Aye. 'Tis forged to kill all monsters should they dare get close to its owner." Colin spared a brief look at the lad. "Would ye like to see it?"

Edmund nodded and moved even closer as Colin pulled the dagger King Louis had given him from his belt. It looked magical with its gold inlaid hilt sparkling in the candlelight.

"That is the magic dagger, Colin?"

"The verra one." Colin turned the hilt in his fingers, staring at it as if contemplating something terribly difficult. "I have no more need of it." He let out a gusty sigh. "I could give it to ye."

"You could?"

"Aye." Colin finally turned to give the babe a stern look. "If ye vow not to touch it until ye are at least six. It loses its power if ye but touch it once before then."

"I will not touch it," Edmund promised meaningfully.

Before Colin could stop it, he smiled at the boy. "Then 'tis yers. I will put it in a safe place fer ye." He looked around the dimly lit room and rose to his feet. The high wooden cabinet partially steeped in shadow would serve well enough. Reaching up, he set the blade where Edmund could not reach it. "The next time ye have a bad dream, the dagger will protect ye."

"Thank you, Colin."

He should have nodded and walked out of the room. The lad was safe and no longer frightened. He shouldn't have stayed in the room an instant longer than he had to.

"Are we friends again?"

Colin closed his eyes. Hell. He'd just given up his favored blade for a child's dreams. Why in damnation did he feel like such a heartless bastard? He knew he was one. Oftimes, he prided himself on it. But not now.

"Edmund." He returned to his seat and kept his gaze steady on the face staring back at him. "I am a soldier and I must prepare for battle so that I won't be hurt."

"Like when Lieutenant de Atre struck you?"

Colin nodded. "I have little time to play, but that doesn't mean we are not friends."

"Edmund!" Lady Gillian's terrified voice startled her son off the bed and brought Colin to his feet. She ran to them and snatched the boy off his feet and into her arms.

"What are you doing in here?" she demanded, glaring at Colin.

"Edmund was crying. He—"

"Oh, my darling..." she cut him off, her tender endearment meant for her son and not for him, leaving him slightly unsettled. "Did you have another bad dream?"

When the babe in her arms nodded, she pulled him closer and cooed against his mop of curls. "Forgive me for not hearing you. Were you terribly frightened?"

"Aye." Edmund yawned. "But Colin gave me his magic dagger."

In the flickering light, Colin watched her eyes widen on him. She looked about to admonish him. What kind of mad savage gave a babe a dagger? But Edmund's next cheerful declaration silenced her.

"Now, when the monsters come, it will chase them away."

"'Tis there." Colin pointed to the top of the tall cabinet to show her that he'd put the weapon where her son couldn't reach it.

"I am not to touch it until I am six!" Edmund added, pulling his mother's attention back to him. "Else it will lose its power."

"Is that so?" She glanced again at Colin. He couldn't tell if what he saw was a hint of a smile softening her features, but the alarm in her voice was gone. "I should like to hear more about this magic dagger tomorrow, Edmund. But now, the hour is late and you should be asleep. Would you like me to stay with you?"

"Nay, Mummy, I am safe now, aye, Colin?"

Hell, what kind of pitiful stuff was he made of that such an innocent query should hook him so deep in his chest? "Aye, lad. Ye are safe."

"Bid good eve to Mr. Campbell now, dearest. I shall see you in the morning." She moved closer to the bed—

closer to Colin—and bent to return the lad to his mattress, but he squirmed to the right and into Colin's arms instead.

For an instant, Colin was lost as the babe wrapped his arms around his neck. He'd been hit in the guts many times, but never like this. On his visit home to Camlochlin, he'd held his nephews and nieces in his arms, but he hadn't saved any of them from monsters. He hadn't felt the uncontrollable desire to protect them from traitorous earls who hated them because they had no fathers.

He looked at Lady Gillian, her eyes fashioned from liquid while she watched her son clinging to him. Hell, he should have left sooner. He should have ignored the lad's weeping and gone straight to bed.

He closed his arms around Edmund and gave him a gentle squeeze.

"I will remember what you told me about us being friends," Edmund promised, pulling back to slay what was left of Colin's steely facade with a wide grin.

Colin cleared his throat, nodded, then tossed the boy onto his bed the way he'd done with his nephews when he'd visited home. Wee Adam and Malcolm would like Edmund. He couldn't help but smile when Edmund squealed with laughter. "Pleasant dreams, Edmund."

"Pleasant dreams, Colin."

Colin turned for the door, ready to get the hell out of there before he was tempted to tell the boy a story next. Damnation, how could he be allowing this to happen? He couldn't let himself go soft. Not now when his war was so close. A war, he reminded himself, he'd had to convince himself over and over in the past two years needed to be fought.

"Mr. Campbell, a word, please?"

He stopped, waited while Lady Gillian kissed her son good night, and then followed her out the door.

The hall was only a tad brighter than inside the room, but Colin had no trouble taking in the alluring glimmer in her eyes, the perfect shape of her mouth when she looked up at him after shutting the door behind her. In all his years at court he'd never wanted to take a lass in his arms and kiss her as badly as he wanted to do to Gillian now.

"I almost always hear him," she said, looking miserable that this time she hadn't. "I—"

"Ye play the lute beautifully."

The soft blush that stole across her cheeks was replaced an instant later by worry creasing her brow. "You heard me then."

"Aye."

She looked away. "I should have been in bed, where I belong."

"As should I," he agreed quietly, catching and holding her gaze when she returned it to him.

"Why weren't you?"

He shrugged slightly, reminding himself yet again how perilous letting down his guard with anyone here could be. "I couldn't sleep. When I left my quarters on my way to the kitchen, I heard Edmund."

"Mr. Campbell," she began, and he realized 'twas the first time they were alone together, the first time she spoke his name. Only, it wasn't his name.

"I would offer you gratitude for seeing to him. He has been inquiring after you constantly and I—"

"I've already explained my absence to him."

"Oh?" she asked stiffly. "Well, would you mind explaining it to me, as well?"

Since when did he have so much trouble remembering his purpose? His duty? Since when did he regret either one—even for a moment?

"As a matter of fact, I would mind," he told her truthfully, noting the fall of a certain tendril of hair along her cheek and wanting to reach his hand out to smooth it away. The quicker he got through talking to her, the safer it would be for all of them. "I'm not given to explaining myself to lasses," he told her, a bit more gruffly than he intended.

Taking a step back, she folded her arms across her chest and cast him a frosty glare. "Is that so?"

"Aye," he said, suppressing the urge to smile at the strength in her stance. She was a fierce lioness defending her cub and he admired her for it. He resisted the urge to offer her his aid at the task. A quick slice along Devon's neck would end that threat.

"You will explain yourself to me, Mr. Campbell."

"Will I now, Miss Dearly?" he countered, fighting to ignore the sheer pleasure he found in studying the shape of her mouth, the delicate angle of her jaw when she tilted her chin at him.

"If you intend to befriend my son and then break his heart, then aye, you will."

He hadn't meant to break the lad's heart. Damn it all to hell. He could sink any one of his blades into an enemy without losing a single night's sleep over it, but the thought of hurting Edmund's tender feelings made him want to apologize. It would be the first time in his life he'd ever done the like.

"I will not be visiting him again."

Her cool expression faltered, revealing her weakness. Unfortunately, Devon knew what it was as well. "Why not?" she asked him. "Is it because he is a bastard, or because his mother is a whore?"

Her words angered him. His anger wasn't directed at her, but at the man who mocked her with them. He wondered what the king would think if he killed William's host before his army got there.

"Go, Mr. Campbell," she ordered quietly. "I was wrong about you. Edmund doesn't need a man like you in his life." She graced him with one more iron-hard glance, then turned to go back inside her son's room.

His fingers closing around her wrist stopped her.

"My decision," he told her when she looked at him, "was made to protect Edmund from any harm that may come to him because of my attention. Words spewed from the mouth of yer enemy, nae matter how vile they are, do not concern me. Nor should they concern ye."

Her flash of anger dissipated as quickly as it had arrived. She stood there, as still as the silence around them. "I . . . forgive me for . . ."

He gave her a brief nod, knowing that whoever he'd pretended to be in the past, whatever role he portrayed so expertly before, was going to be a hundred times more difficult this time.

And this time, he couldn't fail.

"Edmund understands," he said succinctly. "I hope that ye do, as well."

She nodded her head, about to say something else. He didn't wait to hear what it was but turned on his heel and left.

This time, he didn't like who he was.

Chapter Ten

Gillian sat on the rocks watching Edmund fish, or, as Captain Gates called it this morn, angling. One fished with a net, but when he cast a pole, he angled. Gillian had never seen a contraption like the one George handed over to her son. Aye, it was just a stick, but it had been carved quite thin and was as pliable as her skirts. From one end hung a string that looked to be fashioned from a long single thread of linen. Fastened to the end of the string was a gorge, about an inch in length, made of bone and sharpened at both ends.

Her first thought had been how in the world was Edmund supposed to catch fish with such a thing? Then she had wondered something else.

"Where did you come by this?" she had asked her captain.

His answer made her ache from a place that frightened her to death. Mr. Campbell had made it for Edmund. Evidently, he'd been at work on it for a few days, finding the correct wood and whittling it late at night, after his practice. He'd carved the bone, as well, with a warning to Edmund to have a care when touching it.

An angle. The mercenary had made Edmund an angle.

Gillian worried her lip, watching her son bobbing the stick up and down in the water. Twice already, something had nibbled at the tiny bit of rice fastened to the gorge.

She had judged Mr. Campbell harshly. But really, what did she know of men save that they were cold, heartless beings? Why would she have expected anything different, especially from a mercenary? She'd been so angry with him for forgetting Edmund. But he hadn't forgotten him. He had stayed away for Edmund's safety.

She lifted her gaze to where George stood over Edmund, watching the pole for any movement. He had to have told Mr. Campbell that his attentions were dangerous. She couldn't be angry with him for it. Not when he was correct.

Ah, but the morning was too lovely to ruin with the terror of thinking about what her cousin was capable of.

Breathing in the crisp, salty air, she looked out over the estuary instead and contemplated the man sitting on her son's bed last eve. It was astonishing really, that any man in Geoffrey's garrison would care about Edmund's childish fears and seek to protect him from them. A magic dagger. Gillian covered her grin with her hand. It was so simple . . . and so kind. She remembered the way Edmund had reached for him, coiling his little arms around Colin's neck. The thought of it still brought moisture to her eyes. Edmund had never before done the like with any man. The surprise and initial unease on Mr. Campbell's face proved that he had never been the recipient of such gratitude from a three-year-old. But he hadn't pulled Edmund off him, or held him away, as George might have done. No, he'd closed his strong arms around her son and returned his affection.

She closed her eyes now and wrapped her arms around her knees, wondering, before she could stop it, how those arms would feel around her.

"Mummy"—Edmund looked up at her—"you should ask Colin to make you a angle."

"I might." She returned his tender gaze, but the thought of speaking to the mercenary again banished the smile from her lips. It wasn't the rugged symmetry of his fine visage and form that stilled her breath and kept her awake most of last night. It wasn't the way the soft firelight reflected all the different hues of gold and green in his steely eyes when he set them on her, revealing an inner struggle he fought to win against himself.

No, she didn't trust herself to speak to Colin Campbell and not beg him to visit her lonely child because of the way he'd playfully tossed Edmund back into bed—the way a father might have done when bidding his beloved son good night. Because of the way he and Edmund had smiled at each other afterward, as if some bond of trust and affection had passed between them that could not be broken.

Did Colin have children of his own? Lord, she knew nothing about him. All those questions she imagined putting to him to help her gain more of William's favor were forgotten the moment she looked at Colin's face.

Another thought occurred to her now that made her shift her sore buttocks on the rocks. Did he have a wife? She glanced at George and considered a way of asking him without raising his suspicions that she queried for any other reason than simple curiosity.

"He's my friend, Mummy." Edmund grinned around his thumb.

"I know, darling." She winked at him and returned

her gaze to George. "Mr. Campbell knows many games. I wonder if he has children of his own."

"What other games?" George asked, his sharp eyes falling to her.

Gillian inhaled a long, silent breath. Damn her faithful friend for catching her error. She smiled, hoping Edmund remained silent about magic daggers and flying through the air and landing in a downy mattress. "Naughts and Crosses," she reminded her guardian, "hunting crabs, swordplay, angling. He must have little ones back in Breadalbane."

"Nephews," George muttered, turning back to the water. "He mentioned visiting them before he came here."

But was he wed? Had he mentioned a woman? God's teeth, how could she ask without sounding smitten? She would mention Colin no more. In fact, she wouldn't spare him another thought. What did she care anyway if he had a wife? He was a hired henchman, likely with little coin in his pocket. There was nothing he could do to help her, and trying would be too dangerous to Edmund.

"Pull, Edmund!" George shouted, wrenching her from her thoughts. "Pull now!"

She looked at the pole, one end clenched in Edmund's tight fists, and the other dipping low in the water.

"Mummy!"

Gates sprang forward at Edmund's cry and covered his hands before he let go and lost the pole. They tugged one last time and then almost fell backward when a fish sprang from the depths and wriggled frantically from the end of the tread.

Much shouting and jumping ensued—until the fish stopped moving and George informed them that it was dead.

"Why did it die?"

"Come now," the captain said between Edmund's

tears and a yawn. "It's time for your nap." They packed up after that, the thrill of angling losing a bit of its appeal to Edmund, and went home.

Gillian gave the courtyard a brief looking over and then continued on toward the doors, trying to convince herself that she wasn't disappointed at who wasn't there. She would have liked it if Mr. Campbell had seen their fish. That was all. Where was the harm in that? The man had spent two days making the angle. She wanted him to know it had worked.

"Colin!"

She cursed the heart flipping in her chest. She was utterly deranged to let it quake at the thought of speaking to him. But she couldn't stop it. She was completely mad to allow herself to trust that there was good in any man...especially a Highland mercenary, but someplace deep inside her wanted to trust him.

She looked up to find Colin exiting the Great Hall, looking revived and remarkably refreshed for a man bent on training every hour of the day. Edmund broke away from her and ran the short distance to him.

"I caught a fish!"

"I see ye did." Mr. Campbell's eyes settled on her for an instant before moving onward to the limp body caught on his gorge. "'Tis a decent sized one, too."

"Captain Gates helped me."

Campbell met George's level gaze and smiled mildly. "That's what friends do, aye, Captain?"

George appeared only slightly discomfited before he squared his shoulders and nodded. "Of course."

"Colin." Edmund tugged on his belt and waited while Mr. Campbell squatted before him. "The fish died."

"They cannot breathe out of water fer too long, lad."

Gillian liked how he said "lad." She liked how he explained things to Edmund, and that he did so at eye level.

"I don't want to kill them. I want to keep them."

Colin scowled, making his eyes even more mesmerizing beneath his dark brow. He looked at the fish, and then at her son, and appeared to be battling yet another dilemma. "Sometimes, killing is..." His jaw rolled around words he reconsidered at the last instant. "Is not always necessary. I can show Captain Gates how to remove the gorge without harm to the fish. Then ye need only to throw it back into the water."

Gillian smiled. She couldn't help it after seeing the relief and joy on her son's face.

"But ye cannot keep them, lad. They need water to live."

"Come now." George motioned them forward. "The boy is tired."

"Just a moment, please, Captain." Gillian stopped him and looked down at her son. "Edmund, thank Mr. Campbell for his gift."

"There's no need," he told her, straightening.

She looked up, the trace of a smile hovering about her lips, sincere and determined not to fade under his cool regard. "I would have my son appreciate a kindness."

His jaw hardened, but he didn't argue and accepted Edmund's gratitude graciously.

"I have to get back," he said and swept a wooden sword from beneath his belt. "Good day, Edmund. My lady. Captain."

He was gone before Gillian could bid him farewell.

"We must smell worse than I thought," George said, quite innocently, moving on toward the stairs.

Gillian eyed him, then shook her head at his back.

Aye, that's why Mr. Campbell fled their presence like they had the plague. It had nothing to do with her guardian's black warnings to slice him up thinly should he get too close to her.

Ah, dearest George. He meant well.

Chapter Eleven

Colin whirled on his heels and blocked a blow to his head an instant before it would have rendered him unconscious.

"You are distracted, *mon ami*," Philippe Lefevre backed up in his polished boots, lowered his waster, and gave him a pitiful look.

Colin smiled and waited for the Frenchman to regain his breath. "Too much wine with my morning meal." He'd had but one sip, but Lefevre was correct. He was distracted, and Lady Gillian Dearly was to blame.

He knew he shouldn't have made that damn angle for Edmund. He had feared, while he pinched his fingers on the sharp gorge more times than he could count, that he was going soft. But to have her think him kind? To see her smile at him as if he were some sort of champion from his mother's books? Hell, he deserved to have his skull cracked open by Lefevre's blade. Mayhap, 'twould knock some sense into him. What the hell was he doing wasting his time fashioning toys for a lad who pouted at the thought of killing a fish? Unable to sleep at night, haunted by the sound of a lute played by a woman whose son meant more than her dignity?

He swung his waster before him, loosening his arm and scattering his unwanted thoughts. "Ye're not done already, are ye?"

The Frenchman grinned, swept a lock of blond hair off his shoulder, and raised his weapon. "You enjoy being beaten then?" He rushed forward and brought down his wooden sword hard against Colin's.

Aye, battle was what Colin desired. He needed nothing more than the rush of chopping his blade across another, the intensity of avoiding being cut in half, the thrill of knowing he could best any man who came against him. Soon, practice would end and he would stand among the dead, victorious, champion of a cause far greater than love.

But when?

"'Tis a dreary place, this," he said, casting his eyes toward the gravestones rising along Dartmouth's walls. "Does the earl never receive guests, then?"

"Guests?" Lefevre blocked a jab to his ribs and then another to his legs.

"Aye, my cousin in Glen Orchy mentioned other nobles who support Prince William. Yet it appears Devon is alone in this endeavor to see the prince on the throne."

"You mean the invitation." Lefevre drove him back, raining a series of hammering blows upon Colin's waster. The Frenchman was slight of frame, but his strikes were delivered with purpose.

"Invitation?" Colin pretended ignorance...and poor skill, letting his opponent's blade swish across his belly without proper defense. "They are all coming to sign the *same* letter then?"

"The letter has been sent to them." Lefevre corrected, knocking the wind out of him. "It shouldn't be too long now before it's returned and ready to be sent off to Holland."

Then the prince's arrival was closer than they expected. Colin leaped to the right, avoiding a strike to his thigh, and brought his blade down hard on Lefevre's forearm.

His opponent backed away, rubbed his arm, and then came at him again. Colin deflected the blow but was surprised by a counterattack to his calf. Lefevre's waster caught him up on one foot and set his arse to the ground.

He looked up. "How many signatures does the prince require?"

"Seven."

Seven traitors to the throne. Colin wanted their names to give to the king. He rolled away from the thick slab of wood coming at his face and bounded back to his feet, positioning his sword to strike.

"Who are they?"

Lefevre shrugged his shoulders and then held up his hand, giving up the fight. "I need water." He frowned when Colin shook his head at him. "Forgive me for lacking the stamina of a relentless young bull. Age will slow you too one day, *mon ami*."

"Ye are out of form because ye don't practice, not because ye are a few years older than me."

"Perhaps you are correct," Lefevre agreed with an amiable smile. "If we are going to be fighting the Catholics, I should be better prepared, no?"

Colin nodded. "Aye, ye should." Else his long-awaited battle would be over before it began. "And I shall help ye."

From over Lefevre's shoulder, his eye caught Captain Gates exiting the castle. Behind him was Lady Gillian.

"How did you come to be here, Campbell? I thought all you Scots were Catholics."

Colin smiled, returning his attention to his weary comrade. "I thought all ye French were, as well."

Lefevre laughed and handed him over to Gerard Hampton, a much bigger opponent.

"You'll need one of those pistols you carry to stop me." The giant grinned down at him. "And I'll never give you the time to load them."

"Then I shall keep them ready to fire at all times," Colin replied with a friendly grin of his own and readied himself for his next set. He nodded to Gates as the captain passed him, then let his gaze skim over the lady following, not certain why her glance back made him feel more lighthearted than when he'd sat at Duncan Campbell's table and gained proof of William of Orange's treason.

The flash of alarm in her eyes alerted Colin to Hampton's strike. He ducked, pivoted on his heel, and entered the fray.

Hampton's blows would have been painful if he'd managed to land any. His size made him as slow as a fly in molasses, unfortunately giving Colin more time to look at Lady Gillian while she tended to a tiny garden in the cemetery. She appeared as delicate as the blossoms she was planting but he remembered the cool control she possessed while her cousin tried to humiliate her, the fiery pride in her gaze while she played Martin's lute in the Great Hall, the lioness demanding he give account for abandoning her son. Hell, her strength and defiance ignited his blood, tempted him to give chase and conquer.

She wore her hair in a long plait over and down her shoulder to her waist. A shaft of light peeked through the clouds and fell directly on her, as if God's roving eye had spotted something so bonny, He took pause to have a better look.

"I'll take it from here." Captain Gates relieved Hampton and stepped into his place, his sword unsheathed and dangling from his right hand. "Throw down your waster and choose your sword, Campbell." He moved forward slowly, relaxed and fully centered on Colin. "Let us see if your eyes still roam when you're fighting for your life."

He didn't pounce while Colin released his waster and reached for his claymore, rather than the thinner English swords resting uselessly against the western wall. Instead, he took a step back and waited until Colin took position.

"Interesting choice," Gates acknowledged, sweeping his eyes over the long blade.

Colin didn't answer, but circled him, ready for a strike. He had the feeling he wasn't facing the same man from practice a few nights ago. But he was. Gates was clever indeed, mayhap almost as clever as Colin. The captain hadn't needed to best him the first time they met at blades. He'd chosen the craftier path of catching his prey. By watching them first, same as Colin caught his. He was intelligent and dangerous. Colin was going to have to be more careful around him.

"So, Captain, ye're going to try to kill me because of the direction of a few brief glances?"

"No, I'm going to discover how good you truly are to be able to glance away at all." He moved in a blur of speed, bringing his sword left and right, raining sparks around their boots as metal clashed with metal. He withdrew, flipped his hilt to his left hand, and advanced from the opposite direction.

Hell, Colin thought when the tip of Gates's blade scratched his neck as it swooshed by him. He wanted a demonstration of Colin's true skill, and Colin ached to give it to him. But how would he explain why he'd concealed it?

An instant later he didn't care about explanations or anything else. He looked down at the blood seeping through his shirt from a deep cut to his shoulder. He was barely aware of Lady Gillian's demand for Gates to stop, and de Atre's laughter somewhere behind him.

All right then.

Parting his legs, he flipped his claymore into his left hand and balanced on his feet. If 'twas a fight he wanted, Colin would give him one.

They met in a clash of metal, Gates driven back on his heels by the sheer force of Colin's strength. Colin advanced without pause, cutting through the captain's defense with powerful, crushing blows. He blocked every strike to a screeching halt, struck from every angle, swift, precise, and effective.

Gates held him off for more than a quarter of an hour, but 'twas clear he was weary. His reflexes slowed and three times Colin could have delivered a lethal blow. Inactivity was a pitiful reason to lose a war. But this captain didn't care about wars. He was driven by his own purpose: to protect a lady's virtue from the jackals around her...including himself.

Colin lowered his sword. He didn't want a victory over Gates. "I would never harm her, Captain," he vowed.

"You will *bring* harm to her." Gates lifted his blade over Colin's head, forcing Colin to block it. "Do you not understand that?"

"Nae, not entirely." Colin pushed away from him. "I'm not clear on why Devon takes every opportunity to shame her, yet a few mere glances could bring her harm."

Realizing the fight was over, Gates sheathed his blade and rested his hands on his knees, his breath coming heavy. "And I'm not clear on certain things about you."

Colin returned his blade to its scabbard and lifted his gaze to Lady Gillian, who was striding toward them. A coastal breeze snapped her skirts around her ankles and blew tendrils of hair loose around her face. When she reached them, she looked at the blood staining Colin's sleeve and then glared at Gates. She said nothing, which seemed to ruffle the captain's composure more than fighting with Colin had.

"Are you done in your garden?" Gates asked her, straightening.

"I am." She didn't blink but folded her arms across her chest and continued to stare at him.

"Good, then I'll see you to your rooms."

"You will see me to the Great Hall, where I will tend to the wound you inflicted on Mr. Campbell, and then I would have words with you alone."

She was angry. Colin wondered if his injury was the cause and then put the thought from his mind. 'Twas nothing but a scratch. He'd received worse at the Battle of Sedgemoor and had seen to the injuries himself. He didn't need a woman to mend him. He certainly didn't want a woman worrying over him.

"I can see to it myself," he said when Gates did not refuse her request right away.

"Nonsense." She turned her glare on him. "I've tended to the men's wounds before. You are no different."

He didn't know why her words made him scowl, or why he'd just fought the captain with blades instead of just apologizing for looking at her, or why he couldn't look away now.

"I'll have Margaret see to him," Gates finally said, regaining his poise and his breath. "I would have words with Mr. Campbell—"

"Margaret can balance a tray on her hand and her hips in a man's lap," Lady Gillian contended, unwilling to budge on the matter. "A needle and thread in her fingers will likely render him useless while he fights off infection. Now let us go before we draw a crowd and Mr. Campbell bleeds all over the courtyard."

She turned on her heel without another word, leaving both of them to stare after her and then eye each other helplessly. Colin followed first, with the captain muttering blasphemies behind him.

A few men loitered about in the Hall, Lefevre among them. When the French mercenary saw Colin's bloody arm, he laughed and raised his cup to him. Colin acknowledged him with a brief nod and then strode to the nearest empty table.

"Captain." Lady Gillian pulled out a chair and motioned for Colin to sit in it. "I will need a bowl of water and my needles. Please have one of the men see to the task while I examine the wound. Mr. Campbell, remove your shirt."

Colin fell into the chair silently and glowered up at her. He had no stomach for being pampered like some English peacock in need of a nursemaid. But he found his protests caught somewhere between her full pink mouth and the vivid blue of her eyes. Would she be so determined to have a look at him when she saw the number of scars marring his form?

What the hell did he care? Was he losing his bloody mind, worrying over her aversion to his bare chest? So what if she thought him ugly. Mayhap she would quit looking at him and he could get on with his task without thinking about her with every damned breath he took.

"Your shirt," she commanded, standing over him.

He aimed his most deadly frown at her and she bit her bottom lip, either frightened of him or trying not to laugh at his last feeble attempt at dignity. Neither reaction pleased him. Jaw taut, he yanked his shirt over his head and tossed it to the floor.

As he suspected, Lady Gillian's eyes widened before she quickly looked away.

Chapter Twelve

Gillian lived in a castle with more than a hundred men. She'd seen bare torsos before and mended dozens of wounds inflicted upon men she didn't like, or barely knew.

But this was different.

She didn't dislike Colin Campbell, but, God help her, she'd never seen a form like this one before. From shoulders to belly, this was a body honed to perfection, sculpted by daily, rigorous training. Not overly muscular, his lean corded sinew twitched beneath his glistening skin, damp and still wound taut from his morning's exercise.

She let out the breath caught between her chest and her throat and looked away.

Get a grip on yourself, Gillian, she told herself, stunned and disgusted by her base appraisal. *He is just a man. Just like all the rest.*

"I can tend to myself."

His gruff voice dragged her attention back to him. Her eyes lingered over the powerful length of his arm reaching down to snatch something from the floor. An arm that had overpowered George.

"What are you doing?" she asked as he stood up, his shirt dangling from his hand.

"I'm leaving."

"Oh, do stop being a child. I will be extra gentle with you."

His mouth opened into a curiously alluring O before it curled into an indulgent smirk. "Woman, I've dug musket balls out of my flesh with a knife. I don't fear anything ye can do with a needle."

She offered him a cheeky smile in return, though for some reason his declaration and the quiet authority in the way he spoke it made her kneecaps ache. Of course, her weakness could be blamed on the way he stood before her like a statue carved in cold granite. He *looked* like the kind of man who could dig bullets from his own flesh and not flinch.

"Very well." She folded her arms across her chest in defense of his dangerous appeal. "Now that we've established how strong and manly you are, would you sit down and let me tend to you before you bleed all over the chair?"

He didn't protest, but his muscles remained coiled and he was ready to spring back up from his seat. Gillian breathed a silent sigh and moved closer to examine his wound. She didn't like prideful men. In fact, she didn't like men in general. She kept that thought firmly in her mind while she reached her fingers to his flesh.

He flinched, anticipating her touch. They glanced at each other at the same time. Lord, but his eyes were captivating, like twin sunsets ringed by darkness and shadows. Deep, mysterious wells of emotion boiling beneath the surface. However stoic he appeared, his eyes were alive with the storm of passions unleashed. What were they? What moved him, drove him, made him smile? She wanted to know.

"It's deep," she said, blinking away and over his bloody shoulder to glare one last time at George.

What in Heaven's name had come over him to fight with real swords? He'd fought like he was trying to kill Colin. Why? Did it have to do with her? With Edmund? She hoped not. Colin Campbell was far more dangerous than he led others to believe, but he had been nothing but respectful to her and kind to Edmund. She would not have him harmed for things he hadn't done, save for in George's own head. She would speak with him about it later. Her bowl of water had arrived, along with clean rags, and if she didn't set about her work now, she might be too afraid to touch her patient later.

"Who closed those previous wounds?" she asked, dipping a rag in the bowl to begin cleaning around the injury.

"I did," he practically growled at her.

She quirked her brow at him but he'd severed their gaze and looked straight ahead. What was he so angry about? She shrugged a shoulder, suspecting it had much to do with George.

"All of them?" she asked, continuing her work. And there were many. At least six other tears in the arm he was bleeding from now. Four that she could see on the other. A small nick on his collarbone, two large gashes across his chest and three round gouges, the size of musket balls, on his rippled belly. Lord, he'd spoken true.

"You're lucky to be alive, Mr. Campbell."

"Luck had naught to do with it."

"What had it to do with then?" George asked, coming to stand at her side. "Mastery of the sword, perhaps?"

Colin glanced up at him briefly. "A passion fer my life when someone is trying to take it from me."

Gillian listened while she dabbed his shoulder clean. George had been correct in his suspicions about the mercenary. Had this been a test to force Colin into proving his skill? She knew George was clever, but he'd still almost taken off Colin's arm.

"Passion stirs many things in a man," her captain agreed, looking him over slyly. "Let us hope that being a fool is not one of them."

Gillian cut a glance to her friend and then looked up at Lieutenant de Atre when he appeared over her with her needles and thread.

"Lord Devon wishes to speak with you, Captain. I am to escort the lady to her rooms when she is finished sewing this one up."

Gillian didn't look at de Atre while he spoke. Her eyes found Colin's instead. They shared a moment of displeasure at the lieutenant's presence. This time, she looked away first. She nodded to George when he told her to make haste with her task, then set her mind to work as he left the Great Hall.

"Would you like some ale or wine to aid with the pain?" she asked Colin quietly.

"Nae."

"Looks like you've been losing fights for quite some time now, Scot." Lieutenant de Atre laughed, looking over Colin's flesh.

"Lieutenant," Gillian said with annoyance clipping her voice, "if you must stay here, would you be so kind as to remain silent?" *Your voice makes my skin crawl.*

He glared at her as if he'd heard her silent thoughts, then muttered something about her being a cold-hearted bitch and stomped off to join three of his comrades who were sharing some ale.

Gillian's hands trembled as she put her needle to flesh. Sewing a man didn't make her queasy. Being alone with Colin Campbell did. Was she so pitiful then, that she could become so undone by a man simply because he was kind to her son? Or worse, because he had the most piercing, smoldering eyes she'd ever seen? She moved in closer, trying desperately to ignore the pulse beat at his neck, the strength of his jaw just inches away. When he turned his head to watch her work, she almost stuck the needle in the wrong place. Pausing, she drew in a breath and began again.

"Ye don't like him."

She drove the needle through. He ground his jaw.

"He smells like a sewer."

"I've noticed," he said, following the length of thread through his arm.

She relaxed, more because she liked the rich baritone of his voice than because he was finally speaking to her without sounding like he'd rather be doing anything else. His thick, melodic pitch soothed her nerves. She thought she might like to listen to him speak to her all day.

"You fought Captain Gates with your left hand." She glanced at his gaze.

"Aye."

"Most believe such a practice reveals a sinister nature."

"They are most likely correct. My father was referred to as the devil in his younger years."

Gillian smiled. He did not smile back. No matter. In fact, she rather preferred his dispassionate response over the lecherous grins she usually received from the others. "Did you come by the rest of these scars in practice or in battle?"

"Both," he told her, his brow heavy above his eyes as he moved them to the men drinking and laughing on the other side of the Hall. "I wear them proudly."

"And so you should." Her eyes lingered over them before lifting to meet his as he turned them back on her.

"Some find them repulsive."

"Fools. I...I mean"—she stumbled over her words when that unfathomable gaze went warm on her—"they are...you are..." She pierced his skin again and felt his muscles constrict beneath her fingers. "Oh, do forgive me." She let go of her needle and stepped back. "Perhaps I should have Margaret see to you, after all."

"Ye're doing fine." He reached for her hand and pulled her back, setting her poor nerves to ruin. "Continue."

Could she? Everything about him was driving her to distraction. Perhaps if she wasn't standing over him, so close that her leg brushed his outer thigh. She moved around him, to the left, then to the right, but found no position comfortable from which to sew him. She wiped her brow and then realized he was watching her with a curious quirk shaping his mouth. Lord, but he had nice lips.

"I...I cannot seem to find—"

He took her by the arm and moved her between his thighs. "Better?"

Dear God, no, it wasn't better. She felt a bit faint and prayed she wouldn't swoon into his lap. She didn't want to like him. She certainly wouldn't let herself trust him completely. But Lord, she hadn't been so close to a decent man in more years than she cared to recall. "Better," she managed, but didn't move to retrieve the needle dangling from his shoulder.

"Captain Gates is verra protective of ye."

"Hmmm? Oh, aye, he is." She picked up the needle and resumed stitching. "Sometimes, too protective."

"He has his reasons, I imagine."

Gillian caught him eyeing de Atre. "He does," she agreed, following his gaze. "Thankfully, some of them are afraid to even look at me."

"I'm aware."

Damn it to hell, but she stabbed him yet again. "Is…" She forced herself to go gentle on the next stitch. "Is that why he challenged you to swords?"

"That may have had something to do with it."

He *had* been looking at her then. She felt him looking at her now. Something flipped in her chest and made her palms grow moist. Why had he been looking at her? Twice the needle nearly slipped from her hands. "You must forgive Captain Gates. He worries over Edmund."

"And Lord Devon, what does he worry over?"

Gillian finally glanced at him, not understanding his meaning.

"Will he lose yer father's coin or perhaps his military support if ye leave this place?"

She paused her work to look at him fully. What was he saying… "Leave this…?" Her words trailed off and she shook her head. "No. He will lose *me*."

"Woman!" Lieutenant de Atre called from his place across the hall. "Hurry the hell up with that. I've other things to do."

For a moment Colin's expression went so dark on him that Gillian feared he might snatch one of the daggers peeking out from his boots and hurl it into the lieutenant's chest.

"Perhaps it is best if we don't speak of Geoffrey anymore. Edmund will be waking soon and I don't wish to spoil my good mood. Tell me instead how you received some of your wounds."

He looked at her like he wanted to refuse and question her more on things she preferred not to think about. Such as marrying her cousin and never leaving Dartmouth.

"I imagine," she said, stopping him, "your body has many thrilling tales of battle to tell."

She didn't think tending to him could be any more difficult, but when he smiled at her, she felt the defenses that had taken her years to build weaken... along with her knees. It was nothing like the pleasant, though somewhat inconsequential smiles he offered the others here. His gaze on her softened, warming her from the inside out. Oh, his many battles may have thickened his hard shell, but beneath was a man crafted of fire. So hot that his voice dancing across her ears burned her nerve endings like languid flames.

"This"—he pointed to the nick on his collarbone—"was given to me by my sister. She has a treacherous temper."

Gillian smiled back at him, forgetting her frosty shield that helped to keep the men at bay. Forgetting everything else for one blissful moment. "And this?" She touched her finger to a scar running down the length of his arm. "Her as well, or something more dangerous?"

"A thief who tried to rob me on the road."

Oh, what an adventurous life he seemed to have led. Fighting in the king's army, meeting robbers on roads that led wherever he desired.

"Did the thief get much from you?"

"Aye, an opportunity to plead his case before God."

They shared another stolen smile. Gillian thought she might even have giggled.

"And the holes?" She reached for the gouges along his belly before she realized what she was doing.

He pulled her hand back as Lieutenant de Atre appeared beside them.

"Are you done?"

"A stitch or two more."

"Be quick about it, wench. I want my turn against the stray next."

Colin leaned in an inch closer to her and whispered along her ear. "I vow to ye, he will get it."

✢

Chapter Thirteen

*I*nstead of returning to the courtyard, Colin found himself lingering at the bottom of the stairway, looking up. He didn't like the fact that de Atre was bringing her back to her rooms alone. The pig had practically grunted with anticipation, and Lady Gillian had stuck him with her needle three more times before she finished mending him.

He watched them reach the landing and then disappear down the dim corridor. He knew what he was doing when he set his boots to motion. What he didn't know was why he was doing it. He wasn't here to rescue the Earl of Devon's cousin. He didn't even clearly understand what she needed rescuing from, aside from the unkempt swine presently counting the moments before he could begin pawing at her.

Colin hurried the rest of the way. He would simply watch and then report what he saw to Gates. He vowed he would involve himself no further after that. She was Gates's responsibility, not his.

He crept down the hall, blending in with the rest of the shadowy phantoms dancing against the torchlight. As he drew closer to her door, he heard their voices. Lady Gillian's, curt and urgent.

"You may go, Lieutenant."

"Is that all the thanks I get for saving you from having to spend any more time with that torn-up waif? I could see the repulsion in your eyes as you worked, love."

"What you saw was aimed at you, Lieutenant. Now leave my door, please."

Colin watched her hand move to a fold in her gown where the hilt of a dagger peeked out from within. He smiled in the shadows. So, the lass carried a weapon. That pleased him more than it probably should have.

De Atre reached his hand out to her, but Colin didn't wait to see what he meant to do with it—or what she would do with her dagger. Stepping out of the shadows, he caught the lieutenant's wrist in his right hand and pointed a dagger at de Atre's belly with his left.

"Lady"—he offered her a reverential nod—"would ye mind repeating yer request once more? It appears the lieutenant failed to hear ye the first two times."

"Not at all," she replied. "Lieutenant, leave my door."

Colin turned to him, his gaze sharp and hard. "I heard her. Did ye?"

"I'll have your balls for this, Campbell!"

"'Tis more likely that Gates will have yers. But if ye would like to give yer threat a go, ye know where to find me."

De Atre yanked his hand back and stepped away from Colin's dagger, clearing his oily hair away from his face, his dark eyes gleaming with anger. "I'll see you in the courtyard then, stray."

Colin nodded, then watched him pound away toward the stairs. So much for making friends with the men here. Hell, he didn't know how much longer he could have waited anyway before he knocked out some of de Atre's teeth. It had little to do with her.

"Thank you."

He turned to her, knowing he shouldn't, but feeling his control abandoning him yet again. 'Twas alarming how drawn he was to look at her, risking his wits, Gates's fury, and God knows what else.

"I think he's gone now," he said, barely recognizing his own voice. He wasn't a lady's champion. Hell, he didn't possess a single romantic bone in his body. "Ye're...ehm...safe." Him, stumbling over words. What was next, writing her poetry? God, kill him before that day ever arrived.

"I am on my way to check on Edmund," she said hastily when he moved to leave her.

He had to leave. He should leave.

"It would please him to see you. For just a moment. Please, Mr. Campbell."

How could he refuse such a simple request without sounding like a heartless bastard? But that's exactly what he was. He befriended his enemies to gain information and then he left, never sparing them another thought. He'd never offered a lass anything more than a few hours of pleasure, and he rarely even enjoyed that. He had a single purpose—to stop William from ever gaining the throne. He would never sway from it.

"Colin."

"What?" She blinked those huge, round eyes on him. Eyes that had looked at his battle-scarred body with appreciation instead of revulsion.

"My name is Colin."

Her lips tightened around her mouth before she looked away. "I couldn't."

"Of course. Fergive me." He drew in a deep breath he hoped would clear his head. "I shouldn't be here. 'Tis—"

But she was already a few steps away from him, heading toward another door, most likely Edmund's. "You've made an enemy in de Atre, you know."

He smiled, thinking of the day when it no longer mattered who liked him and who didn't—and watching the way her long braid swayed around her shapely rear. He wanted her to like him. God help him. "I'm certain I will get over it."

She looked over her shoulder and laughed softly, almost bringing a halt to his steps. 'Twas the first time he'd heard the sound since coming here. 'Twas soft and sweet, like her.

Och, hell, he didn't care what she was doing to him or how. He wanted to touch her, take her in his arms, and let himself feel something again. "Ye should laugh more, lass," he told her, aware of his defenses collapsing around him and unable to stop them.

She'd stopped walking and turned to him, taken aback by his boldness, mayhap, the sincerity in his smile. But only for a moment. "You're right," she said, her humor restored. "I should. Do you think me a terrible snob that I find little amusement in the Great Hall?"

The flitter of mischief in her eyes told him she was teasing him with her query. She possessed no haughty airs and they both knew it. She was clever though, making him see the foolishness of his advice without calling him an insensitive cad.

And since when did he give a damn about being insensitive?

He blamed his sudden affliction of weakness on his

recent visit home. Seeing his sister and his brothers with their families made him ache—from somewhere in the parts of his heart where he didn't venture—for the same.

"What is it that makes ye laugh then?"

"Many things." She quirked her lips at him, reminding him of how completely beguiling he'd found her while she was torturing his shoulder earlier. "But they are silly and fanciful and nothing I would ever think of telling a dangerous mercenary such as yourself."

Damn it, he wanted to laugh right along with her, and then convince her that he was no danger to her.

But he was.

He was about to remind her when they reached the door. She poked her head inside then reappeared, holding her finger to her lips.

"He still sleeps. Come."

Colin followed her like a lost sailor helpless against the lure of a siren beckoning him toward his pitiful end.

He'd been in this room before, but not while sunlight splintered the dimness through cracks in the shutters. There was not much to see, in truth. Other than a few dolls hand-sewn in the shape of knights, there was little to suggest this was a child's chamber. A wooden table was butted up against the west wall with two chairs pushed neatly beneath it. The table housed books of different sizes, along with parchment and a quill. A small lute and the rod he'd made for Edmund rested against another wall. Four trunks were scattered about and Colin hoped they contained forms of entertainment for the wee lad who resided here. But for the cabinet where he'd hidden Edmund's dagger, a tall bookcase, and the bed where the babe slept, there was no other furniture to be seen.

'Twas dreary as hell.

"He should wake soon," Edmund's mother promised while she unlatched the shutters and swung them open, drenching herself in daylight.

He'd seen lasses more beautiful than she. In fact, there were things about her that some might not find appealing at all. Her cheekbones, for instance, were not sharp or painted to appear that way. The flesh below her eyes was a wee bit puffy, too, as if she wept often—or not at all. Her lips were . . . Hell, her lips were lovely. *She* was lovely, angelic and untainted.

She was trouble.

He dragged his eyes away from her and looked down at the tiny body curled up in his oversize bed. He didn't think his chest could grow any tighter than it already was, but he was wrong. He wished he'd spent more time at Camlochlin. His nephews barely knew him. He'd helped their parents tuck them in, had kissed their wee heads, and silently promised to keep them safe from a Protestant king. But hell, he hadn't been struck with an almost paralyzing desire to protect them the way he felt gazing at Edmund.

And his mother.

"He doesn't usually nap so long," Gillian whispered, appearing beside him to gaze at her babe as if he were the only thing that mattered in their world.

Colin guessed he was.

"I suspect your dagger has made his slumber more peaceful."

He smiled. He couldn't help himself. "He resembles ye," he told her softly, feeling his heart go even softer at the babe's wee features and shallow, even breaths.

"Do you have a wife, Mr. Campbell?"

He turned to her, surprised by her question, and found her assessing him with flushed cheeks.

"Nae. I'm not wed." Hell, why couldn't he stop smiling like a dimwit?

"A pity. You would be a wonderful father."

He shook his head and grew serious, remembering himself. "Nae, I wouldn't, trust me. I don't possess the heart fer it."

"Oh, but you do. You're patient with Edmund, thoughtful and generous. You consider his safety, and he is not even your charge."

Colin wasn't sure of what to say, or how to say it. He wasn't what she believed him to be... what he knew she wanted him to be. She was alone here, raising her son amid mercenaries and soldiers bred to kill. Gates clearly cared for the lad, but he'd managed to remain distant where Colin had failed.

"Why hasn't Gates taken ye both from here?"

"And bring us to his wife?"

Colin's gaze lingered on her for another moment before his eyes fell back to her son.

"We are fine here, Mr. Campbell. Leaving is an option I cannot consider just yet."

Just yet? What did that mean? Did she plan on escaping? If so, with whom? And what did she mean earlier when she told him that her cousin would lose her? What did he want with her? Colin wanted to ask her but Edmund came awake. He couldn't help but return the babe's smile when he saw him.

"Colin." Edmund sat up in his bed and rubbed his sleepy eyes. "Are you bleeding?"

He remembered his bloody shirt and shook his head. "Not anymore, lad. Yer mother mended me."

"May I see?"

"No, Edmund," his mother said. "You may not. It will frighten you."

"No it won't, Mummy."

It likely would, Colin reasoned, squatting in front of the bed. Stitched wounds were an ugly sight, but 'twasn't natural for boys not to see them.

"If 'tis all right with yer mother, in a few days, after it has healed a bit, I will remove the bandage and show ye."

"Will it be all right?" Edmund turned the same eyes on his mother that she had fastened on Colin a dozen times today. Eyes that were difficult to refuse, and that found his while she considered her reply.

"Ye weren't frightened, aye, lady?"

She shook her head and turned to Edmund. "In a few days then."

Edmund grinned at her, and then at Colin. "Have you come to play?"

Colin shifted slightly on his haunches, uncertain of how to reply without disappointing the lad yet again. "I'm afraid I only came to—"

"To what?" Captain Gates's voice brought Colin back to his feet. He stood by the open door, his body poised and ready to pounce. "I'm curious to hear your reply after I warned you about coming up here without me."

"Captain." Lady Gillian stepped forward, placing herself between both men. "He—"

"Let him answer," Gates commanded sternly. "I wish to hear what he has to say before I skewer him."

Colin cast the heavens a frustrated look. De Atre was one thing, but it wouldn't serve well to make an enemy of Captain Gates. He understood the man's concerns, but he didn't want to fight him again. Especially right here in front of Edmund.

"Captain, ye will have my answer in the hall."

"Very well," Gates approved, eyeing Edmund in his bed. "After you." He stepped aside elegantly, clearing a path for Colin to take.

Before he left, Colin bent to Edmund again and winked at him. "You and I will speak another day, friend."

He glanced at Gillian on his way out, then muttered something unintelligible when she picked up her steps behind him. He thought about telling her to stay here with her son, but she took orders from enough men. He didn't want to be another.

"Well?" Gates demanded the instant the door shut behind them. "You have but a moment to speak before I toss you out of Dartmouth on your arse."

"I would wonder why ye haven't already done so to yer lieutenant."

"De Atre?" Gates narrowed his eyes on him, and then on Lady Gillian. "What does he have to do with this?"

"He grew bold after escorting me to my door."

Gates's expression went black in an instant. Even keeping Colin off him in the courtyard hadn't enraged him as much as what he was hearing now. "What do you mean, he grew bold? What did he do?"

"Och, Captain," Colin said incredulously, interrupting her when she would have replied, "surely ye are aware of his desire fer her."

Gates might not possess the endurance for an all-out fight, but he was quick enough to yank Colin's dagger from his belt and point it at his throat.

Gillian leaped for him, but Colin held her back with

his arm. He remained utterly still, his eyes fastened on Gates, waiting, knowing his own reflexes were quicker.

"Rest assured, Campbell, I'm aware of every lewd glance cast her way."

"Mayhap," Colin said calmly, "ye should train yer eyes more toward the fear in hers when ye give de Atre leave to have her alone."

Horror replaced the fury staring back at him, slowly moving from him to the lady he swore to protect. Colin didn't know whether to pity the captain's duty against so many, or loathe him for failing at it.

"What has he done?" Gates asked her quietly, sounding sickened to his soul.

"He has done nothing, George. But he grows ever bolder."

"Why haven't you told me?"

"And have Gerald Hampton take his place when you are seeing to other things? I could never fight off that giant. Or perhaps Mr. Alvarez, whom I suspect would not leave me alive to tell you anything?"

"Gillian..."

She closed her eyes when he lowered Colin's dagger and reached his fingers to her jaw.

"You should have told me. And you—" He looked at Colin again. "It seems *your* eyes have been trained on her well enough to see what I have missed."

"He protected me, George." Gillian's soft voice stole across both men's ears. "I will not let you punish him for that."

Gates nodded and handed Colin back his dagger. "You and I will speak of this after I've seen to de Atre. For now, you may go."

• • •

Gillian watched Colin leave and then turned to George. "I would prefer it if Mr. Campbell escorted me when you cannot do so."

"Absolutely not."

"Then who, George? Whom do you trust?"

Her captain scored his fingers through his hair. He looked more miserable than Gillian had ever seen him. Perhaps she shouldn't have told him about de Atre.

"No one. Not him."

She knew George's fears, but she didn't think Colin would try to take her and Edmund away. She practically had to beg him to spend a moment with her son, and though his smile on her was captivating, he fought the urge to offer it to her.

"Perhaps"—she put her hand to Edmund's door and turned to her captain before she entered it alone—"it is not him you don't trust, but me."

Chapter Fourteen

Colin stepped out of the path of what would have been a sharp blow to his head, and brought the flat end of his waster down hard on Gilbert de Atre's back, bringing him to his knees for the second time. He didn't fight the arrogant pig with the skill he'd used while fighting Gates. He didn't have to. This time, he kept his head and blocked more blows than he issued. Most of the other men had gathered in the courtyard and were watching, and Colin wished to remain underestimated.

Still, he took enjoyment in bringing de Atre to his knees and making him look cumbersome and clumsy in view of the others.

His pleasure, though, came to an abrupt halt when someone shoved him out of the way and filled the yard with the sound of his blade scraping against its sheath as it left it.

"Captain Gates." De Atre held up his hands and dropped his waster. "Whatever Campbell told you—"

"He told me nothing." Gates sliced his sword through the air and cut a deep gash through de Atre's palm. "Lady Gillian did, as she has been instructed to do with all of you." He raked his gaze over the others and brought the tip of his blade back up, catching de Atre across the cheek and lip. The lieutenant finally attacked but only found himself staring down at the tip of Gates's blade butted up against his heart.

"Go near her ever again and I will cut away what I merely wounded today. Do you understand?"

De Atre nodded and stepped carefully away from the blade.

Having proved true to his word to slice open anyone who touched his charge, Captain Gates sheathed his blade and turned to walk away.

Having remained in the yard after Gates took over the fight with his lieutenant, Colin watched de Atre rip a blade from his boot and lunge toward the captain's back. He scowled, thinking that one of them should have killed the disreputable swine. He didn't think too long though, but took off, leaped into the air, and fell on top of the would-be assassin.

They landed hard on the ground, though de Atre absorbed most of the impact since he hit it first. His dagger fell away, useless. Rolling to top position, Colin drew his arm back, ready to break some teeth, mayhap smash a bone. His shoulder locked in pain as his stitches tore open. When his fist fell, it did nothing but wake the lieutenant from his stupor.

De Atre went for a hilt tucked into Colin's boot and pulled it free. Before he had the chance to stab Colin with it though, a fist, appearing from their left, slammed against his jaw and knocked him out cold.

Captain Gates tested his hand for broken bones and then shoved his arm beneath Colin's and helped him to his feet.

They stood facing each other, both knowing they had moved to save the other's life. No words were spoken, but what passed between them was the stuff that bound men together on the battlefield.

"Come on," Gates said, turning for the castle. "Let's have Gillian sew you back up and then we'll share a drink."

"Nae." Colin held back. He didn't think he could sit through another stitching with the lady of the castle without her haunting his thoughts for another se'nnight. He did want to sit with Gates though and find out what he could about the prince.

"I can tend to this myself, but I'll meet ye in the Great Hall afterward fer that drink."

He waited for the captain's agreement, then cut across the yard to the other side of the castle, where the smithy was busy hammering away at swords. Colin hadn't known *how many* swords until he stepped inside. The red shadowy walls were lined with rows of blades of various lengths. More were piled atop shelves and tables.

Clutching his bloody arm, Colin looked around and then at the smith, who paused in his labors to have a look at him in return.

"Expecting a rather large army, are ye?"

"Who the hell are you?" The smith squinted at him and held up the red-hot blade he'd been hammering. "What do you want?"

"Colin Campbell, and I require yer services, old man."

"I don't repair wasters." The smith waved him away and went back to work. "See the woodcutter for that."

"'Tis flesh that needs repairing, not wood."

"Then you'll be wanting the lady."

"Nae, I don't want her," he said above the noise of the fire and pulled on his shirt, exposing his gaping wound.

"She mended me once already, and rather poorly, I might add. I want ye to seal it with yer blade."

"My blade?" The smith held up the glowing metal and shivered. "Are you mad, soldier? That will hurt like hell."

"I'll survive it." What he wasn't sure he'd survive was looking into her eyes again, so close he could almost hear her thoughts. Watching the way her lips moved when she spoke, tempting him to wonder how they would taste against his. Hearing what kind of father she thought he'd make.

'Twas best if he stayed as far away from her as he could.

"Steady hands, then." He took the smith's trembling wrist in his fingers and brought the blade closer to him. "Just seal the wound, aye?"

The smith nodded, but he looked less than confident. Colin guided him closer and then closed his eyes, readying for the pain. He'd done this before, but one never grew accustomed to the pain and the smell of flesh burning.

Colin thought of every distraction his mind could conjure, but finally had to leap away from the smith's touch. He leaned against one of the tables until the wave of nausea passed, then thanked the smith and plunged into the cool air outside. He dragged in a deep breath to keep from passing out, then headed for the Great Hall.

When he arrived, Gates was sitting alone at a table, staring into his cup. Colin picked up his steps when he saw the pitcher and second cup on the table waiting for him.

He slipped into the chair opposite the captain, appearing so suddenly that Gates startled a bit. Colin didn't apologize but reached for the pitcher, poured himself a cup of whatever was in it, and downed its contents. He repeated those actions once more, slammed the cup down on the table, and looked at the man sitting across from him.

"Hell, don't ye have anything stronger here? Whisky?"

Gates shook his head then dipped his gaze to Colin's singed collar. "You burned it closed?"

"Aye, and I could use some damned whisky."

"There might be some in the lower cellar. I'll have a look later."

Good, Colin thought, filling his cup once more with the piss-warm, weak ale. Gates was warming up to him. They always did. The more time Colin spent with someone, the more information they were likely to offer.

"I've been pondering some things, Campbell. I thought we might speak of them."

Colin nodded his consent and brought his cup to his lips.

"I will need to find another who will protect Lady Gillian when I cannot."

Colin guzzled down the ale. No way in hell—

"I don't know who to choose. You know the men, Campbell. Who do you think can be trusted with her?"

Colin regarded him carefully. Gates was clever to ask for his opinion rather than his service. Every man in the garrison who secretly desired her would have leaped at the chance to be her chaperone, and Gates knew it. Another test.

"I think Lefevre would be best."

Gates blinked. "Not yourself?"

Colin contained the smile creeping along his lips. He was correct then. He usually was. Part of what made him the king's best spy was that he could read people so skillfully, understand what they were saying without their having to utter the words. "I wish to practice, not become a woman's guardian."

The captain looked into his cup while he sloshed his

ale around inside of it. He seemed to be weighing his words before he spoke them. "Would your answer be the same if she requested you?"

Damn it, he hadn't anticipated that. She requested him? "Why wouldn't it be?" Colin asked him. "And why press me now, after ye convinced me of the dangers of forming attachments to them?"

Gates finally looked up, with eyes, large and solemn, like a man being forced to do something that went against every bit of good sense he had left in his pitiful head. "Because she is frightened of the other men here, and with good reason. Men tend to desire what is forbidden to them."

"Aye," Colin agreed, shifting to a more comfortable position. "I've been wanting to share a word with ye about that."

"Have you?"

"Aye, I have. Ye warned me that the earl would harm Edmund if she tried to leave. But ye did not tell me why. Will he lose her father's support against the king? And what does William of Orange's arrival have to do with it?"

Gates looked about to answer, but downed his ale first and set his level gaze on Colin across the table. "Why do you allow the men to beat you in the yard when you are obviously better skilled than they are?"

Colin raised his cup to his companion. He wanted answers but he respected the captain's refusal to give them up so easily. "Ye don't believe that 'twas the rage of seeing my own blood that gave strength to my arm then?"

Gates chose not to reply to that, but to ask another question instead. "Why do you fight with a Highland sword and not an English rapier? You said you fought in the English army."

These weren't difficult questions to answer, since Gates wasn't the first man to ask them. Colin almost conceded. But he wasn't one to surrender. At least not until he got what he wanted. "I will tell ye why after ye tell me why Devon continually goes out of his way to shame his ward and spoil her name?"

For a moment, Gates simply stared at him, his eyes narrowing, his jaw tightening. Colin thought he would refuse again.

"She's strong of will. Devon wishes to break her."

Did Colin truly want to hear the rest? His blood was already simmering against her cousin. What if what he learned provoked him further? He already had a cause, and 'twasn't her. He couldn't let it be.

"Why?" he found himself asking anyway.

"So that she will not fight him when he takes her before a priest," Gates continued, keeping his end of the bargain. "He makes her yield through Edmund, but we fear that once he has her, he will send Edmund away."

A man's coarse shout to his friend somewhere in the castle echoed against Colin's ears as he sat staring at Gates. Had he heard the captain right? Devon wished to wed her? It wasn't unheard of to wed one's cousin. Prince William and his wife were related by blood, but Devon was a cruel bastard with little to offer her besides a fortress as cold and dreary as a marriage between them would be.

"Her father would allow this?"

Gates shrugged his shoulders. "Essex has practically disowned her already. And even if he forbids such a union, once William takes the throne, he will most likely agree to give Devon whatever he wants in gratitude for aiding him."

Sitting back in his chair, Colin let what he'd learned

sink in. Aye, William would grant his English lackey what he asked and Gillian would remain a prisoner for the remainder of her life. And what of Edmund? Devon wouldn't keep her bastard son around longer than it took a priest to recite the benediction. But all hope wasn't lost. William couldn't grant Devon a damned thing until he was king—and Colin wasn't about to let that happen.

"Your sword?" Gates arched a dark gold brow at him.

Aye, that. "'Twas a gift from my father. He presented it to me the day I left home to join the English army. He didn't want me to ferget my roots." 'Twas the truth, but Colin had never told it to anyone. If he sought to gain Gates's trust, he knew he would have to give a bit more.

"And have you forgotten?"

Colin shook his head. "'Tis the reason I am here."

Gates regarded him briefly, then pushed his cup away. "The afternoon grows late. I must attend Gill...Lady Gillian."

Colin stood, disregarding his drink, as well, and turned to leave.

"Have you changed your mind?" The captain's question stopped him. "About attending her when I cannot?"

He wanted to. Och, how he ached to protect her. Her and her son. He wanted to spend more time with them, hear their laughter, be a part of the intense love between them. 'Twas passionate, and things had stopped being passionate for Colin long ago.

But he wasn't part of it. He couldn't be. Now more than ever he had to remain dedicated to his task and stop William from taking the throne. "Nae," Colin told him. "I have not."

He was a cold, merciless bastard. And as he left the Hall, he felt like one.

Chapter Fifteen

Gillian wrapped her son's wet body in a heavy drying cloth and lifted him from his morning bath. She pressed her nose to his damp, golden curls and held him close against her.

"My, but you smell good. I thought you might smell like a fish forever."

"I would like to smell like a fish, Mummy!"

She laughed, gazing into his clear blue eyes. "Flies would like it as well if you did."

The door opened as she was crossing her son's room to his bed. She glanced at Margaret, entering with two male servants.

"He's finished with his bath then?" Margaret didn't look up when she spoke, but waited while the two men carried the basin away. Suddenly Gillian felt a sharp pang of pity for her. She knew Geoffrey often took Margaret to his bed. Poor girl. They were both suppressed under the pressure of the same hand. Why weren't they friends?

"Margaret." Gillian stopped her when the servant

turned to leave. "Stay for a few moments, won't you? We can—"

"I have more important duties to see to," Margaret said, barely sparing her a glance. "Some of us do not have the pleasure of reading all day and doing little else."

She left the room, slipping past George as she went. The captain watched her go and then turned to Gillian, who was drying off her son and trying to look unaffected by the servant's rejection.

"I'm not permitted to do anything else," she muttered.

"It's safer that way," her captain answered, entering the room.

Gillian closed her eyes, refusing to let loneliness grip her. "How does Lieutenant de Atre fare?" she asked, gathering her composure.

"I was in a merciful mood. He yet lives."

"Spare me the details now, will you?" Gillian covered Edmund's head with the drying cloth and rubbed his damp curls.

George took a seat at the table and frowned at her first, and then at the door. "Perhaps you can offer to teach Margaret to read."

"Aye, perhaps," Gillian said softly. She stopped drying Edmund, kissed his forehead, and reached for his fresh clothes, which were folded neatly on the bed. Another day almost gone. Another long night to come before it began all over again.

"Have you decided who will follow me about in your absence?" She prayed for him to say Colin Campbell. She knew it was foolish and dangerous, but Edmund so enjoyed his company...as did she. He broke up the day. His smiles, as brief and unwelcome as they were to Colin, made the moments here more bearable. Besides, she told herself, refusing to admit that she'd turned fool again and begun caring for a man, she still had things to learn from him for William.

"Yes, Mr. Lefevre. I will speak to him about it after supper."

Gillian's heart sank but she managed to smile at Edmund while she dressed him.

"You frown," George noted, though she tried not to let him see. No sense in piquing his suspicions about her preferences, or why she had them. "Has he also made advances toward you that you haven't told me about?"

"And what if he has? You still would not choose the man I prefer." Good God, why couldn't she control her own mouth?

"I did choose him," George told her quietly. "He refused."

Gillian's comb paused in Edmund's hair. He refused? Oh Lord, what kind of pathetic fool was she to allow herself the hope of…of what? Becoming more acquainted with a mercenary? To what purpose? He could do nothing to change her life, or Edmund's. She didn't expect him to change it. She only wanted—No, it didn't matter. Mr. Campbell did this for Edmund's sake. He didn't want Geoffrey to harm her child because of his attention. She was happy that he was considerate enough to stay away. But a part of her feared that the Highlander didn't favor her company. What man wanted to sit by a door while she read to her son, or sit on the rocks, waiting hours for a fish to bite? And why in blazes did she care so much if he favored her? She'd allowed her heart to rule her once before and look at where it had gotten her. She would forget him and keep her thoughts straight on things that mattered. Like keeping Edmund with her always…and always thanking

God for George. She knew that the only way Mr. Campbell could refuse was if George had asked him. She smiled tenderly at her friend. He'd asked for her, putting aside his own misgivings for the sake of making her happy. It was nothing less than she would do for Edmund.

Save for one thing.

"Mr. Lefevre is as good a choice as any." She plucked Edmund off the bed and set his feet on the floor. "Unless you allow *him* to refuse you, as well."

George didn't flinch at her mild jab, nor did he defend himself. He simply stepped around her and held open the door. "To the Great Hall then?"

She wanted to kick him on the way out.

The Great Hall was empty when the three of them entered it. Gillian was thankful. She knew how the place sounded, how it smelled, when the garrison was in full attendance. Unfortunately, so did Edmund. Her cousin didn't care if Edmund sat among them during the day. Geoffrey supped with the men only at night.

Her son had to hold his ears during a few of his morning or afternoon meals, when the men's cups were heavy and their shouts to be heard over the clamor were too loud. He hadn't complained though, and she guessed it was because a small part of him enjoyed the rowdiness. He was a boy, after all.

She released his hand when he pulled on hers to run to one of the tables. She smiled, watching him climb onto a hard, wooden chair, then turn in it to wait for her. As much as she hated eating in the Hall, her child liked it.

"Look, Mummy!" He pointed at something on the table as she sat next to him. "It's Colin's game! Want to play?"

She looked up at George, who was taking his seat across from her. "Perhaps Captain Gates will play with you."

George blinked at her, and then flicked his gaze to Edmund, who was staring hopefully at him. "After we eat." He turned to shout for Margaret over his shoulder.

Gillian should take pity on him; after all, it wasn't *entirely* because of him that Edmund would have been happy to play Naughts and Crosses with de Atre if the man had ever asked. It was George's duty to keep the men away from her. But it wasn't Edmund's fault *at all*, and she was tired of him suffering because of it. Why did they need Colin anyway when they had George? It was time he played with her son.

"We will need bread and cheese," she reminded him when Margaret marched toward them waving her apron.

"The food is not yet ready. If you want it sooner"— the serving wench turned her simmering green eyes on Gillian—"the cooks said to tell you to complain to Lord Devon."

"Just bring us some bread and cheese for now," George's voice dragged Margaret's gaze back to him. "And remember that you speak to the daughter of an earl."

Gillian watched her go, then turned to the captain. "She will likely rub something foul on our food now."

He smiled, and then so did she, happy that he was her friend. "I don't need protection from her, or do you think all those long, tedious days of you teaching me how to protect myself fell on a lackwit's ears?"

"They were long and tedious, were they not?" he teased. "It took you almost a month to hold a blade correctly."

She kicked him under the table, but not too hard.

"Mum, can we look for frogs tomorrow?"

"Oh, Edmund, we have to travel all the way to the other side of the estuary for frogs."

"We can do it," her son assured her. "I won't be tired this time, I promise."

A thunderous roar stopped her from giving her reply. She sighed deeply and didn't bother to turn to watch the men spilling into the Hall for their afternoon meal. But Edmund looked, and when he found who he was searching for, he called out.

"Colin!"

Gillian tugged her son's sleeve to get him to face forward in his seat. "Mr. Campbell explained to you that he cannot—"

"Look what I found, Colin!"

Gillian kept her gaze on the table and on Edmund's finger tracing the grooves in its surface. She didn't blink, and for a moment she forgot to breathe when she heard his voice above her.

"Naughts and Crosses." He was smiling. She could hear it. She wanted to look at him, but she didn't dare. She already knew that his was the most compelling face at Dartmouth. Why torture herself further by looking at it? He was right to remain distant and aloof toward her and her son. She was grateful to him for it and angry with herself for not being as cautious. A sentiment she would rectify beginning now.

"Have ye been practicing?"

His husky voice sent fissures down her spine. She bit her lower lip to distract herself from the sensuality of it.

"Aye, with Mummy."

A moment passed in silence, for she heard none but the two voices speaking, and they had both stopped.

"Lady Gillian," the mercenary finally took the matter into his own hands and greeted her.

She neither spoke nor looked at him. She was afraid that if she did either one, she might not want to stop.

"Do you want to play with me, Colin?"

"Edmund." Gillian tugged his sleeve again. "Captain Gates is going to play with you. Bid good day to Mr. Campbell and let him be on his way."

"Lefevre, there you are." George stood up and beckoned the Frenchman over. "I've been meaning to have a word with you."

Damnation, not now. Gillian prayed for Colin to leave. She would hate herself if she interrupted George's order to Mr. Lefevre to protect her and she turned to Colin and begged him to instead.

"You will be guarding Lady Gillian and her son in de Atre's place."

There. He'd said it, and she'd kept her mouth shut.

"*Oui*, Captain."

Gillian looked up, swearing that if her new French escort was grinning at her like he'd just spotted the town whore she would tell him to burn in hell and then leave the Hall with Edmund. With or without George.

But Lefevre wasn't grinning. In fact, he looked rather miserable. Gillian felt the same way and turned, before she could stop herself, to Mr. Campbell, who was still standing over the table.

"Was there something else you wanted?"

His eyes bore into hers. She watched his jaw go hard even as he severed their gaze to smile down at her son and melt her very bones. "Aye, there was. One game with Edmund." He turned to George. "If the captain doesn't protest."

"Not at all," George said, trying not to sound too relieved. "I'm afraid I don't yet know how to play the game."

Gillian shot her captain a glare and moved down a seat to make room for Colin. Margaret returned with a tray of bread and cheese, and Lefevre excused himself, preferring drinking with his friends to learning a child's game.

"I saw de Atre speaking to Lord Devon earlier," Colin said while he broke the bread and cheese into equal pieces. "Or at least, he was trying to speak to him."

Gillian caught the furtive smile George tossed him. She wondered what her captain had done to his lieutenant and if Colin had aided him in doing it.

"I imagine speaking would be difficult with part of his lip hanging off."

"Captain." Gillian hushed him for Edmund's sake. Dear Lord, his lip! Barbaric. "I will not sew him up. Let Margaret do it," she added a moment later, remembering the lieutenant's wet lips and hot, stale breath so close to her.

And what were these smiles being passed between George and Colin about? She thought George didn't like the mercenary. He probably liked him now, she thought, simmering in her chair, knowing Colin was no threat to her or Edmund's safety. She decided to ignore both men and watch the game until their food arrived, then she would leave and return with Edmund to his room.

She almost smiled twice when Colin pretended not to notice a move that would grant him the win. Damn him, why did she find him so likable?

None of them noticed Geoffrey enter the Hall and saunter toward them until he spoke.

"Gates, would you care to explain to me why you sliced open my lieutenant's face?"

"Not at all." George glanced up at him. "He made an advance on my charge while they were alone."

Geoffrey offered him a rapier-thin smile. "Ah, ever the rabid dog, aren't you?"

"It is my duty, if you'll recall, my lord," George reminded him with a thin smirk of his own.

"Yes, of course," Geoffrey muttered, then turned his attention to the table.

"What's this? Games?"

"Just something simple to pass the time, Geoffrey," Gillian told him through tight lips. "In fact, Edmund grows bored with it. Come, darling." She rose from her chair and offered Edmund her hand. "Let's go do something else."

"But Mummy, I am besting him."

Geoffrey must have taken note of which edibles were whose, for he snatched up two nuggets of cheese, both in winning positions, and tossed them into his mouth. "The game is over and you have lost. Now get off your arse and do as your *mother* tells you."

Gillian clenched her teeth and stared in mute fury at her cousin. "Edmund, meet Mummy at the doors, please." She knew the wise thing to do was to keep her mouth shut, but she was past caring. The prince would be arriving in a few short months and then she could speak to him directly about leaving Dartmouth. "I warn you, cousin, mind your mouth. You might wish to wash it out, as well. I do believe your wench, Margaret, besmirched the cheese before she delivered it."

She left the table feeling quite pleased with herself and with the horrified look on Geoffrey's face. She didn't pause while he shouted after her that she and Edmund would be confined to their rooms for the remainder of the day. Let him bellow. Let him try to take Edmund from her for her insolence. She would tear out his eyes and spit on his grave.

Chapter Sixteen

Colin didn't see Lady Gillian or her son for the next two days. Devon had sent for her both nights at supper, but she didn't attend, nor did she leave her and Edmund's rooms. Her absence became a distraction to Colin more so than if she were standing between him and his opponent. She'd spared him a single scornful glance the last time he'd seen her, and it pricked his thoughts constantly that she had been angry with him. Was it because he'd refused Gates's offer to escort her throughout the castle? She should thank him for keeping away from her.

He'd fought like hell for the last two days to keep her from his thoughts and listed each reason he should. He was fashioned for fighting, born to conquer. But he didn't know how to fight himself. For truly, he was his own most grueling opponent, and late on the second night, while he and Captain Gates helped themselves to Devon's finest whisky in the cellars, he threw down his shield and asked about her.

"She pretends illness to stay away from Devon, lest she fling a dagger at his heart," the captain told him.

They both sat on the dusty floor, drinking and equally surprised to have discovered someone he didn't mind sharing speech with for more than one day at a time.

"The dagger she keeps hidden in her skirts," Colin recalled with the slightest quirk of his mouth. "I saw her reach for it when she was alone with de Atre," he hastened to add when the captain eyed him. "Does she know how to use it?"

"She does. She can defend herself if ever she needs to."

"How is Lefevre doing?" Colin asked and sipped his drink. "No open wounds on his person then?"

"From what she has told me, he barely speaks to her. It's a good arrangement. You have my thanks for suggesting him."

Colin nodded, feeling like he deserved no thanks on the matter. If the truth be known, the longer he went without seeing her, the more he regretted his decision. He'd sentenced her to a companion who didn't speak to her. Was that worse than one who wanted to hear her laughter again? He could help her. If he decided to give up his glorious war and help her and Edmund, Devon wouldn't stop him.

He closed his eyes and downed his whisky. Dear God, what was wrong with him? How could he even think in such a way? Give up his war? Nae. Never. He was here for information. He'd won the captain's favor. Why the hell was he sitting here asking questions about a lass instead of getting his new friend drunk and asking about Prince William? He was a general in the king's army. 'Twas time he began behaving like it. His runner would be returning in a few days and Colin needed more information to give him.

"How much longer do ye think we have left to train?" he asked his companion casually.

"Until what?"

"Until our new king arrives."

Gates shrugged his shoulders against the wall he was sitting against. "We don't know. We won't find out, I imagine, until he receives his invitation."

Gates wasn't telling him anything Colin hadn't already heard from his Argyll cousin. The task was getting him to speak of what Colin didn't know, and to do it without any sign of guile.

"How many more must sign it?"

"I'm not certain. One, perhaps two or three." The captain yawned.

Colin filled his cup. "Are these men Catholics?"

Gates held his drink to his mouth and shrugged again. "From what I know, all but one are Protestant."

He downed his whisky, then gave his head a vigorous shake to ward off its spirits. "You Scots certainly like your drinks strong."

Colin cast the keg a disdainful glance. 'Twas piss water compared to his cousin Brodie's brew back home. Still, after as many cups as he and Gates had already consumed, he was beginning to feel the groggy effects of it. He would be careful to drink no more.

"Sometimes," he said, refilling Gates's cup and holding his up, "potent brew is all a man has to keep the winter chill from his bones." He watched his companion swig his drink, then set their pitcher down, along with his full cup, and stretched his legs out before him.

"Might I know any of them?" he asked more boldly, watching Gates's eyes glaze over.

"You know one of them."

"Lord Devon, of course," Colin noted, pressing gently.

"I doubt you know the others, unless you've been entertaining with Lord Edward Russell."

As a matter of fact, Colin knew Russell rather well. He was one of the first officers in the Royal Navy until he fell out of King James's favor five years ago, after his connection to the Rye House Plot to murder King Charles and his brother James was discovered. "Who else?"

"I don't recall." Gates shook his head and then stopped himself when his jaw went green. "Devon's been keeping the good stuff to himself. The bastard."

"Aye, we should piss in the kegs before we leave."

Gates roared with laughter, and so hearty was the sound that Colin found himself joining him.

"I haven't laughed aloud in a long time," the captain said, sobering and closing his eyes. "You are good company, Campbell."

"Nae, 'tis the whisky."

The captain smiled. "I haven't been drunk in a long time either."

"Proof that Devon, bastard that he is, chose the best man to protect his cousin."

Gates opened his eyes and tipped his head at Colin's praise. "A choice he regrets every day. I am no longer his man, but hers, and he knows it. He knows that if he touches her without proper claim, I *will* kill him."

"Why hasn't he simply relieved ye of duty?" Colin asked him.

"There would be nothing simple about it. He'd be dead within the hour, and any man along with him who came against me."

Colin smiled, liking his confidence. "Ye're that good then?"

"Yes, I am."

"I did not see it," Colin teased, after thinking about it for a moment.

Gates shoved him away and they both laughed and shared another drink.

"Tell me, Captain," Colin said after a few moments, looking for, *needing* a reason to dislike his companion enough to fight against him and likely kill him when the time came. He could find nothing. "Why would ye fight on Devon's side when 'tis clear ye would rather see him die at the king's blade?"

"Because James is an unfair king."

"How so?"

Gates didn't need to think on it overly long. "He advocates tolerance for Catholics but that the persecution of Presbyterian Covenanters should continue. My wife is Presbyterian. Her father was slaughtered while attending a field mass in the Lowlands when Charles was king."

"Yer wife is Scottish then?"

"She is. Her family still suffers much in her hometown. James purges from office anyone who thinks differently than he. I fear my wife's family will soon be purged from their homes if James remains on the throne."

"Prince William is just as zealous in his desire to purge the kingdom of Catholics," Colin pointed out impassively. "Is it fair that they will suffer if *he* gains the throne?"

"Of course it isn't, but the world is ruled by arrogant men, Campbell. We are merely their pawns who do what they command whether we believe it right or wrong."

Colin remained silent, thinking about the captain's words. Was it true? Was he merely a pawn? Nae, he believed in the cause he was fighting for. Didn't he? Aye. If Prince William gained the throne, he would likely come after the MacGregors once he discovered that Colin had tried so vigorously to stop him.

"Will ye do nothing to stop William from coming here, knowing he will likely give her over to Devon?"

Gates looked up at him. "Are you asking me to consider her life above the lives of thousands? Would you?"

Colin blinked at him. Of course he wouldn't. Many times throughout history innocents suffered for the good of many. As a soldier, he knew this better than anyone. But then, why couldn't he answer? "Nae," he finally bit out. "I would not."

"She is like a daughter to me," Gates admitted to him. "But neither would I. William must take the throne or my family will suffer."

And mine, if he succeeds, Colin thought. They both wanted to protect their kin. But who would protect Gillian...and Edmund? Would she live out the rest of her life residing in a tower, cut off from the world like a melancholy princess in one of her child's fairy tales?

"I feel like hell now." The captain ran his hand over his head. So did Colin, and it had nothing to do with his drink. Apparently, it didn't for Gates either. "We should go check on her."

Colin shook his head and set down his cup. "What? Nae." Hell, seeing her disheveled and sleepy would surely get him injured on the practice field tomorrow. "'Tis the middle of the night. We're drunk."

"We'll bring the whisky." The captain ignored his protests and tried to rise to his feet.

"She will be asleep," Colin argued, watching the normally collected captain slip back down the wall. "Rapping at her door will frighten her," he pointed out, hoping to appeal to Gates's protective nature.

"I have the key to her rooms." The captain shuffled

through his pocket and grinned, producing the proof of his words.

Colin suddenly knew how Adam felt when Eve offered him the apple. He wanted to see her, to know for himself that she and Edmund were unharmed... but creeping into her rooms while she slept...

"Captain, I don't think we're in the proper condition to enter a lady's chamber."

"We're not," Gates agreed. "But she will forgive such intrusion for the company of a friendly face or two. Believe me when I tell you that encased in her often icy facade, there beats the heart of a dove. Help me up, will you? I'll go without you."

Aye, Colin thought while he gained his feet and then reached down his hand to the captain. He saw her heart clearly whenever her gaze settled on her son. All the more reason not to frighten the hell out of her when she saw her captain as intoxicated as a sailor on leave of duty. What if Gates tried to kiss her? What man in any state, soused or sober, wouldn't be so tempted?

"I'll come," he said, fixing his level gaze on Gates's, "but remember tomorrow that this was yer idea."

By the time they reached the ground floor of the square tower, Colin had almost talked himself into turning around and letting Gates go on alone. How had this happened? How had he let someone, a lass no less, crawl under his skin and veer him off his path? Aye, he pitied her, and pity often softened the heart. But he admired the strength in her silence and the bold defiance in her voice when silence was too difficult to maintain. The radiance of emotion that poured from her to her son attracted him like a moth to a flame. He missed home, his kin, and though Gillian and Edmund were but two, they shared a bond of love that took hold of his heart and made it ache for something more. Why now? Hell, why now?

"I will enter first and wake her," Gates whispered while they crept up the stairs and then down the silent hall. "You look out for anyone. I'll return for you after I wake her."

This was madness, Colin reminded himself for the hundredth time, and looked around for any eyes watching them. He shouldn't have fed Gates so much whisky. But, remarkably, the captain managed to walk with minimal stumbling, and he still knew enough to use caution. What would Devon do if he caught them in her rooms?

Worse, what would become of Colin's poor brain once he entered? He'd picked his way into dozens of rooms before to gain information for the king, but he'd never done the like for the pleasure of seeing a lady. He had to be as mad as Gates for agreeing to this.

"Are ye certain ye want to do this? What if Devon sees us?" Colin asked him again as Gates slipped his key into the door.

"He sleeps in the round tower. He will not hear or see us."

Still, Colin hesitated. "I thought ye didn't want me anywhere near her."

"This is different. I'm here to protect her virtue. Do you have the drink?"

"Aye." Hell, Colin wanted Gates to trust him, but it had nothing to do with Lady Gillian. This wasn't wise, and 'twasn't safe, but he did nothing to stop Gates when the lock clicked and her captain opened her door.

He waited in the hall while the captain disappeared inside. He looked toward Edmund's door and was tempted to check on the lad, then decided against it. He had to gather the information he needed and get the hell out of Dartmouth while he still possessed some good sense. And damn it, but it didn't look like his time here was going to end anytime soon. Gates didn't recall the names on the invitation. He likely didn't know when William was coming or how many men he was bringing with him. Colin suspected the only way to gain that information was to befriend Devon. Hell, that was going to be difficult, since every time he looked at the earl, he wanted to stab him in the gut.

The door creaked open and Gates popped his head out. "Come inside."

He shouldn't. He should run the other way. But then he saw her, standing alone in the soft candlelight, and he stepped inside for a clearer view.

Chapter Seventeen

$\mathcal{G}$illian rubbed her eyes, but when she looked again, Mr. Campbell was still standing outside her door, George was truly beckoning him to enter, and it really was the middle of the night. She wasn't dreaming. The only logical question left to ask herself then was what in the name of all that was holy had gotten into her captain? She could scarcely believe her eyes when she had opened them a few seconds ago and found him hovering over her bed, beckoning her to leave it.

His behavior was peculiar, indeed, for she had never known him to be so exuberant...so cheerful. But when she stepped out of her sleeping quarters, pulling on her outer robe, and saw whom he'd brought with him, she doubted truly waking up.

"I apologize fer the intrusion, Lady."

Colin's voice was real, unmistakably masculine, wrapping itself around her like a warm wool blanket.

"Do shut the door, Campbell," George said, passing him and snatching a pitcher from his hands. "You're letting in a draft from the turrets." He proceeded on to the small cupboard behind the settee and withdrew a cup for her use.

"Wait until you taste this fine nectar, Gillian. Devon has kept it—"

"Captain, are you out of your bloody mind?" she nearly screeched at him. He had to be. Why would he take such a chance with her cousin? Him, the pinnacle of responsibility and worry? "You know no one is permitted in my room after dark. Not even you. If Geoffrey found out—"

"I would be forced to kill him," he interrupted, then glanced at Colin, shutting the door behind him. "Wouldn't I, Campbell?"

Oh, dear Lord. She turned to the mercenary. "You got him drunk."

He hadn't moved from his place by the door and when she spoke to him, she wasn't surprised to see him look away before he answered. "He brought me to the cellars and lifted his cup to his own lips."

"Here you go, my dear." George tapped her arm and held the cup out to her. He smiled as if he hadn't a care in the world. Then he swayed just a bit on his feet.

"Oh, for goodness' sake, sit down." Gillian took the cup and led him to the closest chair before he fell on his arse. When he was safely seated and a little less green around the jaw, she leaned over him and gave his cheek a short smack. Just enough to snap him out of the fog he was trapped in.

"What has come over you to bring yourself and another into my room at this hour? And what do you mean by making friends with Mr. Campbell when you warned me of him shortly after he stepped through Dartmouth's doors?"

"He's good company," her longtime friend assured her, as if she didn't already know. "I thought you might enjoy him."

Gillian turned, setting her gaze on the Scotsman guarding the entrance, and blushed at just how much she might enjoy him. Lord, just looking at him was a pleasurable experience.

"Now please, Gillian, taste the whisky."

Returning to George, she tossed her head back and sighed at the heavens. "Very well, if it will aid in removing the two of you sooner." She brought her cup to her lips and tasted the liquid inside. She didn't care much for spirits but she had to admit this stuff wasn't half as sour going down.

"It is lovely, George. Now I must insist—"

"It is indeed lovely," her captain agreed. "Pity we pissed in the keg before we left." He lifted his cup and grinned at Mr. Campbell, who found sudden interest in her ceiling.

Gillian backed up and fell onto the settee, stunned and unable to believe what he'd just confessed. Indeed, he'd gone mad, and she had the sinking suspicion that Colin had helped him arrive there. She thought about what they had done, imagining them standing over the keg like grinning fools, with no loyalty or fondness for her cousin. She smiled. And then she began to laugh. It was a silly, reckless deed, but blast it all, everything was always so serious. George was always so in control, so guarded against the other men here. What had Colin Campbell done to gain such trust that her captain should bring him here to her rooms?

She turned to him as her laughter subsided and remembered, when he cleared his throat and looked away, that he was not like the other men here. She felt safe in his company.

"Mr. Campbell, are you going to guard the door all evening?"

He glanced behind him at the door as if he'd forgotten where he was, and then stepped away from it and looked around for a place to sit.

Gillian realized the only empty spot was beside her. Her chambers were small and sparsely furnished compared to Geoffrey's rooms. She had but one chair and one settee. She needed no more than that, as she never entertained visitors.

"We won't burden ye with our presence fer too long," he promised, coming to stand before her.

"It is no burden at all." She couldn't keep herself from smiling at him. It was difficult not to when looking at him was like listening to a master lutist playing her favored song.

She politely moved over a bit to make room for him and sipped her drink, trying hard not to choke on it when he sat.

"George, I...Oh, dear." Her captain was asleep—or passed out. Either way, he'd left her alone with the mercenary. "I should wake him."

"Aye, ye should."

Gillian rose from the settee, putting away her hurt feelings that he couldn't wait to be rid of her. It was for the best. If he had a fondness for her, it would be doubly hard not to find him so damned appealing. It was good that he reminded her of the real world in which she lived.

"How is Edmund?"

Her hand hovered over George's shoulder, ready to shake him awake, and then fell to her side. "He's been in a sour mood of late."

"As I would be if I hadn't seen daylight in two days."

"Was I wrong then," she asked, returning to him, "to want to prove to my cousin—"

"Aye, ye were if Edmund suffered because of it."

Her eyes stung, holding back the sudden rush of tears she would shed, she *should* shed, over her pride. Colin, this stranger, was correct, and it nearly brought her to her knees to hear it said.

"I didn't mean to cause ye sorrow," he told her as she dropped back down beside him. "'Tis not my place to advise ye on the raising of yer own bairn."

"I will make certain he leaves the castle tomorrow. I appreciate your candor, Mr. Campbell."

Looking relieved that she hadn't let her tears flow, he sat back and crossed his ankle over the opposite thigh. "Ye call the captain by his familiar name."

Then he wasn't in such a rush to leave, after all. Her heart beat so furiously in her chest that she was sure he could hear it. Lord, but she was pitiful indeed. Had she not allowed herself to walk down this path before? Hadn't she sworn she never would again? Why was it so difficult to remember when she was with him? "Only in private."

"There is no one here but us," he said, lifting his gaze from her mouth. "In truth," he told her, smiling as if he possessed no power at all to stop himself. "I don't much care fer hearing myself being called Mr. Campbell."

"Why not?"

"It makes me feel too proper."

She glanced at him out of the corner of her eye while she brought her cup to her lips. "And you're not?"

"Not most of the time."

But he was always proper with her. She liked him better for it. She was tired of men looking at her like she was the last succulent morsel of lamb left on the table. However, she wasn't entirely opposed to him finding her appealing. In fact, she wished he did.

George let out a rumbling snore that brought both their gazes to him.

"How did you gain his favor?" Gillian asked softly, watching her dearest friend sleep. "He has no friends here."

"I saved him from de Atre's sword at his back."

She blinked at him. De Atre! The lowly bastard! She should thank Mr. Campbell for that. She was about to do so when he continued.

"He returned the deed shortly after."

"I'm thankful for it...for both of you...I mean that he..." She smiled nervously, setting her cup on the low table in front of them, then sweeping her heavy hair off her shoulder. The air around her was stifling. "The spirits are potent. I mostly drink water at supper and am unused to the effects of Geoffrey's drink."

"That's good, since Geoffrey's drink is nae longer suitable to consume."

She laughed. "I'll keep that in mind."

He watched her for a moment, then blew out a soft gush of breath, as if resigning himself to some difficult task. "When I first saw ye, that day on the turrets"— he forged onward despite the shift in her weight—"ye looked...like ye were longing fer something. Is it home? Mayhap Edmund's father?"

"I've given neither home nor Edmund's father more than a thought in four years."

"Freedom then?" he pressed when she said nothing more.

"Just childish fancies." She shrugged her shoulders

and stared at her cup on the table. "Nothing I would care to dull your ears with."

"Ah, ye wish to remain mysterious, then." His mouth curled into a playful smile when she looked at him.

Good Lord, how could a man look so dangerous and unyielding one instant and utterly guileless and inviting the next?

"I'm afraid this castle is too small for mystery, Mr. Cam...Colin." Her boldness made her blush. His eyes drifted over her cheeks, the heated bridge of her nose. She smiled yet again and covered her face with her hand. "Forgive me, I'm not accustomed to—"

"Being dragged out of bed and questioned by someone ye hardly know?" he finished for her, pulling his gaze away.

She didn't want him to stop looking at her. She didn't want him to leave and she knew he would if she remained quiet and childishly awkward in his company. "Tell me something about yourself," she said hastily, "and then we will know each other better."

Now it was his turn to shift position, as uneasy as she was about revealing anything too personal.

"What would ye like to know?"

She lifted her brow at him, curious and surprised at his reply. The plate was bare and she could fill it with whatever she liked. Should she ask him for tidings from England or something to satisfy her longing to know everything about Colin Campbell, the man? "What is your age?"

"A score and two. Ye?"

"Nine and ten."

"Do you reside in Glen Orchy when you are not offering your sword for battle?"

"Nae, my kin live farther north."

"I've never been to the Highlands before," she told him. "Is it as dangerous as others say?"

"Aye, but 'tis bonny there, too." Something about the way he spoke the word "bonny," the subtle catch of his breath, the warmth in his eyes taking in her features, made her stomach flip. Perhaps he did find her appealing.

"Is there someone in the Highlands whom you call beloved?" Blast it, she hadn't meant to be so bold. She reached for her cup, but he leaned over her, stopping her.

"'Twill give ye an aching head in the morn."

His hand covered hers, big, warm, calloused from clutching a hilt hour after hour.

"There is no one." His whisky-sweetened breath washed over her, along with a smile so tender and so close, she wilted at the sight of it. She prayed for strength—something she hadn't done with Reggie.

Lowering her cup back to the table, she separated his hand from hers. "Are you so dedicated to the sword that you have no time for love?"

He moved back and rested his elbows on his knees. He stared down at the hilts poking out from his boots and thought about his answer before he spoke. Finally, he looked up at her. "Aye," he told her, "The sword is my love. I grew to manhood with a blade in my hands."

She looked up from beneath the veil of her lashes and crooked her mouth at him. He had secrets indeed. Would he be so open if she put a different sort of question to him? "One would think a man who was born with a blade in his hands would know how to wield it with superior skill. No?"

His topaz gaze settled on her like embers ready to blaze to life. For a moment she feared she had gone too far. Whatever his motives were for feigning a lack of sword skill, she didn't want to make an enemy of him. She liked his company. Was that so terrible? So dangerous? But he wasn't angry. In fact, he appeared slightly amused by her bold observation. It wasn't the first time she had challenged him without ruffling his feathers. It made her feel even more at ease with him.

"Superior skill takes years to master," he told her, skirting her subtle accusation, but not lying to her about it. "When it comes time for battle, 'twill be my dedication to practice that makes my blade deadly and wins me the day."

She smiled. George was correct. The Highlander was arrogant, clever... and apparently quite dedicated to William. "Prince William is fortunate to have you on his side."

He poured himself more whisky, downed it, and then turned to her. "Captain Gates told me Devon's plans fer ye when the prince arrives."

Lord, why did he have to bring that up? It was the dark cloud that followed her everywhere, every day, in everything that she did. "My cousin believes I am destined to be his. He's always wanted me. I don't know why."

"I can think of a few reasons."

Their eyes met and they shared a brief, slightly awkward smile that made her toes curl in her slippers.

"If you wish to leave Dartmouth—"

She held up her hand. Lord, no. Don't let him say it. She wouldn't get him, and heaven forbid it, Edmund, killed when Geoffrey sent his army after them.

"My cousin will not have his way," she said softly.

He leaned in closer. "I didn't hear ye, lass."

She almost didn't repeat herself. No one knew about

her letters to William. What she was doing was too dangerous. If Geoffrey found out that she was scheming against him with the prince, she had no doubts he would make good on his threats to take Edmund from her and likely wed her sooner.

She slipped her gaze across the table at George. Her dear captain would never have told a soul, but he would have tried to stop her. Perhaps even insist on delivering her letters to the messenger himself.

She didn't know why she wanted to tell Colin her secret. She truly hadn't thought he might want to help her. She couldn't let him, and she wouldn't have to. Not if William stayed true to his word. She wanted Colin to know that she had hope of leaving this dreadful place. To finally whisper the truth, that she'd been doing more than sitting around cowering to her cousin.

"I said, my cousin will not have his way."

He was silent for a moment, giving her more time to consider what she was about to confess. Then he said, "What d'ye intend to do about it?"

She peeked at him from the corner of her eye and wondered if he would laugh at her efforts to save herself and her son the way de Atre, Hammond, or even Mr. Lefevre would have laughed if she told one of them. But he was different. He'd seen her on the turrets and he hadn't told anyone. He'd risked George's fury by following her and saving her from Lieutenant de Atre. He hadn't once mocked her obviously limited strength when she challenged him. He wouldn't laugh now.

"I intend to win William's favor."

That unflappable guard he defended so well fell apart before her eyes.

"William?"

"Aye, the prince."

He stared at her like she had just sprouted another head, and then reined in his composure and returned his expression to mild interest. "Ye believe he would aid ye?"

She nodded. "He vowed that he would."

"Did he? When?"

Her eyes skipped to George, and then back to him. "Many times…in letters. He is my only hope. Geoffrey doesn't know, nor does George. I would ask that you—"

He held up his palm to stop her before she said any more. "Let me understand this correctly. Ye're secretly corresponding with William of Orange? How? What have ye told him?"

"I've given him news carried here by some of the men. I told him that it was not Geoffrey's idea to have him formally invited to England to avoid a war, but my father's."

"Was it?" he asked quietly, sounding a bit stunned, as was, she guessed, to be expected.

"Aye. I told him that despite Geoffrey's claims to the contrary, it was my father's coin and influence that convinced the seven to sign the invitation. My cousin doesn't possess the wit or the means to have seen this through. Yet he intends to take all the credit and win William's favor when he arrives. I must stop that from happening."

Colin was silent long enough to give her heart pause that she had told him too much. He shifted twice more in his seat and then ran his hands over his face. Finally, after dragging a deep breath into his lungs, he spoke. "Ye know the names of the seven then."

"I know the names of six so far," she told him. "The prince and I never discussed the men my father had chosen. There were many, but they needed only seven. I know who they are because Geoffrey enjoys taunting me with the closeness of William's arrival after each of them signs the invitation.

"The Earl of Shrewsbury and the Viscount Lumley were the last two to pen their names. Henry Sydney, Earl of Romney, and Edward Russell were before them."

"So two more are still needed?"

She shook her head. "Only one. The Earl of Danby signed first."

"And the last is nae doubt yer faither."

"No. My father is too much of a coward to rise against the king should William be defeated. That's why he will allow Geoffrey to take the glory for everything. At least, for now."

"Ye speak harshly of him." Colin's voice thickened when he finally looked at her.

"He cut me and my son from him the way a soldier would cut away the head of his most hated enemy."

"And yer mother?"

"She allowed it," she told him without feeling. For there was nothing left. "The only thing that would separate me from my child would be death. The prince is my only hope."

George snored and opened his eyes briefly to smile crookedly at them both before falling back to sleep.

"We should cease this speech," she warned in a low voice.

"Aye," he agreed, sounding somewhat relieved. "Tell me about Edmund then."

She blinked back a combination of stunned disbelief, gratitude, and something that made her heart ache and her eyes burn. No man had ever taken an interest in Edmund.

She began with very basic facts, his age, which stories

he liked best, his favorite games. Colin smiled when she told him that Naughts and Crosses was among them. When he asked about Edmund's father, she told him the truth. She'd been young and foolish, but she would rather have her son than live the life of a spoiled noblewoman.

"You don't miss the courtly life then?"

She shook her. "Do I miss attending balls and feigning smiles at would-be suitors who bored me to tears? No, I don't miss that. Besides, after years of me refusing them all, my father would likely have tried to wed me to some old, stuffy English lord."

He smiled, ensnaring her breath with a glint in his eyes that made them shine like rare jewels. "Somehow I don't think ye would have allowed that."

"That is why I said *tried*."

She decided that his open grin was as deadly as the subtle curl of his lips. They spoke for hours, sharing quiet smiles and even laughter until the sun began to rise beyond the narrow windows.

It was, Gillian decided later when he shook George awake with a warning that they should leave, the most wonderful night of her life.

The only thing that would have made it more perfect was if he'd kissed her.

Chapter Eighteen

Colin narrowly avoided a blow to his middle and ducked as a second swipe nearly took off his head. He held up his hand to stop Gates's advance. Hell, he knew he shouldn't practice this morn with Lady Gillian haunting his every thought. *William of Orange was her only hope.* When she told him of her plans—the actions she had already taken to undermine her cousin and save herself and her son—he hadn't known what to say. She was secretly sending letters to the Dutch prince! Hell, he still couldn't take it in. She was a spy for William, and a damned decent one if Gates truly knew nothing of the correspondence. She'd committed treason against King James. What would he do about it? Nothing. He understood why she did it. What had William promised her? How would the prince save her from her cousin? Would he keep his word? Colin doubted it, and even if William had vowed to take her away from Dartmouth, Colin couldn't let him rise to power.

"You're distracted," his opponent said, sheathing his blade.

Aye, he was. Despite everything his mind told him about staying detached from her, Colin knew he was losing that battle. For he could scarcely wait to set eyes on her again. It wasn't because she possessed the information he needed about his enemies, though, by God, he'd never expected to find what he looked for in her! What else did she know? When was William planning to arrive? He could have asked her last eve, but with all her talk of needing the prince, he couldn't bring himself to question her further. Nae, he simply wanted to hear her voice, look at her, see her smile again. She possessed no airs, but was refreshingly open and genuine. She wanted nothing more out of life than to be happy and to see her son the same. Her beauty called to him, but her character, touched with kindness, boldness, and integrity, tempted him beyond his endurance to resist.

He'd given up trying to forget the way the firelight in her chambers had glimmered off her unbound, abundant waves or the way her eyes danced when she spoke of Edmund.

He hadn't genuinely laughed with anyone since leaving Camlochlin last month. Three years before that. Hell, it had felt good to let down his guard a wee bit—to remember who he was. A man. A MacGregor, passionate about his land, his kin, and his woman. But Gillian Dearly wasn't his woman and his desire for her startled him. It made him feel vulnerable, like a ship sailing aimlessly without an anchor. Last night, it had taken every shred of control he possessed to keep from dragging her to the turrets and kissing her until dawn and then promising her whatever she desired.

"You should have left her chamber last night when I fell asleep."

Colin put away his sword and expelled a weary sigh.

He'd wanted to leave, but his mind, his mouth, and his feet had turned traitor on him. "Ye brought me to her. 'Tis foolish to be angry with me about it now."

"Is it? I see the way you look at her—or try not to," her captain continued. "The way you go soft when you look at Edmund. I warn you, no good can come of it. You may be skilled with a sword, despite your flimsy excuse to the contrary, but you will not be able to keep her safe from Devon if you're thinking of helping her leave Dartmouth."

"I'm not. I simply—"

"Because he would find her wherever she fled. And do you know what he would do to her? To Edmund?"

Nae, Devon wouldn't find her at Camlochlin.

It's a hard truth to conceal when a man loses the last of his mind in a single instant and doesn't know where to begin to find it and gain it back. Colin blinked and looked away, lest Gates's ever-sharp eyes see the evidence of it.

He couldn't take her to Camlochlin. There wasn't enough time to bring her there and return to battle. What would she do there with his kin? She would hate the cold weather and the isolation. She didn't know he was a MacGregor and once she did, 'twas very likely that she would never want to speak to him again.

But suddenly he couldn't stop himself from imagining Edmund running freely in the vast green vale of Camlochlin with children his own age and Gillian laughing at his kin's table, smiling up at him in his bed.

What had become of him? He'd always known his own mind. There was no room for a woman in it—certainly no room for a wife. He was mad for even contemplating the suddenly clear path in his head.

"I would have yer thoughts on something, Captain."

"What is it?"

"Ye're not going to like it."

"Then perhaps you shouldn't put it to me."

Mayhap he shouldn't. Mayhap he should ask the captain to beat him in the head with one of the heavy wooden wasters leaning uselessly against the outer wall.

"I would ask that ye trust me," he forged onward. He would need the captain's assistance in what he meant to do, and since Gates was unaware that William of Orange had already promised to aid his charge, the task would be less difficult if Colin went about it correctly.

"You ask me to trust you," said the captain, "but it's difficult to do so when you evade answering my queries. I've been patient because I don't find you as unfavorable as the rest here, and you're clever. But you are playing a part within these walls, at our table, Campbell, are you not?"

Colin wished for a chair to sit in. 'Twas impossible that Gates had figured him out so quickly. What did he suspect? Surely he was incorrect in his assumptions. Better to find out now though... "A part?" he asked calmly, looking Gates square in the eye.

"You don't like Devon, or the men." He held up his hand when Colin would speak. "Don't take me for a fool and deny it. You aim your practiced smiles at them, but anyone watching you closely enough can see the difference when you speak to Edmund... and his mother. You wear your mask well, Campbell, for I cannot decide which smile you aim at me."

Colin hated to admit it, but he liked Gates. Enough to not want to kill him with the rest, at least. Nae, 'twas more than that. "I hold ye in high regard, Captain."

"That is well received. But it doesn't answer the question of what you are up to."

And Colin wasn't about to tell him. Not the entire

truth of it anyway. "I will tell ye, but as I stated, ye are not going to care fer what I say."

"I'm listening."

"We cannot let her wed Devon."

"We?"

"Ye cannot tell me that ye would sit idly by when that bastard takes her to his marriage bed."

Gates leaned his shoulder against the wall and tossed him a foul look. "But there is no way to stop it. If the prince agrees to—"

"There is a way to stop it," Colin interjected. "But I need yer aid, and yer full trust."

"Go on."

"Would ye do anything to see Lady Gillian and her son safely away from Dartmouth?"

The captain laughed and pushed off the wall. When he reached Colin, his mirth faded into a cold snarl. "I knew you would want to help her. I told you the dangers of trying. Must I set you to a sickbed for the next few months to stop you?"

"Ye could try," Colin warned quietly. "But in the meantime, I will do what needs to be done, with or without yer aid. But I would rather have ye on my side. The moment Devon is wed to her he will put Edmund out." Hell, 'twas true. Mad or not, he had to do something.

"It's too dangerous. I will not aid you."

"Nor will ye stop me."

Gates glared at him with such murderous intent that for a moment Colin believed he might try to kill him.

"With yer aid, I can do this without danger to either of them."

Gates looked mildly ill. "The three of you will be shot down before you leave England."

"Not if two of us still remain. We must get Edmund away first."

"Do you understand that she will never allow you to separate her from the boy?"

"She will if she trusts me. And with yer aid, she will."

Gates went back to leaning against the wall. "I will think about it."

At least he didn't draw his blade. Colin nodded. 'Twas a start.

Later that night, Colin sat quietly in the Great Hall, barely aware of the men around him quarreling about what Captain Gates had done to his lieutenant.

He'd had time to think more clearly about his earlier decisions regarding Lady Gillian. He couldn't help her and he couldn't let William remain in England long enough to do so. His path was set before him and he couldn't take any detours. Not now. He'd waited too long for this. Hell, his entire life had been spent in preparation for the coming, glorious battle. The fate of the throne, of the three kingdoms, rested in his hands. He had to discover what else she knew about the rebellion. Do what he'd come here to do, and then get the hell out of Dartmouth.

The sight of her entering the Hall with Gates a moment later made him doubt the importance of his cause. How was it that each new time he saw her, she grew more bonny than before? His eyes took in every nuance of her: the light footfalls that brought her closer...the swell of her hips beneath her gown of pale coral...her slender waist and full, round breasts...His fingers curled into his palms with the need to caress her, kiss her, claim her. Even if he could get her out of Dartmouth before all hell broke loose, what would he do with her after that?

Letting her distract him was dangerous, but wanting her was deadly.

He looked away, fighting with everything he had left to resist her. 'Twas foolish and reckless to enter her rooms and share laughter and speech with her, no matter what she knew. He knew she was trouble with those wide, seafoam blue eyes and pale pink complexion. His gaze found her again and basked in the long, flaxen braid draping her shoulder, the wee tendrils falling loose about her temples. Hell, he knew she was trouble, but he didn't care... and he couldn't look away.

Until she tipped her gaze from the floor and looked back at him.

Steadying his breath, he turned his most practiced smile on Gerald Hampton as the giant took the seat closest to him. "Apologies, I didn't hear what ye said."

The giant slammed his even bigger fist on the table, summoning one of the male servers. "I said, the bishop of London arrives at Kingswear within the next fortnight." Hampton turned a dark, bloodshot eye on him while his drink was delivered. "You asked about visitors."

Colin blinked. "The bishop?" Hell, it didn't bode well for the king if the bishop of bloody London was inviting the Dutch prince to steal the throne. James was losing his allies and without the church behind him he would likely lose the war. Colin scowled as an even darker thought occurred to him. Lefevre had told him the invitation had been sent to the seven. Why was the bishop coming here? Did his arrival have something to do with her?

His eyes found her yet again as she took her seat opposite Gates. She didn't look up but kept her hands folded in her lap. A swan on a lake of murk and mire. Had Devon decided not to wait for William of Orange's arrival to take her as his wife?

"She is not my burden."

"What's that, whelp?" Hampton finished the contents of his cup and swiped his knuckles across his dark beard.

"'Tis a burden," Colin corrected effortlessly, but cursed himself inwardly. He hadn't realized he'd spoken. When the hell had *that* ever happened to him?

"What is?"

"Having to wait on these signatures before the true king can arrive."

Hampton laughed. "Thirsty for Catholic blood, eh, stray?"

"I came to fight. Not to practice."

Hampton slapped him on the back, then held up his cup for a refill. He eyed Gates, then slumped closer to Colin. "What think you of what he did to de Atre?"

"He did his duty," Colin told him. "As he swore to each of us he would do."

"He nearly cut the lip from his face. De Atre will be scarred for life from the viciousness of his attack. Gates chose a woman over one of his own men."

"A man who tried to stab him in the back."

Hampton's grin was anything but amiable as he settled it on Colin. "Fortunate for the captain that you were there to stop it."

"'Twas fortunate indeed," Colin agreed. "If de Atre had killed him, then as lieutenant, he becomes the man who leads us into battle against our enemies." He stared at Hampton, letting his words seep in. De Atre would keep them alive for a day at the most, and Hampton knew it.

The giant shrugged his massive shoulders and went

back to drinking and laughing with the others. Colin caught Gates's eye at the front of the table and passed him a subtle nod. The captain returned the silent greeting and then turned to watch Devon saunter into the Hall.

With the earl's arrival, the servers waiting along the wall snapped to attention and hurried toward the kitchen.

"What do we have here?" Devon adjusted his wig and pushed Margaret away from his side as he came to stand over Gillian. "My cousin has deigned to sit with us tonight. To what do I owe this pleasure?"

When she didn't answer him, he fell into his seat and smiled at the rest of the men. "She must have missed us. Let us not forget that a whore's place is among men."

Colin sat as still as stone, his fingers itching to rip a dagger from his boot and fling it at Devon's throat. He looked at Gates, infuriated that Gillian's captain said nothing in her defense yet again. He would ask him why later, and to hell what Gates thought of him. He'd begun to respect the man who'd managed, for more than three years now, to keep a pack of wolves from tearing his charge to pieces. But hell, how could he sit there night after night listening to the vile way her cousin spoke to her?

The answer came with his next breath—when Captain Gates rose to his feet and looked down at Devon. His warning was so quietly given, it did not reach Colin's ears. But a warning 'twas by the flash of fear in the haughty earl's eyes.

Unfortunately, the fear did not last long.

Rising from his seat, Devon set his glacial gaze on Gates and ordered in a loud voice, "I want the boy brought to me now. It's time he learned of the circumstances of his birth."

Lady Gillian sprang from her chair to protest. "He is abed and I will not have him disturbed."

Her cousin turned to her slowly, his pitch quiet at first but ending in a roar. "He will not be abed in this castle tomorrow night if he isn't brought to me at once!"

Here it was, her war. Looking up from his seat at the captain's defeated expression, Colin realized that she fought it alone. Gates defended her honor, an admirable trait for any man, but he defended it with caution, always careful not to risk Devon's full anger. He protected Edmund passively but 'twas she who fought constantly to keep her child safe.

Lefevre pushed his chair from the table, apparently deciding that since no one else was moving to the task of escorting the lady back to her son's room, 'twas up to him.

Colin shook his head as if to clear away the madness of involving himself in things that had nothing to do with his war. "I'll bring the boy to ye," he said, standing to his feet and motioning to Lefevre to stay where he was.

Stepping away from the table, he kept his steady gaze on Gates. Over the years, Colin had learned how to gain his enemy's trust. But Gates wasn't his enemy and he wanted it to remain that way. Nevertheless, he wasn't about to stand around and do nothing while Devon opened his vile mouth to Edmund.

"Last eve, our good captain appointed me the lady's escort in place of Lefevre. Since he refuses to obey ye, I will see the duty done."

Devon tossed his head back and laughed, giving Colin a moment to offer the captain a subtle nod. *Trust me.* He willed the captain to hear his silent plea.

"How refreshing it is to find such loyalty at my table."

The earl grinned at Gates, fell back into his chair, and tossed Colin a regretful look. "The captain might slice off your lips for this in the morning, but for now, go, and be quick about it. Gillian, you will remain here with me."

"I'm going with him. Edmund will be frightened—"

"Sit down and be silent, wench," her cousin warned, his eyes as hard and merciless on her as Colin's were before he cut a man down the middle.

Instead of retreating, she took a step forward. "Geoffrey, take heed," she warned him in a soft, low voice. "If you refuse to allow me to tend to my son, he will not be the only one gone from this castle."

"You aren't leaving Dartmouth." He laughed at her.

"I wasn't speaking of myself."

Devon caught her meaning and his laughter faded. So then, he didn't doubt the lass would spill his innards. Huzzah, lass! Colin didn't smile, but he wanted to.

"Such a saucy temper." Less determined to win, but not giving up, Devon laughed again and spread his gaze over his men. "You make every man at this table eager to shove his..."

Thankfully, she didn't listen to another word, but whirled on her heel and stormed toward Colin.

"I wish to speak to you, Mr. Campbell."

She swooshed passed him, leaving him saturated in the scent of wild blossoms and with an icy cold chill down the length of his spine.

Chapter Nineteen

"Why have you done this?" Gillian turned on him the instant they left the Hall.

He stopped short of hurtling into her. "What?"

"Why would you volunteer to subject Edmund to Geoffrey's company?"

"D'ye think yer threats would have kept him in his bed?"

"No," she admitted quietly, looking up into his eyes. "But you near leaped at the task."

"Trust me."

Heavens, how could anyone refuse his low, sorcerer's voice, the eager sincerity in the confident quirk of his lips? She shook her head. "You have no idea what you ask."

"Aye, lass, I do, and fer that, I won't disappoint ye."

Oh, how he tempted her! Was she so pitiful then, that she would believe his promise and put hope in him? It frightened her, but the warmth of his breath falling against her face made her forget why.

"I don't want my child to hear me being called a whore."

"He won't."

She closed her eyes, feeling his mouth so close, anticipating and dreading his kiss. She wanted to know what it felt like to be held in his arms, pressed to his heart. She turned away, fearing that if she didn't, it would be the end of her.

They entered Edmund's room quietly, but her son was still awake. When he saw her in the candlelight and the man behind her, he sat up and smiled.

She couldn't do it. She wouldn't let him hear what Geoffrey intended to tell him. Let him try to take Edmund away for it, she would stab him at the table, push him down the stairs, find a way to poison him. He would never succeed. She blinked away the tears that burned behind her eyes, pushed aside her constant terror of losing her child, sat next to him on the bed, and smiled.

"Edmund," Colin said, coming forward and matching her son's wide grin. "How would ye like to come to the Great Hall tonight?"

"With you?"

"Aye. I've another game to teach ye." He bent his knees and crooked his finger for Edmund to come nearer. "'Tis a secret game though. Only the three of us will know of it. D'ye want to play?"

Edmund nodded enthusiastically.

"Good, put on yer slippers and then I will tell ye of the rules."

"Mr. Campbell...," Gillian began. He held up his palm to quiet her, then rose and crossed the room to one of the candles. She watched him tilt the wax and let it drip into his palm. She caught his smile in the soft firelight and felt her belly tighten. What was he about?

"Did George truly relieve Mr. Lefevre of duty?"

"He did not," he answered, reaching for another candle and doing the same with the wax. "But ye won't be burdened with the Frenchman anymore."

"Will I be burdened with you then?"

He looked up and laughed quietly, sending Gillian's defenses scattering. "Aye, ye will."

"This is going to feel warm," he said, bending to Edmund and breaking off two small pieces of wax from his clump. "But 'twill not hurt." He shaped the bits and moved Edmund's curls away from his ears.

"What's it for?"

"'Twill help ye hear yer own thoughts more clearly. There is much noise in the Hall and this game requires us to think without distraction. We shall all play and at the end of the night, we will remove the wax and tell each other what we thought about."

Edmund removed his thumb from his mouth and watched Colin knead the wax in his fingers. "What should I think about?"

Colin shrugged, "Things ye enjoy doing with yer mother—"

"Or with you?"

"Aye." The mercenary's voice took on a softer tone, as did his smile. "Think about things that make ye happy."

"Puppies?"

Gillian finally smiled in the dim light, understanding now what the hardened Highlander was doing. He was clever and caring, protecting her son from Geoffrey without frightening him. She was so grateful, so enchanted by his tenderness, that she was tempted to leap from the bed and fling her arms around him.

"Aye, puppies will do," Colin replied with a resigned sigh and began fitting the wax into Edmund's ear. "The trick is to ferget whatever else ye might hear and just concentrate on those good thoughts. My mother used to tell me that if we thought about something hard enough and wanted it badly enough, we would have it. One of the rules, though, is that ye don't let others know about the wax in yer ears. If they speak to ye and ye cannot hear them, simply nod yer head, pretending that ye do. Do ye understand?"

Edmund nodded, happy to play. "What will you think about Colin?"

Gillian felt her cheeks blaze when he glanced at her.

"Swords and battle most likely."

He pressed his pliant wax into Edmund's other ear then tested to see how well it worked. When Edmund didn't answer him, he grinned.

"Ye're next," he said, rising to his feet and turning to her.

"I've heard it all before."

"I would rather ye didn't hear it again tonight." He moved in on her and before she could stop him, he fit two fingers under her chin and turned her head, inclining her ear toward him. "It won't block out Devon's voice entirely, but 'twill muffle what ye hear."

His tone was thick and deep, covering her like smoke while his fingers flittered across her lobe. She was having a hard time breathing with him so close, hovering over her. He smelled like the outdoors, like the briny wind and something so male it went straight to her head and left her dizzy. She looked up into his eyes, smiled at him, and watched him come undone a bit around the seams. He tried desperately to mask her effect on him, keeping his jaw taut, his fingers steady, but the evidence of his fondness for her was clear in his silent gaze. It made her heart rejoice and quake with worry at the same time. He couldn't save her or Edmund from their futures and it was unfair of her to hope for it. What if he did something foolish, like knock out a few of Geoffrey's teeth? Her son would suffer for it.

"Mr. Campbell, I—"

"Think of yer lute." He quieted her, leaning closer to her ear. "Or of the freedom ye dream about high atop the turrets."

She nodded, smiling. She trusted him. God help them all. She trusted him.

When he finished with her, she pulled more of her hair loose, covering the evidence of their scheme to ignore her cousin.

She was about to thank him when George plunged into the room, demanding explanation. Colin gave it to him with patience and evidence, showing him the wax in Edmund's ears. Moving toward the door, the men spoke quietly for a few moments. She watched them, noting George's refusal to participate in their game, but at least he didn't look angry. In fact, the two men exchanged what could have passed for a smile.

Before they left the room, Colin worked his remaining wax into his ears and winked at Edmund. Surely, Gillian thought as they walked in silence to the Great Hall together, this was a better alternative than poisoning her cousin.

Geoffrey was quite pleased with himself when he saw them, gloating and no doubt eager to begin spewing his filth without any to stop him. Gillian glared at him, though it was difficult to keep from laughing at him instead. As they sat, she noticed Colin slipping his hand to one ear and then depositing the wax he'd pulled from it beneath his belt. He didn't look at her, or at Edmund, as he gained his chair.

The next hour was a curious mixture of amusement, anxiety, and pure pleasure for Gillian. Amusement in that she could hear her cousin blathering on, but his words had absolutely no effect on Edmund. Her son played his part to perfection, smiling at Geoffrey from time to time, as if he heard him but didn't understand what he was being told. She thought she might have heard her cousin call her son a simpleton, especially after Edmund let out a resounding bark that made the men at the table stare at him as if he'd lost his mind. But she wasn't offended. Let them think what they would. Her son was thinking of puppies and it made her happy. Her own thoughts did the same for her. Ridiculously so, in fact. She had no trouble at all imagining herself laughing with Colin, walking with him while they watched Edmund running around a field carpeted with flowers and butterflies... and a puppy. It was all very sweet, but soon those thoughts turned in another direction. One that made her breath grow short. How would it feel to kiss him? To belong to him? To watch him undress and come to her bed at the end of each day?

No. She was mad to let herself think of such things with him. Trusting him with certain things was bad enough. Losing her heart to him was entirely different, and equally dangerous. So what if he was a warrior, equipped with enough weapons on his person to fight the king's army alone? Or if he was fond of Edmund... or even her? It meant nothing. Still, it was nice to ponder a different life with him, even for an hour.

She refused to pay attention to Geoffrey, even when Colin's expression grew dark from across the table.

George looked just as murderous opposite her. Why hadn't he plugged his ears? They both looked like they wanted to leap over the table and silence Geoffrey forever. No doubt her cousin was calling her a whore and her son a bastard. She tossed him a black look for good measure, and to convince him that she'd heard what he said. Part of her was mortified that Colin should constantly hear such terrible things about her, but presently she was more fearful of her son being witness to his friend killing a man at the supper table.

When Geoffrey turned, bored with his endeavors, and pulled Margaret into his lap, Gillian emptied one ear of wax before speaking to him directly and swept out of her chair. "The hour grows late," she announced. "I'll not have him asleep in his stew."

Her cousin waved her away, his satisfaction in belittling her complete. Both George and Colin rose with her, but Geoffrey pulled his lips away from Margaret's throat long enough to mutter something that made her captain sit back down. She listened more closely when he ordered Colin to escort her alone.

"Prove your loyalty to me and to Captain Gates, Campbell," he said. "Don't touch her if you want to keep your hands attached to your arms. She is promised to another." He slipped his eyes back to her and winked. "Though she's a wanton seductress and likely won't put up too much of a fight if you put your hands on her." He laughed at the flush flaring her cheeks. "My dear, let's be truthful. He's not de Atre, after all."

Gillian met his frosty gaze head on. "Nor is he you, cousin."

An instant of watching his confidence falter was almost worth igniting his full temper. But not now, with

Edmund here. So she lowered her gaze and her head along with it and left the Hall with her son...and Colin's steady footfalls behind her.

"Can we take the wax out now, Colin?"

Gillian gasped at her son's request echoing off the walls and turned, relieved to find the Hall doors had been closed behind them. She laughed nervously a moment later, realizing that Edmund couldn't hear himself, or how loud he was speaking. She thanked God that he hadn't spoken a word at the table.

"I think ye might have won the game, lad," Colin told him, bending to remove the wax balls from her son's ears. "Do ye intend to beat me at everything, then?"

Edmund's laughter filled her ears as Gillian freed the second one. How had such a harrowing night turned into a bit of fun for Edmund? She watched Colin straighten to his full height and reach for Edmund's hand as they headed for the stairs. Who was he? Had God sent him to Dartmouth to fight for the Dutch prince, or to help her and her son?

"Were ye thinking about puppies, then?" Colin asked him on the way to his room.

When Edmund nodded and stuck his thumb into his mouth, Colin shared a tender smile with her over Edmund's head.

"And do you know what else?"

"What else?" the mercenary asked him when they reached his room.

"Catching frogs." Edmund hopped to his bed, then stopped and turned to look at them. "Do you think because I thought about them hard enough they might come true?"

Gillian gathered up her mettle like a shield against

her tears. It would do no good to have Edmund pity his life. Knowing he could not have all that he wanted would make him a better man. Still, it broke her heart to pieces wanting to give him everything.

"Why can't ye catch frogs? 'Tis easy."

Gillian blinked away the threatening moisture clouding her vision when Colin bent to pick up Edmund in his arms. This was becoming dangerous. Being alone with this man, watching him care so tenderly for her son... Dear God, it made her ache for the dreams she had put away so long ago. A father for Edmund. A man who loved them and would never abandon them.

"Frogs live on the other side of the estuary," she explained, coming to stand next to them. "It's too far. Geoffrey won't let us take horses," she added, knowing by the confusion on his face that that was to be his next question.

He didn't look pleased with her reply. "Why can't Gates carry... Och, aye," he amended an instant later. "I've seen the way he carries him."

"Will you come with us when next we go, Colin?"

Level with her son's hopeful gaze, Colin Campbell, curious stranger, hardened Highland mercenary, swallowed and nodded his head as if he had no other choice, and surrendered to a force beyond his control.

"Aye, I'll come with ye."

Her son jumped up and down on his mattress when Colin set him on it.

"It's quite far," Gillian managed, but didn't dare look at him while she bent to settle Edmund to bed.

"I wouldn't object to taking a long walk with the both of ye."

His words, and the slow, husky way he spoke them,

suspended her breath. Afraid that she might already be falling for him, she fought to think clearly. "What about the danger from my cousin for showing us too much interest? You were concerned about it just days ago."

"That was before I decided to guard yer son with my life."

Gillian looked up at him, unable to stop herself, and not wanting to. Had she just heard him correctly? He looked almost as surprised as she at what had just left his lips.

"He needs a guardian," he said, sounding like it was he who needed convincing.

"He has me," Gillian told him, too afraid for all their lives to accept his aid.

"And now he has me, as well."

"Do you think we will catch a frog?" Edmund asked, looking up from his pillow and sparing her from having to refuse his offer.

"I know we will." Colin stood over him, smiling and mussing his curls. "Now off to sleep with ye and have good dreams."

Gillian kissed Edmund good night and then followed Colin out of the room. Alone in the hall, she did all she could to compose herself before she offered him a smile, her thanks, and then a good eve.

"Where might I escort ye next?"

His voice above her set her nerve endings on fire. "To bed. I...I mean...to my rooms. I can get there myself. It's only the next door." She dipped around him. He turned, following her. "Good eve to you." She backed away, looking at him watching her.

"Ye're angry with me."

She smiled and shook her head. "You have my heartfelt

gratitude for all you've done tonight. I will never forget it. But neither can I forget that you're dangerous to me, Mr. Campbell, and to Edmund...in more ways than you realize."

"And ye are dangerous to me, Lady Gillian." He stepped forward, closer. "So much that ye tempt me to run. But I've never run from danger before, and I will not do so now."

She thought about running when he lifted his fingers to her temple, but she couldn't move. She couldn't breathe, or think, or speak. His touch sent tiny sparks throughout her body. He traced the outline of her chin, her jaw with his fingertips—a soft, intimate caress that turned her insides to butter. His gaze poured over her features, taking her in as if the sight of her impassioned him beyond what he could control. He let out a long, deep breath as if he'd been holding it for weeks, perhaps years, and then swept his hands down her arms to her hands.

His palms were as stone, rough and hardened from endless hours of wielding a blade. A titillating contrast to the gentleness of his touch as he lifted her fingers to his mouth. She watched his eyes close while he inhaled the scent of her, felt her heart quicken to the point of making her dizzy when he brushed his lips across her knuckles. When he opened his eyes, it was to bask in the sight of her for a moment or two before he slipped his hand behind her nape and dragged her into his embrace.

Gillian had been kissed by only one other man, and it hadn't been like this. Colin's tongue slid across her lips, then captured her gasp with his mouth. Her body jolted as if he were made of lightning. His arms tightened around her waist, drawing her deeper against his hard muscles while his tongue stroked the softest recesses of her mouth. She went weak in his arms, consumed by a power he hadn't forced upon her, but laid at her feet.

Making it that much more deadly.

For the first time in more than four years she believed she could love a man again. No! She pushed against his chest and broke free of his embrace. "He will kill you. Perhaps truly harm Edmund. You must go." She spoke quickly, avoiding his gaze, his hand when he reached for her again. "Go, and forget that I allowed this. I never will again."

Chapter Twenty

Nothing in Colin's life could have prepared him for the battle he found himself fighting over the next three days. He was a warrior, unmatched and unbeaten against any foe he'd ever faced. He didn't give himself over to weakness of mind or body. He lived a life of danger and risk and never once had he allowed his heart to soften toward anyone.

But his current opponent was not fashioned of flesh and blood, but of stone and of pale flowing locks. Her lips were as soft as he'd imagined. Her breath, as sweet as he'd dreamed it to be. Damn it to hell, but he shouldn't have kissed her.

Worse, he'd wanted to do it again the instant he'd stopped and every moment since.

He'd hoped to have words with her about why he'd been so bold. In truth though, he had no bloody notion about what to say. How did men throughout history explain their hearts to lasses? Why the hell did they have to? 'Twasn't enough that he had no notion of how to demonstrate his affection toward a lass. That he cared for her well-being was crippling in and of itself.

He was likely going to get himself killed over her. Instead of blocking Lefevre's waster this afternoon during practice, he'd almost lost an eye watching her spread a blanket in the midst of St. Petroc's gravestones. She'd caught his gaze twice and tossed him a disinterested glance that left him floundering with weapons he'd been born to wield. Edmund waving cheerfully to him was equally dangerous.

At least Gates hadn't rammed his sword into his gut when Colin explained how he intended on getting her and Edmund out of Dartmouth. He'd even given Colin the benefit of listening to his plan from beginning to end—with only minor variations in Gillian and Edmund's ultimate destination. Colin liked the captain, but he didn't trust him with his identity or Camlochlin's location.

None of it mattered though, because she had made certain to stay away from him and 'twas eating away at him. At every part of him, until he found himself standing in the stairwell late at night, unable to leave while she played her lute in the turrets. Worse, knowing that the men of the garrison were passed out drunk in their beds, he'd managed to convince himself that he was there to protect her from unwanted intruders.

He cursed himself now while he made his way to the round tower. He had to get kissing her, seeing her, out of his thoughts. Right now, the only thing on his mind should be getting her, Gates, and Devon to trust him with their lives, and the lives of others. He'd hoped to have gained Gillian's trust before he set his plans in motion, but he could wait no longer. The sooner she and Edmund were gone from Dartmouth, the better he could concentrate on the annihilation of his enemies.

The earl's trust wouldn't be difficult to win. Colin knew a few things that Devon didn't know—like who was truly behind the plot to bring William back to England. Devon wanted power and he wanted Gillian. To gain both, he needed allies. Powerful ones. While the name Colin's father had given him struck fear into the hearts of his enemies, his mother's offering commanded respect among the English. Colin was not above using it to gain the advantage.

Practicing his smile, he knocked at the door to the Earl of Devon's solar. He adjusted his smile to a cordial one when Devon's voice from the other side invited entry.

"Campbell." The earl looked up briefly from a pile of parchments scattered across the table he was sitting at. "What can I do for you? Be quick in your telling. I've things to see to."

Colin looked around the solar. They were alone. Without waiting for an invitation, he took a seat in the only other upholstered chair in the room. "I came to help ye depose a Catholic king but as each day passes with no enlightenment as to how we shall be going about the task, I grow restless, my lord."

Devon stared at him, looking a bit surprised by his guest's boldness. "You are being paid to prepare for that day. Leave the details of how and when to me."

Colin's smile went bland. The time was perfect to play his hand. "My cousin, the future Earl of Argyll, believes 'twas the Earl of Essex's hand—and not yers—behind William's soon-to-be victory. I was hoping to tell him differently."

Devon dropped his quill and stared at him from behind the table. "What is it you want?"

Not much, really, Colin thought. He already had an idea of when William might be landing. If only one more signature was needed on the invitation, then it would likely be going out within the next few weeks. The prince would be arriving in the summer. But with how many ships at his back? Colin was meeting his runner later tonight and hoped to have a bit more information to give the king.

"Many things, my lord," Colin admitted. "One being my kin's name restored to favor."

"I'm certain it will be," Devon assured him and reached for the silver pitcher at his elbow.

"As am I. The Campbells have always held a place of high esteem both in Parliament and at the king's ear. I wish it to be so again."

Devon eyed him from across the table with a whole new interest. Colin could almost see the thoughts weaving together in the earl's mind. "Of course, I will do all I can to help your family. Whisky? I understand you Scots enjoy it immensely."

"My thanks, but nae."

"It's from my private store."

Colin's smiled remained casual. "Yer generosity is appreciated, but my answer must remain the same. I haven't yet finished practice fer the night."

Devon scrutinized him from behind his cup before he drank from it. "You say you have Argyll's ear?"

"I do."

The earl reclined in his chair, bringing his cup with him. "Perhaps we can aid each other in our endeavors then. I would be in your debt if you put an end to the rumor that this brilliant strategy to see William on the throne was not my doing."

The bait dangled. Now to get Devon to bite.

"Certainly, my lord. I put no importance on gossip."

Grinning, Devon held up his cup and guzzled its contents. "I like you, Campbell. You're not like the others."

"We are as different as night is to the day."

"I knew it was a fortunate day when you stepped upon Dartmouth soil."

"Did ye?" Colin raised a raven brow.

Devon pushed out of his chair and stepped around the table. "Most certainly. A Campbell in my service is fortunate indeed. I would have had speech with you about this sooner but you are forever with sword in hand." He smiled at Colin, who smiled back. "You bear witness of my aid to our new king. Presently favored or not, your family will once again rise to power and I would have them as my allies."

At least the earl was to the point. 'Twould save time. "As would I," Colin told him, willing his triumphant grin to remain hidden. Hell, but men with desires such as Devon's were easy to catch. "I would be happy to tell my cousin of yer many virtues. He admires loyalty and dedication and will hold an ally such as yerself close at his side. But..."

"Yes?"

"There is little I know to tell him."

"Perhaps this will help then." Devon swept a rolled parchment from the table and wiggled it in front of Colin's face—close enough for Colin to take it, and the earl's life with it. But that wasn't what he had come to Dartmouth to do. "Thanks to me, we have all of England behind us, including the Church."

"The bishop comes here to put his name to the invitation, then?" Colin asked, keeping his voice neutral.

Devon nodded and handed it to him as easily as if he were handing him a drink. "Read it so that you may tell your—what do you call them?—kin that it is *my* hand that works hardest to restore a Protestant king."

Colin took the parchment and looked it over briefly, taking careful note of the six names inked at the end. Gillian had had them all correct. Damnation, but this was almost too easy.

"It seems I have my proof," he said, offering a smile and the invitation back to Devon. "When are ye expecting to send it?"

"Within the next month. We hope the prince will land sometime in July."

"And with enough men at his back to take on whatever is left of James's army."

"No doubt." Devon laughed, but gave no numbers. It didn't matter. Colin had enough information to amass his army.

"The king will be in yer debt."

"True enough, if there weren't others who would steal the glory from me." Devon's smile faded into a ruthless snarl. "I intend to silence that mouth as soon as I can."

It wasn't what Devon said, but rather the way he said it, and accompanied by a longing gaze at the door, that chilled the blood in Colin's veins. But he couldn't mean Gillian. He had no reason to suspect that she could have told anyone what she knew. Besides, she wasn't the only one who knew the truth. "Lord Essex has been known to visit Argyll—"

"I speak of his daughter," Devon bit out, turning to reach for his cup. "My cousin."

It took every ounce of self-control Colin possessed to keep his bland expression from faltering. "Lady Gillian?"

He had to know. What did it mean? "What has she spoken against ye?"

"Nothing," Devon told him, moving toward a cabinet on the other side of Colin. "She's penned her words in ink." He pulled open a narrow drawer, stuck his hand inside, and returned with a folded parchment in his hand. "Here is her latest."

Colin looked at it, wishing it were anything but her letter to William. But that's exactly what it was, and he felt the stab of regret at having to tell her that her champion wasn't coming to save her. The prince likely didn't know she existed.

"Letters she wrote to the prince." Devon waved it in the air. "Spreading lies to shame me, spending her nights with the men to pick up bits and pieces of news from whatever land they hailed from." He tossed the missive into the fire and laughed, swinging back around to face Colin. "Asking him not to allow our marriage. She's a shrewd bitch. I will give her that. Almost as clever as she is stubborn and beautiful. I'll delight in it while she tries not to scream beneath me."

Colin wanted to kill him. Very slowly. "How did ye intercept them?" he asked quietly instead.

"I didn't," Devon grinned. "The messenger she thought came from Holland to meet her came from Kingswear. She isn't acquainted with most of the men there, and in the cover of night, they all look the same."

"Clever, my lord."

"Indeed. And would you like to know the best part?"

Colin nodded.

"I pen her in return using William's seal. I have it, you know, to use on the invitation. She believes the prince hates me and will take her from my care."

"Why not just tell her that ye know?"

Devon's grin widened with sheer joy and satisfaction. "This gives her hope. She will be easier to break when that hope is destroyed."

Colin ground his teeth. 'Twas cruel. Crueler than anything he had ever devised for his enemies. "Why?"

"Why what?" the earl asked, returning to his seat.

"Why d'ye want to break her?"

"You see it, don't you, Campbell?" Devon poured himself another drink. "She thinks she's above us all. Above me!" He laughed, swigged his wine, and then slammed the cup down. "She has always looked down her nose at me and all because her father owns more land than mine and has a few more titles. She laughed at me when we were children and I told her of my love for her. Later, she expressed disgust at the idea of sharing my bed...and then, as if to mock me, shared the bed of a peasant." He emptied the contents of another cup down his throat and offered Colin a wretched grin. "But I will have her."

Och, aye, this was what he had come in here tonight to do. His task was simpler than he had expected. He should be thankful, but he wasn't. He was angry, and he hated himself for what he was about to say. "And ye think taking away her hope of leaving will break her more than taking away her son?"

The earl shook his head and stared into his empty cup. "I don't think I would live long enough to enjoy her if I carried out my threats."

Colin didn't think so either. "Perhaps I can help."

Devon looked up, hope lighting his sullen expression. "You know, Campbell, I've been wanting to get rid of that bratling for quite some time."

Colin's smile didn't flicker or fade. His heart did pound a wee bit faster in his chest, pumping charged blood to his veins. He steadied his breathing and watched Devon closely for any sign that he was suspicious of anything—like Colin's heart. He'd never had difficulty veiling his true purpose before. But his heart had never become involved in the past. Did the earl see the longing in his eyes when Colin looked at her? When he spoke of her?

"Do ye have a family in mind that would take him?"

"No one Lord Essex would approve of if he found out."

"I thought Essex didn't care fer the boy."

"The bastard is his grandson nevertheless."

"True." Colin pondered the dilemma for a moment. "How does he feel about the Campbells? My kin would take him."

"To Glen Orchy?" Devon eyed him and when Colin nodded, he thought about it. "Why would they?"

"Future leverage against Essex"—Colin shrugged—"if they should ever require it."

Grin restored to full resplendence, Devon turned toward the flames. "You are ruthless, just like the rest of your family. But then, they didn't rise to their position without leaving behind a few victims."

"More than a few," Colin agreed.

"There is but one issue about our plan." Devon set down his cup and turned to him. "Gillian will never stand before a priest with me if I take her son away from her. She will put her dagger into one of us first."

"Not if you had nothing to do with her losing him." Colin leaned forward in his chair and smiled, not as wide as Devon, but with the same amount of satisfaction. "I'll need a wee bit of time, but before I'm done, she'll be thanking ye fer what is, I'm fairly certain, the only kindness ye've ever given him."

Devon practically drooled. "Do tell."

✣

Chapter Twenty-one

Gillian plucked the strings of her lute, filling the turret stairwell with soft music. Usually her practice helped her forget the gloom of her life, but for the past three nights nothing could drive Colin Campbell from her thoughts. And, oh, how she tried to forget him. His handsome face. His strong, lithe body practicing in the courtyard...hovering over her, holding her close, safe within his arms while he made her forget everything else but the taste of his passion. His smile, and the way it fell upon her as warm as the summer sun, transforming him from a hardened mercenary to a man seemingly lost and addled by his unwanted reaction.

Oh, how she missed him! How she wanted to give in to those silly, reckless emotions that made her palms sweat and her heart quicken. Did he care for her? He certainly touched her, kissed her, like he did. He wanted to protect Edmund, and Gillian wanted to let her heart soar over it. But she couldn't. What if he wanted to take her away next? What if her foolish heart made her agree to go? She knew exactly what would happen. Colin thought he understood Geoffrey, but he didn't. Her cousin would hunt them down without ceasing. And when he found them...Colin couldn't fight Geoffrey's entire garrison alone any better than George could. What if he tried and Edmund was slain in the meantime?

Unable to play with such thoughts plaguing her, she fit her lute under her arm and climbed the rest of the stairs to the turret. She needed the cool night air to clear her mind.

Leaning against the crenellated wall, she looked out over the rocky terrain illuminated by the full moon. It was well past the midnight hour and not a sound disturbed her reverie save for the rushing waves below. She knew what she had to do: stay away from Mr. Campbell and temptation and save them all.

Perhaps after William arrived and saved her from marrying Geoffrey, she would allow Mr. Campbell to court her. Until then, though, she couldn't risk involvement with him.

Lord, but she hadn't been this miserable in three years. Poor Edmund was just as unhappy being holed up indoors. But she would protect him even if it cost him his laughter for a few days. The only one who didn't appear utterly miserable was George. Her captain smiled more, seemed more at ease, and had even taken up practicing until his uniform grew damp from exertion. When she'd asked him if Mr. Campbell's friendship was the reason for his pleasant moods, he stunned her by calling the Highlander "a refreshing change from the half-wits he'd been surrounded by for far too long."

Gillian agreed. Colin Campbell was different from the other men at Dartmouth. She remembered one of her first opinions about him. He'd reminded her of the kind of wolf that stalks its prey in the dark. The kind you don't see coming until it's too late. The garrison seemed to like him well enough. And why wouldn't they, when he constantly allowed them victory on the practice field? He'd won her son's favor, thereby winning hers. And now even her stoic, cautious captain had fallen victim to his guileless charisma.

Of course, she hadn't told George about Colin's kiss. No reason to get the poor man killed, although she wasn't completely certain that her captain would come out triumphant against Colin.

A sound behind her spun her on her heel. The hooded figure standing beneath the entryway nearly stopped her heart. Instinctively, she moved backward until her rump hit the wall. She stumbled for an instant before regaining her balance, but he'd rushed toward her, his hand outstretched, his beautiful face pale beneath the moonlight.

"Lass, I beg ye, have a care."

"You startled me, Mr. Campbell." She remained where she was, refusing his hand. "You shouldn't be here."

"Why do ye avoid me?"

Oh, dear God, why did he care? Why did he sound like her answer was the only thing that mattered to him? She didn't want him to care. It would lead to nothing but sadness. Geoffrey would never let her go.

"You frighten me," she told him, wishing the wind would carry her words away as she uttered them. She hated being frightened. More, she hated admitting it.

"Fergive me," he said quietly, pushing back his hood. "'Tis not my intention to frighten ye. 'Tis what I came to speak to ye about. The other night...I didn't mean to... I should not have..."

She shook her head, agreeing with him and feeling as miserable as he sounded. "You mustn't."

"I'll be more vigilant in the future," he vowed.

"As I am trying to be now." She lowered her gaze, embarrassed by the truth. She'd never been any good with concealing her feelings behind some weighty mask. Now was no exception. She didn't want him to look into her eyes and see the power he had to resurrect dead dreams. If he thought she'd prayed for him, longed for him, he might never give up his quest to guard Edmund.

"I'll leave ye to yer thoughts then."

He moved to go, but Gillian's hand shot forward to stop him. Even in her youth, she had not been this reckless, but the very sight of this swarthy Highland mercenary tempted her to abandon her logic and her fears, and live again. She said nothing, though she'd halted his departure. What was there to say? That she was weak? That being with him was better than being with her thoughts... or her lute? That she...

She caught her breath when he coiled his arm around her waist and drew her up against him. She could do nothing else but watch, heavy-lidded, while his mouth descended on her, tender yet unyielding. She knew with dreaded certainty that she was losing her heart to him. Perhaps it was already too late. Presently, she didn't care. She just wanted to kiss him back. And she did, despite every alarm going off in her head. Boldly, she ran her palms down the hard contours of his arms and flicked her tongue across his in a sensual dance that pulled a groan from deep inside his throat.

He seemed more aware of the effect they were having on each other than she was and withdrew first. "Ye're not going to avoid me fer a se'nnight this time, are ye, lass?" Smiling down at her, he kept her close in his arms, shielding her from the wind.

"Perhaps four days this time." She smiled back. "But if you continue to kiss me like that, I cannot promise it will not be a month before you see me again."

"Then I'll restrain myself, lady. Three days was wretched enough."

Gillian closed her eyes and pressed her cheek to his chest. Oh, she was lost. She couldn't fight this. She didn't want to. "Did you miss my company then, Mr. Campbell?" She tilted her face to his and offered him a playful smile.

He grew serious, as if her question unnerved him, proving to Gillian that he feared losing his heart as much as she did. Why? What would it cost him? She already knew: his life, if Geoffrey discovered it.

"I should go check on Edmund." She broke away from his embrace, hating her cousin more than she ever thought possible.

"I will escort ye to his room. There are things I would speak to ye about," Colin said, picking up his steps behind her when she turned to go.

She should stop him, but she didn't. What harm was there in walking down the stairs with him, even letting him look in on her son if he wished to? He certainly wouldn't kiss her again in her babe's chamber.

Reassuring herself did nothing to stop her hands from shaking when she opened Edmund's door a few moments later. The room was quiet and softly lit with candles burning low on their wicks, but she could see Colin's face clearly enough when he stepped up to the edge of the bed beside her. So then, it hadn't been only her that he'd missed these last few days.

"I understand why ye doubt my ability to protect him," he whispered, turning to arrest her heart with the residue of tenderness for her son warming his gaze. "But if ye knew—"

"I don't doubt that you believe you can," she interrupted gently. "Though you stumble from time to time in the practice yard, you walk with the confidence of a king. You go about conquering monsters with a magic dagger and some candle wax. But Geoffrey is more than a bad dream. You cannot protect Edmund from him."

"I can, Gillian."

"How? How can you when you are not with Edmund all day, every day? Geoffrey has authority here. He needs but to speak the word and any harm could befall my son."

"I would take him away."

Her breath stilled, followed an instant later by her heart.

"I've already spoken to Captain Gates, and he—"

"What? What are you saying?" When her son stirred in his bed, she snatched Colin's wrist and pulled him toward the door. "You want to take Edmund away?"

"Aye. I mean to get him away first, without yer cousin suspecting anything amiss. I will get ye out after that."

She shook her head. What was she hearing? George would never have agreed to this. And if he had, he would have told her.

"I need ye to trust me, Gillian."

With her son's life? No. Never.

"He will be safe, lass. I vow it. Ye must not depend on William of Orange fer yer aid."

"Why not?"

He looked anguished and angry, but he didn't give her a reason for his warning.

"Please, just trust me."

"The hour is late, Colin. You should go."

He hesitated, his gaze drawing her in until she felt tempted to move closer to him. She didn't. She'd kissed him. She'd feared for his life and her sanity. She didn't want to think about him taking Edmund from her...not even for a day. Trust him? Dear God, would that he had asked anything but that.

Chapter Twenty-two

Gillian was summoned early the next morning and escorted by George to her cousin's solar. When she saw Colin already present, standing by the window, she felt a renewed prick somewhere deep in her chest. Why was he here? Did it have to do with Edmund?

"Gillian." Geoffrey's cutting voice raked across her ears. "Your father arrives at Kingswear tomorrow with the bishop and has requested to see you."

Her father? Hope did not hasten her heart. She'd learned during his past visits that he didn't come to bring her home, but only to assure her mother that he'd seen her alive and well. Gillian wondered why Evelyn Dearly cared. Perhaps, she told herself often, her mother secretly wished her daughter and grandson were dead. Then she wouldn't have to be burdened with the idea of Gillian showing up at one of Essex's posh balls with her bastard on her hip.

"We leave first thing tomorrow morning," her cousin continued, oblivious to the tears welling up in her eyes. She didn't know why her body chose to betray her now, and over her parent's detachment.

"Has he requested to see Edmund as well?" she asked, pulling herself together.

Geoffrey rose from his chair and hovered over her. "Why would he?"

Then he hadn't. It didn't shock Gillian, and it didn't change her mind about what she meant to do. "It's time he finally meets his grandson."

Geoffrey laughed, as if in utter surprise and delight at her gall. "Your waif will remain here. I'll not hear another word on the matter. It's time you began obeying me, Gillian. When we——"

Oh, but she was tired of him bullying her. If she were a man, she would have punched him in the mouth. She was also tired of her parents pretending that Edmund didn't exist. It was too easy for them with her locked away here. But not this time. "I will not be going without my son," she said, cutting off whatever he was blabbering. "Tell the earl I refuse to see him. Tell him that nothing you could threaten to do to me or to his grandson could persuade me to look upon his face. He shouldn't be angry with you for too long, dear cousin." She gave his shoulder a tender pat. "After all, you are nothing but a mere messenger."

Fire lanced up Geoffrey's cheeks and blazed to life in his eyes. Fearing she'd gone too far, Gillian lowered her gaze and bit back the remainder of her words until her jaw ached.

But it was too late.

"What a mouthy bitch you are, cousin. You simply don't know when to quit."

She looked up in time to see Colin move away from the window and take a step closer to Geoffrey, the hilts of his many daggers gleaming in the firelight and George's warning glance stopping him.

"But now that you bring up messengers," Geoffrey spat, his eyes as cold and as dark as the fathomless depths of the sea, "do you think the opinions of some wretched whore would sway the mind of a great man? A man like Prince William, for instance?"

Prince William? Why would he say such a thing? Gillian fought the intense urge to flee and stood her ground...keeping her trembling hands at her sides. What did he know? Had someone told him about her missives to the prince? The room spun just a bit when she swung her gaze to Colin—the only one besides her who knew.

He'd betrayed her to her cousin.

"Thankfully for us both," Geoffrey practically sang, appearing to have forgiven her. She knew better. "Not a single drop of your venom has touched him."

She blinked her eyes away from Colin and back to him, hoping she'd heard him wrong. "I don't...What do you mean?"

Geoffrey's tight lips relaxed into a triumphant snarl. "Why, I mean your letters to Prince William. What do you think I mean? I've intercepted them all." He chuckled, watching her fall into the closest chair, her bloodless complexion proof enough of her guilt. "The prince will not be saving you, dear Gillian. No one will."

"What letters? What the hell are you referring to?" It was George who spoke while she tried to remember to breathe and why she wanted to continue.

Geoffrey turned to him, his joyous grin fading. "I was coming to you next, Captain, but I will conclude with you now. I speak of the letters against me that your charge has been penning to the Dutch prince while you were busy teaching her son how to piss standing up."

"Impossible." George almost laughed in his face. "There are no letters—"

"Not anymore," her cousin agreed. "I burned the last of them last eve. Did I not, Campbell?"

Gillian watched, the closest she'd ever come to letting Geoffrey witness her tears, while Colin nodded. Burned. None of her letters had ever reached the prince. How could it be possible? How could everything she'd hoped for, risked everything for, be over so quickly? No help was coming. Her gaze frosted over on Colin. He might not have told her cousin her secret, but he knew what had become of her letters and he hadn't told her. She'd kissed him. She'd allowed him to awaken her dreams. She'd become a fool once again.

"As of today," her cousin continued, "you are no longer Gillian's guardian, Captain Gates." He held up his palm to stop George when her captain objected. "I put you to service to watch her. If you truly don't know about her treachery against me, then you failed miserably at your duty. On the other hand, if you did know about them, that would mean you have also betrayed me. Either way, I need a man I can trust to do what I ask. She will be in the care of Mr. Campbell starting today."

Like hell she would! Gillian didn't wait to hear whatever George was about to say but stood up and swiped a tear from her lashes. She had had enough of sitting around cowering and taking orders from Geoffrey. Enough of fearing what he might or might not do. It wasn't over. It couldn't be. She couldn't give up or give in, now more than ever. Her course may have changed but she still had to fight...for Edmund. Perhaps she would steal into her cousin's room tonight and kill him while he slept.

"Geoffrey, Captain Gates knew nothing of what I was

doing, so don't threaten him." She let him hear the bite
in her warning, unconcerned with the consequences. Let
any one of them lay a finger on Edmund…"As for Mr.
Campbell, I can promise you that no matter how sharp his
eyes are, if he makes a move against me or Edmund"—
she spared the Highlander her briefest glance—"he won't
see my dagger until it's in his heart. In regard to my visit
to Kingswear, you will have to tie me to a horse to get
me there without my son. But I warn you, Geoffrey, you'd
best prepare to explain to the earl why his daughter is so
badly bruised and battered, because I swear I will fight to
my death if I must with whoever tries to bind me. It will
be easier on all if I bring Edmund."

For a moment Geoffrey looked like he wanted to
throttle her senseless. Gillian knew he wanted to. She
wanted to roll up her sleeves and dare him to give it a
go. She knew how to use her dagger *and* her fists, thanks
to George. But being a lady, she refrained. Besides, she
knew how to beat him. She simply had to keep her reaction to him to a minimum.

He took great pleasure in belittling her, and believed
he came out victorious in every battle in which they
engaged. She was certain he'd anxiously waited for the
day when he could tell her how clever he'd been at seizing her correspondence with William. He wanted to gloat
over her helplessness. She wouldn't let him.

Without waiting for his response, she turned to George
on her way out of the solar. "Captain Gates, if you would
please escort me to my son's room."

"That was quite bold," George said when they were
alone in the hall.

"I know. I went too far. I cannot let Edmund out of my
sight for an instant."

"Your mercenary would bring him to my house in Essex."

She stopped and turned to him. "Why did you not tell me that you spoke with him about this?"

"I wasn't certain it was a good plan."

Gillian gaped at him. "And now you do? George, your home is the first place Geoffrey would look for us."

"Not if it was his idea to bring Edmund there."

She shook her head. "What in blazes are you talking about? Are you mad to think I would—" Her words were cut off by the solar door opening and Colin stepping out. She watched him pause when he saw her and then thought better of it and continued his stride in her direction.

"Good, I'm glad I caught both of ye." He turned to George first. "Captain, I had no idea what he meant to do. But now that's he's done it, it makes my plan easier."

"Mr. Campbell." Gillian stepped up to him and tilted her chin. "I have no idea what your plan is, nor do I care. It will fail because I will have no part in it. I don't know what your motives are, but if my cousin can trust you, then I cannot. You are not taking my son anywhere without me and if you ever bring it up again, it will be the last time we speak. Do you understand?"

He had the audacity to let his mouth hook into a smile. "Aye, but would ye be opposed to me telling ye that ye stood like a warrior in there? He wanted ye to break and ye didn't."

She quirked her brow at him, astonished that he would try to compliment her, perhaps continue to win her favor after what he'd done. She would be a fool no more and it was time he knew it. "You took a chance with my heart, then, didn't you? You had no way of knowing my reaction and yet you told me nothing about my letters being destroyed before they ever reached Prince William." He had nothing to say to that, did he? She nodded to herself, angry enough to slap him. "Now that I think more on it, I would prefer if you cease speaking with me from this day hence.

"Captain," she called out as she headed for the stairs. "Please see that Mr. Campbell does not follow me. I fear he might try to kiss me again."

She cringed at the sound of a fist striking bone, and then she smiled when she heard George shout, "To the yard, Campbell, and you'd best prepare for the worst."

"I didn't force myself on her," Colin explained, turning to the captain when they stepped outside.

"I trusted you." Gates's fist came around swinging yet again. This time Colin stepped back, avoiding the blow.

"'Twas a moment of weakness."

The captain scowled even harder and ripped his sword from its sheath. "Then she means nothing to you. You take liberties with her for no reason other than your own desire."

"I didn't say that." Colin ducked, narrowly escaping a slice to his neck. He nearly fell backward when the blade returned to cut him down the middle. Hell, all those nights of practicing together had paid off...for the captain. Pity. Finally, he had before him a man who promised to deliver a good fight, and Colin didn't want to fight him. He'd have to injure the captain to end it.

"I don't know what I feel fer her...," he confessed, knowing that the only way to disarm this opponent was with the truth. In his line of duty, Colin didn't give up many of his truths. But he found that once he spoke this one, he couldn't stop. "'Tis like a madness that plagues me, and it is getting harder to harness every day."

Gates's sword slowed enough to give Colin plenty of time to sidestep another attack.

"Her and Edmund's safety is fast becoming more important to me than anything else. I know ye're angry with me because ye fear fer her, but I will keep them safe. I would not be willing to risk their lives if I wasn't certain of it."

Gates paused in his attack to stare him in the eye. Whatever he saw convinced him of Colin's sincerity. "She will always be my charge, Campbell. No matter what Devon orders."

"I expected nothing less, Captain Gates."

Gillian's champion finally lowered his sword. "How would you keep them safe?"

"With an army more fearsome than anything in England or Holland, and with my skill."

Gates backed away and positioned his blade for a second assault. "Show me then."

"With wood, not steel." Colin reached for the practice swords lined against the wall, and noticed the group of men who had sauntered out of the fortress to watch. Let them see. With five of his best men, Colin could take down this entire garrison, whether they were familiar with his skill or not. He tossed Gates a blunt weapon and, with no other choice but to reveal something more about himself, took position.

They exchanged blows for more than an hour with Gates pressing hard and Colin meeting every strike and parrying every jab. Twice the captain swept him off his feet only to have him roll away and spring back up swinging hard. Colin was impressed by his opponent's ability to remain balanced on his feet beneath the force of Colin's arm. Gates's stamina had also improved, but finally he gave in to a series of powerful, chopping assaults and held up his palm.

"Have I convinced ye then?" Colin asked, tossing his sword away.

"That you're losing your heart to them? Yes," the captain answered quietly enough for only the both of them to hear. "That you can protect them against a hundred men sent to retrieve her? No."

"That's because I went easy on ye." He smiled when Gates laughed, leading him back to the castle. "And my heart has little to do with this. 'Tis my head I can't control."

"Mon frère." Philippe Lefevre clapped him on the back as Colin passed him. "You were *magnifique*. When did you—?"

"Practice, Lefevre. What ye should all be doing more of, aye?"

Colin didn't wait to hear whatever else Lefevre or any of the others had to say about his sudden mastery with a blade, but caught up to Gates, who was entering the castle without him.

"Will ye still help me get her and Edmund out? I spoke to Devon and he is open to my suggestions."

"I never said I would help you," the captain reminded him. "How am I supposed to trust you with her well-being when you can't even admit to falling in love with her?"

Hell. Was it true? He fell behind again, nearly paralyzed with the thought of being so lost. When Gates stopped this time and turned to wait for him, Colin wanted to tell him the truth about everything…everything, in order to remember who he was, what he was here to do. But he couldn't tell anyone. He must remain Colin Campbell and see his duty through.

"You knew about the letters she penned to William?"

Colin nodded, happy for the change in topic, and picked up his step again to join his companion. "She told me of them recently. She'd hoped to convince the prince of aiding her when he arrived. I had no idea Devon had them until last night."

"She didn't tell me," Gates reflected quietly.

"Mayhap she thought ye would try to stop her from sending them."

"I would have." Her captain allowed a hint of a smile to creep around the edges of his mouth. "She may not appear to be, but she's a force to be reckoned with, that one."

Colin agreed. When Devon had told her of her letters to William, Colin wanted to go to her... or smash her cousin's skull into the nearest wall. He knew how difficult it had to have been for her to learn that all her work had come to naught. But she didn't fall to pieces at Devon's feet, as the bastard had hoped. She'd squared her shoulders and tilted up her chin and refused to surrender. God help him, but 'twas beautiful to watch.

"Devon said the prince should arrive by summer." As was becoming a worrisome habit of late, Colin's thoughts returned to helping her. "That's a pair of months away."

"And?"

"And I plan on getting her and Edmund the hell out of here before then. I've already penned a missive to my kin telling them when they are to arrive. They will take Edmund into their care and bring him home. I'll get Gillian out after that."

Gates eyed him narrowly as they made their way to the Hall. "You did this without even waiting for my approval."

"I told ye I would."

"Yes." The captain thought about it for a moment and then sighed with something that sounded like resignation. Colin hoped it was. "You did tell me you would. All right then, how long do we have to get the boy to Essex?"

"Three weeks. Mayhap a month."

"Why not do it sooner? It shouldn't take the Campbells a month to get to Essex from Glen Orchy."

The captain was correct...if 'twere the Campbells who were coming for Edmund and not the MacGregors—who were arriving from Skye. When would Colin tell him... or the child's mother where he truly planned to have Edmund taken? He guessed they would discover it on their own when his father and brother appeared at Gates's door.

"I still don't quite understand how you'll get Devon to agree to let me take the boy to my home," Gates said. "In fact, I don't truly understand why I even trust you."

"What choice do ye have?" Colin asked him on his way to their table. "I am her last hope."

"You sound so certain you can do this."

"I am."

"And what if he sends Edmund off with someone else? How can you be certain that he will do as you suggest?"

"He wants my kin's favor," Colin told him and fell into his seat to await his drink. "To get it, he must keep mine."

Gates smiled at the server setting down his cup, then turned back to Colin. "Your arrogance can be dangerous, Campbell."

"My confidence will see me through it."

The captain studied him from across the table long enough to make Colin squirm in his chair. "So then, you're done with trying to convince me that you're not the most dangerous man ever to step foot in Dartmouth?"

Colin offered him a furtive wink and reached for his ale when the server set his cup before him. "Aye, I've decided to stick with the truth if I am to gain yer trust."

"Arrogant bastard," the captain muttered behind his cup. "God help us all if you're not what you claim."

Chapter Twenty-three

Gillian stood before the esteemed Earl of Essex in Kingswear Castle's Great Hall, dry-eyed and as hard-hearted as his example had taught her to be. He'd aged. The strands of hair peeking from beneath his wig had gone silver and he didn't appear as tall when he stood over her, looking down his nose at Edmund. Instead of speaking with her alone, he granted her an audience during the afternoon meal, which was every bit as lively as it was at Dartmouth. Their speech was curt and customary, her father preferring to hear about life at Dartmouth from her cousin rather than from her. George and Colin sat together, sharing few words and the same disgusted look on their faces when the earl pushed his chair farther away from Edmund's.

Gillian didn't spare Colin a glance across the table. She was through wasting time trusting men. Any man.

"I wish to share a word or two alone with you, my lord." Gillian rose to her feet with her father when he finished eating. She wanted to tell him about what she'd written to the Dutch prince. About what she would tell William when he arrived.

"Sadly, I cannot spare the time, daughter. Pen it to me. I'll have your mother read it."

"As she has read my letters about Geoffrey's lewd desires for me?"

Her father's eyes hardened on her and she wondered how in the world her mother had remained wed to him for so long. "I've spoken to him about your accusations and he has denied touching you. Do you refute that?"

"No." She shook her head, glaring at Geoffrey, who was still seated in his chair. "But I—"

"Then be grateful for him, Gillian. He's the only man willing to take you in with a bas...a child attached to you." He whispered the words and yet each one stung as if he'd slapped her. "Until you agree to let me find a home for the boy, you will remain here."

Gillian smiled, though it cost her almost more than what she had left. Her father wouldn't protect Edmund from anything Geoffrey did to him. He wanted her child gone from her life as badly as her cousin did. "Then bid my sisters farewell from me, for I shall never see them again."

"Don't be a fool, Gillian," the earl ground out his warning, watching her take her son's hand to leave. "Do you want to grow old and die alone, with nothing to your name?"

"If my name was anything but Dearly, I would be content to die tomorrow. But I am determined to wed someone who does not share the same name as yours. Farewell, my lord."

She pushed past him and strode to the exit, pulling Edmund with her. To hell with Lord Essex. If this was what he wanted, than she had a father no more. She wouldn't spend another minute of her life begging for his aid or even thinking of him. She would enjoy the rest of the day, and the different view she got to see a few times a year here at Kingswear.

Edmund freed his hand from hers and ran past her, spotting something and practically squealing on his way to getting a closer look.

"Gillian."

Someone touched her shoulder and she turned to find Colin there, his eyes laden with pity for her.

"I'm fine." She moved to turn away.

"I would have a word with ye."

"Later, I—"

"Campbell?" one of Kingswear's guardsmen said, coming up to them and thankfully distracting Colin. "Where have I seen you before?"

Gillian didn't wait around for the answer but turned to follow Edmund. She saw the piglet, or rather she heard it, while it raced away from her son, down a ravine. Edmund gave chase and Gillian followed him through a stand of trees and back around. Or, at least, she thought they'd come back around.

"Edmund!" she called to halt him from going any deeper into the forest. The piglet kept going, but Gillian picked up her son and looked around. She didn't recognize the trees around her. How far had they gone? No need to panic, she told herself. Colin should be close by. She called his name and was answered by a single lark overhead.

And then a twig breaking to her left.

"Colin?"

The man stepping out from behind the trees, a bit out of breath, wasn't Colin. He wasn't anyone from Kingswear, nor were the other four men who followed after him.

Gillian clutched Edmund to her chest and yanked her dagger free. "Come no closer. The men of my garrison are but beyond those trees."

"We know where they are. We followed you from Dartmouth," the first man said, slipping a dagger of his own from his breeches and smiling at Edmund. "Handsome boy, he is. Come here, little one." He held out his arms and Gillian slashed her blade at him.

One of the others caught her from behind. She screamed before his hand clamped around her mouth. She fought wildly when another man wrenched her son from her arms and handed him over to the first with the knife.

"It'll be quick, I promise."

She bit the hand over her mouth and rammed her heel into her captor's foot. He let her go, but it was too late. She watched in horror as the blade flashed above Edmund's throat.

Something big whooshed by her and then dropped to its back and slid beneath the man holding Edmund. The dagger fell from the culprit's fingers and Edmund followed shortly after. The man almost fell on top of him when he sank to his knees, blood gushing from between his legs.

Gillian dove for her son, snatched him up off the ground, and ran behind a tree. After making certain that his tears were brought about by fear and not injury, she turned to watch Colin, back on his feet, a second man already dead beside them. She turned Edmund's head away from the slaughter that ensued next, but found that no matter how horrifying it was, she couldn't bring herself to look away.

Colin wielded his sword with brutal force, cutting

through flesh and bone and leaving his third victim screaming on the ground. Two more circled him, one to his left, the other to his right. He looked at them both, a purposeful, powerful warrior with cold death in his eyes. He moved to his left, kicked the knife from his opponent's fingers, caught it in his hand, then flung it back at him, sending it through his throat.

Without pausing to disarm the last man standing, Colin snatched him by the throat and with legs braced, pounded the hilt of his sword into the man's face, once and then again, satisfied only after he heard his victim's nose breaking beneath his fist.

The man opened his bloody mouth and spoke something to Colin that Gillian couldn't hear. Whatever he said seemed to enrage Colin further and before she had the time to close her eyes, he sliced his blade across the man's throat.

She couldn't move. She couldn't breathe, watching him. She'd never seen a man so beautifully lethal, so much more dangerous than when he fought against George. Where had he learned to fight with such skill? It terrified her and excited her at the same time.

She breathed, and then stopped again when Colin dropped his blade and ran to her.

"Are ye hurt?" he asked her, reaching to take Edmund from her arms. Whatever beast his fury had unleashed only moments ago was gone, and in its place stood a man whose fingers trembled as they brushed over her son's head. "Are ye hurt, lad? Here, let me have a look at ye." He held Edmund at arm's length and examined him from foot to crown.

"Are they gone, Colin?" Edmund wiped his eyes with his fists and waited while Colin nodded his head and swallowed back a well of emotions no warrior of his caliber was likely accustomed to expressing.

A movement from within the trees propelled Gillian to Colin's side; Colin pressed Edmund close to his chest and produced a pistol from his belt that he held cocked and ready to fire.

George emerged slowly, holding up his hands. He must have witnessed the quick massacre because the color had drained from his face and had not yet returned.

"Who the hell are they?" he asked, eyeing the scattered dead.

"Thieves," Colin told him, swinging Edmund around to his back rather than return him to Gillian. "Let's get back." He retrieved his sword without another word to any of them, then led them back to Kingswear.

"Thank you, Colin," Gillian said quietly while they walked. She didn't realize her teeth were chattering or that her hands were shaking until he looked at her and then swung his arm around her shoulder and pulled her closer.

"'Tis over, lass," he comforted tenderly, though his voice sounded as shaky as hers. "But ye will stay close to us from now on, aye?"

She nodded, pressing her face deeper into his shoulder. He'd saved Edmund from certain death. Oh, dear God, what kind of monster would kill a child? Her knees nearly buckled beneath her at the thought of what would have happened if Colin hadn't been there.

"I'm all right," she hastened to assure both him and George when they offered to carry her. She needed to walk off the hysteria lurking beneath her somewhat calm exterior. She looked up at Edmund and felt a rush of tears fall from her eyes at the way he clung to Colin, his little arms wrapped tightly around his friend's neck.

Colin had slaughtered those who would hurt him. The memory of it would haunt her dreams for years to come. She would never forget the fear in his eyes, the fury, and then the sheer relief when he knew her son was safe.

"I was wrong to be angry with you," she told him, trying with all her strength not to fling her arms around his neck and hold him the way Edmund did. "Forgive me."

He looked at her, and for a moment, nothing else existed in the world but him. Every hard angle of his face softened with something that clutched at her heart. He smiled slightly, then ran his palm down the back of her head. A comforting, intimate touch that made them both catch their breath and left them longing for something more.

Chapter Twenty-four

Colin sat by Gillian's bed and watched Edmund while he slept. His mother had insisted the babe sleep where she could see him, hear him if he needed her. Colin thought 'twas a good idea. He would be happy never to have Edmund out of his sight again.

He listened to the muffled voices coming from the sitting room, but did not join Gillian or Gates right away. He'd never felt fear like he'd experienced today. He never wanted to feel it again. When he couldn't find them... when he heard her screams...Och, God, he'd nearly gone mad trying to find them. And when he did...He rubbed his palm down his face, fighting the fury renewed by the memory of what he'd seen. A blade held to Edmund's wee throat. A look of terrible horror on Gillian's face that he never wanted to see her wear again.

Still, such a memory was better than the alternative. He shook his head to scatter the images of what he would have come upon if he'd arrived just a few moments later. They would have killed Edmund, and his mother after that, and Colin knew why. He still couldn't believe it though. And he couldn't tell the two waiting for him in the next room.

"General MacGregor." The last attacker had known him. He'd known Colin's name. *"The king ordered it. He sends a message..."*

Colin hadn't waited to hear what the message was and ended his miserable life quickly. Too damned quickly.

The king, *his* king, had ordered the death of a mother and her child. Why? He'd been agonizing over the answer since their return to Dartmouth. He would have refused to believe it if he hadn't recently killed the proof. Closing his eyes, he ground his teeth until his jaw pained him. He wanted to ride to Whitehall Palace tonight, smash open the door to the king's solar, and hurl him out the window. Whatever the reason James wanted them dead, he wouldn't have known they resided here if Colin hadn't told the first runner that he wanted safe passage for them.

He'd put them in danger. Today was his fault.

He cursed quietly in the dimly lit room and rose to pace before the bed. Everything he believed in and fought to protect had changed in the ephemeral span of an instant. He'd been stripped of his weapons, his purpose, and left on the battlefield, bewildered and lost. How could he serve a king who would attempt such a thing? Why, James was no better than the man who'd massacred an abbey full of nuns and set Colin's course against him three years ago. What was he to do now? Continue to fight for a man who'd allowed power to turn him into a merciless monster?

"Colin?"

He opened his eyes and leaned down closer to Edmund. "Aye, lad?"

"I had a bad dream."

"So did I. But 'tis over now. I'm here with ye."

"Will you stay with me and Mummy and neber go away?"

"Never."

"Colin?"

"Aye, Edmund?"

"I love you."

"I love ye too, lad."

Och, hell, was this what love did to a man? Did it make his chest spasm, his heart twist and wrench into a mangled mess? He was as helpless against it as he was about thinking of the lad's mother. He looked up at her now, standing beside him. When had she appeared? How much had she heard?

"Mummy, I had a bad dream, but it's over now."

She smiled at her son and leaned down to kiss his flaxen head. "Go to sleep, darling. Colin and I will be in the next room."

She straightened and turned to Colin with gloriously large glistening eyes.

He rose to stand before her and touched his thumb to a tear about to fall from her eyelid. "Dinna' be frightened, lass," he said softly. "All will be well from here on in."

She flung her arms around his neck and buried her face in his shoulder. "You're a good man, Colin. I'm glad you're here with us."

He held her for a time, not really knowing what to say in return. She had bigger enemies than Geoffrey Dearly, Earl of Devon. For some reason King James wanted her dead. He had to get her out of here, and fast.

"I heard what you told him."

Colin felt the gratitude in her voice deep in his bones. He tightened his arms around her, breathing in the delicate scent of her, rubbing his cheek against her silky waves.

"I trust you. I..." She angled her face toward his, her nose brushing softly against his chin. "I can't seem to..."

Bending his head to her, he pressed his mouth to hers and kissed her warm, moist lips. "Nor can I." He wanted to kiss her for ten lifetimes. Slow, meaningful kisses that told her things he didn't know how to say. Things he never thought he would care to utter. The thought of those men hurting her tempted him to kill in a blind rage he feared he could not control.

"Mummy, are you kissing Colin?"

They broke away and smiled at each other. Gillian's softly flushed cheeks made him want to kiss her again and again.

"Go to sleep, my love," she told Edmund, then took Colin's hand. "Come, George would have words with you."

"Wait." Colin pulled her back. "There is something I would have ye know. I learned what Devon had done with yer letters the night I met ye in the turrets. I know what that correspondence meant to ye, and I didn't know how to tell ye the truth. 'Twas cowardly of me."

"No..."

"Aye," he corrected, holding her fingers to his lips. "Better ye had learned of it in the comfort of my arms than in the presence of Devon's unholy humor."

She stared at him, still and silent. And in the flickering light her eyes shone with tears that finally fell. "You're correct. I would have preferred to learn the truth in your arms. Everything I tried to do for Edmund was for nothing. I failed him."

He pulled her in and held her close. She'd risked much and with good cause. It made him want to fight for her, kill for her—he looked toward the bed—for him. Could he denounce the king and give up his war? He felt her tears soak his shirt and held her away to look into her eyes.

"Gillian," he whispered, stroking the back of his knuckles tenderly across her cheek. "Ye told me that I conquer monsters with a magic dagger, but ye, lass, ye fight them with a quill. Remember that when this pain passes. Remember, too, that we can't win the war without an army at our back...or in yer case, me."

She smiled with him and swiped her cheeks dry. Hell, her strength moved him. He would help her. He would be her champion. He was all she had left. His heart would let him do nothing else.

"I can get ye away from here, lass. And I don't plan on letting anyone stop me."

She ran her fingers over his lips and looked him deeply in the eyes. "I would be forever grateful, Mr. Campbell." Taking his hand, she pulled him forward. "Come, George awaits. Let us discuss this together."

Colin followed her out of the bed chamber, grateful for the distraction that talk of rescuing her and her son provided from what plagued his inner thoughts: the treason he felt brewing in his guts for a king who was once his friend. He'd killed for Gillian and Edmund today and he would kill many more if their enemies pursued them. But what would he do if James tried to have her killed again?

He couldn't think on it now. There were other matters to discuss.

When Gillian sat beside Gates on the settee, her captain noted her puffy eyes and pink nose and patted her hand. She'd almost lost her child today. Gates tossed him his thousandth thankful look of the day.

"You spoke of bringing Edmund to your family in Glen Orchy."

How much should he tell them? Would they still trust him after they learned that he was a MacGregor? A spy for the king who had ordered men to kill her? And what about Skye? 'Twas a considerable distance from Glen Orchy. What if Gillian refused to let her son be taken by savage Highlanders who hid in the misty mountains of the north?

"He would be safe. I vow it."

"But how will you get Geoffrey to agree to let him go?" Gillian asked him.

An easier question to answer, but Colin doubted she would be pleased with his reply. "Ye must trust me fer this."

"I do."

He drew in a long breath and let it out slowly. "Ye believe yer cousin was behind today's attack because those men wanted to kill Edmund. I tell ye, Devon had nothing to do with it. True, he would have rejoiced if we had told him how close Edmund had come to..." He couldn't finish the thought aloud. "Yer cousin wants ye, but he doesn't want ye plotting his demise each night before bed. I have promised him everything he desires."

"Me?"

"Aye, lass," he told her truthfully. "Ye in his bed. Grateful to be there."

She closed her eyes and looked a wee bit ill. "The only way he would ever find me grateful to be in his bed is if I were lying there dead."

Colin smiled, enjoying the spark of fire in her eyes. "He wants yer undivided adoration and the only way to get it is to remove Edmund. I merely suggested a way for him to go about it without any blame on his hands. He wasted no time agreeing to it."

"That still doesn't guarantee that he will send the boy off with your family," the captain pointed out.

"He will if Lady Gillian is not entirely opposed to seeing her son go."

"He will never believe such a thing," she told him. "I would never send Edmund off with strangers."

"Ye're not going to. Ye'll be sending him off with Captain Gates fer a visit with his wife in Essex. We will deceive ye into believing that 'tis a temporary arrangement. One that is safer fer Edmund, what with the prince arriving fer war. Ye will agree, though not without the fight he will expect from ye. Ye will not suspect that he and I arranged fer my cousin in Argyll to arrive and take him. Ye will be heartbroken when ye return without yer son, but ye will not hold Devon to fault."

"He will agree to that, Campbell, you clever bastard," Gates finally acknowledged, then turned to Gillian. "He will agree. Edmund could leave here safely."

She nodded and looked at Colin. "Why can I not go with him to your family's home?"

Colin knew the thought of Edmund being taken from her was difficult. It had to be this way, but he wanted her to understand why.

"My kin cannot cross the whole length of England with an entire garrison at their backs without raising more than eyebrows. Their band will be small and they will travel unnoticed and leave the same way. If ye go with them, yer cousin will send both Dartmouth's and Kingswear's garrison, and possibly yer father's after ye. None of ye would likely escape alive." He let the full meaning of his words sink true…precisely, what they meant for Edmund. "'Tis safer this way. But I will reunite ye. Ye have my vow on that."

He wanted to bring her home. He wanted to see her face when she looked upon Camlochlin for the first time, breathless at its splendor. When she realized that nothing could touch her or her son within the impenetrable walls of his father's stronghold. But how would he get her there and return himself to Dartmouth before the prince landed on England's shores? He had to return to fight. Didn't he? No matter what King James had become, William of Orange would be worse for the people of the Highlands.

"Geoffrey will not let me leave once Edmund is gone."

She was right, and he couldn't take the chance of having an army follow him to Camlochlin. He would have to wait until Devon was either dead or taken prisoner before he could get her out. "He will not have a choice," Colin promised her. He didn't want her here a moment longer than she needed to be, but he would figure something out later. At least, with Edmund gone, she would no longer need to cower to her cousin.

"Ye both have an important role to play in this. Can ye do it?"

Gillian nodded. Gates did not.

"What will become of them in Argyll?" he asked, making certain every detail was scrutinized before he agreed to this. Damn him. "Why would the Campbells continue to protect her once William is king? Have you thought this fully through, Colin? I know you care for them as I do, and I'm grateful for it, but I cannot—"

"Captain," Colin cut him off in a firm voice, "my kin will protect her no matter who sits on the throne."

"They are Campbells," Gates persisted. "Other than yourself, I don't trust them."

Colin regarded him for a moment. His father would like this man.

"I need something more from you," the captain forged on. "You fight like a bloody barbarian, and an extremely effective one at that. What I saw today was not the skill of a mercenary, but of something more. Why would King James ever let such a warrior leave his service? Who taught you to fight the way you do? I want answers. I want the truth."

Colin sat back in his chair and wished for a cup of the strongest Highland whisky he could find—so he could feed it to Gates and dull his wits. But hell, the man was doing his duty, and doing it well. Colin couldn't fault him for that. Especially not when it came to Gillian.

His eyes fell on her, looking dreadfully anxious, await-ing his reply. He didn't want to lie straight to her face. But he'd never told this truth to anyone. For three years he'd lived as someone else…a servant to a king he'd stopped respecting long ago. But everything had changed today. If he hadn't traveled with them to Kingswear…

He couldn't think of it, but was he willing to reveal his true identity and risk everything in exchange for Gillian's and Edmund's safety?

"My faither taught me how to fight. I am…" He paused and shifted in his seat, clinging to the deception he'd used to survive and become one of England's most unknown spies. 'Twas difficult, letting go of one of his secrets. The most difficult thing he'd ever done. "My mother is a Campbell. My faither is not."

The room was quiet. Colin could hear them breath-ing. He could almost hear the questions forming in their minds.

"Who is he then?" Gates finally asked him.

Colin looked at him and let out a gusty breath that he felt he'd been holding for centuries. "He is a MacGregor."

The captain's mouth fell open. Gillian studied them both with confusion marring her brow. "I don't understand," she said. "Why would you lie about being a—"

"MacGregor," her captain interrupted, terror and concern vying for dominance over his normally composed features. "What the hell are you doing here, MacGregor?"

A question Colin feared he would be asking himself in the days to come. He couldn't tell them the truth, that he was a general in the king's army. 'Twas one thing to be a MacGregor mercenary, quite another to be a leader of the Catholic king's army. Gates might be here solely to protect Gillian, but would he turn the other cheek if he knew what Colin's true purpose was at Dartmouth? Would Gillian forgive him for deceiving her once again?

Colin wouldn't risk discovering the answer.

"I'm a mercenary, Captain. I need the coin. Would ye have hired me if ye knew my true name?"

"I would have words with you alone."

"And I would have my words never leave this room. My kin are still looked upon poorly and if Devon discovers that I'm not a Campbell—"

"Dear God," the captain breathed, obviously not believing a word he'd just said.

'Twas not difficult to piece together the truth of what he was doing here when one knew that the MacGregors were Catholic. He was their enemy. His gaze slipped to Gillian, praying that she knew little about where Highlanders stood when it came to God.

"Tell me what is going on," she demanded, proving that she didn't know much.

Colin almost sighed out loud with relief. He didn't

want her to know the full truth of it yet. He was James's snake, sent here the deceive them all and kill the man she'd been awaiting for three years...the man who would solve all of Protestant England's troubles. She would never trust him again. Mayhap she would refuse to let him help her.

"Who are the MacGregors?"

Colin eyed the captain, probably more nervously than he'd ever appeared before. Hell, he'd never had this much to lose before.

"They are a notoriously savage clan of Highlanders," the captain told her.

Colin didn't know why the captain did it, but he passed Gates a brief, appreciative nod just the same.

"How savage?" Gillian asked, twisting the skirt in her lap into knots.

"Enough for a king to proscribe them almost to the point of extinction."

Colin straightened his shoulders, recalling the strength of his clan to survive their history and with pride at being one of them.

"And you would trust Edmund with these people?" Gillian challenged, turning to him.

"They are not—"

"You told me," Gates interrupted, apparently not finished with his interrogation, "that you could protect her with an army more fearsome than anything in England or Holland. There are not many MacGregors left in Glen Orchy, and those who remain are scattered from east to west. What army did you speak of?"

Colin wouldn't kill him. After all, Gates had refrained from telling her the truth. But hell, this was what happened when one was as ill prepared as he was for confessions. They opened doors to more questions. "My kin come from farther north."

"How far?"

Colin scowled at Gillian when she spoke, then cleared his throat. "Quite far." Damnation, she was never going to agree to this now. But he couldn't give up. He never had before. When he made up his mind to do something, he always got it done. And he was getting her and Edmund out of here. But first, he had to convince her that he could. "That is why I sent my kin a missive three nights ago, and why I will not move forward for at least another se'nnight. We need time."

"How far?" Gates repeated her question.

"Skye," he confessed, hoping at least to firmly convince the captain that no one would ever find them.

"Where is—"

"Are you telling me that you're kin to the Devil MacGregor?" Gates gaped at him.

"'Twas a name given to him long ago," Colin tried to reassure Gillian when she looked about to spring from her seat to protect her son against him. "No one has called my faither that in over a score years."

"Your father?"

Hell. Colin closed his eyes when Gates sprang from his seat instead.

"The man is your father?"

"We are getting ahead of things here." Colin held up his palms and smiled, doing his best to calm them both. "Please, let us discuss the plan."

"What other shocking revelations do you have to share, MacGregor? What are you doing here? You will tell me the truth."

"Campbell," Colin corrected him with a steely-eyed

stare. "Ye must remember to call me that. As fer revelations, there is only one more. I consider ye my friend—and I am not the kind of man who so considers many."

That seemed to take the wind from Gates's sails. For the first time that night, Colin was glad for the captain's perceptive intelligence. He knew Colin was sincere, and he understood why.

"There are not many to be had. But I will still have words with you alone."

"Nae, there are not," Colin agreed and smiled at him when he sat back down. "And I will be happy to answer each of yer queries when this is all over. Fer now, I ask ye again to trust me."

When Gates nodded, he turned to Gillian, wanting to ease her trepidation. He realized that what he meant to tell her, he hadn't spoken to a soul in three years, when he spoke them to the king. "Captain Gates speaks true about my kin. Our history is a long and brutal one, but 'twas not always by our hands." Telling her felt better than he'd expected, mostly because while his siblings spent hours listening to their mother's tales of legends, he spent his time watching and learning from his father. "My faither escaped the dungeons of my great-grandsire and fled to Skye, where he built Camlochlin, deep in the mountains, enshrouded in mist. A safe haven fer any man, woman, or child who bore their name proudly. He brought war to many, but the proscription is over and we live peacefully now, with laughter and children filling the hills."

Satisfied by Gillian's wistful smile that she needed no further convincing, he turned back to Gates. "Whatever else ye want to know about me, be convinced of this: the lady and her son weigh heavily on me. I want to help them. I vow to ye that they will be safe. My faither is distrustful by nature. There are only two ways into Camlochlin on foot, and one way by water. The battlements are continuously patrolled with guards and cannons facing east, west, and south."

"You have no enemies in the north?"

"Nae, we have a mountain behind us. 'Tis called Sgurr na Stri."

Gillian repeated the Gaelic name, liking the sound of it on her lips, if her smile was any indication.

Colin liked it as well. He described the way the mist rolled down from the Cuillins and how the lavender heather glistened and danced on the moors.

He missed being home. He missed the crisp air and the harsh mountain ranges, the sounds of his father and brothers clashing swords in the practice field.

"Edmund will have to learn how to swim. The children often play in the bay outside the castle."

"He will love it," Gillian said, her eyes closed to see more clearly the world he described.

"Aye," he agreed, watching her and imagining her sewing and giggling with his mother and the other women of the castle. "Ye both will."

She opened her eyes and granted him a smile he feared would someday tempt him to learn how to pick flowers.

"Then tell me again what I must do to deceive Geoffrey and let us be about this, Colin Campbell."

Chapter Twenty-five

Gillian pressed her back to the rocky wall along the coastline and clutched Edmund to her side. She was proud of her son for keeping silent. It also gave her time to think of the man they were hiding from.

She was fairly certain she had fallen in love with Colin MacGregor over the past se'nnight. It scared the blazes out of her. She knew every possible consequence that could come from it. She'd lived and survived the betrayal of it. She never wanted to endure such misery again. But she couldn't stop it from happening. Colin was not just her angel, her champion, her friend. He loved Edmund. Lord, but it was so evident in his eyes, his tender, unguarded smile. He'd spent most of his time with them over the past eight days, giving up his hours in the practice yard for angling, catching frogs, and teaching Edmund how to fashion a ball out of cloth so they could then throw it to each other.

He made her feel alive and vibrant again, even behind the thick stone walls of her prison. He made her forget William of Orange and her cousin's promises to wed her.

Geoffrey didn't suspect their growing fondness for each other, despite the time she spent with Colin. After all, he'd assigned Colin to guarding her. It was Colin's duty to follow her and Edmund around, just as it had been George's duty.

That didn't make their attraction to each other any less dangerous. She'd never wanted to kiss George while she was pretending to dislike him.

The crunch of a boot walking on sand behind her quickened her heart and she smiled down at Edmund, holding her finger to her lips.

"Where could they be?" Colin called out.

Edmund giggled into her skirts.

An instant passed in absolute silence, and then another. She was about to take a peek around the rock to see if Colin had given up seeking them, when he appeared on the other side of her.

"Aha!"

Edmund squealed with delight and Colin picked him up and tossed him into the air. "I found ye both," he said over her son's laughter, holding him comfortably in the crook of his arm.

"I prayed that you would."

He leaned in closer to her and she smiled at Edmund to keep her gaze off the stubble defining the broad angle of Colin's jaw, the exquisite shape of his mouth.

"Did ye now?"

His breath along her ear drew her eyes back to his. "Aye," she told him without pretense. She wanted him to know what he meant to her. She wanted him to promise never to leave her. "I did, for a very long time."

His lips curled and swept over hers—a brief, titillating touch that rattled her senseless.

"Is it our turn to count?"

Colin stared into her eyes long enough to let her know that he wasn't done with this. Then he turned to Edmund and cocked his brow at him.

"Ye know how to count then?"

"One, two, three!" Edmund proved exuberantly.

"Then what are we waiting fer?" Colin put him down and asked him to count slowly as Gillian turned with Edmund to begin.

She heard Colin slip behind the rock wall they were counting from. It was as far as he could get in the little bit of time he had. She smiled and let herself fall as madly, as recklessly, in love with him as any damned fool could get as she ran off with Edmund in the opposite direction to seek him.

They returned an hour late, giving her little time to tend to Edmund before supper. Colin's promise to handle her cousin didn't soothe George's temper, but Gillian guessed her captain was still smarting over being replaced as her escort. Poor George. Geoffrey kept him busy with menial chores that the captain would never have agreed to perform if not for Colin's plan. But he'd done them . . . for her, and she loved him for it.

When they parted, she shut the door to Edmund's room and leaned against it with a wistful sigh. Lord, who would have ever thought supper in the Great Hall with Geoffrey and his men would cease to become her least favorite part of the day? Colin made it bearable. They barely shared a word during their meals, but the secret smiles they exchanged while Geoffrey pawed at the female servers gave new life to her dreams.

Was she dreaming now? Was it truly possible that

she and Edmund were going to leave Dartmouth? Could she still have the life she dreamed about? One where she was free to make her own choices? To come and go as she pleased? Where no one called Edmund a bastard or threatened to take him away? What would it be like in the mountains with a band of notorious Highlanders? Would she want to remain there? Would Colin stay with her? After tonight, how much longer would she have Edmund in her arms before he was taken away?

She thought about it all while she bathed her son and kissed his wet curls. She had to do this. She had to trust Colin. There was no other choice. Edmund would love it in Skye if the MacGregors were anything like Colin. MacGregor. She liked the sound of it, but according to Colin, most scorned it. That was why he had come here as a Campbell. He explained it all to her the day after the attack, while they sat on the rocks waiting for a fish to bite. Gillian had had a hard time believing the details of the proscription he'd described to her. Women branded on the face, their rights stripped bare, their name outlawed.

And the English thought the Scots barbaric?

The MacGregors of Skye didn't frighten her. She was as yet undecided about the cold, harsh mountains though.

"Would you like other children to play with, Edmund?" she asked him, carrying him to his bed and setting his feet on the mattress.

"What other children?"

Would they like him? Would they think him odd because he didn't know any games to play?

"No one, darling." She smiled and helped him into his nightclothes.

"Do they have puppies?"

"They have puppies, sheep, and even chickens."

Gillian swung around, startled to see Colin standing at the door, carrying a tray of food in his hand. She hadn't heard him enter.

"They have an old barn filled with ducks, pigs, and cats. Lots of cats," he told Edmund, coming toward the bed.

"And these cats don't harm the ducks?" Gillian looked up at his profile and felt her limbs go weak when he turned and winked at her.

"They would not dare fer fear of their caretaker's wrath."

"I will like those other children!" Edmund clapped his hands, pulling their gazes back to him.

"We will speak more of them tomorrow, lad," Colin said, taking his hand and swinging Edmund off the bed. "Now 'tis time fer yer supper and then fer yer mother to read to ye before ye set about on yer dreaming adventures."

Gillian frowned, following them to the table. "There won't be time for a story."

"A brief one won't hurt." Colin lifted Edmund into his seat and then turned around to smile at her. "I'll see to it."

And he would. Gillian imagined that he could see to just about anything. She wouldn't worry. For once, she trusted that she didn't have to. "Very well, a brief one then after supper."

She skirted him and headed toward the bookcase before she flung herself into his arms. Heavens—she thought of fanning her hand before her face while she scoured the shelf that was level with her gaze—she'd become the kind of fool she detested and feared. Only this time, she wasn't afraid.

How could she not surrender her heart to a man who patiently answered the dozen questions Edmund put to him while her son ate? A warrior who stood silently while she read from Chaucer, holding her breathless with the tenderest quirk of his mouth when she looked up at him from time to time. He waited while she tucked her babe in his bed and kissed him good eve, and then offered her his arm as he led her to the Hall.

"Remember to revile me in Devon's presence tonight."

She closed her eyes and drew in a deep sigh. "It will be difficult."

When she opened her eyes again, his smile scattered her fears to the four winds.

"Truly, Colin, you must cease doing that."

"What?"

"Smiling. How can I pretend to dislike you when you are looking at me like that?"

"How am I looking at ye?" He laughed softly and clasped his free hand behind his back while they walked.

She moved a breath closer to him. "Like you don't dislike me."

His grin went soft but did not falter. "I will stop when I need to."

"What if I cannot?" She paused, unsure if she could continue to master her emotions as easily as he did. She could barely mask them when she was angry with Geoffrey. What if Colin smiled at her in the middle of flying bread and swinging elbows and she smiled back like some lovesick fool? She would ruin everything.

"Ye'll do it, lass," he soothed, slipping his fingers through hers. "'Tis but a game, and no matter how ye play it, I will not let ye lose."

Was he jesting? How was she *not* supposed to swoon over such chivalry? And those fathomless eyes searing into her, sweeping her away to a forest saturated in the sunlight of a quiet afternoon where only the three of them existed.

She wanted her choices returned to her. She wanted to spend more time with Colin without fear of discovery, and she wanted Edmund to share his life with him too. She didn't doubt Colin's promise, but she wouldn't rely on it alone. "I won't let me lose either."

Gillian wasn't completely certain she could do it, but when they stepped through the doors and entered the Great Hall, her features went as hard as Colin's when she saw de Atre sitting close to her cousin at the table.

"Ah," Geoffrey called out when he saw them, "the whore who thinks she's a queen decides to grace us with her presence."

De Atre smiled and then flinched when he remembered that his mouth was still healing.

"If this frosty maiden is what ye call whore," Colin said, stepping away from her and around the table to take his seat, "then 'tis quite clear my lord has never enjoyed the pleasures of one."

Gillian didn't look up while she sat, but basked silently in the way Colin had defended her and insulted Geoffrey at the same time.

Her cousin didn't take the blow well, especially when a few of his men laughed at him. But as he opened his mouth to defend himself, Colin set down his cup and offered him his sincerest smile.

"I know quite a few who would bend over backward fer an hour with a distinguished earl such as yerself."

My, but he certainly knew how to restore himself to the good graces of his enemy, Gillian thought when

Geoffrey forgot the insult and curled his tight lips into a lewd grin.

"Do you think they would be willing to teach my future bride how to please me?"

Gillian wanted to hurl her plate at her cousin, and then her cup at Colin for the convincing display of camaraderie between them when he laughed.

"Fer the right amount of coin they will direct yer wedding night from the bedside, or in it. Whichever ye prefer."

Beneath the table, Gillian twisted her serviette into a tight knot. She didn't know what was worse, imagining herself in Geoffrey's bed or a whore in Colin's. Both made her feel ill and angry. She had no claim on the mercenary. He never said he would stay with her in his Highland home. What if there was a woman there who possessed his heart...or more than one? She looked at him—quite boldly too, unconcerned with what her cousin thought about it.

"Mr. Campbell," she said, quieting the men around her and dragging Colin's casual gaze to her, "it is difficult enough having to spend my days with you. Do you think you could save this crude topic for a more private audience with your lord?"

Only because she'd spent nearly every moment in his company, enthralled by every nuance of his expressions— as subtle as they often were—did she recognize the playful tip of his mouth and the flecks of gold in his eyes bursting with fire when he settled them on her.

"I could if ye pretend to enjoy my company more."

The game had begun. She almost smiled, but didn't. She would not fail Edmund, or him. He wanted her to revile him, did he?

"Then please, do go on," she said with enough cool contempt to send a chill down the back of every man at the table.

"Screw her sensitive ears," de Atre murmured, trying to position his cup around his sutured lips.

"More sensitive than your mouth, de Atre," George growled at him. "But that can be remedied."

"Don't bother slicing off his nose next." Colin swerved the topic away from whores with a tip of his cup and a murderous slant of his mouth. "He cannot smell himself with it right there on his face."

The brutish Mr. Hampton smacked Colin on the back and roared with laughter, and the conversations proceeded, as they always did, to fighting and whoring.

Thankfully, it didn't take long for her cousin to grow bored with her company. In fact, he looked painfully dulled by everyone around him. He yawned and set off a linked reaction from every man at the table. Almost every man.

Colin, she noted, fighting everything in her being to keep from smiling at him, pulsed with vitality as he looked up at a server about to refill his cup and refused the offer.

Chapter Twenty-six

"Where are we going?" Gillian laughed as Colin pulled her by the hand over rocky crags and down slippery crevices.

"Ye'll see."

In truth, she was only mildly curious about their destination. She was happy to be out of the castle, thrilled by the wind snapping her hair behind her and the smell of the sea, crisp and briny, coming in from the estuary. She knew she should be anxious about Colin's confession to spiking the wine, and Geoffrey waking in his bed in the morning with no memory of how he'd gotten there. Poor George. He was going to be angry. Thankfully, the most the men would suffer was a pounding skull when they woke from their slumber.

"I wanted ye to myself tonight," Colin had told her when she questioned him about why he'd rendered Dartmouth's entire garrison powerless. She would think about what an effective, calculating warrior he was tomorrow. Tonight, she would enjoy her time with him without fear of discovery.

They ran along the rocky coastline, beneath the silvery luminance of the moon, and for a short, exhilarating time, Gillian pretended that they were running away to Camlochlin, running toward Edmund, and freedom, and happiness.

By the time they finally slowed, the coastline had changed slightly with the cliff wall rising higher before them.

"Can ye climb?"

She nodded, breathless by the journey and the raw vigor exuding off Colin in waves. The man possessed stamina that wilted the strength from her kneecaps and made her doubt her claim.

She must have looked about to collapse at his feet, because he swooped down and lifted her in his arms to carry her the rest of the way. She should insist that he put her down, bring her back to the castle, and deposit her alone in her bed. Both Geoffrey *and* George would kill him if they knew he'd taken her away in the cover of night to…She let out a slight gasp when he stopped at the entrance of a cave overlooking the estuary. Light and shadows flickered along the jagged walls from the small, dying fire just beyond the entrance. Her face went hot when her eyes settled on the intimate pile of blankets keeping warm beside the flames. When had he found the time to do all this?

"I thought ye would like it here." His voice was thick with tenderness when he set her on her feet.

"I do, but how did you know I would come?"

He turned her around on the precipice edge to look out at the pewter waves meeting the starry sky. "Because ye fancy dreaming, lass, and the view is better from this angle."

Heaven help her, but yes, she dreamed. She'd never stopped. Through it all, she'd never stopped hearing music on the waves and in the wind. She'd never stopped dreaming of the profound. And here it was. If she wasn't already in love with Colin MacGregor, she would have fallen in love with him then and there for seeing the part of herself she tried so hard to hide. (It proved he had been looking.) And for the care he took in finding this perfect place to take her.

"Am I dreaming now?" she asked, turning to face him.

He was close enough to slip his arm around her waist and draw her closer, until her lips dangled beneath his. "Mayhap we both are." Caressing her cheek, he dipped his mouth to hers.

She sighed into him, savoring the supple yield of his lips and the power in his arms to subdue her so gently. He tasted of spice and desire, and she basked in the sensual stroke of his tongue, the scent of him, the feel of being held with no barriers between them. He took his time kissing her, pausing to smile at her as if he too could hardly believe they had the entire night to spend alone.

He'd planned it all, the cave, the fire, the blankets... all to be with her. But there were consequences to this. As much as she loved Edmund, giving him a sibling now would destroy everything she wanted for him. "Colin, what if...?" She pushed her palms against his chest and broke their kiss.

"Lass," he breathed against her temple when she turned her face away. "I won't be careless with ye." When she looked up at him, his decadent mouth curled into a slow, confident smile. "Trust me."

What fool wouldn't? Every ravishing inch of him exemplified virility in its rawest form. She might be as mad as a hermit, but she trusted him completely, even letting him carry her to the blankets and lay her down on them.

"Ye're smiling, lass."

She looked up at his face poised above her when he joined her on the blanket. "I seem to do that more frequently when in your company."

His smile was sensuous and genuine, searing her nerve endings and making the air hot and thick. "Such things please my ears." His gaze moved over her face, taking in every angle, every nuance, and treasuring what he saw. "I want to hear yer laughter filling the hills. Yers and Edmund's."

She wanted to kiss him, to move him, to claim his heart and run away with him. For now, she would be happy kissing him. She didn't close her eyes when he bent to do as she willed, but watched him come closer, their gazes locked and dusky with anticipation.

Gillian didn't know what drove her madder with desire for him, the intensity of his kiss or the tenderness of his hand moving over her face. He did both as if driven by a need to know her more intimately. When he dragged his mouth to her throat, his coarse jaw scraped her skin and lit her flesh on fire. Neither of the two nights she'd spent with Reggie had felt like this. Colin was a completely different animal, groaning like a hard, lithe leopard while he moved over her, wedging himself between her thighs. He kissed a scorching path down the valley between her breasts, growing tighter in his breeches, as stiff and as hot as newly forged steel against her.

When his hungry mouth found her nipple, he sucked her through the fabric of her gown. She groaned and surged up against his arousal. He bit down around her bud and she gasped, growing wet under him. Instinctively, her legs opened wider, inviting him deeper, tempting him like some lust-starved siren to have his way with her and damn the consequences. He rubbed his confined erection against her crux in a long, slow surge that boasted his size and made her body tremble and her muscles spasm.

She felt his fingers drawing the hem of her skirt up over her knees and then her thighs, and for an instant she feared he would take her. And she would let him. Oh, hell, yes, she would let him. But instead of releasing that glorious beast on her when he exposed her to the flickering light, he licked two of his fingers and rubbed them over her engorged nub. She cried out, arching her spine and finding his weight there above her. He stroked her and dipped inside her until his fingers glided easily from the moisture drenching them.

Her readiness seemed to stir him to madness and he rose up on his knees, lifting her ankle with him. She watched, breath held, heart drumming madly, as his eyes roved up her bare thigh and settled on her glistening center.

His intention dawned on her an instant after he bent his face to taste her there. "Colin," she breathed on a ragged moan while his tongue flicked over her again and again, tightening her until it became almost painful. Pure, raw ecstasy set fire to her blood, and she pushed against his hungry mouth. He answered her plea for something more by closing his lips around her and sucking gently.

Wanton, wicked desires coursed through Gillian such as she'd never known before. Shamelessly, she clung to him, raking her hands through his hair, drawing him close to taste her more fully. She guided his head over her with long, languorous groans, lifting and undulating her hips to take his tongue deeper when he drove it inside her.

Her cries echoed off the jagged walls as she came in his mouth, panting with pleasure, rocking against him as wave after wave swept her away to a place she'd never been.

When it was over, Gillian could barely move. Spent and breathless, she watched him rise to his feet and make his way to the entrance. With his back to her, he worked the laces of his breeches and finally freed himself in the direction of the ocean. She knew what he was doing, but when he turned slightly to have a look at her lying weakly where he left her, he afforded her a view of his flat belly and his hand working the thick shaft of his cock. The sight and size of it silhouetted against the pale moon, and the way he looked at her while he pleasured himself, sent brand-new fissures of heat shooting through her. How could any man look so fit and strong even as he went down on one knee, spilling his seed all over the cave floor?

When he returned to her, tucking himself back into his breeches, she had to bite her lip and look away to keep from inviting him to tear off her gown and make love to her until the morning came. She had no doubt he could accomplish such a feat. But he wouldn't do it. He'd kept his promise, as tremendously difficult as it had been for him. He hadn't been careless with her. It made her want him even more.

But they had to return to the castle. For despite what Colin had done to the wine and the men, Edmund was still inside Dartmouth without her. She'd never been this far from him, for this long. Lord, how was she ever going to send him off to Skye?

She voiced her concerns to Colin as they walked back along the shoreline and he did all to comfort her, promising that she would not be separated from her son for too long. She nodded, praying to God that she was doing the right thing. What choice did she have? At least escaping to Skye would give her time to pen new missives to William. Perhaps, after he witnessed the ferocity of Colin's blade and the dedication to see him on the throne, the Dutch prince might even agree to allow her to wed Colin and remain with him in Skye.

With that thought giving new hope to her heart, she turned and clung to Colin one last time before Dartmouth came into view.

"When, Colin? When will this all end?"

He kissed the top of her head and then released her as he entered the fortress. "We leave fer Essex within the se'nnight, lass. Hold fast."

She promised she would and let him escort her back to her room. She didn't remain inside after he left her, but grabbed her lute and raced up to the turrets. A new song filled her heart and as everyone around her slept, she filled the night with the sound of it.

❖

Chapter Twenty-seven

The next several days were the best Gillian had ever spent at Dartmouth. The nights were even better. She met Colin on the turret stairs every night at midnight. He never disturbed her while she played her lute, preferring, he told her, to listen without distraction.

"It soothes the darker part of me," he'd whispered across her cheek a few nights ago.

"I don't fear that part of you, Colin."

"Nor shall ye ever."

"But I might"—she'd kissed him boldly on the mouth—"like to see that side of you from time to time."

After that, she played a few less *soothing* tunes and found herself snatched out of the light and hauled against his hard body.

She smiled now on her way to Essex...on a horse. She hadn't ridden one in years and her backside was killing her. But what was a sore arse compared with leaving Dartmouth? Colin had done it. He'd played Geoffrey like a master of strings, tactically outwitted him like a general of an elite force. She had also played her part well, refusing to let Edmund leave Dartmouth without her—even if it was just to visit with Captain Gates and his wife for a short time. It wasn't difficult to let her anger spill forth in a convincing display, especially since she knew that Geoffrey fully expected her son to be kidnapped during the visit. She'd finally relented, letting him go on the condition that she be allowed to escort Edmund to Essex. She understood that if she went, Mr. Campbell would have to escort her back alone, but he was going along anyway, so she wasn't inconveniencing anyone.

Geoffrey hadn't agreed to it right away, but after a few words with Colin, he'd had a change of heart.

How had Colin managed it all? A better question, and one that had begun to gnaw at her until she couldn't sleep at night, was why? She remembered the day she met him, when he tried to help her leave Geoffrey's solar. And later, when he kept Lieutenant de Atre from her in the courtyard. How many times after that had he stepped up for her? Whether with guile or the skill of his arm, he'd been protecting her from the beginning. Who was she that such a man would consider her?

She thought it would be difficult to trust again, but Colin had proven his loyalty to her over and over again. It felt good to hope again, to love again.

Edmund surely loved him. But they were sending him off with strangers. What would her son's life be like with people he didn't know and without her there to see to him? Lord, she was going to miss him. What would she do without him to take care of? Colin had promised to reunite them, but how long would it be before she saw Edmund again? She'd spoken briefly to Colin about her escape. She had no idea how he meant to get her away from Geoffrey without her cousin sending both

Dartmouth's and Kingswear's garrisons after her. He'd asked her yet again to trust that he would, and she did.

"What troubles ye, lass?"

She loved the way he called her lass. She loved the way he looked at her, as if each time he set his eyes on her was the first time. Like nothing else in the world could ever touch him, but her. And he knew it, and had accepted it.

"Silly things," she assured him, looking away so he wouldn't see in her eyes how desperately she wanted her and Edmund to stay with him forever.

"He'll get along fine," he promised patiently, although it was the hundredth time he'd done so.

"I know."

"Do you think your father will be among those making the journey?" George asked Colin on the other side of her.

"'Tis likely. The moment he knows someone needs protection, he sets himself to the task."

"You are much like him then," Gillian said, meeting Colin's gaze and letting herself smile openly at him. She couldn't help it. She didn't want to.

"In many ways, aye, I am."

"I would like to meet him." George yawned, shockingly uninterested in their inability to keep their eyes off each other.

"As I look forward to meeting yer wife," Colin replied, finally looking over her to their companion.

Gillian listened while they shared friendly words and laughter. Imagine, George giving himself over to laughter! Astounding. How was it possible that a mercenary from an outlawed clan could change their lives so quickly? There were things about him...contradictory things…that tugged at her logic…like the fact that he claimed to fight for a Campbell cause even though his family on Skye clearly meant more to him than any in Glen Orchy. The way he practiced compared to the way he fought. The amiable smiles he cast on Geoffrey while those brimstone eyes remained cool and untouched by anything given to him in return. His battle-scarred hands resting gently over Edmund's tiny ones, holding the reins, and her heart along with them.

What did logic matter when her son was safe for the first time in his life?

They made camp that first night of Edmund Dearly's freedom deep in the woods. The small fire did little to illuminate their surroundings, or to provide Edmund with a feeling of security while small creatures scurried around in the darkness or hooted from the treetops.

When, after two stories, his eyes were still as wide as saucers, Colin plucked him from Gillian's lap and set him down against the tree under which he was sitting.

Gillian listened while he told her son of a legend who lived long ago. She watched him, moved by the rich, lilting tone of his voice, and the story he chose to tell.

"Then King Arthur came out of his tower, and had under his gown a jesseraunt of double mail, and there went with him the Archbishop of Canterbury, and Sir Baudwin of Britain, and Sir Kay, and Sir Brastias: these were the men of most worship that were with him. And when they were met there was no meekness, but stout words on both sides; but always King Arthur answered them, and said he would make them to bow."

"Isn't Malory's King Arthur the same man believed to be Gildas's Aurelius Ambrosius?" Gillian asked him a little while later. Somehow, it didn't surprise her that

Colin knew about the war leader who saw victory over the Anglo Saxons. Or that the part of Malory's *Le Morte d'Arthur* he chose to recite was when King Arthur was preparing for war. What she did find utterly mesmerizing was the way his arm curled around Edmund's shoulder and ended with their hands intertwined above her son's lap. It was an image Gillian had tossed aside years ago. The sight of it now moistened her eyes.

She blushed, mortified by her tears when Colin turned his smile on her. "Ye know of Arthur then?"

"Of course," she told him. "He is Edmund's favorite hero."

"He is my mother's, as well."

"She taught you well then, Mr. MacGregor."

He laughed, a deep, alluringly husky sound she would put music to later. "I'm afraid I paid little attention to her lessons in chivalry."

"I disagree," she said. "You remind me of him."

He turned away from her worshipful gaze, granting her a view of his beguiling profile against the firelight. "I'm not a hero, lass."

"But that…," she whispered softly, careful not to wake George when he shifted on the other side of her, "…is exactly how a hero would reply."

They entered the rural borough of Thurrock several days later, just before dawn. Gillian had grown up a few leagues away and she recognized the shadow of the old blockhouse, built by Henry VIII, and rebuilt two years before she left Essex. It stood firm and solid in the midst of farms and marshland along the Thames.

But for the bark of a dog somewhere in the distance, the world slept and tempted Gillian to join it on her horse.

She yawned and took comfort that soon they would reach George's manor house and she could rest her head on a pillow and not sleep with her ears alert to every unfamiliar sound.

She didn't hear the click of the pistol ahead of her, but Colin did. The golden splash of morning fell upon him as he reached down and plucked a dagger from his boot. He flipped it over in the air, caught it by the tip of the blade, and prepared to fling it.

George's command stopped him. "Harry Thompson," her captain said, turning to their assailant next, "what the hell are you doing aiming a pistol at me?"

"And who might you be that I shouldn't?" The old man squinted, the growing light doing nothing to aid his vision.

"I'm George Gates, Harry. Now put down that damned weapon before I have my friend remove it from you himself."

"Captain Gates!" Harry shoved his pistol into his belt and bid him off his mount. "We weren't expecting to see you for another few months."

"I know," George said, dismounting and taking hold of his reins. "I thought my wife might enjoy seeing me a little early."

"Indeed she would," old Harry Thompson agreed. "But perhaps she wouldn't mind waiting a little longer while you and your companions share a cup of mead with me. I haven't enjoyed any company since my Liz passed last summer."

George began to decline, but Gillian stopped him. Of course they would give the poor man some of their time. She knew George would be angry, but perhaps less so if he thought she did this for Edmund's sake. Her captain might not display his affection for her son openly, as Colin did, but George loved him nonetheless. "Mr. Thompson, if you have a goat, I would be most grateful for a cup of milk for my son."

They followed the farmer to his home, with George muttering something unintelligible under his breath, and Colin smiling. Gillian took a seat at a small, carved wooden table just off the kitchen and hefted Edmund into her lap. She listened to their host while he told them about losing his wife and offered her aid in anything he needed while she was here. She knew she'd made the correct decision to visit with old Harry when Edmund tasted what was in his cup and then downed the rest and asked politely for more. With little to graze but shrubs around gravestones, no goat survived at Dartmouth. George tried to keep one after Edmund's second year, when she ceased suckling him, but the beast died and her breasts went dry.

She turned her smile on her captain and he nodded, agreeing that the visit was worth it.

Only one thing could make Edmund discard his cup and leap from her lap. Somewhere outside a dog was barking.

"It's Mary Tanner's bitch calling for my Brutus," Harry said when Colin left his seat next. "She hasn't let him be since she delivered his whelps. Just like a woman, eh?"

"This Mary Tanner," Colin asked him at the door, "she is yer neighbor?"

"Aye, she lives just down the road a ways."

Colin glanced at Edmund first, and then moved his gaze to Gillian. "I'll return shortly."

He was gone before any could protest. Edmund raced

away to the window and Harry Thompson picked up his previous tale where he'd left off.

Just when Gillian had decided that there was no hope in getting away from their lonely host before nightfall, Edmund shouted Colin's name and sprinted for the door. Gillian followed, helping her son open it. What they saw before them stopped them both in their tracks.

Colin held a puppy out to Edmund. An adorable little bundle of ashy brown fur and scruffy ears. Between his dangling hindquarters, his tail wagged so furiously he near squirmed out of Colin's grasp. Edmund took a step forward.

"Ye can keep this one, lad."

They left Harry's farm with a promise to return soon for another visit.

"He liked Edmund," Gillian pointed out, waving to the old man as they trotted off.

"Aye," Colin agreed, looking down at the top of her son's downy head and the fur bundle clutched in Edmund's arms. "Who wouldn't?" He brought his smile back to her as their gazes met. "But 'tis likely ye who will restore life to the man."

Gillian canted her horse closer to his, drawn by the desire to kiss him. She might have been bold enough to do it if George hadn't galloped past her.

"Quit pining for each other and let's make haste. We are almost there."

"Who has been pining for his wife for the last six months?" Gillian called back, laughing and feeling more grateful for this day than any other. She flicked her reins to catch up with him, but Colin's hand on her arm stopped her. He drew their horses close, and without caring if

George happened to turn to them or not, pulled her in for a brief, beguiling kiss. He withdrew with the promise of more to come in his scalding eyes, and then took off, leaving Edmund's voice on the wind.

"Do you love Mummy?"

To her utter disappointment, she didn't hear Colin's reply. What were the Highlander's feelings toward her? What were his plans for her after he brought her to Camlochlin? She'd never asked, and he'd never offered to tell her. Would he stay with her or return to the nomadic life of a mercenary? So he cared for Edmund. That didn't mean he wanted a son. He was young and fit and led an adventurous life, escaping danger and sending would-be thieves to their Maker.

She forced herself to smile when she reined in her mount between them and George leaped from his saddle and ran to his front door.

Colin dismounted, taking Edmund with him. After setting her son on his feet, he came to her and helped her out of her saddle.

"We are truly doing this," she said, held aloft in his arms for a scant moment before he set her down next.

"Aye, we are."

His smile was so fearless, so confident, that she allowed her heart to quake at the dreams he restored. She wasn't going to be forced to wed Geoffrey. She would never again have to worry over losing Edmund. They were free!

She took his face in her hands when he released her and pulled him down, a little closer to her upturned face. "Thank you."

Whatever reply he meant to give her appeared lodged in his throat. He swallowed and opened his mouth to begin again but she stopped him, sealing his lips with a stolen kiss. When she felt his arm snake around her waist, she broke free, smiling at him.

"Don't think that George won't still cut off your hands if you touch me."

With a slight slant of his lips and a golden glint in his eyes, he rattled her to the core. "Then I shall have to get ye away from him before the night is over."

"I'm certain you can think of a way," she said quietly over her shoulder when he picked up his steps behind her.

They entered the house together just as Sarah Gates rushed forward from the stairs, pulling her grinning husband behind her. She was as lovely and youthful looking as Gillian remembered, with deep mahogany hair plaited into a thick braid that dangled over her shoulder, and large, luminous dark eyes.

"Lady Gillian, what a wonderful surprise this day has been. Not only does my George return to me, but he brings you with him." Sarah was a petite woman, but her embrace encompassed Gillian in warmth. How long had it been since she'd had a woman with whom to share words, secrets?

"And this must be Edmund!"

Gillian watched while her son was scooped up off the floor. She cringed inwardly, praying he wouldn't begin wailing. He didn't like being carried, save by Colin.

Thankfully, Edmund kept his thumb in his mouth during the entire introduction, which served only to encourage more cooing.

That is, until Sarah glanced up and took a closer look at Colin. She backed away, clutching Edmund to her, while she dipped her eyes to the array of weapons he had strapped to his body. "And who is this?"

Gillian eyed him standing beside her, his hands folded behind his back, his features hard as stone. He appeared much like he had the first day she met him. Heavens, if this was how he greeted ladies, it was no surprise that he wasn't already wed.

"This is Colin Campbell," George told his wife. "He's a—"

"MacGregor. Colin MacGregor."

Gillian was tempted to elbow him in the ribs so he would smile at the poor woman.

"—a friend of mine," George continued. "He's taking Lady Gillian and her son away from Dartmouth."

Sarah Gates's mouth fell open and she turned to her husband. "And you're letting him?"

He sighed deeply and took her hand. "Come, let's show our guests to their rooms. I shall explain everything to you later."

"Are you certain he can be trusted?" Sarah whispered to the captain on their way up the stairs. "He looks quite dangerous."

"He is. But not to her or the babe."

Following them up the polished wooden stairs with Colin in back of her, Gillian smiled at their hushed words and thanked God for the hundredth time for sending her one of his warring angels.

Please, she beseeched, *don't ever call him back.*

Chapter Twenty-eight

Colin dipped his head over the basin in his room—just down the hall from Gillian's, in Gates's lavish manor house—and rinsed his cleanly shaven face with the cool water. He'd done it. He'd gotten Gillian and Edmund out of Dartmouth.

It had been difficult for him since they left. The moments he had alone with Gillian were brief. He missed kissing her on the turret stairs, and every time she but smiled at him while they rode, he ached to have her in his arms again. Many times during their journey to Essex he had contemplated telling Gates that his feelings for her were deeper than either of them had feared.

He didn't want to bring her back to Dartmouth, but he had to. He had to remain on the path he'd set or Devon would come after them.

His path. When had it become so indistinct? When had her and Edmund's safety become his duty and desire above all else? He understood now why his brothers had been so willing to cast aside their pride, and everything that came along with it, for their women. He'd wanted no part of such weakness and spent his years either training or on battlefield to avoid it. But it had found him and once it had, he was shocked to find that it actually made him feel more invincible.

He was certain he loved Edmund. He'd never seen such pure joy on any face as on Edmund's when he'd handed him that pup. He'd never felt his heart, his muscles, and his bones go soft all at the same time. He wanted to protect him, raise him as his son, and teach him to grow into a strong man.

He was doomed and he knew it, but it was what he felt for Gillian that frightened him most. It was what he would do to the king, his old friend, if James came after her again that kept him awake at night. It was the danger he was willing to risk to himself and to his kin by defying whoever sat on the throne in the days to come that convinced him that his heart was no longer his own.

He ran his wet palm over his head, then gave his head a brisk shake to dry off...and mayhap shed him of his constant thoughts of her. What if she didn't share his feelings? What if she gave in to his kisses because she was grateful to him, and nothing more? What the hell would he do then?

A soft rap on his door yanked him from his troublesome thoughts.

"Colin?" Her sweet voice on the other side brought a smile to his face.

Hell, he was revolting. Truly.

Opening the door only made him feel worse. This couldn't be his heart slamming against his ribs like some peach-faced whelp that had just set eyes on his first goddess. It couldn't be his mouth opening to utter words he'd never spoken to anyone before.

"Hell, lass, but ye rob the seas and the stars of their beauty."

He watched the scarlet hue burn across her cheeks and found himself willing to recite every chivalric word his mother had ever burned into his head if she would continue to look at him the way she did now.

"Thank you." She offered him a dainty curtsey, then turned her bonny face up to his. "Forgive my boldness, but Edmund is already below stairs with his puppy and I hoped you would escort me to breakfast. George promised that Sarah is quite skilled in the kitchen."

He thought about pulling her into his room, bolting the door, and feasting on her. He wanted to undress her slowly, carry her to his bed, and make love to her. His body twitched with the need to do it. But he would be as bad as Edmund's father if he did...unless he wed her. What the hell would he do with a wife? What kind of life could he give her while he was off fighting this king or that? What if he died on the battlefield and left her alone with even more bairns at her ankles?

"I'd be happy to escort ye," he said, stepping out of his room and closing the door behind him. "But ye don't need a chaperone here. Ye're free to come and go as ye please."

"And I came to fetch you."

'Twas astonishing how quickly the quirk of her mouth, the way the light flickered over her eyes, made him forget everything else. He held out his arm and waited while she looped her hand around the crook of his elbow. He didn't have to pretend to be someone else here, away from his enemies. But he hadn't been Colin MacGregor for so long, he'd forgotten how.

"You look quite pensive today," she noted as they

walked down the corridor together. "What are you thinking about?"

He smiled in spite of himself and answered truthfully. "I was thinking about how ye have cast me into uncharted waters."

"Oh?" She tossed him a playful glance. "Are you trying to say that you've never met anyone like me?"

"Aye," he admitted. She was perceptive. He added that to the list of things he valued in her while the sight of her lips, dangling there beneath his, parted slightly, tempted him to forget the shame he could possibly bring her. "And how dangerous my desire fer ye is."

She looked deep into his eyes, laying him bare before her. Whatever she saw warmed her smile. "You're correct," she said softly, moving a bit away but not disengaging her arm from his. "And more concerned for my good name than I. Are you certain there are no wings beneath your shining armor?"

He shook his head. "Trust me, lass. If I had wings, they would not be white."

His gaze traced the sleek contour of her neck when she tossed back her head to laugh.

"I don't believe it."

He moved in closer, mayhap to taste her pulse with his tongue. "Ye make me ache to prove it."

They grew serious when his lips fell to her throat. Her lusty sigh nearly snapped his control right there in the hall.

"Campbell!"

Gillian broke from his touch at the snap of Gates's voice. But the captain wasn't angry. He did his best to mask his apprehension when he turned to Colin calmly and said, "I think your family has arrived."

• • •

Much to Gates's disappointment, the MacGregor chief was not among the four horsemen reining in on his front lawn. Colin was satisfied with whom he saw though, knowing Edmund would be in safe, skilled hands on the journey home. No one took protection as seriously as his eldest brother did.

"Rob," Colin greeted the tallest among them as he swung his long claymore over his hip and dismounted first. " 'Tis good to see ye."

Colin pounded his brother on the back, then turned to Connor Grant, his brother-by-marriage and once captain of the King's Royal Army.

"How's my sister?"

"Short-tempered," Connor told him, with a smile deepening a dimple on either side of his face. "She threatened to cut out my heart with a dagger if I ever tried to get her with child again."

"Becoming a mother fer the third time hasn't changed her then," Colin noted, then moved on.

When he saw his cousin Will MacGregor, he expelled a slight sigh. "Better ye than Tristan, I suppose."

"Why?" Will met his feigned disdain with a spark in his eyes that promised no mercy. "D'ye think I canna' irritate ye with a wit as sharp as yer brother's?"

Colin shook his head. "Ye lack his natural ability to the task. I rarely want to kill ye. Let's keep it that way, aye?"

Will laughed and shoved him out of his way to hand his reins over to Gates's stableman.

"Ye must be Lady Gillian Dearly."

Finlay Grant. Hell. Colin turned to watch Connor's younger brother—and the demise of every young lass at Camlochlin—step around him and tip his cap to Gillian, who was standing at the door. 'Twasn't, according to his brothers when last Colin had visited home, that Finn took advantage of his admirers. He was no rogue. He was a poet. And a dashing one at that.

"Yer description in Colin's missive was sorely lacking, my lady," Finn crooned while his pale yellow hair fell free around eyes as green as Ireland after a rainy spring. "Rest assured, I will remedy that."

"Bard." Colin's steady voice gave Finn's mouth pause above her knuckles. "Yer duty is to recount yer laird's deeds, not to seduce lasses with yer pretty words."

"'Tis his visage that wins hearts," Will warned him with a grin. "Ye best keep him away from her if ye mean to keep her."

"I don't—" Colin didn't finish, but turned to her instead and changed his mind about what he meant to say. "Finn." He glanced at his longtime friend. "Back off."

Finn did as requested but with eyes wide with disbelief and then humor as he turned his radiant grin on the others.

"What's this?" Naturally, 'twas Will who laughed first. Colin would teach him a lesson for it later. "Has someone finally conquered that lion heart of yers?"

"I'll be happy to let ye judge how stout my heart is, Will."

"Practicing?" Captain Grant asked him, coming to stand in front of Gates.

"Every day," Colin told him.

"I'll see how diligently ye have been at it," Rob said, brushing past him. He bowed before Gillian and smiled at the same time, catching sight of Edmund running around them with a puppy hot on his heels. "Fergive my brother's poor manners." He introduced himself and the others and moved to Gates next.

"This is Captain George Gates," Colin offered hastily, poor manners or not. "Of the Royal Horse Guards," he added, hoping his brother would catch his inflection and not mention Colin's being a general in the king's army. "He is a trusted friend."

Rob looked the captain over from foot to crown, then clapped him on the shoulder. "A trusted friend is always welcome."

Sarah Gates looked about to pass out right there in the grass when Rob moved on to her next. Unlike Colin though, he eased her nerves with a smile as warm as the thick woolen plaid draping his shoulders.

Gates invited them inside and waited to enter behind them with Colin. Edmund rushed by them all with what he was now calling Aurelius scraping the floor to keep up.

"My Sarah is blushing like a milkmaid. What is that one called who laughs with her?"

"Connor."

"He's quite handsome."

Colin regarded Gillian's captain with a doleful look. The man could fight off an entire garrison single-handedly for almost four years, but 'twas his wife who brought fear to his eyes.

"Her heart is yers," Colin pointed out with some sort of morbid fascination piquing his curiosity. Was this what was to become of him?

"So then," Gates said, eyeing Rob as he swung his mantle off his shoulders, "the thought of Gillian at Camlochlin without you doesn't trouble you?"

Aye, it did, now that Finn seemed to be taking a liking to her.

"We will sleep in here tonight," Rob announced, entering the sitting room.

The captain and his wife followed them inside. "My servants are happy to give up their beds for the night."

Rob smiled and unbelted his scabbard. "This room will serve fine. We'll sleep on the floor. We havena' come to put anyone oot. We killed a few rabbits on the way, so we willna' be a burden at yer meals."

Gates appeared somewhat awestruck and slightly disturbed, like he had to have been mad to involve himself with such men.

His wife, on the other hand, didn't seem bothered in the least by all the virility in one room. "Nonsense," she promised him. "You'll be no burden at all. Will they, George?"

Colin smiled at the scowl on Gates's face...until he looked at Gillian and found her smiling at Finn.

"Something other than warm water might be well received though," Will interrupted both men's dark thoughts.

"I have whisky," Gates informed them and called to one of his servants. "I helped myself to some of Devon's unspoiled brew before we left." He winked at Colin as the servant went to the task.

"Good man," Colin tossed back at him, already returning his attention to Finn, who was beckoning for Gillian to come sit by him.

"Brother." Rob dragged his attention away from Gillian accepting Finn's offer. "We have much to discuss. Take a seat and bring wee Edmund with ye."

"Why didn't faither come?" Colin moved across the room and sat next to his brother. He kept his eyes on Finn.

"He's off visiting Connor Stuart in France with Mother, Graham, and Claire," Rob told him.

"Rob's chief now," Will said, producing an apple from his bag and biting into it.

"Well, 'tis about damn time," Colin offered, unfazed by the news. As firstborn, Rob had been preparing his whole life for the duty of protecting the clan. Colin had no doubt the MacGregors of Skye would be safe in his brother's capable hands.

They raised a toast when the whisky arrived, then settled in to hear Colin tell them of Gillian's dilemma.

"Ye will remain at Camlochlin fer as long as ye care to stay," Rob told Gillian, then winked at Edmund, who was sitting at Colin's feet with Aurelius lying beside him.

"Ye're no' afraid to come with us, aye, lad?" Will asked Edmund, then handed him another apple when Edmund shook his head.

"Colin told us there were other children at Camlochlin." The men looked together at Gillian when she finally spoke. A light blush stole across her cheeks at the sudden attention she was being given, and Colin wondered how such a delicate sparrow would fare with the women of Skye. She eased his thoughts a moment later though, when her blush faded and she faced all four Highlanders with fearless determination to continue. "What will it be like there for my son?"

"He'll have chores," Rob told her, watching Edmund bite into the fruit, the sound perking Aurelius's ears, "as the other children do, and many to play with in between."

"My son Malcolm"—Connor offered her a reassuring smile that brought the flush back to her face—"along with Adam and Lucan, Rob's and Tristan's lads, are about the same age. He'll fare well."

She nodded and turned to Colin, rendering him a wee bit breathless with the gratefulness of her smile.

Unfortunately, Will caught his moment of weakness and kicked him with his booted foot. "England has softened ye."

Colin regarded him with a wry look. He might have let a lass into a place no one had tread before her, but that didn't mean he couldn't still beat Will MacGregor's arse to the ground. "Let's go find out how much, aye?"

✣

Chapter Twenty-nine

*G*illian sat on a bench with Edmund and Aurelius at her feet and watched, her heart beating madly in her chest, while Colin and Will went sword to sword in George's front yard. It wasn't enough that Colin nearly swiped off his opponent's arm several times, or that the other three Highlanders watching cheered every time blood came close to being spilled. She could almost ignore George's sharp intakes of breath while he paced a few inches away, swearing every now and then about Colin's superior skill and deadly accuracy. She silently agreed that he could have beaten half the men at Dartmouth on his own, and wondered vaguely why he hadn't.

But none of it mattered now, save for the sight of him. He'd exchanged his breeches for a woolen plaid much like the one the rest of the Highland men around her wore, belted at his waist and swinging about his bare muscular calves while he tumbled and rolled to avoid blows to his shoulders and head. He was terrifying and mesmerizing to watch. As agile as a leopard and as merciless as a lion. He came at Will over and over, slicing, hacking, with barely enough control to keep from striking a truly damaging blow. Legs apart and slightly bent, feet braced to the ground, he stopped Will's advance like a wall, and then answered with a brutal assault of metal against metal.

When it was over, with the larger of the two Highlanders yielding first, the victor turned his molten gaze on her. She nearly quivered as the heat of battle burned into something even less tamed. It sparked a flame somewhere in the center of her belly that made her whole body burn. She refused to blush though. To blazes with propriety. She'd been proper for four years. She wanted to be herself, free of shame and retribution.

She wanted Colin MacGregor. She wanted him in her arms, in her bed, hard and naked, doing to her whatever he wished.

She smiled at him from across the yard and he almost lost an ear to the edge of his brother's enormous claymore.

"Poor form, Robbie." Colin leaped away and felt for his lobe.

"I'm no' English," the chief said, hefting his sword over his head. "Neither are ye, so dinna' fight like one and disappoint me." He brought his giant blade down onto Colin's and drove his youngest brother to his knees.

But Colin didn't stay down. Scraping his blade across Rob's, he slipped away, relieving the pressure to the heavier claymore and sending it deep into the dirt. Without wasting an instant, he bounded back to his feet and whirled his blade in a powerful arc before striking the other and almost separating Rob's hands from his hilt.

The brutality of their practice made Gillian pull Edmund's face into her chest and tempted her to look away with him. For they held nothing back, swinging and striking with lethal intent, sending dust and sparks flying around them.

Colin's sheer power alone made him captivating to watch. The force of his lightning-quick parries, the fluidity of his wrist while the rest of him remained tightly wound and ready to spring in whichever direction his feet pointed him.

But clearly, Robert MacGregor hadn't been named Chief MacGregor for nothing. He regained himself after each assault with a loose shrug and positioned his blade for the next round. "Ye remember yer trainin' well."

"I told ye, I practice every day."

"He doesn't practice with any of us like that," George mumbled quietly as he made his way past her.

Colin fought hard, but several times Rob caught him with the tip of his blade across his chest and shoulders. When little remained of Colin's shirt—and Gillian's heart along with it—but tatters, he tore it off and flung it away.

"Och, his flesh is testimony that even death does not want him."

Gillian blinked and turned toward the cherubic grin of Finlay Grant. Good Lord, but he was gloriously beautiful, the antithesis of the dark, deadly warrior who had saved her.

"Fortunate for death," she smiled back at him, certain that no woman could resist doing so, and then turned back to Colin. "It would have to fight me for him if it did."

"Ye love him then?" Finn asked, his voice setting music to the air and finally making her blush when she nodded, admitting to someone that she did.

"Does he return yer affection?"

"Would it be so unlike him if he did?" she asked,

seeing the surprise that lit Finn's eyes like twinkling emeralds.

"Aye, 'twould. If ye knew him—"

"I do know him."

He laughed and then pointed to Colin. "I mean the way we do."

Gillian looked in time to see Colin turn away from her and smash his blade so hard into Rob's that he drove his brother back. Without pause, he delivered a combination of hammering blows in rapid, forceful succession. Every counter Rob attempted was halted by another crushing assault.

And then Colin caught her eye and lost the fight.

"Well." Finn bounded to his feet and dusted off his plaid when Colin took up his steps in their direction. "I'll leave ye to yer beloved." He was gone before Gillian could open her mouth to reply.

She returned her attention to the man coming toward her and took in every inch of his tightly wound physique as she rose to her feet to meet him. Never in her life had she been so attracted, so beguiled, by a man that the mere sight of sweat glistening down his heaving chest could near buckle her legs.

"Well done," she said softly when he reached her. "Were you hurt at all?"

"Nae," he answered, then saw Finn hurrying toward the house and cast him a dark scowl.

Was he jealous? He looked angry and a bit... worried. Lord, Gillian thought, gazing up at him, he had nothing to fear. Colin's face was the one she adored. When his eyes fell back to her, they robbed her of breath. For in them she saw the residue of a warrior, and the longing of a man.

"Have I thanked you yet, Mr. MacGregor?" She smiled at him, hoping he saw her heart in her eyes.

He smiled back, forgetting whatever troubled him. "Fer what?"

"For everything. For becoming my friend, and for loving my son. For a future I can look to with anticipation. For a puppy."

"Ye dinna' have to thank me fer those things, lass." He moved closer to her, scorching her with the heat of his body.

What were they speaking about? Gillian couldn't remember and she didn't care. "I like the sound of your voice." Goodness, was that herself she was hearing purring against the warmth of his lips like a contented kitten? Was this her body trembling with desire for him? Unaware of George, or Colin's kin, or even Edmund. She wanted to kiss him, to feel the strength in his arms caressing her.

But that would have to wait.

He was dragged quite literally away from her by his brother and hauled beneath his arm. Gillian composed herself and glanced in George's direction before following the two men inside. Edmund turned and waved to her from high atop the chief's shoulder. She blew him a kiss and waved back.

They were an interesting and unique brand of men, these rough, rugged Highlanders, Gillian thought while sharing supper with them at George's table that night. They laughed with ease and without malice. Their speech was not crass or offensive, though it did not lack any amount of boisterous enthusiasm when they spoke of fighting. Edmund did his share of talking once questions were put to him about his interests. They listened to him and patiently answered questions of his own.

"Does you know how to play Naughts and Crosses?" Edmund asked the chief.

"I am the Naughts and Crosses champion," Colin's eldest brother boasted. "Do ye challenge me?"

Edmund laughed and then nodded.

"Just a moment." George held up his hands. "No one is going to carve up my table."

"Carvins' hold memories when yer memory fails ye," Will murmured and cast the smooth surface of the table a disapproving look.

"Chess then?" Rob stood up, causing Gillian to crane her neck as she followed his ascent. The smile he aimed at George was every bit as beguiling as Colin's. "I saw a set in yer sittin' room. D'ye know how to play chess, Edmund?"

"No."

"Come then." He waved his hand and turned to leave. "'Tis time ye learned."

The rest of them followed, carrying their drinks and their merry mood with them. Finn offered her his arm, apparently deciding that he didn't really need two. Colin didn't remove his blade but merely shoved Finn out of the way instead. Finn winked at her, ignoring Colin's lethal stare, then disappeared into the sitting room.

Colin stopped before they entered next and turned to the golden-haired captain behind them. "Connor, will ye see Edmund to bed when the game is done? I would have words with his mother."

"Go." Connor waved them away. "Before I lose a brother."

Before Gillian could protest leaving Edmund to the

care of strangers, she found herself being pulled in the opposite direction. And really, why should she protest at all? Edmund was going to live with them and rely on them until Colin brought her to Camlochlin. They were kind to him, and they were Colin's kin. Edmund would be fine.

She didn't question him when he led her to the stairs. She missed the turret shadows and their forbidden kisses.

"MacGregor."

They both stopped and looked down the stairs at George and Sarah.

"I wish to speak with her alone, Captain," Colin said, assuring her trusted guardian that that was all he meant to do. Gillian hoped he intended more than that. "I will speak with ye after that."

Gillian thought George might protest. It didn't matter if he did. She wanted this. Whatever it was...whatever it meant...she wanted it and no one would stop her. But her captain said nothing and finally moved on to join his guests.

Left alone, they turned down the hall and out of sight. Gillian hoped Colin would sweep her into his arms and kiss her senseless. When he slowed his steps but kept on walking, she stopped him and waited until he turned to look at her.

"What is it you wish to say that brings such trepidation to your face?"

He laughed softly, but the sound was left hollow by his pained expression. "The understanding that I have become so transparent, fer one."

She moved closer, unable to stay away, and lifted her hand to his face. "Would you hide from me as you do with others?"

He looked into her eyes, deeply, meaningfully. "I would do anything fer ye...and it scares the hell out of me, Gillian."

It wasn't what she'd asked him, but his reply warmed the deepest chasms of her heart just the same. He had already done everything for her and she gave him her heart in exchange. She wanted him to take it. She prayed that he would offer her his in return.

"Colin," she whispered as his mouth dipped to hers. "I love you."

She was almost certain she saw him smile an instant before he kissed her. Oh, but he did not simply kiss her. If he did, she might be able to forget him someday if he, too, left her. His soft lips branded her, his hungry mouth consumed her, opening to take her more fully. He set fire to her blood with the silken stroke of his tongue. She answered by pushing up against him and sighing into his mouth when his strong arms closed around her.

He resisted her, calling up that mastery of self-control he'd revealed in the yard today. She could feel him reining in something he didn't trust near her. Not his heart. For she might be young, but she was a woman. And a woman knows when a man's heart is already involved. He cared for her and Edmund. It wasn't that which frightened him and kept him guarded. Was it the dark beast that cut down five men to save Edmund? The part of him soothed by the music of her lute. Was his passion unleashed so dangerous then?

She wanted to discover the answer herself.

Curling one arm around his neck to keep him close, she ran her other hand down the hard planes of his chest and belly. His bare flesh singed her fingers and curled her toes. She opened her mouth and accepted his slow, sinuous tongue. He groaned against her, his body growing harder, tighter in her hands. She tossed back her head, breaking free of him to draw a breath. When his teeth raked over her chin, then down her throat, he made her quiver with desire.

"Gillian," he spoke her name on a ragged groan, "what I want to do to ye…"

"Do what you will."

"Nae." He straightened and stared down into her eyes. "Yer life is in my hands. I won't put ye in more danger."

That was it then. Like the night they spent together in the cave, he restrained himself because he was afraid of being careless with her. To think that she held such power over a man who cut musket balls from his own flesh made her tremble with emotion. "Colin"—she took his face in her hands—"my life is my own. You gave it back to me."

"And now that you have it, you would hand it over to me?"

"Aye." She smiled, tilting her head up to kiss him. "Mine, and my son's. Now please—"

He scooped her up off the floor and carried her down the hall.

"—take me to your room."

Chapter Thirty

Firelight reflected in his eyes as he kicked the door to his room shut and then bolted it. Gillian's muscles convulsed with the thrill of being alone and locked away with him. She wasn't afraid or coy. He'd resisted her for her sake but now his body pulsed with hunger for her.

She would make him wait a little longer. When he reached for her again, she stepped back and pulled at the laces of her gown.

His gaze darkened on her, searing her blood, making her ache. He made no move to rush at her, but stood by the door, his hands clenched at his sides. Her past faded from her memory, and looking at him before her with the soft glow of firelight accentuating his twitching muscles, she felt that every moment in her life had led her to this one. To this man who risked his life for her, who killed for her. She wanted to belong to him, and he to her. She wanted to bear his children and watch him love them.

Shifting out of her gown, she drew in a tight gasp as it fell around her feet and his plaid rose away from his knees.

She stood before him in her thin white chemise, her breathing suspended. "Colin...I..."

He closed his eyes, as if still trying with one last effort to resist her. Now she knew why, and it made her love him all the more.

"Gillian," he spoke her name on a ragged groan, opening his eyes to look at her. "There are things I would tell ye first."

She rushed to him instead and he caught her in his arms. "Tell me them later." She traced the muscles of his chest with her fingertips, her mouth. "For now, all I want is you."

She slipped out of his reach when he tried to pull her closer. He'd made her surrender all her doubts and fears, throw down her shield and trust him. She wanted the same from him. She wanted to see him. The true, unguarded man or beast beneath his iron control. By the fire smoldering in his eyes, she knew it wouldn't take much longer.

"I know a bit about swordplay, you know." She circled him, slipping her finger beneath the wool wrappings around his waist.

"D'ye?" he asked, following her with his eyes.

She nodded and tilted her mouth to his ear. "You were magnificent to watch. Now"—she slipped behind him and purred along his nape—"I would see more of you."

She gave his plaid a sharp tug and stepped away to watch its descent to the floor. She scored her gaze over him, from his dusty hide boots up to the backs of his sturdy thighs. He had very nice thighs. His arse was fine to behold, as well. Blushing, she stepped around him and examined him full-on.

Good. Lord.

"Oh my." She brought her palm to her chest and regarded his large cock jutting heavenward, swollen and ready to take her. She smiled, wanting him to do it, wanting to climb all over him, surrendering herself to her warrior.

When he continued to resist what his body clearly wanted, she bent to retrieve her gown. "If you would rather I leave..." She closed her eyes in sheer ecstasy when he snatched her off the floor.

His control finally snapped with a harsh grunt and the tearing away of her chemise. Their lips collided with possession and pleasure, for both of them, in equal measure. She straddled him in the air the moment she was free, coiling her arms around his neck and her thighs around his waist.

He held her suspended in his palms, his hands caressing her hips, sliding over her buttocks. He grazed his teeth along her throat, her cries of delight making him harder between her legs.

She arched her back, hovering above the bed to offer him more. The strength of his arm keeping her aloft thrilled the breath right out of her. When he captured her tight nipple in his mouth and sucked, she buckled in his embrace. He showed her no mercy and sucked the other just as hard. When she thought she could stand no more without begging him to lay waste to her, he flicked his tongue and began a more sensual assault, licking, tasting, relishing her breasts and then her mouth.

She felt his hot shaft, thick and long against her crux, and wiggled over it. His body pulsed in her hands as he cupped her buttocks and rubbed his full, throbbing length against her one more time. And then, lifting her in one hand and dragging her to his hungry mouth with the other, he thrust himself inside her, again and again.

His body surged into hers, each stroke bolder, longer, deeper, lifting her toward the heavens. Gillian cried out at the pain of not having been with a man in four years, but soon, the rhythm of his hips and the force of his upward thrusts heated her muscles and every other part of her. She relaxed and opened her eyes to find him gazing at her. Ruthlessly, he clenched her arse and guided her up and down, stretching her tight sheath around him to take him deeper until she took all of him. He made her gasp and pant and almost fear what she had so carelessly set free. But his eyes, staring deeply into hers, revealed the beast he truly feared. It was his heart, and the knowledge that he'd lost it.

"Do you love me, Colin MacGregor?"

His fine mouth slanted into a smile against her teeth. "Have I not told ye a hundred times today already that I do?"

When she shook her head, he kissed her and set her down beneath him in his bed. "Aye, I love ye, Gillian Dearly. 'Tis nothing to smile about," he warned, sinking deep into her again. "I'm a cold-hearted bastard."

"Not with me." She reached up to touch his face with both hands, unable to believe that she had won such a man. "Not with Edmund."

"Ye've made me soft, lass." He dipped his gaze to her lips and then closed his eyes to kiss her, setting her heart and her loins ablaze.

Lifting her hips, she coiled her legs around his waist and met his sinuous plunges with equal fervor. Breaking their kiss, they stared into each other's eyes while their bodies rocked and pitched like waves cast about in a tumultuous storm. If this was what he considered soft...

She held him close, moving her fingers over his shoulders, hard and corded beneath her touch. Down the flare of his back, pausing to trace his battle wounds, and then smiling at the thrill of cupping his buttocks while he nailed her to the bed.

Her soft cries dragged a low, throaty groan from him. He spoke, his mouth hungry for her. "I dream of ye, and now ye're here with me."

He dreamed of her. Lord, she never wanted to be parted from him. She wanted a lifetime of nights like this. Cleaved to him, body and soul, feeling the weight of him, the strength of him as he swept her away, across the sea and above the clouds. To a place where love was real and never disappointing.

The tender glide of his fingertips along her temple, and down her cheek as he prepared to kiss her, drove her wild with love and desire. Or perhaps it was the way he caressed her mouth, taking his time to taste every inch of her while he slipped his other hand down her back and pressed her hips closer to his. Lord, but he was big and as hard as newly forged steel. When he gritted his teeth and turned away from her to delay the effect of sliding all that cock in and out of her, she quivered in his arms.

So, she thought, stroking the backs of his thighs while he moved her in a slower, deeper kind of dance, even in the heat of passion, the beast was patient.

And merciless.

With a seductive curl of his lips and a molten glint in his eyes, he ground his hips into hers, stroking the nub of her passion with his hot flesh.

"Ah, lass, am I dreaming now?" He thrust into her hard, once and then again. "Or is this truly yer wet, wicked sheath so tight around me?"

She arched her back, taking him from tip to hilt as the world as she knew it burst into radiant light. She twitched against him then dug her fingers into his shoulders as her muscles clenched and throbbed around him. Fighting the urge to score her nails down his back, she met his plunges

with resistance, unsure of the deluge threatening to over-
come her. She cried his name and heard him swear, trying to rein in his control.

It was her undoing.

Tossing back her head, she answered his last slow,
salacious stroke with a soul-stirring shudder that shook
her beneath him.

She looked up to find him watching her, his expression
sorely pained. When she smiled, sated from her passion,
he sprang away from her, holding the head of his shaft
in his hand. Leaning back on his haunches, he released
himself and shot a stream of his seed straight up into the
air. The deep-throated growl he emitted with it tempted
Gillian to take in the full sight of him, spent though she
was. He kept his hands on the mattress behind him, jutting himself toward the ceiling while three more spurts
left him shaking.

He'd kept his seed from her. She understood why he did
it. A short while ago, she loved him for it. But now, when
passion's fire had been sated and left her with embers, she
realized that wedding her would solve the issue of impreg-
nating her with another fatherless babe. Clearly, he had no
thoughts of making her his wife. He said he loved her, but
many things were said in heated moments.

Gillian watched him sit up and then leave the bed to
fetch a rag on his table, near a wash basin. She remained
silent while he cleaned her, and closed her eyes when he
wiped himself next and climbed in beside her.

She wouldn't weep. She shouldn't have expected so
much from him. She thought she'd learned her lesson.
Still, he'd done so much for her already...If one night
with him was all she was allowed, she would make the
most of it and hold her head up high in the morning.

Chapter Thirty-one

"Tell me about your family."

Lying in his bed facing her, Colin smoothed a golden tendril away from her cheek and smiled at her. "My *kin*."

The way she worried her brow at his correction made him want to tighten his arms around her and pull her close. But he'd already been too rough, too demanding, with her for one night. He'd never relinquished all control in the past—in any undertaking. No one knew the true force of the fires that formed him. But her confidence in seducing him stirred his blood in a way no one else ever could. Her surrender was more satisfying than any victory in battle would ever be. He'd taken her too quickly, too eager to conquer, to relish every moment, every movement. He wanted her again.

"Are there many different words I must learn?"

"I'll speak them to ye every day," he promised. "By the time ye get to Camlochlin, ye'll know them all. But first, fergive me if I hurt or frightened ye tonight."

Her smile spread over her face, so close to his he could

taste her breath. "You didn't." She closed her hand around his as it dipped to her mouth and kissed it. "It was perfect. I shall never forget it."

He didn't intend to let her. Something within him stirred back to life at the thought, but he stayed it, utterly content to simply look at her, speak with her.

"Now tell me of your kin. Are there many women at Camlochlin?"

"Aye," he told her quietly, tracing his fingertips along the fine curve of her lips. "My mother will nae doubt gather ye beneath her wing from the moment ye set yer feet on the ground. If not her, then my aunt Maggie surely will. Pray 'tis my mother."

They laughed in the firelight while he told her tales about his kin, from his cantankerous cousin Brodie Mac-Gregor to the youngest addition to the MacGregor clan, his niece Caitrina. A few times while he spoke, the pure joy and longing in her eyes made Colin ready to surrender all to her. He had to rein in his heart and think logically. He shouldn't have taken her body, but at least he'd kept his seed from her, ensuring that in the event of his death, she would have no more bairns out of wedlock. Aye, he intended to fight. He had to, especially if war came to the Highlands.

"Edmund will hate having to leave."

He wasn't certain he'd heard her right. "Why would ye leave?"

She looked away, trying to shield her sudden melancholy behind her thick lashes. "There will be no reason to remain there if I can convince William that I..."

William? What the hell did he have to do with her anymore? Colin should tell her the damned truth. That William was a merciless bastard who'd once ordered the death of an abbey full of nuns, and that he intended to stop the prince from gaining the throne and doing the same to every other Catholic in the kingdom. He'd meant to tell her earlier, when he thought she would be content to live with him at Camlochlin. When he thought she had given up her hope in the man he came to destroy. "Gillian." He cupped her face in his hands and prayed she saw what she meant to him in his eyes. He had no talent with words, the way Finn did. How could he tell her that he'd known from the moment he stepped foot in Dartmouth, that her hope in her prince was lost?

Someone rapping at the door startled her out of his arms. She sat bolt upright in the bed even as he reached for her.

"We are retiring, MacGregor," Gates called from the other side. "I've come to escort Gillian to her room."

"I'll see to it myself, Captain," Colin called back to him when she didn't object. "And I'll have a private word with ye about it tomorrow."

Silence clung to the room while Gates considered his options. Then he said, "Very well. Tomorrow then. Good eve, Gillian."

"Good eve, George," Gillian called back, her cheeks ablaze in the flickering light. She looked at Colin watching her and her smile grew along with his.

"So"—his voice dipped, along with his gaze when he leaned in to kiss her, forgetting about William and wars—"ye want to spend the night with me then?"

"As many nights as we can," she whispered back.

Endless, infinite nights if he had his way.

"I will win ye, lass," he told her, growing hard against her thigh.

"You already have, Highlander." She licked the crease in his chin and then kissed his lower lip.

She moved like a sensual whisper beneath him, firing up his blood, searing his veins. He took her slowly this time, kissing her with slow, deliberate leisure that quickened her breath and made her tremble for more. He feasted on the supple warmth of her breasts and the tight buds peaking each. His cock, between her legs, ached, but he did not rush into her.

He wasn't prepared when she pushed on his shoulders and rolled him onto his back, but he liked it. When she straddled him, nestling the shaft of his cock against her scalding sheath, he was tempted to pull her back by the wrists and impale her to the hilt.

"Such a powerful warrior," she purred, running her hands over his chest and undulating her hips, "powerless beneath me."

Colin bent his knees on either side of her and slid his palms over her buttocks. Naked male desire curled his lips as he shifted her position an inch and then thrust the full length of his dripping cock deep into her.

"Oh!" She gasped over him, clutching his shoulders, her long hair falling around her face. "You are not so powerless after all."

Colin didn't care about power, only taking her more deeply, getting enough of her to satisfy the hunger that consumed him. Coiling one arm around her waist, he held her close while he guided her rump up and down his stiff, scalding erection until he almost burst inside her.

He pulled her mouth to his and thrust his tongue inside, matching the deep gyrations that heaved her upward. When she bit his lip, he rolled her onto her back, without withdrawing from her, and spread her legs wide beneath him. He watched her accept him, enjoy him, and he marveled at the wonder of her exquisite beauty. When her muscles tightened and convulsed around him and she cried out in her ecstasy, he tossed back his head and reached down deep to delay his own eruption.

"You love me," she said sometime later, wrapped in his arms, "but you will not claim me."

He had already claimed her. According to the law of the Highlands, she was his if he wished it. And he did. Aye, he wanted her to be his wife, his and no one else's, forever. But he had to tell her the truth first. Och, hell, when had he become such a coward?

"Gillian, there is a war coming. I—"

"Don't speak it!" She leaned up on her elbow and pressed her fingers to his mouth. "Tell me you will leave Geoffrey's service. Even if you don't want me after this, the thought of you dying in battle..."

"I do want ye."

"I couldn't go on if you perished," she continued, not hearing him. "According to Geoffrey, the prince has so far assembled more than three hundred ships. One less mercenary will make no difference."

Colin's face remained impassive despite his thudding heart. More than three hundred ships so far? Och, the battle would be a great one. "What else has Geoffrey told ye?"

She shrugged, clearly not interested in the dealing of politics. "The prince needs funding for the invasion and has secretly taken up negotiations with burgomasters in Amsterdam. He has also sent an envoy to Vienna to ensure the support of the Holy Roman Emperor, Leopold the First."

Colin felt sickened that the church would side with William. He wasn't surprised though. Truly, James had become a tyrant to the people...and to him.

"So you see?" she continued. "You are not needed."

He shook his head, battling the voice in his head that mercilessly reminded him that this was what he'd been waiting for all his life. "King Louis of France will send ships to aid England. William's three hundred ships will not be enough to ensure his victory."

She turned away to hide the glimmering blue of her eyes. "Forgive me. I have no right to ask this of you. I know you're loyal to William, as am I."

He wasn't loyal to William and he wished she wasn't either. He could tell her every coldblooded thing he knew about the prince. He could assure her that William cared only for his own gain and would likely never agree to help her in anything she asked. But he didn't. He couldn't bring himself to cause her more disappointment. "Ask what ye will of me," he said quietly instead.

She returned her dreadful gaze to him only for an instant before closing her eyes. "Let the war be fought without you."

Could he? What would it mean for his kin if he deserted the king? What did it say about him that he was lying there considering such a thing? But he was. For her. Sadly, King James had become what Colin despised most in men of power. The desire for self-aggrandizement, even at the cost of those they swore before God to protect. But the king was the father of Rob's wife, Davina—and that made him kin. As such, and since his decisions would affect his daughter, he was less likely to bring hardship and war to the northern clans, whether over religious laws or political ones. Colin had to fight this war to ensure his kin's safety...and now she and Edmund were a part of them.

"My enemy threatens the things that matter most in my heart," he told her truthfully. "If I have the power to stop him, should I not try?"

She nodded and drew closer to him once again. "Aye, I suppose you should. Tell me," she said, fitting her leg neatly between his and holding him closer, "what matters most in your heart?"

"My freedom."

She nodded against his chest, then kissed it. "Freedom to do what?"

"To choose the way I want to live, to believe what I want without fear of consequence."

"I would fight for that too."

"Ye have," he told her softly. "And ye've won."

They slept for a time after that. Once, Gillian had awakened from dreams of losing Edmund. Colin held her close, promising that he would never allow it. He watched her while she returned to more pleasant dreams, studying the rhythm of her breath, the shape of her mouth, the curve of her nose. He hoped the women at home wouldn't be envious of her beauty, but he suspected 'twas a foolish hope. She stole the breath from his body and made his heart all soft and pliant.

He woke her twice, unable to keep his hands from touching her. She didn't protest, or accuse him of being the beast his stamina proved him to be. She took him fully, deeply, matching his fervor on her back, on her knees, draped across his chest while he took her from behind, and later, with her back pressed against the wall.

Twice he almost didn't withdraw, almost gave in to the temptation of casting his glorious battle to the four winds and living out the rest of his days herding sheep and fathering bairns with Gillian.

Twice he almost surrendered it all with one momentous thrust.

Almost.

Chapter Thirty-two

Gillian woke from a dream of Colin to find him already out of bed and tying the laces of his breeches. He smiled at her from across the room while she stretched and then blushed, recalling the night they had spent together. It was magical. It was...It was morning! Edmund was leaving her today! She sat up, crying his name and pulling on her chemise.

Colin was there instantly. "I willna' keep ye from him long, lass. He'll be safe. Ye both will."

"I know," she said, pressed to his chest. "But what will I do without him until we are reunited?"

He withdrew to scald her insides with a provocative quirk of his mouth. She blushed softly, loving him for so easily taking her mind off the day ahead. Lord, but he was an amazing, insatiable lover. Of course, she had only Reginald Blount to compare him with, but it didn't matter. The pleasure she'd experienced with Colin was like nothing else in her life. He exhilarated her with his body and conquered her heart in his passionate embrace. She never wanted to be parted from him. The idea of it was as terrifying as losing Edmund.

"When you are done fighting…"

"Aye?" he pressed gently when she grew quiet.

"I would wait for you. That is, if you wanted me to."

"What about William?"

She looked up at him, wondering how he'd managed to conquer all her fears and doubts about a man, about love, and be so willing to cast away her pride to keep him. "What do I need of a prince if I had you?"

He smiled. Soothing and melting her heart at the same time. "I want ye, lass." He drew her chin up for a kiss that moved her deep within and set flight to her heart. "I'll work diligently on ways of convincing ye so that ye never doubt it again."

Then he did mean to stay with her. Perhaps wed her. Relief flooded through her and she fell against him, his and his alone. "I would bear your sons, Colin. I would follow you to the ends of this earth."

"'Tis where ye'll be going, lass," he told her, dipping his mouth to hers. "As fer bearing my bairns"—he pressed a series of slow, teasing kisses to her lips—"I'll be happy with daughters. I already have a son."

Oh, but how she loved…Edmund! "We must make haste!" She broke away from his arms and shot out of bed to get dressed.

On the way out the door though, she stopped one last time and turned to him. "Grant me one more thing."

"Ask it."

"That you will love me until the end of your days."

He pulled her close and brought her hand to his lips. "I fear I will love only ye until long after that."

She drew away with a smile teasing her mouth. "You fear much…for a Highlander."

He took off behind her down the hall toward Edmund's door. "I can assure ye that I fear less than many other men."

She giggled in front of him. Such an arrogant man he was. "But much more than most when it comes to matters of your heart."

He caught up with her and leaned in to her ear. "My heart has been newly awakened. It may take the rest of my life to grow accustomed to it, but the way it beats fer ye promises a swift victory."

At his side, she closed her eyes and pinched her own arm. When she opened them again, George stood in her path. Or rather, in Colin's. Without a word, his fist flew past her and felled Colin to the ground.

She was about to admonish him for his violence when she caught a movement out of the corner of her eye, and then another on the other side. Rob and Will MacGregor moved closer, ready and quite able to take George down if he lifted his hand again.

Colin pushed to his feet and wiped a stream of blood running from his nose. "Leave him. He's within his rights, fer now."

"Ye mean ye're no' goin' to hit him back?" Will's handsome face contorted with disgust.

"Not this time," Colin said, flicking a glance to George.

"Then you better have promised her something," George warned, standing his ground, "and you better keep your word."

"I did," Colin tossed over his shoulder when he passed him and reached Edmund's door. "And I intend to."

"The lad breaks fast with the captain's wife in the sittin' room," Rob told him when he and Gillian found Edmund's room empty.

"Intend to what?" Will asked, loping behind them when they all headed down the stairs.

"We'll speak of it when I return home."

Rob and Will exchanged a curious look over Colin's head when he bent to catch Edmund in his arms.

"Ye're comin' home?" It was Connor Grant leaning against the doorway who asked him.

"Eventually," Colin answered, and then gave the rest of his attention to Gillian's son.

Eventually. It could mean so many things, Gillian thought, returning Finn's smile and following the rest into the sitting room. Eventually, after he rescued her from Dartmouth? Eventually, after a year or two of fighting in a war? She watched him set Edmund down on his feet, and then bend to tell him something that made Edmund's head bob up and down. Edmund needed him. She needed him.

"We want to make an early start," Rob said, tossing his thick plaid over his shoulder.

Lord, did she not even have an hour with her son then?

She scooped him up when he ran to her next and kissed his downy head until he squirmed in her arms. She was doing this for him, she told herself over and over while she gave him instructions on behaving properly. "Mind what you're told by the chief and his wife," she told him, kissing him again and finally setting him down, "and don't forget your manners. Don't chase Aurelius into any dangerous places, and eat all your greens. I've packed along your magic dagger so if you're fright—"

"He'll do fine." Will took Edmund's tiny hand. "If he's frightened, we'll see to him."

It wouldn't do for Edmund to see her cry, but the task became impossible when Colin squatted before her son.

"Take care of Aurelius. He'll be depending on ye."

"I will," her son promised, sounding as determined in his task as Colin was in his.

"Yer mother will be along soon."

"You too?"

"Aye," Colin told him. "I've much to teach ye."

Gillian held herself together while her son curled his chubby arms around Colin's neck and held on while Colin kissed his head.

"Go on with ye now." Colin rose to his full height and watched while Will led him to the door.

Rob was the last to leave and he stopped to assure her one last time that no harm would come to Edmund.

Colin followed them out, turning to look at her, knowing what he saw in her eyes was about to erupt. When he shut the door, it did. George was there, holding her in silence when she wept. She needed no more assurances. She simply needed to cry, and her dearest friend let her do it.

"Rob." Colin stopped his brother before the new chief leaped into his saddle behind Edmund. "There is something I need to tell ye."

After a dark, knowing glare, Rob folded his arms across his chest. "I thought so. My suspicion is that 'tis somethin' I willna' like hearing and that is why ye waited until now to tell me."

"I nae longer support the king." Best to just get it out there and deal with the outcome as it presented itself.

Rob stared at him as if doubting his ears, then he looked around at the others, who, having heard their exchange, appeared just as dumbfounded.

"Why?"

"Because his thirst fer power has poisoned him.

Because he would murder a mother and her babe to invoke fear in others."

He didn't need to tell his brother which mother and babe he spoke of. Rob slanted his gaze to Edmund, who was waiting for him atop his horse, clutching Aurelius in his arms.

"Ye know this fer certain?"

Colin told him everything, and Rob considered it all before he spoke. He was about to make one of the most important decisions as chief of their clan.

"The king will not send men to Camlochlin to pursue me if I desert," Colin told him confidently. He knew there was one thing that still meant more to James than power. 'Twas his daughter. "He's bound to us by blood."

"Aye," Rob agreed and swatted him on the back. "But do yer best no' to make enemies with him just the same. And dinna' tell Davina yer reasons fer leavin'."

His kin would stand by him. Colin hadn't doubted it.

"And William of Orange and yer war?" his brother put to him, painfully reminding Colin of what he'd been preparing for for three years. "Will ye remain at Camlochlin when ye bring her home?"

Colin looked toward the manor house and tightened his jaw. "The prince is another matter. I don't think he will ferget my service to James so easily."

"Verra well, then," Rob said, swinging into his saddle and lifting Edmund and Aurelius into his lap. "Do what ye must. Just stay alive."

Colin assured him he would, then reached up and took Edmund's hand in his. Hell, he didn't want to say farewell to him. Of all the things he'd prepared for in his life, caring for a child so deeply wasn't one of them. "Don't chase Aunt Maggie's animals."

"I won't," Edmund promised, swiping tears from his eyes.

Colin had never shed a tear a day in his life and he sure as hell wasn't about to do so now. But his heart ached in a way it never had before. He smiled—lest, God forbid, he should do anything else—patted Aurelius on the head, and stepped away when Rob's snorting mount sprang forward.

Passing him, Finn paused his mount and tossed him a resplendent grin. "Do not fret over the lady while ye're off fighting. I will look after her."

Colin cursed him as Finn dug in his heels and took off after the rest, his laughter filling the air behind him.

Like hell he would.

Turning for the house, Colin spotted Gillian at the door, her hands clutched to her chest. He could see her pink nose from where he stood and he knew how hard this was for her, how hard the days ahead would be for her. He would help her through them and crush anyone who tried to take her from him, including a silver-tongued, flaxen-haired bard.

When had he become a lady's champion? Hell. 'Twas downright pitiful. He moved toward her, bending on his way to pluck a poppy from the grass.

Chapter Thirty-three

The journey back to Dartmouth was torturous for Gillian. Nothing could fill the gap of Edmund's absence, and she traveled the first few days in silence. She liked listening to Colin and George talk about their families, and most nights she was able to fall asleep without weeping.

Funny thing about weeping. You can go for years without wasting a single teardrop on an undeserving soul. But let someone you cherish be taken from you and the floodgates crumble like leaves in the fall.

She missed Edmund's voice, his sweet smile, the way he felt in her arms. George was wonderful, as usual, even refraining from speech when, after the first night, Colin lay down beside her and took her in his arms. He did the same every night thereafter, filling her embrace, and her thoughts, with something other than her son.

"Have I told ye about my sister Mairi's courtship with Connor Grant?" His low voice soothed her nerves like a flagon of fine wine. "They loved each other as children and..."

He kept her from thinking about what she no longer had and made her long for her future in Camlochlin. By the end of their journey, she knew just about everything there was to know about the MacGregors of Skye. How they lived and loved, and what Edmund was likely doing at any given hour of the day.

It helped. Sharing clandestine kisses while George snored beside the fire helped. They did nothing more intimate than that, though on several occasions their desire for each other made it near impossible to resist. But they did—for her honor's sake, Colin whispered to her while he tenderly kissed her eyelids, her nose, her mouth.

For now, being in his arms was enough.

She knew she would have to be strong in the coming days, but she didn't want to release her sorrow completely. She would need it when she faced Geoffrey if all was to go according to plan.

Gerald Hampton and Philippe Lefevre met them at the gates. The former sneered at Gillian's bloodshot eyes until she wanted to rip her dagger from her skirts and hurl it into him.

Followed by their escorts, they went to Geoffrey's solar immediately to tell him the tragic news. Edmund had been kidnapped by a band of pistol-toting thieves. There was nothing any of them could do. Gillian wept while she begged her cousin to send his army to Essex to help in hunting the men down. Of course, Geoffrey refused.

"I need my men here," he told her, feigning remorse. "We'll send word to your father, though. I'm certain he'll be eager to retrieve the boy."

Gillian eyed him through her swollen lids, hating him more than she thought she ever could. Oh, but she was tired of him and his hatred for Edmund. This vile excuse for a man believed the Campbells of Argyll had taken her son. He'd helped arrange it! He sat here now thinking he'd won. He'd gotten rid of her child to make room for his own and his scant smile when he looked at her over his cup proved that he gloated over it.

"Of course he will," she said in a low, scathing tone, finished with cowering. "For he loves Edmund as much as you do."

His self-important sneer was like poison to her soul. It had eaten away at her for four years, always threatening to consume her. Edmund saved her from becoming what Geoffrey wanted. Colin saved her from becoming what she feared most.

"Why do you sound cross with me, Gillian?" Her cousin's sharp gaze cut to Colin's. "It wasn't me who snatched your son. Was it, Campbell?"

It was at that exact moment that Gillian realized something was wrong. What had she done? Why did she anger him instead of sticking with Colin's exact plans?

"They came in the night, my lord," Colin said beside her, his voice unshaken, his expression impassive. "We don't know who they were."

"Precisely." Geoffrey turned back to her and rose from his chair. "As terrible as this all is, we must find a way to put it behind us and start anew."

Dear God, she was going to be ill. She closed her eyes and turned her head away from him, calling up her strength not to stick him with her dagger while he moved closer to her.

"You're correct, Geoffrey," she told him softly, taking a step back. "I'm not cross with you. I'm upset. Surely you understand. I would retire to my room and—"

"Gillian," he purred from only a few inches away.

"You'll remain here with me. There are some things we need to discuss. I've waited patiently for your return and now I'm about to burst just at the sight of you."

From the corner of her eye, she saw Colin's fingers inching toward the hilt of his sword when Geoffrey walked around her and stopped to inhale her hair.

"I thought seizing your letters to William was my crowning glory in breaking that inflexible spine of yours. But truly, I've outdone myself this time."

"What you talking about, Geoffrey?" she asked, pulling away from his hand when he reached for her.

He glared at her a moment before his smile returned, bubbling into laughter. "You will *never* outfox me, Gillian. Neither with a prince nor a jackal sent by the king to deceive me."

The scrape of Colin's blade leaving its sheath snapped Gillian's attention to him. She watched the claymore's ascent and then its sleek metal flashing in the firelight as he brought it back down on the sword pointed at his back.

Mr. Lefevre's arms shook at the impact. He paled, as if he hadn't felt Colin's strength a hundred times already in practice. Gillian realized he hadn't.

"I am no fool, *mon ami.*" The French mercenary purposely dropped his sword and bowed out of the altercation.

"Gillian!" George shouted and rushed forward as Geoffrey moved behind her, his blade at her throat. A sharp blow from the hilt of Gerald Hampton's sword stopped her guardian.

Gillian cried out as George fell to the floor, unconscious. Colin eyed the tall man standing over his fallen body with a murderous glint in his eye that would have frightened an entire regiment of men.

Hampton winked in response.

Fear engulfed Gillian, but she had to keep her wits about her before anyone else was injured. She didn't think Geoffrey would kill her. He wanted her in his bed, not buried in the cemetery. It was Colin's reaction that frightened her more. He dropped his claymore and stilled his arms at his sides.

Behind her, Geoffrey cursed Lefevre, then drew her head back with a tug on her hair. He dipped his lips to her ear, turning her stomach when his hot breath touched her. "I've halted yet another one of your devious schemes, my darling betrothed."

She nearly fainted at the frantic pace of her heart. Did he speak of Edmund and Skye? No. He couldn't know. "Geoffrey, I beg you, explain."

"Explain?" Geoffrey pressed the edge of his blade to her throat. "I would prefer to convince you." Thankfully, he didn't spend much time sharpening his weapon the way Colin did with all of his. "Make another move," he warned when Colin inched forward, "and you will be showered with her blood."

Colin didn't need a weapon in his hands to look deadly. His body was as tight as a bowstring, his eyes sharp, and his senses honed to perfection. But he obeyed and didn't move, or speak, or seem to breathe.

"Now let's see," Geoffrey sang, victory won, "where shall I begin? How about with John Smithson? Gillian, dear, you wouldn't know him, but your Highlander might."

"I don't," Colin growled.

"You met him at Kingswear. He is one of my guardsmen. He certainly knows you. He says he fought at Sedgemoor, on Monmouth's side. Most of his battalion was slain under the command of a most ruthless Catholic general, a MacGregor, who, according to field gossip at the time, was a personal favorite of the king's."

Gillian blinked at Colin. Damn it, but they had been fools to underestimate her cousin. He knew Colin's true identity. He knew…Did he say a personal favorite of the king's?

"You were quite clever, General," Geoffrey continued, keeping her close.

General?

"You almost had me believing you were doing all this for me and the good of my name. I imagine my lovely cousin believes the same. Tell me, Gillian"—he pressed his mouth against her ear—"did you know he is a spy for the king? Sent here, I assume based on the questions he's asked of the other men and myself to gather information about the prince's arrival? Did you lure him to your bed with information about the prince? The names on the invitation, perhaps? Or did you fuck it out of you? I understand he's very good at gaining the information he requires. His expertise, I am told, is gaining the trust of his enemies."

Gillian kept her gaze steady on Colin. Her knees nearly buckled when the warrior retreated and the man looked away. Was it true then? Was he a spy for the king? What had she told him? Her vision blurred with the sharp, familiar hook of doubt and disappointment she was used to. She'd told him everything she knew. Was that all he'd wanted from her?

Colin, look at me! She wanted to shout at him. Information couldn't have been all he desired from her. She'd looked into his eyes while he'd made love to her. She'd seen beyond his cool veneer to the passions that fired him from deep within. She desperately needed to see that now.

"How could you do it, MacGregor?" Geoffrey implored, even though Gillian could clearly hear the smug enjoyment in his voice. "How could you use her for information? Make her think you care? What did you promise her?"

He promised her everything. Everything.

"She told me nothing." Colin's eyes flicked back to hers for a brief instant and then cooled to a deadly frost on Geoffrey. "I offered her nothing in return fer it, save to get her and her son out of Dartmouth before I set hell upon it."

Silence clung to the room, void of even the slightest snicker from Mr. Hampton as Colin's words fell like stones at their feet, rattling them a bit from their foundations. Geoffrey's blade trembled at her throat but did no damage, as his anger swelled away from her and onto the arrogant Highlander.

"Thank you for the warning, General MacGregor," he chuckled, refusing to be outwitted by anyone. "I shall prepare for battle."

Was that the hint of a smile she caught snaking Colin's mouth? There he stood, his secrets revealed to his enemy. Exposed to the heart of the woman he said he loved, and yet, he stood boldly, so filled with self-assurance that he made certain everyone felt the conviction of his words when he spoke them.

"I'm afraid there won't be enough time fer that."

"Well," her cousin countered, suddenly sounding less confident and a bit more desperate, "I will have defeated you in at least one of your endeavors. I dispatched a dozen of my men to Essex two days after you left."

Gillian stiffened against him. No!

"To what purpose?" she heard Colin ask, his voice a low rumble.

"To dispose of her bastard and the men who made off with him."

Gillian didn't wait to hear what Colin would say or do.

Her logic fled from the fury and terror rising up inside her. Dispose of her son? Why then, she had nothing left to fear. The game had just changed.

"Geoffrey, hear me, you vile son of tavern whore." She gritted her teeth and held up her palms to stop Colin's advance when the edge of his blade scraped her flesh. "If you're going to kill me then you had better do it now. Because if you don't," she continued calmly, at the edge of madness, "if Edmund is harmed, I will make you suffer and die a terrible death. Whether on the tip of my dagger, in your wine, or in my own body, and I have to suffer and die with you. Rest assured, I will poison you."

"Then I should simply admit defeat then, eh?" Geoffrey angled her head so he could smile at her. "If I can't have you in my bed, what good are you?"

"None," she promised, staring him straight in the eyes. "It's me, or you, or both of us. If Edmund is dead, there is no longer a reason for my breath. So choose."

He lowered his mouth to her ear and said in a quiet voice, "And relinquish my shield against a savage who wants my neck between his teeth? No. Instead, I think I will let you watch your false hero die."

"No more threats, Geoffrey." She shoved her hand into the fold of her skirts, produced her dagger, and without pause in her breath, jammed the blade into his side. "Only cowards make them," she murmured, stepping away from him when he crumpled to his knees. "And I am done with being one."

She spared Colin a brief glance to let him know his course was open and ducked out of his way. She hoped he would do whatever he meant to do quickly so that they could make haste and head toward Skye. Perhaps it wasn't too late to save Edmund.

Chapter Thirty-four

There wasn't time for Colin to pause to appreciate how incredibly braw his Gillian was. Hampton was coming at him, his heavy sword lifted high over his head, ready to strike. Colin ducked beneath the whistling slice of metal and came back up, feet braced, arms outstretched in opposite directions, and a pistol in either hand. One was tilted directly in Hampton's face, the other aimed at Devon.

"Drop yer blade, Hampton. I'm feeling merciful today and may let ye keep yer head."

"Kill him!" Devon screamed, clutching the hilt of the dagger buried deep in his side. "His flintlocks aren't loaded!"

When Colin cocked both hammers, Hampton's eyes opened wide, hopefully with the memory of Colin's warning that he would keep his pistols ready at all times. The giant's sword clanked to the ground.

"Get beside him." Colin motioned Hampton toward his cowering master. Och, but he wanted to kill the arrogant Earl of Devon. Here. Now. His body trembled with the desire to cut open his throat. The bastard had sent a dozen men to kill Edmund. A dozen against four warriors from Skye. 'Twas almost insulting. Colin knew Edmund was safe, but that didn't change the fact that Devon had tried to have him killed.

"Go ahead and shoot then," Devon challenged from the floor. Aye, Colin thought, and alert the rest of the garrison to the solar. Night had fallen and most were likely too drunk by now to cause a decent stir, but with Gillian here, he wasn't about to take that chance.

"I'll come back and kill ye later." He flipped his pistol over in his hand and brought the finely crafted handle down on Devon's temple with a resounding whack. "Move," he warned Hampton as he stepped away, "or I'll kill *ye* now."

He called Gillian to stand behind him while he pushed at Gates with the tip of his boot, his eyes darting to Hampton and then to the door. "Come now, friend. On yer feet," he said when Gates opened his eyes and pulled himself to his knees. "'Tis time to go."

He was about to lead them out of the solar when he heard sounds he was well familiar with coming from somewhere outside. The thunder of horses followed by shouts of command and firing muskets.

His army had arrived.

Hell.

Not now. Not with her here. He didn't trust the king not to kill her. He had to get her away. Snatching her hand, he pulled her toward the door.

"What is it?" Gates asked, holding his hand to his head and following them down the hall with Lefevre hot on their heels.

How could he tell them? In his pursuit of his glorious

war, he had sought the trust of many. Once he'd achieved it, he didn't care what scars his betrayal left in his wake. But Gillian and Gates were not his enemies, and it tore at the fibers of his being to have to admit to deceiving them.

"I am..." He closed his mouth and began again. "My army arrives. A wee bit sooner than I had expected but here they are." This wasn't the time for apologies. They needed to move.

"Why are they here?" Gates asked him, keeping pace as Colin ran, pulling Gillian behind him, down another winding corridor.

"They are here to take Dartmouth," Colin told him honestly, heading toward a hidden stairway. During his nightly investigation of the castle, he'd discovered every exit. The stairs around the next passage would lead them to the back of the castle, close to the smith.

"Then it's true."

Colin closed his eyes for an instant at the sound of Gillian's voice, unsteady and unsure. He knew what she thought of him and he hated it. But there would be time later to convince her that she was wrong.

"Aye, 'tis true." He tugged her down the stairs, scanning his eyes over the shadows cloaking the bottom landing. "But now, ye must be away from here. They will surely kill Gates and they will not stop when they get to ye."

She stopped him when they reached the last step, her eyes wide and moist in the dim torchlight. "What about Edmund? He said—"

"Edmund is safe," he promised her, swiping his thumb over her cheek. "My brother may likely have killed the entire dozen men Devon sent after them on his own. Either way, Edmund rides with the MacGregors and the Grants. Nothing will harm him."

When she nodded, looking a bit more hopeful, he hurried her to the exit.

"This was all to stop William then?" Gates opened the door, spilling moonlight into the hall. "It should have been clear to me that you were no mercenary," the captain told him as Colin passed him on the way out. "But you convinced me otherwise."

Pausing, Colin turned to look at him. They were friends. Colin suspected…he hoped they would remain so for many years. "Would ye have trusted me in getting Gillian and Edmund away from here if ye knew the truth?"

Gates stared at him for a moment, then shook his head and closed the door behind him. "But you should have told me nonetheless."

"Where are we going?"

They all turned to see Lefevre waiting for direction.

Hell, another man Colin found tolerable and would prefer to see live. Still, he didn't trust him enough to let him accompany them to Essex, and then on to Skye.

"We're parting ways, *mon frere,*" Colin told him, patting him on the arm. "I suggest ye get yer horse and move yer arse in that direction if ye want to get out alive." He pointed southeast. "I trained the men who are about to storm the castle."

"How do we get our horses?" Gates whispered as the sounds of men's voices drew closer. Soon, the army would surround the fortress. "The stable is in full view."

"We have to run for it one at a time." Colin surveyed the distance. "We'll stay close to the shadows and walk the horses out. The men will be busy fighting. They won't see us. I'll go first."

He sprinted close to the castle walls, avoiding the

swath of moonlight illuminating the narrow path to the stable. Inside, he turned to watch Gillian make her way to him next. Behind her, the sound of battle drew his attention long enough to miss the movement to his right.

"What's this?" Lieutenant de Atre swerved from his path to his horse and blocked Gillian's advance. "Have your champions abandoned you?"

"As you are about to abandon your friends, Lieutenant," Gillian accused quietly.

When de Atre reached for her, Colin forgot the army and everything else and strode out of the stable toward them.

"With all the clamor inside, no one will hear us," the lieutenant snarled.

"De Atre!" Colin shouted, sliding his claymore from its scabbard. "What were ye told about touching her?"

The lieutenant whirled around looking somewhat startled, until he saw who it was. "Running off with the whore while the captain fights the king's men? Clever." He smiled. "But I'll take her from here."

"Draw yer weapon," Colin warned him and then stepped back to wait.

De Atre laughed and freed his sword with gusto. "This time, I'll give you no quarter."

"And I'll do the same," Colin promised with a dark smile, then stepped aside to avoid a blow to his ribs. Och, how he wanted to take his time and convince de Atre that he was correct not to trust a Scot. But there was no time to waste.

He brought his sword down hard three times, twice on his opponent's blade, lighting their faces with sparks, then deep into de Atre's belly.

Colin watched the lieutenant's stunned expression as

his body slumped to the ground. He pulled his sword free and met Gillian's horrified gaze.

"Move."

She ran around him and he followed. A moment later, Gates joined them, cursing de Atre to Hades on his way to his horse. Lefevre left the shadows last and Colin watched to make certain no one saw him.

The clash of swords rang through the night, accompanied by shouts and screams as his army butchered Dartmouth's garrison. He was supposed to be with them.

"Colin?"

He turned to Gillian, watching him from her place beside her mount. "Get your horse and let's be away."

He nodded, turning back to the fray one last time. He moved toward her, then stopped as a rider passed his vision in the distance. Colin knew him by the set and breadth of his shoulders and the swatch of gray hair, pale in the moonlight.

The king was here to watch the battle from the cliffs just beyond the castle perimeter. He was here, and he would be looking for Colin.

"Take her to Essex." He spun around to Gates. "By now my brother knows that my identity has been discovered. He will send someone back to yer home to warn me."

"You're not coming with us then?"

He looked at Gillian but before he could answer her, she turned away.

"I understand," she said quietly. "You fight for the king."

"I fight fer my kin," he said, moving toward her.

"Well, you got what you came here for. I'm indebted to you for all you've done for Edmund and me. Farewell,

Colin." She tugged on her reins, ready to go. Just like that.

He knew what she thought of him. He'd used her, and now he was done with her. Nae, he wouldn't let her part from him believing that. He stopped her with a hand on her arm. "Aye, I got what I wanted, and now I know what it is. 'Tis ye, lass. I should have told ye who I was, what my purpose here was, but I was afraid."

She looked about to weep all over him. He would have waited while she did. "You?" she laughed instead, the sound hollow and laden with misgivings. "Afraid? Come now, Colin, you can do better than that."

"I was afraid of losing ye." He pulled her back when she moved to leave yet again. Was she going to make him grovel at her feet? Hell, he would do that too. "Ferget why I came here, Gillian. Ye changed my heart and made it a better place."

She looked up at him, clutched in his arms. "You lied to me."

" 'Twas the hardest thing I've ever done. But nae harm has come from it."

Again she tried to wrangle free of his hold. "None that you can see."

Och, hell. He knew he'd hurt her. Gillian needed to trust him, and he'd taken that from her. He would make it up to her if it took him the remainder of his days. "Listen to me, my love." He took her face in his hands when she veiled her eyes from him. "I'll never deceive ye again. I know I ask ye a difficult thing when I ask ye to let me be the man in yer life who never lets ye down again. The father Edmund never had."

His heart sparked with hope at the tears running down her face and he bent his head to kiss her. Her mouth tasted of salt and uncertainty and it broke his heart that he had done this to her.

"I will need more convincing when you return to us," she whispered when he withdrew.

He smiled, wanting nothing more in life than to spend every day with her. But there was something he needed to do first.

Chapter Thirty-five

$\mathscr{J}$ames, king of the three kingdoms, sat in his saddle and gave the fortress before him and the surrounding countryside close examination. So, this was where William planned to land his ships. The estuary was large enough to hold an entire fleet. How many men would his nephew bring with him? Would he bring his wife, James's daughter Mary? Or would she wait to return to England until her father was dead or deposed and the new king sat on the throne?

He shook his head as the roar of the surf blended with the sounds of battle in the castle ahead. If he lived to be sixty, he would never forget the pain of Mary's betrayal. He knew he should never have married her to a Protestant, relative or not. He thought he could forgive her when proof of William's intentions to take the throne had been brought to him. But she never answered his letters, and recently, he'd learned that she'd poisoned his youngest daughter Anne against him. He thanked the saints, as he often did, that Davina lived with the MacGregors, far removed from politics and the courtly life. Davina was his true firstborn heir, but she could never rule, especially with a Highlander for a husband. Imagine, a MacGregor ruling England!

Thankfully, James no longer needed Davina, for soon he would have a son to rule in his name. A son he would have to protect from William, and from his enemies in the church. Colin's last missive naming the bishop as a traitor had been quite disturbing. He would have to mend relations with the Anglicans once this business was over. Thank the saints the French were on his side. The French, and Colin MacGregor.

James smiled in the moonlight, imagining that the screams coming from within the castle belonged to William's men instead of Lord Devon's. Soon they would, thanks to his clever general. The king wanted to be here when William landed and was met by the Royal Army. He would praise Colin for thinking of it later and offer him the Earldom of Essex for killing William with his own blade. A title would suit Colin, and once James was again secure on the throne, there were going to be many titles made available.

"Jameson," he sighed, tired of waiting and eager for victory tonight, "go inside and see what keeps General MacGregor from coming to me with news and some heads."

He watched his escort ride off into the dwindling melee, then startled at a sound to his right.

"D'ye truly think if I was inside, this fight would still be going on? My men are insulting me."

James grinned at Colin, stepping out of the shadows. He wasn't offended that the Highlander didn't offer him the bow he was due. When he met Colin three years ago, the arrogant young warrior had remained stubbornly upright. It had been one of the first things James had liked about him. Thinking of that day and all the days since with Colin at his side filled the king with a measure of regret. With William gone and no longer a threat, Colin's visits to Whitehall Palace would become less frequent.

"Do you know," the king said, happy to see him, "you are the only man I have trusted since my brother Charles died?"

"And yers, my lord, was the only trust I truly sought since I left my faither's home."

The king nodded, accepting the compliment with grace, and then gave him a careful looking over. "Then tell me why you are not covered in blood and Dartmouth is still unsecured."

"'Tis as good as secure. Devon lays wounded and likely unconscious in his solar, and most of his men are poorly skilled."

"That doesn't speak well of our soldiers," the king snorted.

"Killing takes time." Colin shrugged, setting his eyes on the castle, their color matching the torchlight that illuminated it on all sides in the darkness.

"How did you know we were coming this night?" James asked him, chilled suddenly by the cool disregard Colin offered the men he'd dined and drunk with for the last month and a half.

"I didn't."

"Then why is Devon wounded and unconscious in his solar? Was it not by your hand?"

"'Twas by my hand and the hand of his cousin."

The king raised his eyebrows. "The woman?"

"Aye," Colin said, turning those wolf-colored eyes on him. "The woman ye sent mercenaries to kill."

James's breath quickened with a momentary flash of anger that his commands weren't carried out. But it was soon replaced by the kind of unease one might feel when the dead passed through them. He didn't like the feeling at all and he didn't like the way the man who was almost a son to him was looking at him now. The same way he looked at his enemies. Ready to stand, face, and conquer whatever came against him.

The king regarded him, wondering if he had been a fool not to fear him all these years. Was it possible then? Had his resolute general fallen for Lord Dearly's daughter as James had suspected? Damn it to hell if he had. "How do you know it was I who sent them?"

"One of them told me before I nearly severed his head from his body."

"I see." James's fingers tightened around the pommel of his saddle. If this were any other man but Colin MacGregor, his head would be rolling down the cliffs for making a king squirm. "You know her father, the Earl of Essex, planned this entire uprising?"

"Is that why ye ordered the slaughter of a woman and her babe?"

"No." James didn't appreciate explaining his actions to anyone, let alone a soldier. But Colin had always been truthful with him. He deserved the same. He also deserved to be flogged for his boldness. Fortunately, James was terribly fond of him. "You are the closest thing I have to a son, only better, because you are loyal to me to a fault. Like a father—and with the matchmaker who is my dear wife—I had anticipated a courtship for you, and hoped, of course, that you would choose a Catholic noblewoman as your bride. But there were no women who held your interest at court for longer than a night.

None abroad whom you ever found worth mentioning to me in missives. Until you came here." He cast Colin an indulgent smile. "She distracted you, General. She's a Protestant, and eventually she would have poisoned your mind against me. I see that you're angry about it and I—"

Colin's impassive expression didn't change when he shook his head. "I am disappointed."

"Remember to whom you speak," the king warned in a low tone.

His general returned his gaze to the castle, stared at its walls for a moment, and then said softly, "I wish I could."

James bristled in his saddle. He'd had enough. "You stand here and insult me, the only man I would ever allow to do so. But I warn you, try me no further. Your Captain Drummond is inside fighting without you. You will tell me now why that is."

"Verra well then, I will," Colin said, turning slowly back to him. "I'm going home."

For a moment, James simply stared at him, doubting the good of his ears. He couldn't be serious. Home to Camlochlin? Now? With William set to arrive within the next few months. "You cannot."

"With respect, Your Majesty, I am. I am nae longer convinced of the purpose of my sword. I know 'tis to protect, but 'tis nae longer to protect ye."

James's mouth opened into a tight O. "I'll have you hanged for desertion."

A smile, much like the one he offered his men in Whitehall's tiltyard before he set them on their knees, quirked Colin's lips. "Will ye? How d'ye think my kin would feel about that? Rob is chief now. I've spoken to him about my decision and I have his support. With all of England and the church against ye, d'ye truly want to make enemies of the MacGregors?"

"Do you threaten me?" James nearly choked on the words as they left his mouth. "Is this about Lord Dearly's daughter? Do you threaten to leave my service, my well-being, even denying me from seeing my daughter?" His voice rose to a roar. "Over a woman?"

"I don't wish to threaten ye at all," Colin said, his voice remaining infuriatingly calm. "My brother's wife makes us kin and fer that, I would see nae harm brought upon ye. I only wish to leave England."

"But William is coming! You would allow a Protestant to sit on the throne?"

"I would prefer his swift defeat," Colin admitted, providing James a measure of relief. "But not fer the reasons ye would like to believe. Ye have let the lusty siren of absolute power lure ye into tyranny."

"Your head might just roll tonight, after all."

Colin had the supreme audacity to step closer to the king's mount and continue speaking. "If I don't tell ye, friend, I fear no one will until ye're seeking refuge in King Louis's courts."

James found that despite his anger, he could still smile at him. "You've never lacked balls, have you, Colin? I've always found it quite refreshing in comparison to the spineless subservience of my court." Yes, this young rooster bowed to no man. He would do as he pleased and without hesitation go to war with anyone who tried to stop him. James didn't want such a battle. He had too much to lose. Namely his throne. "I do what I must for our faith, son," he said, growing serious. "As I always have. Doubt the conviction of my actions if you must, but help me defeat the Protestant usurper before you leave

England's service. Help me stop William and I will grant you anything you wish."

"My lord!"

They both turned to Captain Richard Drummond as he raced his horse toward them from the castle.

"General," Drummond acknowledged, dismounting and spreading his gaze over Colin's unbloodied shirt before returning it to the king. "Dartmouth is ours. Lord Devon has been spared as you requested and awaits you in the Great Hall."

"Any word on our victory at Kingswear from Lieutenant Willingham?" James asked.

"I'm certain it will arrive momentarily, my lord," Drummond assured him.

"How many men did you dispatch to Kingswear?" Colin asked his second in command, then followed that query with half a dozen more, proving to James that leading an army still fired his blood.

"We missed your presence inside, General."

"Ye did well without it, Captain." Colin's stony expression softened just a bit, but James noted it.

"Your general wishes to leave my service," the king said, ignoring MacGregor's murderous glance and trotting away. "Come inside with me, Colin. At least hear your men's views on a decision that could cost them their lives."

Stopping on the cliffs with George and her mount at her side, Gillian watched Colin speaking with the king and another man. She couldn't hear their words, only the wind and the roar of the surf...or was that her heart pounding in her ears? She knew why he wasn't coming with her to get Edmund. He had a war to win. The wind whipped away her tears but she swiped at her cheeks anyway. She tried not to think about him dying in it. He said he would be the man in her life who never let her down again. A father to Edmund. She wanted it more than anything she'd ever wanted in her life. Was he sincere? He'd lied to her. Could she ever trust him again? Aye, she could. His eyes had never lied to her. But what did it matter? He was a general in the Royal Army. He had to fight King James's war against William whether he wanted to or not. He had tried to tell her, that night in George's guestroom, coiled in each other's arms. He'd asked her if he should stand idly by while his freedom was threatened. She understood his meaning more clearly now. The MacGregors were Catholics, and they had already been proscribed once before. Who knew what new laws a Protestant king would decree upon them? Colin fought for his kin and their freedom, and he would willingly go to war to protect them.

When she saw him following the king into Dartmouth, she tried not to feel abandoned again. His choice might be for a noble cause, but what if he was killed? She would weep for him every day and never wed. For what man could ever take his place, or love her son the way he did? What would she do without him in Camlochlin, with people she didn't know? Where would she go if they asked her to leave? It made her angry that he'd remained behind. Anger, she reasoned while she mounted her horse and steered it north, was better than suffering the terrible weight of her conquered heart. She'd allowed it. She had no one else to blame for letting down her guard and allowing another man fill her with fanciful dreams.

"Do you think he will live through a war with the Dutch?" she asked George when biting her tongue became too painful.

"I've no doubt he could bring victory to James with his sword alone," her captain told her while they wove their way carefully over the bluffs.

"Aye, you're correct," she breathed gustily, feeling a bit relieved. "He will live."

"And William will be defeated."

She could feel George's eyes on her, silently asking her if she realized what his victory would mean. She did. England's Catholic king would remain. The punishments he had already ordered against the Protestants would worsen for their disloyalty, beginning with lesser sects like the Cameronians...and the Presbyterian Covenanters.

"Your wife's family will suffer if King James remains on the throne," she answered his unspoken question. "And Colin's will suffer if he doesn't. All this killing over religion. Do you think God approves?"

"No," her companion said quietly.

"Nor do I." She shook off any more thoughts of what they could not change and flicked her reins, taking off along the sandy shore. "Now let us go find my son and pray that I won't have to ride back here and kill Geoffrey myself."

Chapter Thirty-six

As Colin had predicted, his brother had sent the bard Finlay Grant back to George's manor house to warn him that his identity had been discovered—and to get word to them that the child Edmund remained unharmed in the chief's care just outside of Essex.

Gillian wasn't surprised when George insisted that Finn take her on to the others without him. She hadn't expected her captain and his wife to come to Camlochlin with her. She also hadn't expected the day when she was to be parted from her dearest friend to come so quickly. How did one prepare for such a day?

"Remember me fondly, my dear captain." She flung her arms around his neck and did not fight back the tears she would shed for him. "As I will always remember you."

Their departure was brief, with her eager to get to Edmund and Captain Gates warning Finn to guard her with his life.

Eight days and seven nights later she knew George would have been relieved at the way Colin's kin guarded her and Edmund, never letting them out of their sight.

Gillian didn't mind such stringent attention. They were nothing like the men of Dartmouth. Though they shared drink around the fire at night, they spoke kindly and courteously to her. Edmund liked them too, preferring to ride with one of them instead of with her on some days.

And Lord, but they were a handsome bunch. Not as handsome as Colin, of course, but she could barely look at Connor's slow, double-dimpled grin without it spinning her head just a little. Rob was infinitely more dangerous in appearance, with shoulders a league wide and hair as black as a raven's wing. Will's eyes glittered like diamonds in the sun when he laughed, which was often, and usually at someone else's expense. And Finn. Heavens, what could she say about Finn, save that she was certain he felled many hearts in Skye?

"We ride hard, I know," Finn told her one night after catching her rubbing her bottom before settling in by the fire. "We will reach Glenelg by morning and be in Camlochlin by nightfall."

If that was supposed to make her feel better, it failed. It wasn't the idea of starting a new life in a strange place with people who probably wouldn't like her because she was a Protestant that set her to weeping each night as she snuggled close on the hard ground with Edmund. She had prayed that Colin would change his mind about fighting and head out after them. But if he had, he would have caught up with them by now. He wasn't coming, and the thought of never seeing him again left her aching with despair.

She didn't speak of him. The others did it for her. She learned much about Colin from the warriors traveling with her, and everything they told her further convinced her that battle came above all else for him.

"He fears nothin', that one," Will told her after they

crossed the narrows by boat the next morning and docked in Kylerhea. "Dinna' fret over him. He'll turn up alive and well in a year or two, after the war."

Passing them on his way to retrieve his horse, Connor smacked Will across the back of the head and glared at him. "Ye're an insensitive lout, Will. Ye need a woman in yer life."

"I have plenty," Will called back, then took off after him.

Finn came up behind her, singing a ditty about the chief and his ability to keep his breakfast in his belly where it belonged during their boat ride. He winked at her as he mounted his saddle and began the next stanza, aiming his voice at Will this time:

"The chasm of hell comes quickly, auld friend...
Tread cautiously 'round every bend.
The cliffs of Elgol are deadly to all...
But none turn so green when the chasm is seen,
as Will while he prays not to fall."

Gillian couldn't help but smile at the light banter between Finn and Will as she fit her foot into her stirrup. Two large hands closed around her waist and lifted her the rest of the way. She turned and offered her thanks to Rob, whose color had returned to his face once he was back on solid ground. She watched him scoop up Edmund and Aurelius and set them down in his saddle before he followed.

"Colin spoke fondly of your wife," she said, needing a distraction from more agonizing thoughts...and the notion of crossing deadly cliffs.

Rob favored her with a smile so much like Colin's that she nearly wept. Again. Damnation, but it seemed that once the floodgates had opened they would never close.

"I'm surprised he told ye of us," the chief said. "I'm surprised by many of the decisions he's made of late."

She eyed him doubtfully. "Are you surprised that he remained behind to fight? All I've heard for a fortnight is how he has waited and trained for his glorious battle."

"I dinna' think he remained behind to fight fer the king."

"Why else would he?"

Instead of answering her, Rob shifted his vivid blue eyes from her to the downy top of her son's head. "Love shows nae mercy to a man. When 'tis true, his dreams and desires become meaningless if she is no' a part of them. Colin gives up his war fer ye, and I must tell ye, Lady Gillian"—he smiled at her—"I sit in awe of the lass who has won my brother's heart."

Having mastered the skill years ago, she held back the tears welling up in her eyes. She would not let them fall in front of the MacGregor chief. He was pure, raw strength, born and bred in the harsh seclusion of the mountains, as were the women. She would not appear soft and weak to any one of them.

"Giving up his war would mean desertion." Lord, the thought of Colin being hanged nearly shattered the last of her control. She glanced down at Edmund petting his dog.

"The king will let him go," Rob said softly. The confidence in his voice pulled her attention back to him.

"How do you know?"

"Because I'm his daughter's husband and he doesna' want a battle with his kin in the north."

His daughter's husband? Hadn't Colin told her Rob's wife was called Davina? "How..."

"Ye will discover the whole truth of it at Camlochlin."

That was fine with her, since her head was already spinning in every direction. She needed to stay focused on what was important. "If he has left the army unhindered, then where is he?"

"I dinna' know," Rob admitted, skimming his eyes over the vast hills around them. "But if he means to return to ye, he will. Nothin' will stop him. Trust me."

She wanted to. The sheer authority with which he spoke convinced her that she could. Until they rounded the end of Loch Slapin and the cliffs of Elgol filled her vision. She tilted her head up and almost turned her horse around. Dear Lord, she hadn't been in the saddle in almost four years. She could never maneuver the animal around precarious footing.

Thankfully, her chaperones didn't expect her to. After Connor helped her into his saddle, he tied her mount to his, leaped in front of her, and told her to hold on.

She did. For her life. She kept her eyes squeezed shut and stopped breathing at least fourteen times when Connor's horse bucked and neighed, not wanting to go forward. They pushed along in a single row up the narrow precipice, Rob and Edmund in the lead, with Will directly behind him, and her and Connor third. At the rear, Finn's voice rang out along the rocky wall in an ode to his chief.

"Your brother seems to recall every heroic deed Rob has ever performed," Gillian noted, her face pressed against Connor's back and one ear toward the bard. His voice, as angelic as his countenance, was distracting and soothing.

"Aye, and I'm tempted to smash him across the head with the flat of my blade. It's as irritating as hell."

"Finn," Will called over his shoulder, "sing something aboot Connor. He's pouting."

Much to Gillian's horror, Connor turned around in his saddle, taking his eyes off the pebbly path.

"Don't sing about me or anyone here. I know all the damn tales, and after hearing them a thousand times, I wish we'd died in them."

"Fine then," his brother quipped. "But I cannot recall what I sang fer ye. Are ye certain I immortalized ye in verse? If not, I can make something up."

Dear God, Connor laughed. Gillian was too afraid to open her eyes to see how close to the edge they had come.

Finally, he righted himself, but Gillian's prayers of thanks were interrupted by Edmund's shout that they were in the clouds. She didn't dare open her eyes to see if he was telling the truth.

After what seemed a hundred lifetimes, Connor stopped his horse and turned to her. "We're home."

Opening her eyes, Gillian saw nothing but sky and jagged mountaintops. Then she looked down. The vale rolled out before her in a lush array of heather and wild daffodils. Cottages of various sizes dotted the countryside with men and women working around them, beating blankets or hanging laundry out to dry. Some of the men pounded leather while others pulled their boats in from the glistening bay to the west. Sheep and cattle grazed the misty hills with lazy abandon, and everywhere Gillian set her eyes, she saw children.

Gillian decided that she'd never seen any place more beautiful than this. More than just a safe haven nestled within the mountains, the fortified castle rose up out of the side of Sgurr na Stri with dark, jagged towers piercing the mist rolling down from the Cuillins. Guards patrolled the battlements and shouted below when they saw their chief returning from the cliffs.

"It gets frigid here in the winter," Connor told her, leading them down into the vale. "Ye and yer babe are welcome to stay at Ravenglade with me and Mairi. Or if ye prefer, I'm sure there's plenty of room at Campbell Keep with Tristan and Isobel."

"I'd like to stay here." Gillian sighed with contentment. Oh, how she wished Colin were here so she could thank him, kiss him...

"There's my wife," she heard Connor tell her with a slight catch in his voice. He pointed to a dark-haired beauty waving at him from the castle entrance. "She's going to like ye. If ye love Camlochlin, then ye'll have a friend in her."

Within an hour, Gillian had more friends than she'd had in all her years put together. The women of Camlochlin were nothing as she'd imagined. Unconcerned with her religious preference, they welcomed her into their fold like a sister they hadn't seen in years. Colin's aunt, Maggie MacGregor, wasted little time getting to the bottom of what Gillian and her son were doing here—which left the other women eyeing her with something resembling admiration widening their eyes.

"Colin can be as cold as a stone wall," his sister, Mairi, pointed out, rubbing her swollen belly while she and Rob's petite wife, Davina, walked with her toward another of the hundreds of rooms inside the castle. "I miss him terribly. I pray that he is..." She sniffed, cursed, and then wiped the moisture from her eyes.

"There now." Davina, whom Gillian had learned was King James's firstborn daughter, gave her sister-in-law's arm a tender pat. "We've all agreed that Colin can take care of himself. He would be insulted if he knew you worried over him."

Gillian smiled, knowing she was correct, and stepped inside a massive chamber to meet Tristan and his very pregnant wife, Isobel.

"Aunt Maggie is seeing to the children, but she will be here momentarily," Mairi told her brother when she reached the bed where Isobel lay clutching her enormous belly. "How is she?"

"The pains are more frequent. I've sent for the midwives." Tristan looked up from beneath weary lids and blinked at Gillian. "Who is this?"

Gillian's knees nearly gave way beneath her. Save for his shoulder-length hair and the worry creasing his dark brow, he looked so much like Colin, she thought she had to be dreaming of his return.

"Colin's," he said, sounding more astonished after Mairi filled him in than if his wife had just delivered twins. "'Tis truly a day fer miracles."

"The miracle," his wife groaned and writhed from the bed, "will be if someone gets this babe out of me sometime this century!"

"That is why we are here, sweeting." Maggie swept into the room with two midwives following close behind. She excused her nephew, who refused to leave until he kissed his wife and whispered words of encouragement to her.

Gillian took up her steps to leave behind Tristan. This was a sacred event to be shared by close family. She would find her way around, eager to explore without footsteps trailing behind her.

Davina stopped her. "Stay, I implore you, and help us welcome our newest addition to the clan."

Lord, but Gillian understood why Colin's tone had softened when he spoke of this woman. With hair the same color as the pearls around her neck and her wispy frame, her ethereal beauty reminded Gillian of the fairies of lore. She was the chief's wife and the king's daughter, yet her demeanor was demure, her tone soft and inviting. She was being kind and Gillian liked her for it. But she would not intrude.

"I should see to my son."

"Edmund is off playing with the children," Maggie informed her while she carefully rolled down Isobel's blanket. "He is safe. You needn't worry."

Pausing at the door, Gillian cleared her burning throat and blinked back a fresh spring of tears. Playing. Her son was playing with other children. She needn't worry. She smiled as a surge of happiness welled up inside her. She never wanted to leave this place. With or without Colin, she would make a life here for her and Edmund. And, oh, she thought, rolling up her sleeves and joining the others around the bed, it felt good to do womanly things with other women.

"What do you think of Camlochlin, so far?" one of them asked her while Maggie fed Isobel some tea and propped her pillows.

They all glanced at her, awaiting her reply.

"I know it may sound silly, but I feel like I've come home."

"It doesna' sound silly at all." Across the bed, Mairi smiled at her. They all did.

Aye, she was home. At last.

※

Chapter Thirty-seven

*A*nd surely you don't mean for us to travel over those cliffs."

Colin looked at Gates across the fire. "Of course not. We will make our journey over the hills. I'll tell ye all about Elgol's cliffs so that ye'll understand the nature of the landscape ye'll be calling home."

"Is it very cold?" Sarah Gates asked him, snuggling closer to her husband and reaching for her sister's hand.

"It can be, aye," he told her honestly. "And quiet."

Sarah's kin, consisting of her mother, Helen Harrison, her two brothers and their kin, and her younger sister, Leslie, all wore the same pensive expression.

"Well," her eldest brother said, breaking the silence around the campsite, "it's better than being arrested or shot for our beliefs as our father was."

On this, they all agreed. Gates's in-laws had already lost much.

"But your people are Catholics too, are they not?" Sarah's mother asked. "Why would they take us in?"

Aye, the fact that these people were active Covenanters wasn't going to go over well with his kin. He and Mairi used to go out at night and hunt members of these small anti-Catholic sects, and now here he was bringing almost a score of them home.

What choice did he have? 'Twas either ensure their safety—which he couldn't do unless he brought them to Camlochlin—or watch Gates go off into battle against the king's men.

He sure as hell wasn't about to do that. He and Gates were friends, and besides that, it would make Gillian very happy to have her captain remain in her life.

"They'll take ye in because I will remind them that ye suffer, same as they did."

They shared a light supper from the provisions the Harrisons had taken with them when they left their homes. It had taken much to convince them to leave but finally they'd heeded George's warning. The king had made a promise in Colin's presence, just after he commanded Lord Devon's immediate death, that all Protestant divisions would end at his fist. If they wanted a bloody war, he would give them one.

"Ye must come now," Colin reminded them as he lay his head down in the grass. "I willna' be returning this way again. Ye'll have peaceful lives, and if William succeeds at taking the throne, ye can return to yer homes."

It was another reason he wouldn't bring them to Camlochlin across the cliffs, though it cut a day of traveling. None knew the pass; it was kept reserved for kin alone. A MacGregor needn't worry about arrows in his chest when he returned from the cliffs. The hills, though, they were reserved for strangers. Most times, unwanted ones. He would have to ride ahead and wave his plaid to signal his peaceful arrival until he was more clearly recognized.

"We're coming," Sarah said, speaking for the rest of them with their approval.

"Get some sleep then. We ride for Glenelg in the morning." Colin closed his eyes, then opened them again a moment later and ground his teeth at the stars.

It sickened him to think how his heart accelerated in anticipation of setting his eyes on Gillian again. Or the way his belly tightened from the inside out when he thought of holding her in his arms. He was a warrior, for hell's sake, not some peach-faced whelp.

But he missed her like hell.

"Colin?"

"Aye?"

"You have my thanks in this," Gates said. "In getting *all* of us out of England."

Colin closed his eyes and thought about everything that had happened since leaving Gillian at Dartmouth. Having little choice to do otherwise, James had relieved him of his duty. Colin was going home, either as a deserter, or as the man who gave the king back his daughter and who had the power to take her away. He'd met Gates on the road back to Essex and warned him of the king's intentions. It had taken almost a fortnight to gather the captain's wife and her kin in Norfolk, and another fortnight to reach the Highlands. He was bone weary, but knowing Gillian and Edmund were waiting for him drove him onward.

He tapped his hand on the ground and opened his eyes again. "George, do ye think she's fergiven me?"

He heard nothing for an eternal moment but the sharp snap of twigs in the fire. The captain couldn't have fallen asleep already. Mayhap he didn't want to answer with the truth he suspected.

What if she hadn't forgiven him? What if she couldn't?

"I know I kept much from her, but—"

"From both of us," George finally spoke. "How did you manage to remain so guarded and determined to your purpose? I couldn't have done it," he said in a humble tone. "Not if I loved her. I would have broken and told her whatever she wished to know. I admire your strength of will."

Colin lifted his head off the ground and laughed at his friend. "Are ye jesting? My strength of will was shattered the day after I met her. As fer remaining determined to my purpose," he said, sobering at the truth of it all, "do ye think I came to Dartmouth to fall in love with my enemy's cousin and snatch her from his hands? Nothing has purpose anymore but her . . . her and Edmund." He fell back to the earth and the stars twinkling at him. "There is nothing to admire, my friend."

This time it wasn't Gates who answered him, but Gates's wife. "I disagree."

Colin paused his mount at the top of the crest as the sun began its slow descent over Camlochlin. His heart stalled a little at the raw beauty of a sky bursting into flames of bronze and yellow. The gossamer mist rolling off the mountains high above captured the light and painted the vale in shades of warm umber and lavender. How could he have ever been so eager to leave this place?

There were still many people outdoors, either finishing their daily chores or sitting out to admire the coming evening. He was still too far off to make out if Gillian was among them.

Unfolding his plaid, he swirled it over his head and dug his boots into his horse's flanks. A horn sounded and a fiery arrow pierced the sky above the orchid whitecaps of the bay. He slowed a bit and gave the guardsmen time to recognize him while he scanned the vale from the shoreline to the braes of Bla Bheinn to his right.

That was where he saw her, leaving his sister's unfinished house with Aurelius barking around her skirts and Edmund and Malcolm running ahead of her. They hadn't seen him yet and he slipped out of the saddle to watch them a wee bit longer until they did.

He was glad Gates wasn't here yet to witness whatever the hell was wrong with him that his eyes should well up like a lass's. He gritted his teeth, then let out a resigned sigh. This was what love did to a man. It made him feel more alive than ever before. It made him a father who had done everything to see that his son enjoyed his childhood. It changed a warrior into something better and stronger— a husband.

He lifted his hand and welcomed the rush of warmth that near melted his heart all over his ribs when Edmund spotted him and took off shouting his name. He watched Gillian recognize him and pause in her merry steps as if she'd seen an apparition.

Hell, he'd missed her. He moved toward her, drawn by a power he knew no man could conquer. He reached Edmund first and lifted him high in the air and then kissed his curly crown on the way back down.

"You came home."

"Aye," he replied, lowering Edmund's feet to the ground while Gillian closed the gap between them. Hell, he'd missed her face, her wary smile, the way her eyes searched his and found everything he'd ever wanted to be. "To ye, if ye'll have me."

She smiled, forgiving him all and setting his heart

aflame. "Aye, Colin MacGregor. I'll have you. But what of your war? What of the king?"

He caught her up in his arms and, looking into her eyes, fell in love with her for the hundredth time. Every day without her had been dull and endless. "Let the kingdoms fight for their king if they choose to. They will fight without me." Aye, what was battle? What was war compared to the thrill of starting a new life with her, to becoming a father to Edmund? "I love ye, lass," he told her, dipping his head to kiss her. He'd dreamed of kissing her for a fortnight. He wanted to kiss her for a lifetime. He sighed with pleasure as their lips met and she went soft and willing in his arms.

They would live here, safely guarded by mountains and mist and, most deadly of all, MacGregors. Let England fall to the Protestants.

He had bairns to make.

COAL CITY PUBLIC
LIBRARY DISTRICT
85 N Garfield Street
Coal City, IL 60416

Author's Note

On November 5, 1688, William of Orange landed with the Dutch army in southwest England. The bishop of London crowned him, together with his wife, Mary, at Westminster Abbey on April 11, 1689.

Upon William's accession to the throne, the acts of proscription against the MacGregors were renewed, and it was not until 1775 that the penal statutes against them were finally and permanently repealed.

Dear Reader,

I'll never forget the excitement and the obsession of getting the first MacGregors of Skye from my head and on to paper. To this day, I tear up when I think of Callum and Maggie, and what Camlochlin meant to them in *Laird of the Mist*—the book that lit the fire that still burns strong. I was ecstatic to write the next chapter in the lives of this fearsome, mighty clan. I think it's safe to say that I fell head over heels for every hero in my Children of the Mist series. I swore that no warrior after Rob would make my heart race the way he did. Tristan proved me a terrible liar. Connor distracted me until all I could think about was the slant of his dimpled grin, and Colin...well, let me just say, that he'll live forever in my heart.

And because of you, loyal readers, the outlawed MacGregors will live on in at least four more installments in my new series, Highland Heirs.

With the proscription reestablished by King William III, the MacGregors are once again outlaws. Yes, they were stripped of their rights *again*. Don't worry, this defiant clan doesn't go down so easily. The next generation is no less troublesome and terrifying than their predecessors were. Most of the time though, they prefer to battle neighboring clansmen and an occasional fleet of pirates rather than ride all the way to England to kick the arses of men who wear wigs. There are, however, those more audacious heirs who have been known to ride hard through the glens and straight into London's tawdry brothels or private balls to strike at their enemies while their noble heads are absent of wig, and their arses of hose. Which is exactly where we meet our first heir of the series.

We'll begin with Edmund Dearly, who as a young child melted my heart in *Conquered by a Highlander*. He's all grown up...and so much more than brawn. He's a poet, a musician, and a patriot. But first and foremost, Edmund is a MacGregor. He bears the name of his adopted clan proudly, outlawed or not. He'll fight for the Highlands and die for his clan. But an excursion into hostile territory and into the arms of a seemingly innocent servant will put to the test everything he's learned...everything he holds dearest to his heart.

We'll meet Caitrina Grant, daughter of Connor and Mairi from *Tamed by a Highlander*, and stowaway aboard a ship belonging to the son of an infamous pirate. We'll sail with her across the high seas as she tries to retrieve something he stole from Camlochlin. But Captain Alexander Kyd will not relinquish her heart so easily.

In a tale I'm extremely eager to write, we'll get to know Abigail MacGregor, niece of the reigning Queen Anne and daughter of Rob and Davina from *Ravished by a Highlander*. Part of my excitement over this story is due to the hero. You see, I know this one already...and quite well. Captain Daniel Marlow didn't join the queen's army to escort ladies to England, especially ladies who believe that the Pretender James Stuart is the rightful king of England. Jacobites. They are everything he despises, but every time he looks at Abigail he's reminded of some ancient Pict queen who refuses to surrender to her Roman foes, and before long the need to possess this haughty handmaiden begins to drive him mad. But when he discovers that royal Stuart blood flows through her veins, will he follow his heart or the duty he swore to the throne when the queen orders him to return to Camlochlin with an army and end the threat of any Catholic heirs once and for all?

The series will conclude with the tale of Adam Mac-Gregor, eldest son and reluctant heir of Camlochlin's chief. Tall, dark, and drop-dead gorgeous, Adam would rather rob cattle and ride lasses than fight for his name. When he's forced to marry a stubborn Highland MacLeod lass, he thinks his life couldn't get any worse, until he begins to fall in love with her. But it's when she ventures away from Skye and is arrested for bearing his name that Adam's character is tested and he learns what it truly means to be a MacGregor.

Dear reader, I hope you'll come along on this newest journey into the lives of Camlochlin's children. Whether they battle on the field, on the sea, or in the bedchamber, they live and love with the unbridled, untamable passion that belongs only to heirs to the Highlands. And who knows what mischief the rest of the MacGregor clan will get into?

Enjoy!

Paula Quinn

Davina Montgomery has
lived most of her life sheltered,
locked away in an abbey.
When her home is attacked, she
picks up a bow and aims at the first
man she sees: a fierce and
undeniably sexy Highlander...

Please turn this page for an excerpt
from the first book in the series,

Ravished by a Highlander

and discover how it all began.

Available now

❖❖❖

Chapter One

*H*igh atop Saint Christopher's Abbey, Davina Montgomery stood alone in the bell tower, cloaked in the silence of a world she did not know. Darkness had fallen hours ago and below her the sisters slept peacefully in their beds, thanks to the men who had been sent here to guard them. But there was little peace for Davina. The vast, indigo sky filling her vision was littered with stars that seemed close enough to touch should she reach out her hand. What would she wish for? Her haunted gaze slipped southward toward England, and then with a longing just as powerful, toward the moonlit mountain peaks of the north. Which life would she choose if the choice were hers to make? A world where she'd been forgotten, or one where no one knew her? She smiled sadly against the wind that whipped her woolen novice robes around her. What good was it to ponder when her future had already been decreed? She knew what was to come. There were no variations. That is, if she lived beyond the next year. She looked away from the place she could never go and the person she could never be.

She heard the soft fall of footsteps behind her but did not turn. She knew who it was.

"Poor Edward. I imagine your heart must have failed you when you did not find me in my bed."

When he remained quiet she felt sorry for teasing him about the seriousness of his duty. Captain Edward Asher had been sent here to protect her four years ago, after Captain Geoffries had taken ill and was relieved of his command. Edward had become more than her guardian. He was her dearest friend, someone she could confide in here within the thick walls that sheltered her from the schemes of her enemies. Edward knew her fears and accepted her faults.

"I knew where to find you," he finally said, his voice just above a whisper.

He always did know. Not that there were many places to look. Davina was not allowed to venture outside the Abbey gates so she came to the bell tower often to let her thoughts roam free.

"My lady—"

She turned at his soft call, putting away her dreams and desires behind a tender smile. Those she kept to herself and did not share, even with him.

"Please, I..." he began, meeting her gaze and then stumbling through the rest as if the face he looked upon every day still struck him as hard as it had the first time he'd seen her. He was in love with her, and though he'd never spoken his heart openly, he did not conceal how he felt. Everything was there in his eyes, his deeds, his devotion; and a deep regret that Davina suspected had more to do with her than he would ever have the boldness to admit. Her path had been charted for another course and she could never be his. "Lady Montgomery, come away from here, I beg you. It is not good to be alone."

He worried for her so and she wished he wouldn't. "I'm not alone, Edward," she reassured. If her life remained as it was now, she would find a way to be happy. She always did. "I have been given much."

"It's true," he agreed, moving closer to her and then stopping himself, knowing what she knew. "You have been taught to fear the Lord and love your king. The sisters love you, as do my men. It will always be so. We are your family. But it is not enough." He knew she would never admit it, so he said it for her.

It had to be enough. It was safer this way, cloistered away from those who would harm her if ever they discovered her after the appointed time.

That time had come.

Davina knew that Edward would do anything to save her. He told her often, each time he warned her of her peril. Diligently, he taught her to trust no one, not even those who claimed to love her. His lessons often left her feeling a bit hopeless, though she never told him that, either.

"Would that I could slay your enemies," he swore to her now, "and your fears along with them."

He meant to comfort her, but good heavens, she didn't want to discuss the future on such a breathtaking night. "Thanks to you and God," she said, leaving the wall to go to him and tossing him a playful smile, "I can slay them myself."

"I agree," he surrendered, his good mood restored by the time she reached him. "You've learned your lessons in defense well."

She rested her hand on his arm and gave it a soft pat. "How could I disappoint you when you risked the Abbess's consternation to teach me?"

He laughed with her, both of them comfortable in their familiarity. But too soon he grew serious again.

"James is to be crowned in less than a se'nnight."

"I know." Davina nodded and turned toward England again. She refused to let her fears control her. "Mayhap," she said with a bit of defiance sparking her doleful gaze, "we should attend the coronation, Edward. Who would think to look for me at Westminster?"

"My lady..." He reached for her. "We cannot. You know—"

"I jest, dear friend." She angled her head to speak to him over her shoulder, carefully cloaking the struggle that weighed heaviest upon her heart, a struggle that had nothing to do with fear. "Really, Edward, must we speak of this?"

"Yes, I think we should," he answered earnestly, then went on swiftly, before she could argue, "I've asked the Abbess if we can move you to Courlochcraig Abbey in Ayr. I've already sent word to—"

"Absolutely not," she stopped him. "I will not leave my home. Besides, we have no reason to believe that my enemies know of me at all."

"Just for a year or two. Until we're certain—"

"No," she told him again, this time turning to face him fully. "Edward, would you have us leave the sisters here alone to face our enemies should they come seeking me? What defense would they have without the strong arms of you and your men? They will not leave St. Christopher's, nor will I."

He sighed and shook his head at her. "I cannot argue when you prove yourself more courageous than I. I pray I do not live to regret it. Very well, then." The lines of his handsome face relaxed. "I shall do as you ask. For now though," he added, offering her his arm, "allow me to escort you to your chamber. The hour is late and the Reverend Mother will show you no mercy when the cock crows."

Davina rested one hand in the crook of his arm and waved away his concern with the other. "I don't mind waking with the sun."

"Why would you," he replied, his voice as light now as hers as he led her out of the belfry, "when you can just fall back to sleep in the Study Hall."

"It was only the one time that I actually slept," she defended, slapping his arm softly. "And don't you have more important things to do with your day than follow me around?"

"Three times," he corrected, ignoring the frown he knew was false. "Once, you even snored."

Her eyes, as they descended the stairs, were as wide as her mouth. "I have never snored in my life!"

"Save for that one time, then?"

She looked about to deny his charge again, but bit her curling lip instead. "And once during Sister Bernadette's piano recital. I had penance for a week. Do you remember?"

"How could I forget?" he laughed. "My men did no chores the entire time, preferring to listen at your door while you spoke aloud to God about everything but your transgression."

"God already knew why I fell asleep," she explained, smiling at his grin. "I did not wish to speak poorly of Sister Bernadette's talent, or lack of it, even in my own defense."

His laughter faded, leaving only a smile that looked to be painful as their walk ended and they stood at her door. When he reached out to take her hand, Davina did her best not to let the surprise in her eyes dissuade him from touching her. "Forgive my boldness, but there is something I must tell you. Something I should have told you long ago."

"Of course, Edward," she said softly, keeping her hand in his. "You know you may always speak freely to me."

"First, I would have you know that you have come to mean—"

"Captain!"

Davina leaned over the stairwell to see Harry Barns, Edward's second in command, plunge through the Abbey doors. "Captain!" Harry shouted up at them, his face pale and his breath heavy from running. "They are coming!"

For one paralyzing moment, Davina doubted the good of her ears. She'd been warned of this day for four years, but had always prayed it would not come. "Edward," she asked hollowly, on the verge of sheer panic, "how did they find us so soon after King Charles's death?"

He squeezed his eyes shut and shook his head back and forth as if he too refused to believe what he was hearing. But there was no time for doubt. Spinning on his heel, he gripped her arm and hauled her into her room. "Stay here! Lock your door!"

"What good will that do us?" She sprang for her quiver and bow and headed back to the door, and to Edward blocking it. "Please, dear friend. I do not want to cower alone in my room. I will fire from the bell tower until it is no longer safe to do so."

"Captain!" Barns raced up the stairs, taking three at a time. "We need to prepare. Now!"

"Edward"—Davina's voice pulled him back to her— "you trained me for this. We need every arm available. You will not stop me from fighting for my home."

"Orders, Captain, please!"

Davina looked back once as she raced toward the narrow steps leading back to the tower.

"Harry!" She heard Edward shout behind her. "Prepare the vats and boil the tar. I want every man alert and ready at my command. And Harry..."

"Captain?"

"Wake the sisters and tell them to pray."

In the early morning hours that passed after the massacre at St. Christopher's, Edward's men had managed to kill half of the enemy's army. But the Abbey's losses were greater. Far greater.

Alone in the bell tower, Davina stared down at the bodies strewn across the large courtyard. The stench of burning tar and seared flesh stung her nostrils and burned her eyes as she set them beyond the gates to the meadow where men on horseback still hacked away at each other as if their hatred could never be satisfied. But there was no hatred. They fought because of her, though none of them knew her. But she knew them. Her dreams had been plagued with her faceless assassins since the day Edward had first told her of them.

Tears brought on by the pungent air slipped down her cheeks, falling far below to where her friends...her family lay dead or dying. Dragging her palm across her eyes, she searched the bodies for Edward. He'd returned to her an hour after the fighting had begun and ordered her into the chapel with the sisters. When she'd refused, he'd tossed her over his shoulder like a sack of grain and brought her there himself. But she did not remain hidden. She couldn't, so she'd returned to the tower and her bow and sent more than a dozen of her enemies to meet their

Maker. But there were too many—or mayhap God didn't want the rest, for they slew the men she ate with, laughed with, before her eyes.

She had feared this day for so long that it had become a part of her. She thought she had prepared. At least, for her own death. But not for the Abbess's. Not for Edward's. How could anyone prepare to lose those they loved?

Despair ravaged her and for a moment she considered stepping over the wall. If she was dead they would stop. But she had prayed for courage too many times to let God or Edward down now. Reaching into the quiver on her back, she plucked out an arrow, cocked her bow, and closed one eye to aim.

Below her and out of her line of vision, a soldier garbed in military regalia not belonging to England crept along the chapel wall with a torch clutched in one fist and a sword in the other.

THE DISH

Where authors give you the inside scoop!

♥ ♥ ♥ ♥ ♥ ♥ ♥ ♥ ♥ ♥ ♥ ♥ ♥ ♥ ♥

From the desk of Paula Quinn

Dear Reader,

I'm so excited to tell you about my latest in the Children of the Mist series, CONQUERED BY A HIGHLANDER. I loved introducing you to Colin MacGregor in *Ravished by a Highlander* and then meeting up with him again in *Tamed by a Highlander*, but finally the youngest, battle-hungry MacGregor gets his own story. And let me tell you all, I enjoyed every page, every word.

Colin wasn't a difficult hero to write. There were no mysteries complicating his character, no ghosts or regrets haunting him from his past. He was born with a passion to fight and to conquer. Nothing more. Nothing less. He was easy to write. He was a badass in *Ravished* and he's a hardass now. My dilemma was what kind of woman would it take to win him? The painted birds fluttering about the many courts he's visited barely held his attention. A warrior wouldn't suit him any better than a wallflower would. I knew early on that the Lady who tried to take hold of this soldier's heart had to possess the innate strength to face her fiercest foe...and the tenderness to recognize something more than a fighter in Colin's confident gaze.

I found Gillian Dearly hidden away in the turrets of a castle overlooking the sea, her fingers busy strumming melodies on her beloved lute while her thoughts carried her to places far beyond her prison walls. She wasn't waiting for a hero, deciding years ago that she would rescue herself. She was perfect for Colin. She also possessed one other thing, a weapon so powerful, even Colin found himself at the mercy of it.

A three-year-old little boy named Edmund.

Like Colin, I didn't intend for Edmund Dearly or his mother to change the path of my story, but they brought out something in the warrior—whom I thought I knew so well—something warm and wonderful and infinitely sexier than any swagger. They brought out the man.

For me, nothing I've written before this book exemplifies the essence of a true hero more than watching Colin fall in love with Gillian *and* with her child. Not many things are more valiant than a battle-hardened warrior who puts down his practice sword so he can take a kid fishing or save him from bedtime monsters…except maybe a mother who defiantly goes into battle each day in order to give her child a better life. Gillian Dearly was Edmund's hero and she quickly became mine. How could a man like Colin *not* fall in love with her?

Having to end the Children of the Mist series was bittersweet, but I'm thrilled to say there will be more MacGregors of Skye visiting the pages of future books. Camlochlin will live on for another generation at least. And not just in words but in art. Master painter James Lyman has immortalized the home of our beloved MacGregors in beautiful color and with an innate understanding of how the fortress should be represented. Visit PaulaQuinn.com to order a print of your own, signed and numbered by the artist.

Until we meet again, to you mothers and fathers, husbands and wives, sons and daughters, sisters and brothers, and friends, who put yourselves aside for someone you love, I shout Huzzah! Camlochlin was built for people like you.

Paula Quinn

Find her at Facebook
Twitter @Paula_Quinn

♥ ♥ ♥ ♥ ♥ ♥ ♥ ♥ ♥ ♥ ♥ ♥ ♥ ♥ ♥ ♥

From the desk of Jill Shalvis

Dear Reader,

From the very first moment I put Mysterious Cute Guy on the page, I fell in love. There's just something about a big, bad, sexy guy whom you know nothing about that fires the imagination. But I have to be honest: When he made a cameo in *Head Over Heels* (literally a walk-on role only; in fact I believe he only gets a mention or two), I knew nothing about him. Nothing. I never intended to, either. He was just one of life's little (okay, big, bad, and sexy) mysteries.

Then my editor called me. Said the first three Lucky Harbor books had done so well that they'd like three more, please. And maybe one of the heroes could be Mysterious Cute Guy.

It was fun coming up with a story to go with this enigmatic figure, not to mention a name: Ty Garrison. More fun still to give this ex-Navy SEAL a rough, tortured, bad-boy past and a sweet, giving, good-girl heroine

(Mallory Quinn, ER nurse). Oh, the fun I had with these two: a bad boy trying to go good, and a good girl looking for a walk on the wild side. Hope you have as much fun reading their story, LUCKY IN LOVE.

And then, stick around. Because Mallory's two Chocoholics-in-crime partners, Amy and Grace, get their own love stories in July and August with *At Last* and then *Forever and a Day.*

Happy Reading!

Jill Shalvis

http://www.jillshalvis.com

http://www.facebook.com/jillshalvis

3 5920 00183 6756

♥ ♥ ♥ ♥ ♥ ♥ ♥ ♥ ♥ ♥ ♥ ♥ ♥ ♥ ♥

From the desk of Lori Wilde

Dear Reader,

Ah ,June! Love is in the air, and it's the time for weddings and romance. With KISS THE BRIDE, you get two romantic books in one, *There Goes the Bride* and *Once Smitten, Twice Shy.* Both stories are filled with brides, bouquets, and those devastatingly handsome grooms. But best friends Delaney and Tish go through a lot of ups and downs on their path to happily ever after.

For those of you hoping for a June wedding of your

own, how do you tell if your guy is ready for commitment? He might be ready to pop the question if...

- Instead of saying "I" when making future plans, he starts saying "we."
- He gives you his ATM pass code.
- He takes you on vacation with his family.
- Out of the blue, your best friend asks your ring size.
- He sells his sports car/motorcycle and says he's outgrown that juvenile phase of his life.
- He opens a gold card to get a higher spending limit—say, to pay for a honeymoon.
- When you get a wedding invitation in the mail, he doesn't groan but instead asks where the bride and groom got the invitations printed.
- He starts remembering to leave the toilet seat down.
- When poker night with the guys rolls around, he says he'd rather stay home and watch *The Wedding Planner* with you.
- He becomes your dad's best golfing buddy

I hope you enjoy KISS THE BRIDE.

Happy reading,

Lori Wilde

loriwilde.com

Facebook http://facebook.com/lori.wilde

Twitter @LoriWilde

♥ ♥ ♥ ♥ ♥ ♥ ♥ ♥ ♥ ♥ ♥ ♥ ♥ ♥ ♥

From the desk of Laurel McKee

Dear Reader,

When I was about eight years old, someone gave me a picture book called *Life in Victorian England*. I lost the book in a move years ago, but I still remember the gorgeous watercolor illustrations. Ladies in brightly colored hoopskirts and men in frock coats and top hats doing things like walking in the park, ice-skating at Christmas, and dancing in ballrooms. I was completely hooked on this magical world called "the Victorian Age" and couldn't get enough of it! I read stuff like *Jane Eyre, Little Women,* and *Bleak House,* watched every movie where there was the potential for bonnets, and drove my parents crazy by saying all the time, "Well, in the Victorian age it was like this…"

As I got older and started to study history in a more serious way, I found that beneath this pretty and proper facade was something far darker. Darker—and a lot more interesting. There was a flourishing underworld in Victorian England, all the more intense for being well hidden and suppressed. Prostitution, theft, and the drug trade expanded, and London was bursting at the seams thanks to changes brought about by the Industrial Revolution. The theater and the visual arts were taking on a new life. Even Queen Victoria was not exactly the prissy sourpuss everyone thinks she was. (She and Albert had nine children, after all—and enjoyed making them!)

I've always wanted to set a story in these Victorian

years, with the juxtaposition of what's seen on the surface and what is really going on underneath. But I never came up with just the right characters for this complex setting. The inspiration came (as it so often does for me, don't laugh) from clothes. I was watching my DVD of *Young Victoria* for about the fifth time, and when the coronation ball scene came on, I thought, "I really want a heroine who could wear a gown just like that..."

And Lily St. Claire popped into my head and brought along her whole family of Victorian underworld rakes. I had to run and get out my notebook to write down everything Lily had to tell me. I loved her from that first minute—a woman who created a glamorous life for herself from a childhood on the streets of the London slums. A tough, independent woman (with gorgeous clothes, of course) who thinks she doesn't need anyone—until she meets this absolutely yummy son a duke. Too bad his family is the St. Claire family's old enemy...

I hope you enjoy the adventures of Lily and Aidan as much as I have. It was so much fun to spend some time in Victorian London. Look for more St. Claire trouble to come.

In the meantime, visit my website at http://laurel mckee.net for more info on the characters and the history behind the book.

Laurel McKee

Find out more about Forever Romance!

Visit us at
www.hachettebookgroup.com/publishing_forever.aspx

Find us on Facebook
http://www.facebook.com/ForeverRomance

Follow us on Twitter
http://twitter.com/ForeverRomance

NEW AND UPCOMING TITLES

Each month we feature our new titles
and reader favorites.

CONTESTS AND GIVEAWAYS

We give away galleys, autographed copies,
and all kinds of exclusive items.

AUTHOR INFO

You'll find bios, articles, and links to personal websites
for all your favorite authors—and so much more.

GET SOCIAL

Connect with your favorite authors, editors, and
other Forever fans, and share what's important to you.

THE BUZZ

Sign up for our monthly romance newsletter,
and be the first to read all about it.